Praise for T.J. MacGregor and her previous thrillers!

DARK FIELDS
"A top-notch suspense novel . . . The true magic of this book is that the reader can become so wrapped up in the plot that he can't figure out who really committed the murder. . . . MacGregor's writing style is unique."
Mystery Scene

DEATH SWEET
"The weaving of the two plots is skillfully done, and the resolution well-executed."
The Drood Review of Mystery

ON ICE
"Chilling."
The New York Times Book Review

D0720033

Also by T.J. MacGregor
Published by Ballantine Books:

DARK FIELDS
KILL FLASH
DEATH SWEET
ON ICE
KIN DREAD

DEATH FLATS

T.J. MacGregor

BALLANTINE BOOKS • NEW YORK

Copyright © 1991 by T.J. MacGregor

All rights reserved under International and Pan-American Copyright Conventions. Published in the United States of America by Ballantine Books, a division of Random House, Inc., New York, and simultaneously in Canada by Random House of Canada Limited, Toronto.

Library of Congress Catalog Card Number: 91-92191

ISBN 0-345-35768-X

Manufactured in the United States of America

First Edition: December 1991

For Rob and Mom and Dad
and
in memory of Chris Cox
editor, friend,
&
fellow traveler.
We'll miss you.

"You have to learn to do everything,
even to die."

—Gertrude Stein

"To be or not to be is not the question;
it's the answer."

—Fred Alan Wolf

Lake Okeechobee
November 16
Friday

THE WIND WHIPPED across the lake that night, as noisy as a ghost in chains. It rattled the windows in the attic where Kate Bishop was sorting through boxes of Christmas ornaments, whined under the eaves, and screamed across the dark, flat emptiness that surrounded the ranch. She hated the sound of it.

By tomorrow, the mud around the lake would be rippled like black aluminum, the tall grass would be flattened against the ground, and dirt would cover the wings of Jack's plane, tied down between the house and the barn. The air would taste of dust, the front porch would be slick with it, she would find bits of dirt embedded in the screens. Except for the trees around the house, there was nothing to stop the wind or slow it down. No buildings, no homes, no city. Between the ranch and the nearest town more than thirty miles away there was mostly marsh, farmland, water.

Kate set aside a box of wrapping paper and ornaments, wondering what it was about the desolation that appealed to Jack. And where was he, anyway? It had been his idea to go through everything up here and toss out what they didn't need. But a while ago, before the wind had risen, he had gone downstairs to get them each a beer. Before he'd returned, she'd heard a car drive up. The screen door had slammed shut as he'd gone outside to greet whoever it was.

She'd heard voices and figured a couple of mechanics from the Belle Glade airport had finally arrived. The Bonanza's oil pressure had been too high when they'd flown here yesterday and Jack wanted it checked out before he flew her back to Palm Beach tomorrow. It irritated her, though, that the mechanics hadn't gotten here earlier. Their presence infringed on her evening with Jack.

No sense in doing all this alone, and besides, she was thirsty and it was hot up here. Jack had never gotten around to installing the AC vents. As she started down the ladder, four shots rang out with utter clarity, one after another, as evenly spaced as the tick of seconds on a clock. She froze, hands gripping the sides of the ladder, heart pounding, waiting for something that would release her—another shot, Jack's voice shouting that there had been an accident, anything. But there was only the wind, and she panicked.

She scrambled back into the attic, jerked the ladder up behind her. The light went out, the dark pressed against her, her knees seemed to take root in the floor, her fingers curled in on themselves. She waited. The wind paused as if to catch its breath and the silence thickened and grew as oppressive as the dark. She didn't know how long she remained like that, motionless, her nails cutting into her palms, her life suspended.

When she couldn't stand it anymore, she unfolded slowly, limbs creaking, joints stiff, and stretched out on her stomach. Ear to the floor, she listened.

Water gurgled in a pipe. She heard no voices, no footsteps. She didn't allow herself to think about what the shots meant or why Jack hadn't appeared. What mattered now, this instant, was the location of whoever had fired the shots. The men might be standing in the closet beneath her, gazing up at the square of wood in the ceiling, aiming their guns. In a second or two an explosion would rip apart the floor and she would die up here with the dust and old boxes of Bishop family memorabilia. She wasn't afraid to die, but she didn't want to do it here, tonight.

Shifting, she turned her head toward the windows. If she could get one open, she could climb out onto the roof and— What? Just what could she do? Leap to the plane? Drop three stories to the ground and race for the safety of the barn? Panic stumbled around inside her, a beast with two heads, two mouths. The mouths opened and out came the wind again, louder than before, stronger than before. It shook the house as if to knock her out of it, as if she were miniaturized, a doll, a mote of dust.

She dropped to her stomach once more, pushed forward with her toes, a fish swimming through dust. She patted around until she found the seam of the square hole into which the folding ladder fit. She wrapped its rope around one hand and pushed down on the wood just enough to crack the trapdoor.

Fresh air rushed into her nostrils, tinged with the scent of mothballs from the closet below. She pressed down flat against the floor, started to shout for Jack, didn't dare. She hesitated, then slowly uncoiled the rope from her hand.

When she ran out of rope, she pushed forward on her stomach and pushed down on the top step, fixing the ladder against the closet floor. She waited for the house to tell her if the men were still inside. If they knew she was here. But it coveted its secrets like a selfish child.

Kate rolled onto her knees, turned so her back was to the hole, held on to the edge. Right foot to the top step. Left foot. She released her grip on the edges of the hole, tightened her fingers over the top step. From then on it was easier, but she forced herself to move slowly, afraid that a board might creak, that she would give herself away.

The noise of the wind receded as she descended into the closet. She sensed the door was ajar, but then why wasn't there any light from the bedroom and the hall? Why was it as black as spoiled fruit in here? The power, she thought. The wind had knocked out the power.

Or the wires had been cut.

She crawled into the bedroom. Heard something banging. A shutter? The screen door? She couldn't be sure and waited again, sweat oozing down the sides of her face. When the wind paused, the noise stopped. The awful silence hissed around her, a toxic gas.

Into the hall now. The blackness was excessive, a fathomless hole. She oriented herself—railing to the left, a table with a vase and books on it to her right, the throw rug and the stairs just ahead.

Easy, go easy, she thought.

Kate grasped the banister. Pulled herself to her knees, Listened again. Her memory of the wind echoed in the stairwell. A cold draft slithered over her knuckles. Now, move now, and her hands dropped, one over the other, faster and faster. She smelled water. Wood. The stink of her own fear.

At the foot of the stairs, she sensed something to her right. "Jack?" His name curled into the air, a wisp of smoke, a question that began to dissolve the moment it was spoken.

It was answered with a groan.

Kate scrambled over to him, hands slapping the wooden floors, his name stuck at the tip of her tongue as she touched his face, his hair, his chest. She smelled blood. Felt it at his mouth. His lips moved, a pair of little fish slick with blood. He was trying to speak. She leaned closer. "What? What?"

"Cat."

"I'll get help, don't move, I . . ."

"Shro . . ." He coughed and she lifted his head. He sucked at the air, words whistling through his teeth. "Shro . . ."

She held his head, cradling it, whispering, "I don't understand, Jack, oh God, you'll be okay, you . . ."

"Schrödinger's cat." He gripped her hand, struggled to raise up, coughed again, breath wheezing in his chest. He slumped to the floor and, just like that, went still. Kate said his name. Shook him. Screamed at him. Begged him to move, breathe, something, anything, anything at all, please. But there was only the wind, wailing its way toward sunrise.

1

THE PALM BEACH County jail was flamingo pink and trimmed in black like a funeral announcement. The grounds were beautifully landscaped with plants that flourished in the heat—Mexican heather, marigolds, dracaenas, purslanes in violets and reds. But it was still a jail, Quin thought, and it depressed her to be there. This was not the future she and Kate had envisioned for either of them twenty years ago. This was what happened to strangers you read about in the morning news.

As she opened the car door, the heat washed over her. It smelled and felt like wet cotton. She gave herself a moment to acclimate to it after the cool interior of McCleary's car. The Miata was only a month old, everything in it worked, and it drove like a dream. But when you were six months pregnant, exiting required a precise coordination of movements: a swivel of the buttocks, a swing of the legs, a strong grasp on the edges of the door, a good push. Graceful it was not.

She punched the buzzer outside the jail's rear entrance, noting the video camera perched to the right above her. Its singular eye tossed her image back to her—body shaped vaguely like a pear, her round face as damp as a leaf, her umber hair frizzed into a bush from the heat. Her cheeks were as pudgy as a squirrel's, cute on a kid, not on a forty-year-old woman. But her clothes were the worst of it.

They were as wrinkled as a Shar-Pei's face, but they'd looked that way before she'd even bought them. The khaki slacks gripped at the ankles and bulged at the belly. The checkered shirt had a silly tie at the throat that she'd taken off and now the collar wouldn't lie flat. And this was one of her nicer outfits.

But maternity fashions were never made with fashion in mind. Skirts had horizontal stripes that exacerbated her bulk. The dresses made her weep. And even an iron couldn't help the fabric. Sooner or later some entrepreneur was going to make a fortune designing reasonably priced maternity clothes in pretty colors, in fabrics that looked and felt and smelled nice.

But not during *her* pregnancy.

She leaned on the buzzer until a female voice said, "Yes, sorry. I had two phones ringing."

"Quin St. James to see Kate Bishop."

"ID, please."

She fished in her bag for her private detective license, held it up to the camera. The door clicked and she pushed through, into air that was blissfully cool. The woman who had spoken was sitting in a bullet-proof glass cage and looked to be nine months pregnant. She asked Quin to pass her ID through the slot.

"You can pick it up on your way out, ma'am."

"Thanks."

Quin glanced around for a chair, but there weren't any. Just the white walls, the glass cage, the ubiquitous video cameras, one in each corner of the room. Even Dade wasn't quite this security conscious.

"I've told them to put chairs out there," the woman said. "But you probably won't have to wait long. When's your baby due?"

"February." Quin leaned into the wall and slipped her feet out of her shoes. They were swollen and ached like hell. "What about you?"

"In two weeks, but I swear it feels like he'll be here this afternoon."

Quin laughed. "I know the feeling."

"You know what yours is yet?"

"A girl."

"Did you have an ultrasound or an amnio?"

"Both."

They chatted about their respective pregnancies, exchanging stories with the ease of men who had been to war together.

6

This instantaneous intimacy was a curious phenomenon Quin had discovered early in her pregnancy. Women who were complete strangers would strike up conversations with her in grocery stores, malls, on the beach, for no reason other than the fact that she was pregnant. She'd been privy to all sorts of baby and motherhood trivia and to personal accounts of labors and deliveries and postpartum depressions.

Sometimes the stories were amusing and instructive; sometimes they were not. When they weren't, it was because they contained an element of horror she could do without—the thirty-hour labor that ended with an emergency C-section, the preemie whose neonatal bill totaled fifty grand, the infant who had cried constantly for six months.

Regardless of whether the stories were good or bad, Quin invariably felt that she'd been initiated into an exclusive club where the only criterion for membership was pregnancy. This alone seemed to entitle her to other women's scraps of wisdom, admonitions, and unsolicited advice.

"Kate Bishop a friend of yours?" the woman asked.

"We roomed together in college."

"Oh." Her thinly plucked brows lifted. Her mouth twitched with disapproval. "I was here when she was brought in. I was real surprised, I can tell you. I figured if something like this ever happened to the Bishops, it would be David or Stephanie. I guess you've met them, huh?"

Jack's brother and sister. "Actually, no. Why one of them?"

"Well, David used to be a musician and you know how *they* are."

"Drugs, sex, and rock 'n' roll."

"Yeah." She laughed. "Something like that. He's just an odd duck, real reclusive. I heard he's got a handful of rich clients he advises on stocks and investments and whatnot, and the rest of the time he does charity benefits for sick kids. And his sister . . ." The woman clicked her tongue against her teeth. "She lifts weights. Competes in all that stuff, too."

Quin, recognizing an opportunity for information, said, "And Jack?" As though she'd never met him.

"I don't know. Different from the other two. I took the call from the ranch caretaker that morning." As if she were a witness to a historical event. "He doesn't speak very good English when he's calm, but that morning he was so upset, I could hardly understand him. A lot of our officers were out with the flu and I had to raise Lou on the radio."

"Lou?"

"Lieutenant Garrison. He'd just worked a double shift, but he drove all the way out there."

A conscientious man, this Garrison. "How come?"

"How come what?"

"How come he drove all the way out there after working a double shift?"

"He and Jack went to high school together, he knew where the ranch was." She shrugged. "That's his job."

Quin knew that if she stood here long enough, this woman would tell her every detail of Kate's incarceration since her arrest eleven days ago. What she had eaten, who had visited her, what she had done with the long hours each day. But a policewoman arrived to take her back to the cells.

The holding area for female prisoners wasn't as grim as Quin had expected. Colorful wall murals depicted lush jungle scenes with tigers peeking around leaves and birds flitting through shadows. Light streamed through windows that overlooked the jail grounds. The only other people in the room were a woman in prison blues sitting with a man in a three-piece suit who had attorney written all over him. They were the only people who wore three-piece suits when it was ninety-six in the shade.

Ten minutes passed. Her stomach rumbled with hunger, so she walked over to the vending machines that lined the walls. She had never lacked an appetite, but now she was a slave to it, a servant indentured to the tiny being inside her whose craving for food surpassed anything she'd experienced when she wasn't pregnant. The baby didn't seem to be too particular about what she ate, as long as she did it frequently and grandly. But the machines were filled with forbidden things. Doritos, Mars bars. Coffee.

Forget caffeine. She allotted herself one cup of coffee a day and she'd already had it. And forget beer, wine, onions, radishes, most citruses, Cokes, too much sugar. Forget all that. It either wasn't good for the baby or it gave her heartburn.

Her body was no longer her own. It was a vehicle she shared with someone she had never seen, touched, heard, or smelled. It was an object of considerable interest to her doctor, his nurse, her health insurance company. But it didn't belong to her now. Sometimes she felt it might never belong to her again, that the pregnancy would stretch into a year, then two years, like an elephant. She would become a medical anomaly.

She finally settled on a can of tomato juice and carried it back to the table. She eyed the clock. Fifteen minutes down now. What was taking so long?

Quin hadn't seen Kate since she and Jack had spent a weekend with her about a year and a half ago, during her separation from McCleary. The lapse was due to circumstances and distance and not to any breech in the friendship; that would probably outlive them both. Besides, they'd kept in touch courtesy of Ma Bell.

When Kate had called last night, Quin and McCleary had just gotten back from a trip up north, where they'd spent Thanksgiving with his parents, his sisters, and their respective families. So she hadn't heard about the murder and the news couldn't have come at a worse time. They were in the process of moving from Miami to the Palm Beaches and there were a million things she should have done yesterday. But for Kate she would have gone halfway around the world.

The woman who entered the room was not the Kate Bishop Quin had last seen. That Kate had been pretty; this woman shocked her. She looked shorter than five foot four, as if her bones had shrunk. Her face was as pale as a new moon, her hazel eyes possessed the wariness of a cornered animal, and her hair, which used to fall to her shoulders in black waves, was now ear-length and wild. It was as though some vital hormone had run amok inside her, turning her skin to tissue paper, permanently creasing the corners of her eyes, weighting her cheeks until the flesh sagged on the bones.

At least her smile hadn't changed. It was quick, brilliant, the wink of sunlight on snow. Quin pushed up from the table, towering over her by nearly half a foot, outweighing her by forty or fifty pounds. They hugged hello, hugged hard. Kate was all bones; she felt as fragile as a bird. Quin's protruding stomach made the hug awkward and they both laughed nervously and stepped back.

Kate looked at her stomach and shook her head. "God, you did it. You really did. I never thought you'd be the one who would, Quin."

"And when she's twenty, I'll almost qualify for Medicare."

Kate made a face and dismissed the age factor with a wave of her hand. "Who cares. You look terrific. You've got that mysterious glow they always talk about in the same breath as pregnancy."

"I don't just look fat?"

"You look pregnant."

"I feel like a house."

Kate touched her fingertips to Quin's stomach. "It's so hard. Does she kick yet?"

"All the time."

"Have you named her?"

"Two dozen times."

She laughed and asked how McCleary was, asked as though they were sitting in a café over coffee. "He sends his love," Quin said, then squeezed Kate's hand. "I'm so sorry about Jack."

Her smile faded, her pretense vanished, and she sank into one of the hard wooden chairs. Her fingers fumbled for the pack of cigarettes in her shirt pocket. "I was arraigned yesterday morning, and I'll get out tomorrow on bond. I know it shocked the prosecutor and the arresting officer, but my attorney contends the judge thinks the evidence is weak, Quin. That's a good sign." She said this as if to convince herself that the evidence was weak. "I've got the best criminal attorney in the state. A woman. I like her. She's very forthright, doesn't pull any punches. She says if we go to trial in Palm Beach, chances are good I'll be convicted and get life or the chair, so she's working on getting the trial moved. The press has been . . ." Her voice fell, and she stabbed out the cigarette she'd just lit. "The bastards have crucified me."

"What can we do to help?"

A frown burrowed between her eyes, and they seemed to sink a little in her cheeks. "That's not why I called you. I just needed to talk to you."

"Christ, Katie, you're the oldest friend I've got and this is what Mac and I do for a living, all right? So don't pull that pride crap on me. Anyway, you're the only person in the world besides Mac who can put up with me when I'm hungry."

Her laughter was that of the twenty-year-old optimist with whom Quin had lived during her last two years at the University of Florida. Free-spirited Katie with all her causes: the war, the women's movement, abolish the draft, the environment before it was fashionable. Endowed with inexhaustible energy, she had graduated with honors in sociology, the field that encompassed everything that interested her.

She went on to earn a master's degree and a doctorate, and, at twenty-seven, began teaching at the University of Miami, where she remained for three years. When it started to cramp her style, she quit to travel. Her money ran out two years later. Stateside again, restless again, she looked around for something she knew nothing about that would interest her as much as traveling and sociology did. She found it at the Center for Near Death Studies on the U of M's satellite campus here in Palm Beach. It was where she had met Jack Bishop nearly four years ago.

He was the psychiatrist on the research staff, a man from an old-money Palm Beach family who was as bright as Kate, as curious as she, her complement in every way. Quin had liked him enormously.

"I don't think there's much you can do," Kate said.

"You're going to let these bozos convict you? Someone *framed* you."

"I don't want you to—"

"Look, the only perfect crime I know of in the last thirty years is D. B. Cooper's stunt, parachuting from thirty thousand feet with the ransom money. If you look long enough and deeply enough, you eventually find some detail that was neglected. So why don't you just tell me what happened that night, okay?"

Her smile was weak, watered down, but Quin took it as a

11

good sign. "You must be hungry. I hear that edge in your voice."

"I'm famished. Start talking."

And Kate did. Her hands moved constantly, restless white moths that fluttered over and around her pack of cigarettes. She lit one after another, twisted her wedding ring around on her finger, stopped talking, started, stopped again. Despite everything that she'd gone through since the murder, she was very precise about the order of events, the time, the details. But that was hardly surprising. Kate had always been decisive.

"Doesn't Schrödinger's cat have something to do with physics?" Quin asked when she finished.

"Quantum mechanics. It's an experiment that illustrates the paradox of quantum physics and the different views among quantum physicists."

"Was physics one of his interests?"

"One of many. You know how he was, Quin. He'd find one little detail in some obscure book and try to relate it to everything else in the universe."

Yes, Quin thought. Jack was always reworking the cosmos. "So tell me about this cat."

There was supposedly a long-standing dispute between classical physicists and quantum physicists, she said. The classical group believed that a thing either was or it wasn't. The quantum group believed a thing wasn't there until you observed it. In Schrödinger's experiment, a cat was placed inside a box. A device of some kind was placed in the box that would release a gas which would kill the cat instantly. A random event determined whether the gas would be released and there was no way of knowing what happened inside the box except by looking inside it.

"The classical camp says the cat is either dead or it's not. The quantum camp claims the cat exists in a kind of limbo, represented by a wave function, which contains the possibility that the cat is dead and also the possibility that the cat is alive. When you open the box and not before, one of these possibilities is actualized. The wave function of the possibility that didn't materialize then collapses."

Quin, who had a particular fondness for cats, wondered why

Schrödinger hadn't used some other animal for his example. Schrödinger's rat, for instance.

"The third interpretation of this experiment," Kate went on, "is called the Many World Interpretation of Quantum Mechanics. It says the wave function doesn't collapse at all, that the cat is both alive *and* dead. In other words, reality splits into two branches—one in which the cat is alive and one in which the cat is dead."

It made perfect sense to Quin that there could be a version of herself who had never gotten pregnant, never left Miami, even a version who had never married McCleary. Many Worlds: sure. But it was a weird thing for a near-death researcher to think about as he was dying. She said as much, and Kate agreed.

"The only think I can figure is that Jack was already caught up in the experience of dying and was trying to communicate what it was like. The random event would be his getting shot and the paradox . . ." She hesitated, tapping her knuckles together, then reached for the pack of cigarettes again. "Well, he'd been studying near-death experiences for fifteen years, Quin, and still believed there was nothing after you died. That it was all a big fat zero. But maybe as he was dying he realized he was wrong. Paradox."

"What's your motive supposed to have been?"

"Money, naturally. That's the Palm Beach way." Her voice crackled with cynicism. "Whenever someone dies under mysterious circumstances in this town, money seems to be the first motive people seize on."

"How much do you inherit?"

"I'm not sure of the exact figure. Maybe around five million. His brother and sister get the house. It's been in the family for years and I signed a prenuptial agreement waiving any rights to it." She paused again. "See, he was shot with my gun. I didn't even realize it was missing from the house until a couple of weeks ago, and I didn't bother reporting it."

"What kind of gun?"

"A snub-nosed .38 Smith & Wesson."

"Have you seen the coroner's report?"

"My attorney has. Jack was shot twice through the back.

13

One slug penetrated his lung. His bloodstream was loaded with androgens—male hormones. They were prescribed for his hives. But the coroner told my attorney that these levels couldn't be explained for a case of hives. His exact words were that Jack was probably 'one horny son of a bitch.' ''

"Was he?"

She averted her eyes, hesitated. "More so when we first got married." Now she looked at Quin again. "We'd been having a few problems."

It was news to Quin. "You never mentioned it."

"It started about the time you and Mac separated. I figured you had enough problems of your own."

"Wonderful. And there I was unloading on you."

"Your situation was worse, believe me. Mine was just . . . well, here we were, working eight and ten hours a day together, then we'd go home and bicker about stupid things. In the beginning we used to spend our weekends out at the ranch or just puttering around the house and we were happy with each other's company, you know?

"But over the last year or eighteen months, he started going to the ranch by himself on weekends. When we stayed in town, it seemed our personal time was always shared with other people. Sometimes Jack's brother or sister would drop by on a Saturday with dates, then some of their friends would show up, then friends of friends, and pretty soon we were having a party. I got tired of it. Sometimes I just left and checked into a hotel for the night. Other times I'd go see friends." She shook her head. "I don't know, Quin. Maybe if this hadn't happened, we would've gotten divorced."

"How were things between you the weekend he was killed?"

"Better than they'd been in a long time. We had Thanksgiving dinner at the ranch, just the two of us. He was going to fly me back Friday morning because I had an interview with a client. But the oil pressure was screwed up on the plane, so he called the Belle Glade airport to see if a mechanic could come out and check it over. That's who I thought had stopped by Friday night."

"Was he close to his brother and sister?"

"There were the usual sibling rivalries, but basically they were close. His sister can't stand me, though. I think she's always seen me as the intruder into the Bishop clan."

"How much is the house worth, Katie?"

"Seven or eight million. And no, forget that line of thinking, Quin. Neither of them killed Jack for money. They inherited plenty when old man Bishop died, and now Stephanie's gym is flourishing and David's got a brisk investment-counseling business."

"You have any idea who might have killed him?"

Softly: "None."

Other people had come into the room now and it wasn't as easy to talk freely. Quin took down names and phone numbers for Kate's attorney, her and Jack's colleagues, his brother and sister, anyone who might be a source of information. She asked Kate if she needed a ride home tomorrow when she was released.

"Thanks, but David's going to pick me up."

"Give us a few days to get moved into the house and the office and then we'll get started on this."

"I want to pay you."

"Don't be ridiculous."

"Then I don't want you working on this."

This was familiar ground now and they began arguing with the tenacity of sisters, each convinced that she was right. In the midst of it Quin started to laugh and held up her hands. "Okay, you win. Really. We'll bill you."

Kate, whose stubbornness was legendary, wouldn't hear of it. "I insist on paying something in advance."

"No."

"Quin, don't give me a hard time on this. You all just bought a house and the baby's costing you a mint because you don't have maternity insurance. So just let me do this my way, okay?"

"How do you know I don't have maternity insurance?"

A corner of her mouth dimpled with amusement. "Because I know how you are." She named a figure that was absurdly high. "Consider it an investment in my goddaughter's future."

"Subterfuge," Quin mumbled.

"You got it." She glanced around and stood. "I'd better get going."

"I'll call you tomorrow and we'll see you in a couple of days."

Kate hugged her again and then was gone.

2

McCleary had spent three weeks looking for office space within their budget and the search had paid off. The location was perfect.

They were two blocks off Ocean Drive, the millionaires' row of Palm Beach, and four blocks north of Worth Avenue, the equivalent of Rodeo Drive. The office was flanked by a jewelry store and a bakery that perfumed the air with cinnamon from dawn till dusk. The street was quiet, with a small park directly across from them and plenty of restaurants within walking distance.

McCleary strolled through the four rooms, furnished and operational since yesterday. Most of the furniture was glass and chrome and wicker, things from their Miami office that endowed the place with a familiarity that suited him. Some items, like the bookcase in his office, had specific memories attached to them. For a man who had lost twenty years of memories not so long ago, it was important to be surrounded by objects whose history was linked with his own.

The bookcase, for instance, had been a birthday present from Joe Bean, who was now at the helm of their Miami firm. Some of his paintings hung on the walls, and these, too, were links with his past. The acrylic landscape of hills and a barn at dusk was the view outside the kitchen window of his folks' place in upstate New York. The charcoal drawings of Quin had been done at different points in their marriage, reminders of where the relationship had been and where he hoped it was going.

There was one drawing, though, that mystified him every time he looked at it. A self-portrait, a quick sketch in pencil.

It had been done when he was still in Homicide at Metro-Dade. He was bearded, as he was now, weighed about the same as he did now, a hundred and seventy-five, and was running three miles a day, as he still did. But the eyes of the man in the drawing were not the eyes of the man he was now. There was something forbidding about those eyes, something dangerous, as if he had been living closer to the edge than he'd realized. Too many years in Homicide in Miami could do that to a man.

Or maybe it was simply Miami. Toward the end he had begun to envision that city as a tireless sprawl without boundaries or parameters. Streets emptied into each other or curved back on themselves or simply ended, stymied by the lack of space. People seemed to live in a perpetual state of alertness, as though the city were at war or about to suffer a disaster of one kind or another. It depleted them, scooped them raw inside, made them tense and often unfriendly.

But it wasn't a city you just *left*; it was much too interesting for that. You had to be fleeing something. Crime. Traffic. Overpopulation. Racial strife. Deplorable schools. Higher insurance rates. All of the above.

Their move, precipitated by their reconciliation after a seven-month separation and Quin's pregnancy, had placed them in the ranks of middle-class refugees who pushed farther north into the Florida peninsula every year, seeking what they hadn't found in Miami. Yes, the Palm Beaches were only a hundred miles north and were plagued by many of the same problems Miami had. But it wasn't as bad here. The county was more affluent, the crimes tended to be less heinous. But, more important, Palm Beach was their second chance.

The bell over the door rang as it opened and Harold Javitt, who owned the bakery next door, sailed in with a tray of cinnamon rolls and two cups of expresso. "Morning, Mike. Brought some goodies for you and Quin."

"Great. Thanks. I think she's out back."

Javitt, a spry little man with thick spectacles and thinning gray hair, set the tray on the front desk. McCleary hoped his business was brisk this morning. Otherwise he would stick around and launch into one of his convoluted tales of Palm

Beach history. The movers and shakers of bygone years, the fire that had leveled the Breakers Hotel in 1925, the myriad scandals. He knew it all, every scrap of gossip that had crossed his threshold in forty years of baking pastries on this street. And once he got started, it was difficult to shut him up.

"I knew I smelled cinnamon rolls," Quin said as she came into the room. "Thanks, Harry."

"Don't mention it, little lady."

She beamed at the *little*. For *little*, McCleary thought, Quin would sit through a pitch for life insurance. She alternated between marveling about the physical changes of her pregnancy to mourning the demise of her pre-pregnancy body. But to McCleary she had never looked lovelier. Her skin was creamy, her hair shone, and her eyes, pale blue in the center and ringed by a deeper blue, seemed to gleam like moist stones.

"There's a certain way you have to eat them to really appreciate the taste. You mind?" Javitt asked.

Quin shook her head, and Javitt picked up a knife, a fork, and uncapped the butter dish he'd brought with him. He slathered each of their rolls in butter, then sliced them up into tiny bite-sized pieces. He stabbed a piece on either fork and held them out. "Now try these."

He was absolutely right about the taste, and he watched them wolf down the rolls, beaming like a proud father. "When my wife was pregnant with our oldest son she ate two of these every morning, Mike. You should see that boy now. Thirty-two and strong as a bull. Smart, too. I put all kinds of vitamins into them and that flour isn't refined. Best there is. Nothing in those rolls to hurt the baby."

Over Javitt's shoulder, McCleary saw a man who was all brawn and muscle getting out of a county sheriff's car in front of the building. He stood there a moment, hoisting his pants, and glanced around, probably assessing the neighborhood. Lt. Lou Garrison, McCleary thought, ten minutes early for their appointment.

McCleary had phoned him four days ago, after Quin's visit with Kate, and Garrison had suggested they meet here at the office on Saturday, his day off. McCleary had pressed for an earlier meeting, but Garrison said he couldn't, he was going to be at a law-enforcement seminar in Orlando. So in the interim McCleary had spoken with the coroner and Kate's attorney and they'd both given him some background on Garrison. The coroner liked him; the attorney didn't.

Garrison strolled through the door with the proprietary air that characterized the old-time cops who figured they had seen it all. He whipped sunglasses off his hooked beak of a nose and introduced himself. His voice boomed. He pumped Javitt's arm, Quin's, McCleary's.

Twenty years as a state trooper had etched deep lines of cynicism into his face—crow's-feet at the corners of his dark eyes, brackets at the sides of his mouth that deepened when he spoke, a pair of creases that shot down either side of his nose. McCleary wondered if he would have looked like this if he hadn't left Metro-Dade seven years ago, after a decade in Homicide.

Javitt departed and the three of them settled in the sitting area near the window—McCleary and Quin on the wicker couch, Garrison in the wicker chair, arms thrown open and resting along the edge. His body language literally shouted that he was willing to answer questions about Kate's arrest, the murder, any of it. But there was something patronizing in his manner that McCleary found vaguely irritating—the seasoned cop breaking bread with the new boy in town, already on a first-name basis. *Mike* and *Lou*, old home boys. And he completely ignored Quin; he evidently thought of her as The Wife and of McCleary as The Detective. She sat there, watching him, unusually quiet.

"The way I see it, Mike, is there's two things you got to remember about the Palm Beaches. West Palm is where peons like us live. Palm Beach is the rich man's Disney World. Only thing separating them is a bridge, but it might as well be a goddamn continent. And the folks here in this Disney World figure the rules the rest of us live by don't apply to them."

"Meaning Kate Bishop?"

"Naw, not Kate specifically. I'm talking about all of them. The Trumps, Rockefellers, Kennedys, take your pick. You cruise up and down Ocean Drive sometime and take a *real* close look at some of those houses, my friend. Trump's place has a hundred and fifteen rooms and he paid more than eleven million for it. A bargain compared to what it's worth now. It used to belong to Merriweather Post.'' McCleary knew his face was blank because Garrison leaned forward. ''You know, of Post cereal.''

He was annoyed now, as though McCleary's obtuseness were a personal affront. ''So we're talking the kind of money that equals the national budget in some countries. The Bishop home isn't like Trump's place by a long shot, but the family's cut from the same mold, if you know what I mean.''

''Did you know the old man?''

''Hell, yeah. And the granddaddy, too. Shrewd, those two. The granddaddy was pals with the likes of Flagler. He made all his money in real estate. Jack's daddy could be a real charmer when he thought he might get something out of it. But inside he was a mean son of a bitch. I reckon that's partly why those kids of his turned out so weird. And don't misunderstand me, I liked Jack. He wasn't hung up on all that class-conscious shit you find in this town. But he was an odd egg, studying this near-death stuff and all.'' He grinned. ''I mean, who cares. When you go, you go. Finito.''

How nice that at the ripe old age of—what? forty-one? forty-two?—Garrison had already resolved one of the major philosophical questions.

''Who called the police that night?''

''Not that night, the next morning. The ranch caretaker, Eduardo, arrived around five-thirty and found Kate sitting on the front porch, Jack's body propped up in a rocking chair beside her. She told Eduardo that she and Jack were going to watch the sun rise. That he liked watching the sun rise. Eduardo took one look at Jack and ran inside to use the phone. It didn't work, so he drove over to the migrant camp and called the station. I got there about an hour later. I took her in for questioning.''

''What was the caretaker doing there so early?''

Garrison shrugged. ''I guess he's there every morning at that time.''

''When was Kate charged?''

"When one of my boys returned to the station with a snub-nosed .38 that was found in the weeds near the barn. We ran a make on it. Her name came up on the computer. Her prints were the only prints on it. So I pressed charges and that was that."

"She says the gun was stolen."

Garrison snorted. "She says, she says. That's just what I mean about these Palm Beachers, Mike. They think that because you tell them something is true, you should believe it. So if it was stolen, how come she never reported it?"

"She didn't realize it was missing."

"Right." He guffawed; it made his cheeks puff out. "And if you believe *that*, my friend, then I've got some land to sell you." He sat forward again, his *Let's Be Up Front About This* posture. "It's like this. Kate killed him for money and stuck around because she figured it would make her story more credible. Now, I got no personal beef with Kate. But a man's been murdered and he was a friend of mine."

"High school, right?"

"Yeah. Then he went on to Dartmouth and I became a cop. But it didn't make any difference with him and me. Like I said, he wasn't uppity."

While it was true that Bishop had had one of those magnanimous personalities that cut across divisions of class and education, McCleary couldn't imagine him socializing with Garrison. Volleyball on a beach, maybe, or Sunday football and a couple of beers for old times, but not what Garrison was implying with the *him and me* line.

"Look, I can appreciate Kate trying to save her ass, Mike. Hell, who wouldn't do the same in her shoes? But there's only one truth here. The verdict on Kate Bishop is in."

There was never just one truth when it came to murder, McCleary thought, and the verdict wasn't in until the jury said it was.

"What do you think?" McCleary was standing at the window, watching Garrison pull away, and spoke to Quin's reflection in the glass, standing next to him.

"He's got a bad attitude about women."

McCleary laughed. "Besides that."

Quin rubbed a bright red apple against her skirt, then bit into it as she stepped out of her shoes. "He made my feet swell and that's never a good sign."

"You think he's got an angle?"

"You ever met a cop who doesn't, Mac?"

"Sure."

"Yeah? Who?"

"Me."

"You don't count. You're not a cop anymore." Her eyes followed a thin, elegantly dressed woman down the sidewalk. "I think Garrison is one of those people who could fall on either side of the fence. Maybe he was just doing his job, maybe there's more to it. We just have to play it out." She giggled suddenly. "Here. Quick. She just kicked."

He pressed a hand to her belly and she covered it with her own, both of them waiting for the baby to kick again. "She needs a name, Quin."

"You like Amy?"

"Too little-girlish."

"How about something exotic, like Maya?"

"It'd sound weird with McCleary, but it might not be bad for a middle name."

"There." She moved his hand lower on her stomach and to the right. "She rolled. Maybe she'll do it again."

McCleary's image of his daughter was the same one that had appeared on the screen of a computer when the doctor had performed an ultrasound for Quin's amniocentesis. A large head, the long crook of her spine, her tiny feet and hands, the steady beat of her heart, a little astronaut floating in her dimly lit and clamorous world, tethered to his world by a lifeline.

Then he felt it, a soft, swift flutter. It made him think of a field of butterflies, all of them lifting into the air at once, rising toward the sky, the sun.

Miraculous and mystifying, it humbled him.

The house was a symbol to McCleary.

It represented everything that had gone right in his marriage since he and Quin had reconciled last summer. It was *their* home, whereas the house in Miami had been Quin's before they'd met.

The place was only two years old, custom-built by a family who had worked for Pratt and Whitney in West Palm. It was a single-story that seemed larger than it actually was because it was so open. Huge windows, Mexican tile floors, a tremendous backyard shrouded with tropical plants, a little paradise.

The yard sloped down to a small lake. It wasn't the kind of lake he'd known as a kid in Syracuse, but it was still a body of water that created an illusion of rural living. Ducks visited frequently, a pair of great white herons occasionally flew in at dawn or dusk, and sometimes a flock of wild green parrots from Christ knew where dropped by to roost along the shores. It was the nearest thing he'd known to country since he'd moved to Florida twenty years ago.

The house, unlike the office, was still in shambles: boxes that were half unpacked, furniture in the wrong places, things in need of repair. But as he stood at the far end of the living room, he could see it as it would be. It was like staring at an empty canvas when he had a vague idea for a painting and could perceive a hint of form and color, an outline of what the painting might become.

"Hey, m'man," said Joe Bean, be-bopping out into the living room with a pair of Coronas in hand. "You look like you need a cold brew."

Bean was as thin as his name suggested, with skin the rich black of coal and a relentless energy that kept him moving to the rhythm of some internal beat. He had taken the afternoon off to help them unpack. McCleary doubted an afternoon would do it but appreciated the help.

"Thanks, Bean."

"*Salud.*" He clicked his bottle against McCleary's. "Kate and Quin said the final decision on the pizza was two large, one with everything on it except anchovies, the other with just cheese and black olives. I don't know how we're going to eat two of them, but I never argue with Quin when it comes to food."

"Wise man."

Bean opened the sliding glass doors and they stepped outside. "I like Kate." He sipped from his beer as he gazed out at the lake. "If she's a killer, Mac, then my skin's as white as yours."

"I agree. What'd you think of the file?"

"The killer knew him well. That's how it feels to me."

McCleary didn't ask why he felt that way; there was no explaining a hunch. "Anything else?"

"The arresting cop—what's his name?"

"Garrison."

"Yeah, Garrison. He followed procedure by the book. In fact, he followed procedure like he was reading the manual while he was doing it. Any time it's played that close, it bothers me." They started down the sloping backyard toward the lake. "How well did you know Bishop?"

"Well enough to like him, but not well enough to know who might have killed him or why."

They stopped at the edge of the lake. The stew who lived to their right was weeding the plants around her AC unit. To their left lived a retired army captain and his wife. Both neighbors were obsessive about property lines. The stew had made it clear she didn't want McCleary to plant a hedge too close to *her* property, thank you very much. The captain had told McCleary how he had to pull a gun on his last neighbor because the guy refused to take down a wall he thought was on *his* property.

But the land in front of them was unencumbered. Rays of peach light shot across the surface of the still waters. Crickets chirruped, begging for rain. A black bird swooped low over the lake and landed in the cluster of tall grasses on the other side. This wasn't a place to discuss murder.

"You know, I've got a hunch this case is going to make Miami look like a vacation," Bean remarked.

"Murder is murder whether it's Miami or Tahiti."

"You know what I mean."

Yes, he knew. Some murders were straightforward and uncluttered, like simple arithmetic. If you followed A to B to C, you would eventually reach Z and your killer. McCleary, weekend artist, thought of uncluttered murders as one of the primary colors. Blue. Other murders were a bit more complex.

They detoured, you encountered blocks, you had to be innovative. These were secondary colors, like turquoise or yellow.

Then there were murders like this one, apparently simple, apparently solved as far as the cops were concerned. But these could have endless twists and surprises and nothing was ever what it appeared to be. These were the absence of light, color, shape. These were black holes that could crush you to death and spit you out like space debris. Yes, he understood exactly what Bean meant.

3

CLICKER WAITED FOR darkness the way other men waited for money or fame. He understood its rhythms, its moods, its tricks. It was his element.

His mother used to say it went back to a pattern he established as an infant, when he had his days and nights all mixed up. He would sleep from eleven in the morning to eleven at night and be awake for the next twelve hours. His mother had repeated this story numerous times when she was alive, and in her voice Clicker had always heard what she didn't say. The strain, the fatigue, the tension his sleep habits had caused between her and Clicker's old man. She had thrown it in his face whenever she was angry with him. She had blamed him for being different. Perhaps she had even hated him for it.

What's a clicker, Ma?

My secret name for you.

But why Clicker?

Nothing else fits.

I don't get it.

You're like the clicker on the camera. I'm never sure what I'm going to get when I press the button.

Button, button, he thought, smiling as he loaded a rock into a slingshot. Who's got the button?

He tracked the squirrel that scampered through the moonlight toward the scattering of brush near the barn, and when it paused, he let the rock fly. It slammed into the squirrel's head. The creature emitted a shriek of pain, pitched sideways, twitched for a moment, then went still.

Clicker walked over to it, kicked it in the side to make sure it was dead. Its bright, shiny eyes were open, staring vapidly toward the moon. Its front teeth were partially visible. The tail was thin and scrawny, like the body. A flatlands squirrel. The worst kind. For the most part, they eschewed trees and lived in scrub brush and tall grass that grew around Lake Okeechobee.

He leaned closer, staring into its tiny eyes. Death was there. Clicker could see its flitting shadow, could almost hear its soft, wicked cackle, and knew he would feel the air stir at its passage if he touched the squirrel. Animal or man, he thought, death always stuck around for a bit, smug and cocky, like the bully on the block laughing. *Ha-ha, you can't catch me. But I'll catch you. I sure will.*

"Don't bet on it, fucker." Clicker grabbed the squirrel by the tail and hurled it into the bushes behind the ranch. The vultures would find it. The fire ants. The field mice. He hated squirrels. He'd been bitten by one when he was kid. The goddamn thing had taken popcorn from his extended hand, then grabbed his finger and nearly chomped off the end of it. Since squirrels were notorious for carrying rabies and this one had escaped, he'd had to take a series of rabies shots. That was in the days when the shots were given through the lining of the stomach, with a needle as long as his arm. He could still feel the ghost of that pain.

His hands felt soiled now, tarnished, infected. He stuck his sling into his back pocket and hurried back inside the Bishop ranch to wash up. He remembered to open the door with his handkerchief so he wouldn't leave fingerprints.

Once he'd washed his hands, he wished he had some extra clothes with him. The squirrel probably had fleas and suppose the fleas had jumped onto him when he'd touched it? Flatland fleas. Okeechobee fleas. Nasty fuckers. Just in case, he stripped in the kitchen and shoved the clothes and his black canvas shoes into the washer. Kate's washer. When he lifted the lid, he used his handkerchief. He longed to touch it with his bare fingers, but that was against the rules. Survival anywhere depended on adhering to certain rules, a certain code of conduct.

He added detergent, turned on the washer, lowered the lid. Then he padded naked into the kitchen. Kate's kitchen at the ranch. It was a good feeling, being naked in her space, in air that had touched her, in air she had breathed. It made him hard.

The phone. He hadn't checked in with her yet tonight. He

placed the hanky over the receiver, picked it up, covered the mouthpiece with a paper towel, and punched out her number. She answered on the second ring, her voice drugged with sleep. "Yes? Hello?"

"Kate?"

"Yes, this is Kate. Who's this?"

His hand strayed to his groin. In his head he saw her: Kate in a pretty nightgown that had slipped off a shoulder, her breasts pressed up against the silk, her throat like marble. Like alabaster. Smooth as the inner surface of a shell.

"Did you get my drawing and the note? I—"

She hung up. It was a physical pain, as if she'd stabbed him with a knife. He slammed the receiver down, hating her, loving her, needing her.

One small squirt from the bottle fixed him up fine. Jack's elixir. Oh yes siree. The drug zipped through his blood, electrifying him. He moved restlessly through the rooms where Kate had been, his fingers aching to touch what she had touched. But rules were rules and these were quite explicit:

—Leave nothing behind that can be traced to you. No prints, sperm, spit, strands of hair, no flecks of skin under the victim's nails.

—Keep your weapon simple. If possible, use someone else's weapon.

—Have a solid alibi.

Uncomplicated rules. But the buzz in his head was so loud, he had to think about them, enumerate them.

Touch nothing.

But the murder was done. The place had already been dusted for prints. What harm would it do? He flexed his fingers, wincing at the ache in his joints. They wanted to touch. Needed to.

His fingers trailed lightly over surfaces Kate had touched. A dresser, a tabletop, a glass. His body sang. Kate started to fill out in his mind; he was creating her anew from the residue of the self she'd left behind. His love would improve her. It would thicken her black hair, round out her hips, plump up her breasts. He was preparing her for the day when she would come to him, offer herself to him, and he would take what was rightfully his. What Jack had stolen from him.

Master bedroom. The beam of his flashlight skimmed objects and furniture that were precisely arranged. He sat at the foot of her bed, a water bed. It rolled and rocked with his weight. His head sank into the feather pillows, into the scent of perfumes and shampoos and powders. He extended his arms at his sides and closed his eyes, absorbing the parts of her that remained against the sheets, the spread.

Her hair, a dark shadow against pastel sheets, her long fingers with sculpted nails, the pale curve of an arm, a dimpled knee—all there for the taking. But other images rose unbidden: Jack beside her, touching her, kissing her, making love to her. It infuriated him and he leaped off the mattress, went downstairs and pulled his clothes out of the dryer. He dressed and returned upstairs, hating Jack for disrupting his pleasure.

The bastard had been dead—what? How long? He had killed Jack on November sixteenth; this was Sunday, December second. Sixteen days, then. The bastard had been dead sixteen days and he still haunted Clicker. As he slid open a drawer in her dresser, he thought about how he would one day eradicate all traces of Jack from this room. He didn't know how he would do it, but he would. An exorcism, a purging.

Inside the drawer, everything was neatly arranged. Slips folded here, panties there, shorts in the middle. He picked up a pair of panties. Lightweight cotton, not silk. Cut high on the sides and low in front. Not good enough. He wanted silk. Impractical, marvelous, erotic silk. He found a pair, rubbed it against his cheeks, let it slide through his fingers. A pair of scissors he found in one of the drawers did the trick. *Snip, snip*, and the crotch fell away.

Mine, he thought. She's mine.

He arranged the silk panties in with the others so that she wouldn't see them the second she opened the drawer. He wanted it to be a surprise. Like his calls. Like the drawing, the note, the other things he had in mind.

Into the closet now. So many clothes. She never had to pack a thing to come to the ranch; everything she could possibly need or want was already here. He eased a turquoise robe from a hanger. The silk slipped through his fingers like water. He pressed his face into it, inhaling the fragrance of her skin. Then he snipped holes in the front, where her breasts would be, and returned it to the hanger.

He flashed his light up at the square in the ceiling that led to the attic where she had hidden that night. He was tempted to go up there, to pull from that closed, dusty air what it must have been like for her. But there wasn't time. He didn't want to be here if the caretaker happened by to check on the place.

He drove back into town, negotiating the road slowly because he was still high. He went straight to his darkroom.

One wall was papered in photos of Kate he'd put up while she was still in jail. Snapshots, blowups, posters, some in color, others in black and white. In the pictures where Jack had appeared, Clicker had cut him out. Jack didn't belong here now. He wandered through his private gallery, feasting on the sight of her. Kate in shorts and a halter top; Kate in a string bikini; Kate in a cocktail dress; Kate in her myriad moods and personas, posing just for him. She was his, all right; she just didn't know it. Yet.

He took his time, studying her expressions, trying to guess what she had been thinking when each photo was snapped, what sort of mood she'd been in. It was no more than he'd done dozens of times, but he never tired of it. She was his project, his passion, his obsession. If Jack had taken the time to study her as Clicker did, maybe he would still be alive.

And maybe not.

Chew on that one, Jack.

When he reached the last photograph, his high had gone a little flat. He wished there were more pictures. He wished she were here, watching him, talking to him, laughing with him.

All things come with time, he thought.

Even Kate.

"Too bad, golden boy," he whispered to Jack's ghost, and laughed. "Too goddamn bad."

4

IT HAPPENED SUDDENLY, while Kate was on her way to the mailbox Monday morning. One moment the air she breathed was ordinary, just sticky and hot, and the next moment it was struck through with sunlight that was brilliant, breathtaking, miraculous.

She drank in the blue December sky, the deep green of the Norwegian pines in the front yard, the crimson of the hibiscus flowers on the tall hedge that enclosed the property. Color, so much color. And the light. In jail, she had forgotten the quality and texture of the light in South Florida. That sharpness, that perfection, that sheen like varnish on everything it touched.

She looked down at her hands, at the diamond ring that caught the light, fractured it, tossed it off again. The cluster of tiny rubies around it glistened and danced. In jail, the ring had been taken away from her, and for the five days she'd been there her fingers had felt naked, flayed, stripped to the bone. Every time she had reached to twist the ring, touch it, her heart had broken again.

In jail, the belt on her jeans was removed so that she couldn't hang herself. She was given a blanket, a small pillow as flat as an envelope, a bar of rough soap, a tube of toothpaste that tasted like flour, a toothbrush with bristles as hard as a Brillo pad. Her purse, like her ring, had ended up in the property room at the police station, minus two quarters for calls on the public phone. One to her attorney, the other to Jack's brother. A few items had still not been returned to her.

The cell was dismal—a toilet without a seat, a barred window near the ceiling, twelve empty bunks, a sink with a dark ring around the drain. Every day a volunteer had wheeled a cart down the hall with paperbacks and cigarettes and gum on it. The books were free, the cigarettes and the gum were not. She had read and smoked, losing herself in stories that had nothing to do with the real world, with her world. She had read to keep from thinking about Jack. Jack as he lay dying, Jack dead, Jack murmuring "Schrödinger's cat," the conundrum.

The seventeen days he'd been dead felt like months, like lifetimes.

Her ebullience hissed away so fast, she felt instantly weak, boneless, dry. A strong wind could have lifted her like a leaf and pulverized her. She hurried on down the walk, past her red Cherokee Jeep in the driveway, past Jack's black Porsche, through air that was simply ordinary again. Her eyes burned with tears that refused to fall.

The heat poured over her like molten glass. She grabbed the mail from the box and didn't linger at the curb for fear someone was watching the house. Nosy neighbors, the same reporters who left endless messages on her machine, cops, a spy from the prosecutor's office, Jack's killer. Or the same someone who had called the house every night since her release from jail.

The person—a man, she was sure it was a man—had never spoken until last night. Until then, it was just his breathing, the sound of the sea in a shell, filling the hollowness, connecting them. She'd forgotten to turn on the answering machine last night and when the phone had rung at midnight, she'd picked up. His voice was a whisper. *Did you get my drawing and the note?*

Inside the foyer, she dead-bolted the door and rifled through two days' worth of mail, looking for something that didn't belong with the bills, the magazines, the usual correspondence. But there was nothing. Of course not. Pervs who called did not also send drawings and notes through the mail.

The silence in the house rose up around her, a wall. In its way this silence was just as bad as the sound of the wind in the attic that night. She felt, suddenly, that it would crush her if she tried to endure it too long, and was grateful she had someplace to go today. It would be her first day back at the center since Jack's death. She needed to be there. Needed to root herself in work. Work had always been her haven.

The phone rang, shattering that silence. Her recorded voice was an echo of her former self, quick and cheerful. Certain her caller wouldn't break with tradition and phone mid-morning, Kate went into the kitchen and picked up the receiver.

The voice on the other end belonged to Ray Wolfe, one of her co-workers at the center and a man she'd been involved with before she met Jack. He had been on vacation when Jack was killed and this was the first time she'd talked with him since he'd left. Like the rabbit in Alice in Wonderland, he seemed to be forever pressed for time. He spoke in short, rapid bursts like gunfire, telling her how sorry he was about Jack, asking if she was okay, why hadn't she called him, when was he going to see her?

She didn't want to go into everything over the phone and told him she would see him in a while and they would talk then. "We can have lunch after the Lewis interview, Katie. That shouldn't take more than an hour."

"Lewis?" She couldn't place the name.

"The gardener who got bitten by the rattler."

She remembered now. Lewis was a referral from a counselor at West Palm General, where he had been rushed after he'd been bitten and where he had died. Jack had done the initial intake interview on his near death experience and had worked up the psyche profiles. She was supposed to have interviewed him the Friday after Thanksgiving, then had changed it to Saturday when the plane had developed a problem.

"If the one o'clock interview's a problem, just say so and I'll call him back and reschedule. Or I can do it."

"One's fine, Wolfie. But it's been a while since I read the background info on him. You'll have to update me when I get there."

"Got everything right here." He paused and she knew he was pacing back and forth in front of his desk now, winding the telephone cord around his hand, releasing it, winding it again. He was probably eyeing his pocket watch, then the pile of papers on his desk, irritated that he was spending so much

34

time talking to her. But Wolfe, despite his hurry, was one of those people who couldn't skip on to something else until he was satisfied with what he was working on. And at the moment she was his project. "You didn't tell me if you're okay, Katie."

"I've been better."

"I didn't get in until late last night and didn't know anything until I got here this morning."

"We'll talk, Wolfie. And don't worry, okay? I'm not going to drink arsenic as soon as we hang up."

"Very funny. I'll see you later."

She thought she heard the soft *click* of his pocket watch as it closed. She hung up, her hand lingering on the receiver, fingers twitching to punch out her brother's number, a part of her wanting to accept his offer to fly down and stay with her until "this was over." But that would mean his wife and their three kids would come also. It would mean her parents would arrive. She loved them all, but right now she would suffocate in their good intentions.

She would call Quin, she thought. Just to talk. To root herself in her life before Jack. She wondered how Quin would act in this situation if *she* had been charged with McCleary's murder. A gruesome thought. But she'd always wished she possessed that dark, frenzied humor that seemed to carry Quin through the worst of times. It was a kind of irreverence that protected the core of who she was.

Whereas Quin's first reaction to everything was impulse, emotion, Kate had always struggled to balance emotion and intellect out of fear that she would become too much one or the other. And it had blunted something in her, she thought, some essential instinct.

She drew her hand away from the phone. Get on with your life, she thought, and hurried up the wide oak staircase. When she reached the doorway of the bedroom, the room she had shared with Jack, she stopped. That clarity of perception flooded through her again, just as brilliantly as it had outside, and she realized that her memories of this room were never as vivid as the real thing.

In her mind, the cathedral ceilings weren't as high, the windows weren't as large, and the colors of the Southwest motif were never as lovely. Her memory had cheated her by diminishing colors, shapes, textures, and she wondered if eventually it would also cheat her of her memories of Jack.

Kate tossed the mail on the bed and tried to avoid looking at the photograph of him on the dresser. She showered, changed into a cotton skirt and blouse, and finally couldn't avoid the photo.

It had been taken during a weekend at the ranch a few months ago, when they'd driven out to a meadow near the lake for a picnic. It had been a hot, windy day, with a sky that was a pure, undiluted blue. The drought hadn't yet turned the surrounding countryside to the ugly brown it was now. Jack had been sitting in the shade, reading, and had glanced up just as she'd snapped the picture.

She'd captured the dichotomy in him that had so often mystified her. Here was Jack the analytical shrink. Here was the Jack who had often trotted off to work with his socks falling around his ankles. Here was the brooding Jack, the Jack who had been lover, seducer, husband, friend.

She pressed her thumb to the photo as though something of him lingered in the image. He wasn't a handsome man. But his face was a map of strong, bold lines, each with a story. You had to look at him twice to make sure you had seen what you thought you had. It was a face she had loved almost from the first time she'd seen him nearly four years ago.

She'd been in a hurry that day, late for a meeting with visiting researchers and psychiatrists, not paying attention to where she was going. By the time she realized she'd entered the center parking lot through the exit, a black BMW was leaving and she swerved to avoid hitting it. The driver swerved at the same time, in the same direction, and Kate had smashed into the passenger side.

A tall, lanky man with a stoop to his shoulders leaped out, his face bright red with anger. Shaken, Kate hurried over, apologizing before she had even reached him.

"I'm really sorry. I didn't see you."

"Sorry? Christ. You must've been driving with your eyes shut. That's the exit."

"Hey, I swerved to avoid hitting you and then *you* turned in the same direction."

His smile then was quick and magnificent, and it transformed his face. "How would you know to swerve if you didn't see me?"

He was poking fun at her now, she was sure of it. All she wanted was to settle this as fast as possible and get to her meeting. "Look, I'll pay you out of pocket for damages. Otherwise my insurance will go up."

"I'll pay."

"You will?"

"Sure."

Suddenly it was no big deal. "How about if we just forget it ever happened?"

"Only if you have dinner with me tonight."

She laughed. Dinner. Right. "I don't even know your name."

"Jack Bishop. I'm psychiatry." As in *I'm American* or *I'm crazy*. He stabbed a thumb toward the center. "I'm supposed to be in a meeting in there."

"So am I."

His brows lifted, looping over his eyes at an odd angle. "You're psychiatry?"

"Sociology."

"From where?"

"Here."

"Oh, you teach here on campus."

"No. I'm a researcher in the near-death studies. If you're supposed to be in there, how come you were on your way out?"

"I detest meetings. Let's go have breakfast or lunch or something."

She laughed. "I can't. I've got to present a paper."

"So do I. But I detest presenting papers."

"What's your paper on?"

"Elation associated with near-death experiences."

"I thought you said you're a psychiatrist."

"I am. But I have a group of patients who've been through NDEs. You sure you don't want to have breakfast?"

They both laughed, and it had started then, started in the parking lot with the two of them surrounded by crumpled chrome and scraped paint, and had rolled through several months of turmoil. She didn't like his sister; he was jealous of the men in her past. She couldn't get used to the things he took for granted—the servants, the mansion, the cars, the conspicuous consumption; he thought most of her friends were boring.

Neither of them could escape the prejudices of their backgrounds. Jack was Palm Beach born and bred and had grown up in a family where emotional distance was the norm. Kate had been born and raised in Tallahassee, in a tight-knit family that was comfortable yet not rich.

But their differences had as much to do with their diverse backgrounds as with their individual needs. She tired of playing second fiddle to his patients, of waiting for calls he forgot to make. Jack, accustomed to getting what he wanted when he wanted it, expected her to be available when he was free.

Their splits and reconciliations were as cyclic as the phases of the moon. When she refused to have anything more to do with him, he dogged her relentlessly. He left funny notes on her windshield, sent huge bouquets of flowers, sat at her table in the campus cafeteria even though she might not speak to him for the entire meal. During those times she became his mission, his passion.

After one particularly virulent argument, he showed up at a campus workshop she was teaching on death and dying. When she asked him what he was doing there, he stood up and asked her to marry him, asked right there in front of twenty-two nursing students who applauded. Kate was so appalled, she dismissed the workshop, then lit into him. The next morning at the center she found a package on her desk that contained a diamond ring surrounded by tiny rubies with a card that read: *I apologize. But the offer still holds. Say yes.*

Kate wrapped it up and sent it back via one of her student assistants. That afternoon Jack walked into her office at the center and shut the door.

"C'mon, Jack, don't do this."

"Just hear me out, Kate."

"I've heard you out before. We're too different. It won't work."

"We don't know if it'll work or not because I've never tried. Let's live together for a while and see what happens. All I want is a chance." A job had opened up at the center, he said, and he felt it was his opportunity to get out of private practice and focus on research. "Whether I take it depends on you."

"Do what you want."

"Look, if living together doesn't work for us, I'll get out of your life. I promise."

Because she loved him and wanted to believe it would work, she said she would think about it. For a day, she'd analyzed it to death, spinning scenarios of what he might do, what she might do, what they might do to each other. But in the end these things were only possibilities and the fact was that he had taken steps to leave private practice, which had eaten up all his time. So she called him the next morning and said she was willing to try if they got their own place. She didn't want to live in his house, in that mansion haunted by his mother's tastes and his father's neuroses. Fine, he replied, fine.

Six months later, they were married.

They didn't live happily ever after.

As Kate stepped outside to leave for the campus, a red Corvette sped into the driveway, tires spitting gravel. The top was down and Jack's sister was clearly visible behind the wheel, her very short black hair as shiny as the 'vette's hood. She hopped out and marched to the front of the car, inspecting it for dents, nicks, scratches from the gravel.

"The gravel doesn't kick up if you're going more slowly, Stephanie."

She strutted toward Kate, the twenty-eight-year-old baby of the Bishop family, six feet of bones and sinew who cut an imposing figure even in gym attire. Tight pink shorts hugged her hips, a shimmering violet top covered breasts the size of pimples, and violet leg warmers climbed up her calves. Her leanness was curiously asexual. Zip her into a pair of denim coveralls, Kate thought, pull a wide-brim hat down over her hair, slip shades over her eyes, and she could pass for a man, one of those bamboo-thin young Cubans who wore gold chains and hung out in Domino Park in Miami's Little Havana.

She stopped just short of the porch and tilted her sunglasses back into her hair, eyeing Kate with undisguised disdain. "Even a cherry pit can do considerable damage if it hits in the right place." The nasal quality to her voice flattened her *A*s and grated on Kate's nerves. "The thing ought to be paved."

"The hood looks fine to me."

"You can't possibly see it well from there, Kate."

Stephanie, the pugilist. "You didn't stop by to talk about your car."

She folded her long arms at her waist. "The coroner is releasing Jack's body to me and I'll be making arrangements for the cremation and memorial service."

A hole opened up in Kate's heart, but she didn't say anything. She'd been charged with Jack's murder, after all, and to Palm Beachers she was the outsider who'd killed one of their own. Some mountains were simply too large to be moved.

"Did you hear what I said?" Stephanie snapped.

"Do what you want."

"What I *don't* want is you at the funeral."

Kate brushed past her and felt the burn of Stephanie's eyes against her spine.

5

DEATH, AT LEAST in the abstract, had always held a certain fascination for McCleary, and he knew exactly when it had started.

The summer he was five, his father decided it was time for him to take a more active part in the functioning of the farm. His job was to care for the chickens—clean the coops, collect the eggs, feed them, keep them warm in the winter and cool in the summer. It was enjoyable until the afternoon his father showed him how to wring a chicken's neck.

McCleary could still remember how the bird's wings had flapped as his old man placed one of his large, powerful hands at the base of the bird's neck and, with the other, twisted hard and fast, snapping the neck right off the body. He dropped it, and for a few seconds the creature stumbled around, blood pouring out of the place where its head had been. Then it toppled over into the dirt, inches from where its head lay. It was the single most grotesque thing McCleary had seen in his five years and he promptly dropped to his knees and threw up.

For days afterward, he thought about the chicken, its severed head, the way its tiny black eyes had peered upward, unseeing, and puzzled over where it had gone. He knew his mother had cooked the body, that they had eaten it for dinner, but what had happened to whatever it was that made a chicken a chicken, the thing his parents called a soul? Heaven, his mother said. A special place for chickens, his father told him. Nowhere, his grandfather said.

In one form or another, he'd been wrestling with that question ever since.

During his decade in Homicide, his beliefs had run the

gamut from death as an annihilation of consciousness to the Eastern view of the survival of consciousness and a series of lives in which bodies were exchanged like clothing. His beliefs now resided somewhere in between. He suspected the truth would probably be found along that elusive border between life and death. Kate's territory. And Jack's.

Near-death experiences.

McCleary had read articles about it, had talked to cops who had been clinically dead and to crime victims who had nearly died. But he'd never been inside a facility where the experience was actually studied and knew this wasn't the way he had imagined such a facility would look. This building resembled an old Spanish mission.

The structure was one story, a perfect square the color of coral, with eaves and windows trimmed in chocolate brown. A trellis covered the front walk and was blanketed in bougainvillea vines bursting with bloodred blossoms that also littered the walk like confetti.

The lobby walls were pastel, music played softly in the background, brightly colored fish in a tremendous aquarium swam through their silent world. Sunlight streamed through sliding glass doors that opened onto a courtyard lush with tropical foliage. It was all perfectly orchestrated to create an atmosphere of serenity.

When he asked to see Sam Dayton, the head of the center and Bishop's close friend, the receptionist said he was with someone at the moment. Would he like to wait in the library? En route, McCleary passed Bishop's office, his name burned into a wooden plaque on the door. He doubted that Garrison had searched it; as far as he was concerned, the murder was closed. Since the hall was deserted at the moment, McCleary tried the knob, it turned, and he slipped inside.

The air was cooler here than in the hall, and still, utterly still, as if the room were holding its breath, awaiting someone, anyone. He guessed no one had ventured in here since Bishop's death.

Nothing in the room indicated that it had been inhabited by a psychiatrist. There were no diplomas on the walls, no fancy furniture, no M.D. after the Bishop on the nameplate. It was in keeping with the Bishop McCleary had known, the Bishop who hadn't felt the need to impress people with credentials or titles.

A photograph of Bishop and Kate stood on one corner of the desk. On the other was a wire basket that contained two blank legal pads, several memos on patients Bishop had seen or intended to see, a two-year appointment book with notations like *Call F. Chaney for follow-up interview* and *Recommend Mrs. Howard for weekly NDE sessions*. Business as usual.

But Bishop was dead and somewhere there had to be evidence that business had *not* been proceeding as usual. This didn't have the feel of a thrill killing or a serial murder and it didn't look like the work of a certifiable crazy. That meant he was looking for a pattern of some kind that would lead to a motive.

There was a finite number of motives for premeditated murder and these motives fell under four broad categories: greed, passion, revenge, a cover-up. The problem with Bishop's murder was that, right now, the motive could fit into any of the groupings. Considering Bishop's net worth, greed was a good contender. That would make the brother and the sister the likeliest candidates. But what about professional greed? Perhaps Bishop was on to something with near-death experiences that even Kate didn't know about. That would finger Sam Dayton and Ray Wolfe.

Passion: another woman? Although Bishop and Kate seemed to have had a good marriage, that didn't exclude another woman, maybe someone Bishop had known before he met Kate. Personal experience had taught McCleary that much. After all, when Sylvia Callahan had sailed back into his life during a homicide investigation several years ago, his relationship with Quin had never been better.

But passion might also mean a man who was fixated on Kate. A man like Wolfe? For some reason, he and Quin had seen more of Kate when she was involved with Wolfe than when she'd been married to Bishop. McCleary felt he knew him better than he'd known Bishop, but that didn't exonerate him from suspicion. The first rule in any homicide investigation was to assume nothing.

Revenge? A former patient, perhaps. Someone Bishop had been treating when he was in private practice.

And a cover-up? It could encompass all of the categories. It implied secrets. It implied information withheld, knowledge that was used against someone else in blackmail, something illegal.

McCleary took the appointment book with him when he left and ducked into the men's room to examine it more closely. Locked in a stall, he studied it and noticed three details that had eluded him before. Once a month, usually on a Monday or a Wednesday, Bishop had jotted *Lunch*. That was all, just *Lunch*, and never at the same time. Every other month, a Thursday, Friday, or Saturday was circled in red.

In the first half of the appointment book, which covered last year, he found the same initials scribbled nine times: *BG*, and next to them, *Fargo*. There didn't seem to be any pattern to the dates or days. In one of these entries was an additional notation that read: *Bonanza 100 Hr. Check*. He didn't know what Fargo referred to, but the town nearest to the ranch was Belle Glade, which had a general aviation airport. McCleary remembered flying in there one weekend when Bishop had picked up him and Quin and brought them back to the ranch.

Patterns.

McCleary stuck the appointment book in his back pocket and left the stall.

Except for his height, which was probably about six three, and his eyes, Sam Dayton was rather ordinary looking.

He was in his late thirties, didn't have an ounce of fat on him, and wore clothes that looked as if they'd come straight out of the dryer to his body. His nose was too long, his mouth was too wide, and his high forehead was exacerbated by a baldness that reached halfway back on his head.

His eyes were extraordinary, an intense, compelling blue, the focus of his face. You could look into them, McCleary thought, and know that everything he had experienced—every triumph, every sorrow—had been absorbed into that blue and was preserved there, remembered in excruciating detail.

His memory was so good, in fact, he could recall what Bishop had been wearing the day they'd met nine years ago, at a near-death seminar in Orlando, when Bishop was still in private practice. He could remember that Bishop had taken his coffee with three sugars and cream. That kind of detail.

He had a habit of smoothing his hand over his balding head, as if searching for the hair that was no longer there. McCleary, whose own hair was thinning, sympathized completely. As they talked, he moved around a lot, straightening papers, books, pouring coffee, explaining the framed drawings on the walls.

All depicted some phase of the near-death experience. Half had been done by adults and the other half by kids. Dayton touched his hand to a transparent globe near the window, where continents stood out in bright relief, mountains lifting and sloping into valleys, oceans swirling. The tiny red flags that dotted it pinpointed the various countries where near-death studies were now underway.

"Research has really burgeoned in the last decade," he said, sitting back finally at the edge of his desk. "And most of the people I know who are researching the field are as obsessed as I am."

"Like Jack," McCleary remarked, recalling some of his conversations with Bishop.

Dayton laughed. "Hell, Jack made *my* obsession look like a game of tiddlywinks. And the strange thing is that he had never had an NDE."

"Is that a prerequisite for obsession?"

"It helps." Eighteen years ago, he said, he ran out of air while scuba diving in a sinkhole in central Florida. For some reason he became disoriented and forgot he was wearing a weight belt. Had he removed the belt, everything would have been fine. But he didn't and every time his head popped through the surface of the water, the weights dragged him under again. "I was choking and trying to keep water from entering my mouth, but I was so exhausted from struggling, I think I just gave up. By the time my partner got me out of the water, I had stopped breathing. He figures I was dead for close to four minutes before he resuscitated me.

"It literally changed my life. I was twenty at the time, in college, majoring in engineering, with a minor in women and drinking. After my NDE I went into psychology and started looking for other people who had been through what I had." When he graduated, he worked in a hospice for several years counseling terminal cancer patients. He wrote a book on it, was invited to teach at the University of Miami, and eventually pitched his idea for the center to the trustees. "This was around the same time Kübler-Ross published her landmark work on death and dying and suddenly everyone was interested in the field. The trustees went for the idea and here I am. In 1982, a Gallup Poll estimated that eight million Americans had had an NDE. That estimate seems extremely conservative now."

"How'd you and Jack get to know each other?"

"He had a patient who had gone through an NDE and thought she would benefit by talking to other people who'd had the same experience. He referred her here. I needed someone with a medical and psychiatric background to draw up profiles, so he helped me out. It started like that right after the seminar where we'd met. Then when he decided to leave private practice, I hired him."

Their approaches to the field were quite different, but oddly complementary. Dayton already knew what he believed about death, so his goal was to document the common denominators in NDEs that cut across racial, religious, and cultural backgrounds. Jack, he said, believed there was nothing after death, that the visions of tunnels and lights and beatific beings were hallucinations. "Synapses firing and chemicals running wild. And he desperately wanted to be proven wrong. So for him the research was extremely personal." He paused, rubbed his finger under his long nose. "Maybe too personal."

"In what way?"

"Oh, I don't know. It just seemed to me that sometimes he flirted with death, like a kid taking a dare. He took some unnecessary chances in that plane of his, flying during electrical storms, that kind of thing. Kate tempered that streak in him, though. She was good for him in that way."

46

"You have any idea what Schrödinger's cat meant to him? It was the last thing he said before he died."

Something flared in Dayton's eyes that McCleary couldn't decipher. "He was *alive* when she found him?"

"Not for long."

"Jesus. I didn't know. She didn't mention it. Schrödinger's cat is a physics thing."

"That represents paradox."

"Right. And for Jack the term symbolized the paradox of this kind of research. There will always be people who say NDEs are involuntary responses, like the twitch of a muscle when the body's in its death throes, or that NDEs are dreams. And there will always be people who believe it means that consciousness survives death. It's possible he was already experiencing the things he'd always believed were involuntary and realized he'd been wrong, so the paradox had become personal."

"But why a physics term?"

"It was one of his interests." Dayton glanced at his watch. "If you've got the time, let me show you around, then you're welcome to observe one of our interviews with an NDEer. He's a twenty-four-year-old gardener who was bitten by a rattler. It killed him on the way to the hospital. Ray's with him now, but Kate's supposed to interview him when she gets here."

"Sounds interesting."

"They all are, Mr. McCleary." Dayton pressed his hands against the desk and pushed himself to his feet.

"Was Jack involved in any kind of research that might have led to a breakthrough in the field?"

Dayton understood what he was really asking. "Something someone would kill for."

"Yes."

"If he was, I didn't know about it."

It was, at best, an evasive answer, but McCleary let it pass. As they walked out into the hall, he asked how closely Kate and Bishop had worked together. It varied, Dayton replied. Bishop drew up psychological profiles based on a battery of tests he conducted and on information about a client's family, employment, hobbies, and so on. "Then Kate does the initial interview about the NDE and follows up as necessary. She evaluates the data from a sociological standpoint. Ray Wolfe, the other psychologist, and I do a lot of the mundane tasks. We choose a random number of clients and try to piece together a more complete picture of what has shaped them by talking to family and friends and professional associates. So although the four of us were all dealing with the same clients, we had separate duties and approaches to it."

"Where do you stand on the murder charge?"

"Are you serious?" Incredulity thickened his voice, deepened it. He stopped, his palm rubbing hard at his pate, his eyes pinned on McCleary. "You *are* serious." He shook his head. "Jesus, I've known Kate ten years, Mr. McCleary. She isn't capable of killing anyone. You should know that as well as anyone. Your wife roomed with her, for Christ's sake."

Interesting the way he'd turned things around, McCleary thought. "I *do* know it. I just wanted to be sure where you stood."

"Now you know."

Dayton started walking again and McCleary followed. "You have any ideas who might have killed him?"

"None."

"Maybe a patient he angered?"

"The people he dealt with liked him immensely."

"How about his brother and sister? They stand to inherit a lot of money."

"Kate knows more about their relationship with Jack than I do, but I rather doubt it."

"Were there any other women in his life?"

"If there were, I'd be the last person he'd tell. It would have compromised all of us."

Not quite true. Kate would have been the last. But McCleary kept his opinion to himself, and they walked on in silence.

6

1.

WHEN YOU COMPARED a map of the Palm Beaches with a map of Miami, Quin thought, it was obvious that the former was the place for someone who lacked a sense of direction. Even a moron could find his way around. And yet she was hopelessly lost, something that had rarely happened to her in Miami.

She'd somehow missed the bridge to Palm Beach and ended up in the parking lot in front of Lake Mangonia in West Palm. If she could believe the sign, this lake supplied most of the city with drinking water, which probably explained the absence of motorboats. But there were dozens of Windsurfers racing across the glassy lake, their sails puffed out. They looked like a regatta of bright-colored butterflies.

Quin munched on a handful of Cheerios—her OB's suggestion, they were low-cal—and spread her map open against the steering wheel. She found the lake on the map but wasn't sure if she was on PGA Boulevard or Australian Avenue, so she got out and started down toward the road to look for a sign.

Cars were pulling into the lot in droves, sailboards strapped to racks on the roofs of their cars. Her aging Toyota and a brown Firebird two rows back seemed to be the only vehicles that didn't have racks. Windsurfers were about evenly divided among men and women, and the women, naturally, all seemed to be slender and gorgeous, with deep tans. She was the elephant who had lumbered into a herd of sleek panthers, and longed for her prepregnancy body.

Her hipbones were a dim memory; her usual weight of a hundred and nine now stood at a hundred and thirty-eight; her navel had popped out, dark as a chocolate chip; she couldn't recall the last time she had slept on her stomach; her hunger was never satisfied; and there was a constant pressure on her bladder. The one advantage was that after years of a boob size of 34A, she was now 34C. Surely that counted for something.

She found a sign for Australian Avenue and, on her way back to the car, ducked into the restroom. When she came out a few minutes later, a man was crouched at the back of her car. She wouldn't have thought anything of it except that he was wearing a jacket and slacks, which made him as conspicuous in this crowd as she.

Quin paused next to a van and pretended to fix her sandal as she watched him. It was difficult to tell whether he was looking for something that had rolled under her car—a coin, maybe—or whether he was up to no good. For the moment, she assumed it was the latter, and when he stood, she moved to the other side of the van where he wouldn't see her. She gave him two minutes to get where he was going, then strolled out from the protection of the van, barely resisting the urge to glance around.

Once she was inside her car, she adjusted the rearview mirror, then the side mirror. She glimpsed him getting into the Firebird and thought suddenly of the Fort Lauderdale author who had lost a leg when he'd started his car and it exploded. The police had determined that it was the work of a homemade device attached to the ignition but had yet to find who'd done it. Then there was the ex-cop in Miami who was blown to kingdom come on an intracoastal bridge when the timer went off on the bomb fixed to the underside of *his* car. South Florida war stories: she always seemed to remember them at inopportune times.

Yes, it was paranoid, part of her Miami mentality, but just the same, she got out and walked around to the trunk. She opened it, leaned inside as though she were looking for something. A car pulled up behind her, radio blaring, and stopped. "You leaving?" called a teenager.

She realized he had blocked the Firebird's view. "Yeah, I am. But just stay where you are for a minute, okay?"

"Sure thing."

Quin crouched, rocked onto her knees, then onto her hands,

her belly sagging as she patted around the tailpipe. The indignity of it all, she thought. She felt something, got down on her elbows, craned her neck, peered up. A homing device. No sense in alerting this guy, whoever he was. She left the gizmo in place, rocked back onto her knees, grabbed hold of the fender, and pushed herself up.

She slammed the lid of the trunk and waved to the kid. "Thanks. Be out of your way in a sec."

He backed up; the Firebird was gone.

As she headed east toward Palm Beach, she kept glancing in the rearview mirror; no sign of the Firebird. Just before she drove over the bridge, she swung into a gas station and removed the homing bug. It was a standard apparatus, available at your local spy-supply store or police headquarters. She left it on top of the paper towel dispenser in the ladies' room. Let the sucker chew on that one for a while.

David Bishop's home was an old Florida bungalow built in the Twenties. It had a carport instead of a garage, a yard that was lush and wild with tropical foliage, and awnings over the jalousie windows that looked like hooded eyes. Hardly the abode she'd imagined for a successful investment counselor. But it fit the man he had once been. D. L. Bishop, a musician who had burst through the back door of the New Age music scene nearly a decade ago. Cuts from his *Distant Horseman* album had provided the background music for a low-budget film that was an unexpected box-office hit and sent the album to the top of the charts. The music was visceral, haunted, disturbing; people either hated it or loved it. Quin happened to love it and suddenly wished the circumstances under which they were about to meet were different. A friendly introduction from Kate over cocktails or coffee, for instance. The fact that she was approaching him as a possible suspect hardly boded well for an enduring friendship.

She heard music as she followed the winding path through a jungle of palms and mango trees. It was a cut from the *Horseman* album called "Nirvana," an instrumental composed entirely of flutes. It eddied and flowed, like water rush-

51

ing over smooth stones in a stream. Odd that he would listen to his own music, though.

A man who looked nothing like the photos of D. L. Bishop opened the door. No skintight jeans, no shoulder-length hair, no crazed glaze in the eyes. Except for the gold earring in his right ear, this Bishop could have been a Wall Street attorney on vacation: longish sandy hair that had been professionally styled, the Bishop high cheekbones and square, stubborn jaw, eyes the color of ice.

When she introduced herself, his face lit up. "The famous Quin, sure. Katie's college roommate. I've been hearing about you ever since I met Katie. This is a real pleasure. C'mon in."

Even her cats didn't give her *this* kind of reception.

The house was expensively furnished, but nothing matched. An Oriental chest stood next to a genuine Louis XIV couch, a teak rolltop desk shared a wall with an oak bookcase. An old RCA TV, relic of the Fifties, was next to the latest model of CD players.

Under the window, lined up on a long, low redwood shelf, was a collection of finger puppets and three marionettes. Two of the marionettes—a three-foot rabbit and a basset hound—had no moveable parts.

"Jinx and Brownie," David said, noticing her interest. "And this is Leia, after the princess in *Star Wars*." He held up a third marionette that had hinged everything—neck, eyes, limbs, fingers. Even her knuckles were hinged. Her hair was long, very blonde. Her eyes were startlingly blue, with thick dark lashes. "She's the star of every charity benefit I do."

"She's beautiful." And spooky, Quin thought. There was something too real about her, the way she blinked and moved when David manipulated her.

"Say hello to Quin, Leia."

Those big blue eyes blinked, and in a voice that was a perfect imitation of Kate's, she said, "The lady who eats all the time."

Quin laughed. "You got it."

"That was rude, Leia."

Another blink of those baby blues and she cocked her head,

peering at David. "Katie told me so. And she also told me Quin would be coming to see you to talk about Jack."

"That *is* why you're here, isn't it?" He looked at her now, his eyes as blue as Leia's, but infinitely sadder.

"Yes. If you feel up to it."

"Of course he feels up to it." Leia still spoke in Kate's voice; the effect was eerie.

"Back to the shelf, Princess," he said.

"Noooo, noooo," she sang. "I hate the shelf. The shelf is boring. Jinx won't play with me. . . ." Her voice trailed off, softer and more distant now, as though she were in another room.

"How do you make her sound far away like that?"

"Practice mostly. You learn to talk by not moving your mouth very much. There's no such thing as a ventriloquist who can throw his voice. Mainly it's finding substitutions for words that start with *p* and *b*, because those are tough if you can't move your lips. Have a seat. Can I get you something cold to drink?"

"That'd be great, thanks."

He returned from the kitchen with two tall glasses of lemonade and got right to the point. "I really don't know what I can tell you about Jack except that he didn't have any enemies that I know of."

"I'm looking for a motive, not enemies." Was there something he was researching that might prompt someone to kill him? David didn't know. He didn't talk much to his brother about his research; David found the topic unpleasant. What about ex-patients? Clients he had at the center? He didn't know. In frustration, Quin blurted, "What about people who will benefit from his death?"

David tugged at his earring, smiled a little. "Oh, you mean like Kate, my sister, and me?"

"There're other ways to benefit from someone's death besides money and property."

"Look, I know you're a friend of Kate's and I know this is what you do for a living and I know you mean well. But, frankly, I don't have a clue who killed Jack or why. I always thought that people who were murdered—at least this kind of

53

murder—had something to hide. But as far as I know, Jack's life was what it appeared to be. He was married to Kate, he was obsessed with this near-death stuff, he loved flying. Period.'' He shrugged, palms facing upward as if to catch something. ''I don't know what else to tell you.''

2.

Ray Wolfe, as lean as a totem pole and as graceful as the creature whose name he bore, was alone in the lab when Kate hurried in. He was peering through the video camera he'd set up for the Lewis interview, and only his head of curly hair was visible, a dark Brillo pad streaked with soap.

He lifted a hand in greeting, then raised up, gray eyes burning with questions he would hold until lunch. ''Good to see you, kiddo.''

''You, too, Wolfie.'' The scent of his after-shave seemed to fill the room, a musky odor, the same he'd been wearing for years. ''How was your vacation?''

''Okay.''

That meant he and Marsha, the woman he'd been living with, had probably fought the entire ten days. ''Just okay?''

''Yeah.'' He scratched at his bushy, graying mustache and gave her one of his *Let's not talk about it* looks. His face, which was already expressive, became as complex as an emotion.

A little more than four years ago, they had been lovers with a future. Then she had met Jack and her future had changed and Wolfe was history. But they'd remained friends. He'd seen her through rough times with Jack; she'd always been around to patch him back together when one of his numerous affairs went haywire, which was often. The friendship worked, even if the nothing else had.

''Tom Lewis isn't here yet?''

''He's in the bathroom. Smile for the camera, Katie.''

She waggled her fingers but couldn't muster a smile. ''Tell me about Lewis.''

He picked up a clipboard. ''Clinically dead for a minute and thirty-four seconds. He was resuscitated with the good ole electric paddles and came out of it babbling about what he'd seen. He doesn't have any religious framework to explain what happened to him. His family thinks he's lost it. High school education. Jack tested his IQ, which clocks in above average, at one twenty-six. Extroverted, lacks ambition.

"For some reason Jack must've quizzed him on the basics, because he made a note in the file that he didn't think the NDE would yield anything new."

How odd, she thought. Specific guidelines had been set up to minimize the usual criticism that rode tandem with near-death studies. This was particularly important in the event of a breakthrough. Whoever saw the patient initially was not supposed to ask anything about the NDE because it could be construed as leading the person, as planting suggestions, which could make the data biased. Also, the first telling of the experience was usually the most spontaneous, and they liked to have it on videotape.

"I'll talk to him afterward," she said. "Why don't you get him?"

"I always get the shit work."

"That's Marsha's line."

"Marsha, Marsha. She didn't know how good she had it. She left midway through the vacation, and when I got back last night, her things were gone."

This was uttered with a mixture of disdain and regret; Wolfe apparently couldn't make up his mind what he thought about it yet. If his normal pattern held true, he would spend the next six weeks tearing the relationship apart and examining every detail, looking for what had gone wrong. Unless he met someone else first, which was probably what would happen. Wolfe was never between women very long. They were drawn to him like fleas to a dog's back.

"What happened?"

"She's twenty-three and I'm forty-two, that's what happened. I mean, Kate, to her the Weathermen are guys on the local news who tell you tomorrow is going to be partly cloudy, the draft has something to do with the wind, and she got Richard Brautigan mixed up with Richard Bach. She was like someone from another planet."

Who made you feel young, Kate thought.

"And we'll talk about it over lunch," he finished with a wink, and went off to find their subject.

Tom Lewis looked like a gardener: tan, brawny, with eyes the color of fertile soil. His arms were covered with thick black hair, and more black hair poked up from the collar of his shirt. He was wound up like a spring and, throughout most of the interview, wore a path across the tile and chain-smoked.

He talked easily and fast about the snakebite and the events that led up to it. But when he reached the part about the ambulance, his voice faltered. "I was, like, still conscious in the ambulance. I knew I was getting oxygen, I could hear the medics talking, and I didn't hurt. But then, just before we got to the hospital, I think, I felt this weird pain in my chest, two million rubber bands twisting around my heart. Then the rubber bands, like, popped all at once, and that's when it happened."

"It?" Kate asked.

Smoke drifted from his nostrils. He glanced uneasily toward the video camera, which Wolfe was operating, then back at her. "When I died." The last words seemed to stick to his tongue. "The pain in my chest was gone, and I felt really light, like you do when you're floating on a raft in the water, with the sun pouring over you."

Another hesitation, then he launched into his journey through the dark tunnel toward the light, the most well-known component of the near-death experience. He compared it to a scene in *2001: A Space Odyssey*, a sensation of being sucked in and holding your breath and just grabbing on to your chair.

"Then there was light everywhere. Incredible light that vibrated, that filled up with colors and seemed to . . . to take on different shapes, dissolve, fill up again. I kept thinking *This is God, it's gotta be*, you know?" He laughed nervously. "I mean, this *had* to be God. Nothing else could be this . . . this beautiful. Then I realized I was hearing music. Not harps, no shit like that. It was . . . ." He stopped, as if listening to his memory of the music. "I don't know. I can't describe it. It's not something I heard with my ears, but with my . . . Well, this is going to sound weird."

"Go on," Kate prodded.

"It seemed I could hear it through my skin. Through the soles of my feet. Through my hands." He paused. "See, I told you it was weird."

"Not at all, Tom. The music you're describing is fairly common. Do you remember how you felt at the time?"

His eyes filled with tears. He looked quickly down at his feet, lit another cigarette, swiped at his eyes. "Wonderful," he whispered. "I felt wonderful."

While he was listening to the music, he saw his grandmother, who had died five years ago. She stepped out of the light and asked him if he had made up his mind. "And right then I knew what my whole life was. I could see it. And I knew she could see it, too, and so could the other people inside the light and it scared me. I felt . . . naked. My grandma was, like, well, trying to get me to look at something else, and when I did, I realized I was looking at other lives I had lived." He started to laugh again. "Weird shit, I told you this was weird shit."

Reincarnation was, for the purpose of their research, placed under a heading Sammy Dayton called *Spiritual Orientations of NDErs*. This simply illustrated that NDErs were more open to the concept after their experience than before, thus bypassing the touchy philosophical and theological implications.

"My grandma urged me to . . . to review my life and then . . . then told me I needed to decide if I wanted to go on living or to die."

This threshold, this particular crisis point, was also common. Once the decision to return had been made, the experience usually ended. "I knew I was back in my body, okay? They were electrocuting me with those paddles. But a part of me was . . . Christ, a part of me was out there, I mean, man, I was *soaring*, because I knew I had died and I knew I was back and that nothing in my life was ever going to be the same again."

"Did you feel any regret about the decision you'd made?"

"Regret?" He laughed. "Shit, no. I was ecstatic to be alive."

A little later, when it was just the two of them in the lab, Kate questioned Lewis about his initial interview with Jack.

Besides the tests and the questions about his family and childhood, what else did they talk about?

"He wanted to know how I felt when I realized I had died and come back. I told him, but he didn't understand how I could be ecstatic about being alive since I was in so much pain and had just left a place that was incredibly happy and peaceful."

"What'd you tell him?"

"That I had to die to realize I wasn't ready to die. Once I understood I was alive, it was such an unbelievable rush I was hardly aware of the pain. Dr. Bishop seemed kind of confused about it."

"Confused how?"

"Well, he kept telling me I felt ecstatic because I'd found out there was something after death. But that wasn't it at all. I mean, it's fine to know that when you die that's not it, but I was soaring because I was *alive*."

For most people, it was the knowledge that death wasn't the end that left them ecstatic; this made Lewis something of an anomaly. So why did Jack note the opposite in the file? And why hadn't he followed procedure?

Kate gave Lewis the name of the woman who headed the NDE support group in the area and recommended he attend one of their weekly meetings. They scheduled a follow-up for next week, then he left.

Kate went into her office, which was off the lab, to wait for Wolfe to return from whenever he'd gone so they could go to lunch. She drew the room's familiarity around her like a cloak. The soft leather chair, the pastel walls, the large window that overlooked the pines, bookcases, a Woodstock poster David had given her. Her space.

A ton of mail had arrived in her absence, all of it tossed haphazardly on her desk, probably by Wolfe, who never had the time to do anything neatly. It was mostly brochures and catalogs, but there were a couple of letters, probably from former patients. One envelope looked as if it had gone through the wash before it was mailed. When she opened it, a crude crayon drawing of two stick figures slipped out with a sheet of paper. The woman—head as round as a tennis ball, triangles for breasts, stringy hair—was leaning over as the second stick figure, a man, screwed her from behind with a cock nearly as long as his leg.

A sheet of paper accompanied the drawing. Typed neatly in the center of the page was:

> YOU'RE GOING TO LOVE IT
> WHEN I DO THIS TO YOU.
> THAT'S A PROMISE.

The words blurred and her fingers jerked across the paper, balling it into a tight wad. *Did you get my drawing and the note*? Wasn't that what her caller had asked? She flattened out the sheet, read it again. Nothing had changed. The message was still there, typed in caps, black against white.

"Kate?"

Sammy Dayton filled her doorway, his head barely an inch from the top of it. One hand was in the pocket of his wrinkled slacks, the other was moving back over his balding head. As always, he seemed larger than life to her, the way a father would to a child. And, like a child, Kate's first impulse was to leap up, wagging the drawing and the note at him, and seek refuge in his arms. Instead, she slipped them under a book, got up, and hugged him hello.

He held her at arm's length, towering over her, and searched her face with eyes that had always seen too much. "You could have called me after it happened, Katie."

You're going to love it . . .

"And told you what, Sammy? That I'd been arrested for Jack's murder? You couldn't have done anything."

"I could have been there for you."

. . . when I do this to you . . .

She felt like reminding him that she'd been out of jail for five days now and he hadn't phoned her until yesterday. But there didn't seem to be any point in bringing it up. As she stepped away from him, he said, "I didn't realize Jack was alive when you found him, Katie."

She nodded. "I guess you saw one of the McClearys, huh."

He stabbed a thumb toward the lab. "Mike's out there now with Ray. We were observing the interview with Tom Lewis."

"What'd you think?"

"Pretty typical."

She started to tell him what she'd just learned from Lewis, but McCleary and Wolfe appeared just then. "Hi, Mac. What'd you think of the grand tour?"

"Like Woody Allen said, 'I'm not afraid of dying. I just don't want to be there when it happens.' "

Kate laughed. "You're not alone."

"Mike's going to join us for lunch," Wolfe said.

Like the old days, she thought. Life Before Jack. "You coming with us, Sammy?"

"I already ate, thanks."

It was simpler than that. Sammy hated crowds. Even now, with four of them in her office, which was barely large enough for two, Sammy stood apart, shifting his weight from one foot to the other, looking uneasy.

Kate herded everyone through the door, then took out the drawing and the note and folded them to show to McCleary later.

That's a promise.

7

AT EIGHT TUESDAY morning, Clicker was exactly where he was supposed to be, where The Plan said that he must be.

Seated on a bench in a park two blocks west of Ocean Drive, he had a good view of the McClearys' office. Except for an occasional passerby, he was alone in the park, dressed like a tourist in a flowered shirt and shorts, with a baseball cap pulled low over his sunglasses.

His camera was on the bench next to him, with a sack of popcorn balanced on top of it that he was feeding to the pigeons. They fluttered and pecked and cooed at his feet. His slingshot was also in the bag; he had an urge to pull it out when he spotted a squirrel scampering toward him. But he couldn't very well kill the little fucker here in a public park, now could he. So he kicked out his feet, scaring it and the pigeons away.

He aimed his camera across the street at the office windows. He didn't see anyone moving around inside. Good. He was afraid they might have parked in the alley in back and entered through the rear door. If they did, he would probably be sitting here until lunch, since the pictures had to be taken today. The Plan was as specific as the rules of the game.

He shifted the camera to the bakery next door. It had a large picture window like the McClearys' office and for a few minutes he amused himself by watching the old man inside. The six-hundred-millimeter zoom lens was so powerful, Clicker could see the frosting swirled on top of the tray of cinnamon rolls.

8:22. A Mazda Miata as red as a rooster nosed into a space at the end of the block. Clicker snapped a picture of McCleary as soon as he stepped out of the car. That beard, those shades, the neatly pressed slacks: he could be a celebrity on vacation in Palm Beach. There were a lot of celebrities in Palm Beach. They shopped on Worth Avenue, lived in mansions that were sealed up eight months out of the year, were chauffeured around in Rolls Royces or limos but drove Chryslers, not Mazdas, if they were incognito.

Now McCleary's wife appeared, huge as a house, her hair like polished teak. Clicker preferred slender women, but there was a certain beauty about a pregnant woman that intrigued him, and about this woman in particular. The Nikon's motor drive whirred, clicking away as the McClearys headed toward their office. Although they weren't one of Jack's mistakes, they were in the way, they stood between him and The Plan, and that simply couldn't be.

The photos would be nice, he could tell already. Such a happy pair, these two. Such togetherness, blessed today, on the fourth of December.

He waited until they had gone inside, then emptied the bag of popcorn on the ground and strolled off through the park, bound for Worth Avenue. It was an ideal time of the day to walk. Not too hot yet. Plenty of people on the streets. He looked at everything as a tourist would, especially when it came to the women.

The Palm Beach woman possessed a particular look that other women tried to emulate but couldn't quite master. The clothes. The hat. The sunglasses. The perfect makeup and the spa-toned body. But most of all she was marked by the way her body whispered, inviting you to look but not touch.

It was not a manner that Kate had ever mastered.

By 8:55, he was across the street from the Beach National Bank, leaning against the wall of an alley between two buildings. He knew that Pearl Hanley would appear at nine on the button; promptness was one of her many virtues. She would park her snazzy silver Porsche in the bank lot down the street. She would move past the shops on Worth Avenue with the hubris of a woman who had known their cool, sweetly scented interiors all her life. It was one of the lies Pearl had perfected so well, she had come to believe it herself.

The truth was that she had married money, had studied the Palm Beach look and mimicked it until she could pass for the real McCoy. When she and her husband had gotten divorced, he had offered a generous settlement. She had gotten greedy and had taken him to court. The judge was a friend of her husband's and she had lost. An old story in Palm Beach. Now she was VP in charge of Christ knew what at the bank, a cushy job that paid well and had great perks.

No doubt about it. Pearl was one of Jack's biggest mistakes.

Now here she came, strolling up the road, hips swiveling just so, dress hugging the right places, black hair moving as she moved. He took a dozen photographs on the same roll of high-speed black-and-white film that he'd used for the Mc-Clearys. Color was fine for certain situations, but not for this.

When she ambled through the entrance of the bank, he felt an odd loss, like the grief he might experience for someone he used to know who was dying.

He put the camera back into the case and hurried through the alley, pleased with what he'd accomplished. As his mother used to say, it was important that a man loved his work, and he certainly did love his.

8

1.

INLAND, THE DAY was already a scorcher.

The sun beat against the endless farms around Lake Okee-chobee, waves of heat undulated inches above the pavement, and the Miata's AC was straining. Quin knew that if it quit, her body's thermostat was going to go haywire. "We should've taken my car, Mac."

"Sure. And we'd be stranded about ten miles back."

"At least my air works."

"Bess's air is working fine."

"She's hiccupping."

"Don't worry about it, Quin. If she quits, we'll find a bar with central air-conditioning . . ."

Not out here they wouldn't.

". . . and we'll wait until dusk to drive to the airport, when it's cooler."

"You don't have to be crabby about it." She looked over at him. The set of his mouth told her that the Miata's AC had little to do with this conversation. She decided he was irritated by air-conditioning in general, which probably meant their first electricity bill for the house had arrived. Two weeks' worth. "How much was it?"

"How much was what?"

"The Florida Power and Light bill."

He glanced at her. "Who said anything about FP&L?"

"How much, Mac?"

McCleary turned his attention back to the road. "A hundred and sixty-two dollars and fifty-five cents. It'd be half that if we kept the air at eighty instead of seventy."

"Eighty? Jesus, I'd roast."

"You haven't even tried it."

"I don't *have* to try it. I know what's comfortable. And if we didn't have to keep the bedroom window half open, the bill would be a lot lower."

"I can't stand sleeping with all the windows closed and freezing my ass off in the middle of a heat wave."

"Well, you're not pregnant."

"I know, I know. And you've got one and a half times as much blood in your body."

Twice the volume, she thought. But why belabor the point? The best policy in this situation was to just ignore him. She looked out the window again. In the distance, off to her right, she could see the dike that kept the waters of Lake Okeechobee contained. It had been built in 1928 after a killer hurricane had ripped through and dumped so much rain, the lake had spilled over its shores and devastated the surrounding communities. The mud left in its wake was black and rich and had turned the area into the best farmland in the state. It had also left it hopelessly rural. Quin felt a brief, nostalgic stab for Miami, for its noise and traffic and its confluence of humanity.

Belle Glade Airport appeared at the southeastern edge of the lake, a postscript that probably hadn't changed much in fifty years. It was little more than a landing strip with a flight center, a couple of gas pumps, and a hangar.

As they got out in front of the flight center, the hot wind whipped across the tarmac. Sand stung her arms like dozens of mosquitoes, her hair blew into her eyes, the front of her maternity blouse flapped. She understood Kate's remarks now about the wind out here. It was a wild, primitive thing, ubiquitous and cruel in its indifference, and it was a relief to get inside the building.

Ten or twelve people were sitting around in the coffee shop, maps spread open on tables. Students and flight instructors, she guessed. Why anyone would want to fly in wind like this was beyond her.

Half a dozen more people were standing around a weather map in the flight-service office down the hall. While McCleary went in to find out if there was anything or anyone out here called *Fargo*, Quin wandered to the picture window that overlooked the airfield. At least thirty small planes were in the tie-down area and another four waited for takeoff on the strip. She counted three yellow crop dusters with open cockpits and bi-wings that reminded her of giant dragonflies. Busy little airport for being in the middle of the boonies.

She pushed through the double doors out onto a wide porch that ran along the back of the building. Signs marked different flight-service outfits: glider rides, hot-air-balloon rides, crop dusting, a flight instruction school, an air ambulance, and FARGO FLIGHTS & CARGO.

Maybe Jack Bishop had been flying drugs for Fargo. Sure, a real Miami scenario. Prominent shrink and near-death researcher murdered over drugs or laundered money or both. Damn unlikely, but so far the only leads they had were the drawing and note Kate had received and the notations in Bishop's appointment book. Fargo, a lunch date every Monday and Wednesday, and on alternate months a Thursday, Friday, or Saturday circled in red. Patterns Kate hadn't known about.

In fact, the people who supposedly had known Bishop best seemed to know the least about the details that counted. Kate had promised to dig out the records of his former patients, which they hoped would prove more illuminating.

Inside Fargo Flights, business certainly wasn't booming. Except for an old codger behind the desk who was paging through an aviation magazine, the place was as empty as a bar during Prohibition. The old man kept dipping his hand into a box of vanilla wafers and she wished he would offer her one. But he didn't even glance up when she asked if Fargo was around. He lifted an arm and pointed at the window. "He's under the cauling of the red Pitt out there on the field."

Except for the yellow crop dusters, the majority of planes in the tie-down area were painted red or red and another color. She didn't see any open caulings. "What's a Pitt?"

The codger raised bemused eyes. He was wearing coveralls stained with grease and chewing on the end of an unlit cigar. "An aerobatic plane." He padded over to the window and tapped the glass. "Fourth plane in the second row. Bi-wing, single engine. Looks like it dropped out of World War II. Don't see Roy now, though. He might be in the plane."

She thanked him and stepped outside just as McCleary came around the corner. "Fargo's out there."

He grinned. "That was quick."

"Find out anything?"

"The guy who works in the weather office says Fargo runs a flight school and transports produce from the farms around here to Jacksonville and Miami. He also has the Texaco franchise, so he's doing real well."

"We playing this straight or what?"

McCleary rubbed a hand through his beard as they started across the tarmac. "Jack's Bonanza is tied down here. I've heard it's for sale. How's that?"

"Fine, unless he asks you for a deposit. Then you can tell him we can't buy it because of the electric bill."

"Okay." McCleary laughed. "We'll compromise. I'll shut the bedroom window at night if you turn the air to seventy-five."

"Fair enough. Let's go buy that Bonanza."

McCleary caught her hand and gave it a quick squeeze.

Fargo climbed down from the Pitt as they approached the plane. Quin thought he looked like a sunburned hick farmer approaching middle age: dark shades, denim coveralls stained with oil and dirt, a paunch that attested to a love of beer or food or both. He had a wrench in one hand and a pair of pliers in the other.

"Morning," McCleary called over the noise of the wind.

"Help you with something?" His faint southern drawl fit the sticks image.

"Hope so. I understand Jack Bishop's Bonanza may be for sale."

"I haven't heard, but it wouldn't surprise me much. The missus is the only one in the family who doesn't fly and the plane's a beauty, all right. Parked right over there." He pointed to a low-wing plane that was white and red, a peppermint stick, with a split tail like a peace symbol. "She's one of the nicest planes out here. Tip tanks, pressurized cabin, seats six. Jack took great care of her. She was out at the Bishop ranch the night Jack was killed. Next day, his brother asked me to fly it back here. I've got the key if you want to take a look."

"Thanks. We'd love to."

"If everyone in the family is a pilot, why'd the brother ask you to fly it back?" Quin asked.

Fargo shrugged. "Eccentric family, ma'am. Either of you pilots?" He spoke loudly as the three of them crossed the windy field.

"Yes," Quin lied. "But we're actually looking at planes for a client. What do you think a fair price is?"

He named a figure; it sounded outrageous.

They stopped in front of the plane and Fargo climbed up onto the wing to unlock the door. "Have a look inside."

Quin knew zip about planes, small ones or otherwise. But she had flown in this one a couple of times with Bishop and saw that he'd still pampered the craft the way Palm Beachers did their poodles. Leather seats, an instrument panel loaded with electronic gear, carpeting so thick it invited bare feet, and the plane's call numbers engraved on the glove box. N-929.

"Log book's right there in the glove compartment if you want to take a look at the hours, maintenance, and whatnot," Fargo called.

She squeezed behind the wheel; the cockpit of a Bonanza was no place for a stomach the size of hers. The wind blew the door shut. She left it closed and removed the logbook from the glove compartment. The first entry was dated two years ago, long enough to detect patterns, if there were any. She slipped it in the pocket of her skirt and climbed down.

"She's a beauty, all right. Have a look, Mac."

While he was inside the plane, she asked Fargo if he thought the family would be willing to come down in price at all. "Depends on who's selling it, ma'am." He brought a Baggie out of his pocket with vanilla wafers in it, proffered it, then helped himself. "Quit smoking about six weeks ago, and whenever I get the urge for a butt, I have a wafer." He patted his stomach. "But the damn things are making me fat."

Ha, she thought. You don't know squat about fat, buddy. "Won't Mrs. Bishop be selling the plane?" she asked.

"Probably. But I was thinking that if Jack's brother or sister were doing the selling, the price'll be higher."

"Why's that?"

"They're greedy."

"Sounds like you know the family well."

"Known them a while, what with the ranch so close here and all and the three of them being pilots. But Jack's the one I knew best. We had a flying club going for a while. Real likeable fellow and a fine pilot. Damn shame how things turned out."

"You ever meet Mrs. Bishop?"

"Met her but don't know her. Seemed real nice."

"You think she killed him?"

Fargo rubbed his sunburned face. "No way. Funny thing about guys like Jack, though, is that you get this impression of them being one way and it turns out they're something totally different."

"Different how?"

He shrugged; she could almost smell his regret at having made the remark. "Oh, I don't know. You hear things out here. No way to tell how much truth there is to them."

"What kinds of things?"

He flipped up his sunglasses, amused. "You always ask so many questions?"

"Professional habit, sorry." She didn't say which profession and he didn't ask. "But you read the paper and it tells you one thing and you talk to people and hear something else."

"That's what I mean about things you hear. There's been stories for a long time about wild parties out at the Bishop ranch. Women, sex, drugs. But knowing Jack . . ." Fargo shook his head. "It just didn't fit."

"Parties the Bishops threw?"

"I don't think the missus was around. Assuming the stories are true."

She wanted to ask for names, addresses, phone numbers, and to hell with pretense. Probably would have asked, if McCleary hadn't joined them. "You have a photo of the plane that we could show to our client, Mr. Fargo?"

"I think there's one on my bulletin board in the office. You're welcome to it. In the meantime, I'll find out who you contact about the plane."

"Thanks, we appreciate it."

As they headed back to the building, the wind buffeted them. "Wind always this bad out here?" McCleary asked.

"During the winter it gets like this once or twice a week. Worse out on the flats."

"The what?"

"Death Flats. Real bleak place the army used to use for training. It's about thirty-five miles southwest of here. Not much there anymore. An abandoned fire tower and some old Quonset huts. Seminoles named the flats way back after the Spanish massacred part of their tribe." He pushed open the door to the office.

The old codger was still behind the desk, paging through his magazine as if time in here had stalled. Fargo walked past him without a word, without a glance, and Quin wondered if she was the only one who saw him.

Fargo's cramped office stank of smoke and burned coffee. Butts overflowed the ashtray, papers were strewn across the desk, photos overlapped each other on the bulletin board. A friendly mess, Quin thought, feeling at home.

"Here we go." Fargo unpinned a picture from the bulletin board and brought it over. "Good shot of the plane."

Fargo, Bishop, and two other men stood in front of the Bonanza, hamming for the camera. "The flying club?" Quin asked.

"Yeah." Fargo grinned; the memory was evidently a pleasant one. "We were a weird group, all right. Wayne Shepard's a crop duster up in Indian River County, Frank Abalonee was a buddy of Jack's, in investments or something, real serious type, but a hell of a pilot."

"You hear those stories from one of these guys?" Quin asked.

"Stories? Oh, about the parties. Yeah. From Shepard."

Well, goddamn. A lead. The pilot of a crop duster in Indian River County shouldn't be too hard to find.

What's he talking about? asked McCleary's eyes.

Later, said her shrug.

Fargo said they could have the photo; he had another somewhere. He looked around the office as he said it, frowning slightly, as though seeing the room for the first time. "You want me to call you when I find out if the plane's for sale and all?"

The question was addressed to McCleary, confirming Quin's suspicion that, out here in the sticks, the lines between men and women were clearly drawn. "We'll call you," McCleary replied. As soon as they were outside, he said, "*What* stories?"

She laughed. "I was wondering how long it would take you to ask."

"I suppose you've got the logbook, too. I couldn't find it in the glove compartment."

She slipped it out of her skirt pocket and held it up, a prize. "For this you buy me dinner."

"Done. Now tell me about this story."

"Dinner at the Breakers."

"We can't afford the Breakers."

"Happy hour with free hors d'oeuvres at the Breakers?" she asked hopefully. "And the thermostat at home on seventy-four?"

"How come I have the feeling I just lost this round?"

"I take it that's a yes?"

"Only if we put the air on eighty during the day when we're not there."

A fair compromise, she decided, and related her conversation with Fargo.

9

1.

THE WIND AWAKENED HER.

For a moment, Kate was sure she was back at the ranch, in the attic, waiting. But she recognized this wind. It blew in off the ocean, sweeping across water, sand, sea oats. Day after day it coated windows in salt, rattled screens, swept through the house with gross indifference. It was like a slovenly pet, tolerated because it was familiar, because it provided a measure of comfort, because it was better than air-conditioning.

Jack had always kept the house sealed up like a tomb, with the thermostat on sixty-five. Kate liked to throw open all the windows in the house and switch on the ceiling fans. It meant dust, damp sheets, air that swelled with the scent of salt and fish. But what was the point of living on the ocean if you couldn't smell it? Taste it? Feel the salt between your fingers when you rubbed them together?

She turned on her side, wanting to slide back into sleep again. But the bed now seemed too huge and the silence too vast and deep. It seeped from the walls, from the empty rooms, from the downstairs. She hugged the pillows on his side, scissored her legs around one, burrowed her face into the other, and wished she had a pet, a big, fat, fluffy cat that she could hold, stroke, whisper to. But Jack hadn't liked cats. Jack had no time for pets. In the last year, Jack had barely had time for her. If they hadn't worked together, in fact, she might not have seen much of him at all.

She wondered if it would have been different if they'd had a child. He would have made time for a son or a daughter, wouldn't he? But whenever she had broached the subject, he'd made a million excuses. He didn't want to share her, they had careers, kids tied you down. So she had stopped mentioning it and here she was, alone.

The depth of her loneliness, her grief, the reality of her solitude, appalled her. In her mind, behind closed eyes, she conjured up Jack's face: his creased forehead, the curve of his ear, the long line of his jaw, his mustache, his nose, and finally his eyes. Compelling eyes. She had always loved his eyes.

Now, the rest of him. She sketched in the details of shoulders, arms, and hands, testing her memories, which would have to last the rest of her life. She imagined his hands against her, at her throat, cupping her face, caressing her. He had enjoyed making love in the morning, waking her from a sound sleep with just the barest touch of his hands. Those times, she thought, were slow and sweet.

But other times their lovemaking was darker, strange, an act that slid dangerously close to something that terrified her because she liked it. With silk scarves tied lightly at her wrists, they had played out roles of domination, submission. Jack whispering: *Let go, Katie, let go*—until the pleasure was so extreme, it became pain. Then, it was as if Jack were holding a mirror to her innermost self, telling her that this, too, was part of who she was.

You're going to love it when I do this to you. . . .

She threw back the sheet, stumbled into the bathroom, and slammed the heel of her hand against a faucet tap. She splashed cold water on her face, but it didn't help. She still felt as though she were shrinking, dying, and any second now she would fold up like a suitcase and a person she'd never met would wheel her off and she would be nothing but other people's memories.

Like death.

White light, tunnels, ethereal music, the ghosts of the departed—lies, all of it, otherwise she would feel Jack's presence, wouldn't she? If even a fluff of him had survived, she would know it, wouldn't she? She pressed the heels of her hands against her eyes, waiting for him to touch the back of her neck, to whisper to her, to make himself known. The doorbell rang, startling her, and she started to laugh. She would walk downstairs and open the door and Jack would be standing there in his bloodstained shirt, smiling. *It was all a mistake, babe.*

She backed away from the sink, her hands jerking over her arms, and hurried into the bedroom. She pressed her face to the window screen and saw David peering up. A sign, she thought. It was a sign that Jack's soul had leaped into his brother's body. Sure, why not? Death was a tale of possession, even stranger than *she* had imagined.

"The key's under the bougainvillea pot, David. I'll be down in a minute."

Kate pulled on shorts and a T-shirt, brushed her teeth, drew a comb through her hair. Perhaps when she walked into the living room Jack's eyes would peer at her from David's face, his voice would speak to her with David's mouth. David would become the instrument of a dead man, and her life would plunge into madness.

But the music she heard before she reached the living room could come only from David's fingers. It was "Für Elise," beautifully rendered and as strangely haunting as the cuts from his *Distant Horseman* album. It did justice to the Steinway piano and mocked the thick formality of Oriental rugs, brocade curtains, and the dark, lacquered Oriental furniture.

The room was exactly as it had been when Mrs. Bishop had died, as if preserved under glass like a butterfly. Kate detested it. But David, dressed like a businessman in a three-piece suit, fit the room.

"Hi, cutie." He didn't look up.

"Hi yourself." She sat beside him on the piano bench, and when he switched to "Chopsticks," she joined him on the upper octave. Unlike Stephanie, he'd never viewed her as an intruder into the Bishop clan and she loved him for it.

"Stephanie's an asshole. I want you to come to the memorial service, Katie. Besides, if you don't, it'll look bad."

"I'm sure that's exactly how she'd like it to look."

"Probably."

"And since when do you care how things look to other people?"

He stopped playing and twisted the gold earring in his right ear. Just then, she *did* see a glimmer of Jack in his face, but it was only the family resemblance. The square, stubborn jaw, the high cheekbones, the perfect bow of the mouth, the depth of the eyes. The traits were combined in such a way so that he was the most physically attractive of the three Bishops, a Neil Young from the Sixties. Perhaps if he'd stuck with his music, he might have sculpted the sounds of the Nineties for a new generation, just as Young had helped define it for people who came of age in the Sixties.

"This is different," he said.

"Not really. The press has already convicted me. Whether I go to the memorial service or not isn't going to mean anything."

"To me it will."

She hugged him quickly. "You had breakfast?"

"Hours ago. But I'd love some coffee."

"Coming up."

As she stood, he said, "I met your old roommate. I think I'm on her list of suspects."

"Don't be ridiculous."

He smiled a little, shrugged, and then his hands flew across the piano again, not just playing music but releasing it, as if he were excavating some secret place within the piano itself. She waited for him to pause and offer an opinion on who might have killed Jack. But when he didn't, she wandered into the kitchen, the sound of the music following her, disturbing her almost as deeply as what he had not said. But maybe he didn't *have* an opinion. Or, worse, perhaps deep down he believed she had killed Jack.

While the coffee perked, she stared through the window over the kitchen sink. She thought of the lost weekends when she'd stood in exactly this spot, surrounded by friends of David's and Stephanie's and friends of their friends, music and noise and laughter swirling around her, wondering how she was going to get from this hour to the next without making a scene. Many times she'd simply gone upstairs and occupied herself until it was over. Sometimes she had left and driven over to the center. Occasionally she and Wolfe had gone out for drinks. Twice she'd checked into a motel.

But no matter how she'd dealt with it, she and Jack had

always argued afterward. He accused her of being antisocial; she said there had to be limits. This issue was never resolved because the parties had ended as abruptly as they'd begun. But those months had nearly killed their marriage and nothing had been right since.

"You be needin' some help, lady?"

She laughed and turned. David's Ray Charles finger puppet bobbed up and down on his thumb. He wore tiny sunglasses and was decked out in a little tux. Next to him, riding David's index finger, was Ella Fitzgerald in a slinky white gown. His puppets and marionettes were the stars of his charity benefits, a hit with adults and kids alike. They predated his brief career in music, and when his inspiration had dried up, if that was, indeed, what had ended his career, the puppets had filled the creative void.

"Ray, good to see you."

The puppet bowed. "Morning, ma'am."

"I love your gown, Ella." She set the mugs of coffee on the table. "White's definitely your color."

"I thought black was my color. But thank my manager, it was his idea."

"He has good taste."

Ella peered at David "You hear that? You have good taste."

"I always told you that, El. But you never listen to me, you know."

"You can't believe everything your manager tells you."

"Time out, sweetheart." He dragged the puppets on the table. "I've got a Christmas benefit coming up and I need some new characters, Kate."

"How about Wes Craven?"

"It's a *musical* benefit, not an ad for *Nightmare on Elm Street*."

"So expand. Have characters from movies. Superman, Batman, the Joker, Indiana Jones."

His face lit up. "Indiana. Hey, I like that. Indiana with a little bullwhip and a fedora . . . Yeah, this is going to work great." He slipped Ella back on his finger. "What do you think, El?"

"You's the boss, honey, but I just don't see what any of them folks got to do with music."

"Me neither," piped Ray Charles.

"Bye, kids." He shoved them both back into his pocket. "Dissension in the ranks."

Kate laughed. "I'm glad you stopped by."

"You may not be five minutes from now. Did Stephanie tell you about the developer?"

"Her visit wasn't a social call."

"A developer made an offer on the house."

"Which house?"

"This house."

Oh. Jack's house. She had expected something like this, but not so soon.

The developer, David went on, had already bid on the Laker place and the Dakota estate, which lay to either side. Those houses, like this one, had been built in the Thirties. "If the deals are consummated and if the developer agrees to pump ten million into beach conservation, the county has agreed to rezone for multiple dwellings."

Condos rising like beehives from the Bishop property. To Jack, who had inherited the place from his parents, who had loved it and tended it, this would be a travesty. "The vultures didn't waste any time."

"They got in touch with Stephanie when you were in jail. They're offering eight million. Steph wanted to know where we stand legally."

"Oh, c'mon, she knows damn well it belongs to you two now. You can do what you want with it. I'm just allowed to live in it until you decide what to do."

"I've told her I'm against selling."

"Don't be on my account."

"Look, the only thing four million means to me at this point in my life is that the IRS and my ex-wife get most of it. I'd rather the house stay in the family."

"Whatever you want to do is fine with me. At this point, the odds are good that I'll be going to prison."

"Don't be ridiculous. That's one place you *aren't* going."

"I am unless we find who killed him, David."

Here it was, another opening, another chance for him to offer an opinion on who had killed Jack. But he didn't give one and the subsequent silence was awkward. Sounds filled it: the tick of the clock, the ice maker in the freezer spitting out ice, the drip of a faucet somewhere in the house.

Kate suddenly craved the very solitude that until now had been a kind of curse. She had things to do before she went to work—dig up the old files on Jack's former patients, pay bills, clean out his closet, decide what to do with his clothes. Functional chores that would make her grieving easier. But even as she mentally enumerated the details, she felt the prickling, nagging fear of David's presence.

David, who had always been her ally, her friend, was now a great yawning question mark.

2.

The Bishop ranch was only fifteen miles from the Belle Glade airport, but it seemed like a long fifteen miles to McCleary. The hot, humid breath of the wind blew dirt, leaves, and dry twigs across the deserted road. Its voice alternated between an irritating whine and a low, soft moan that at times sounded almost erotic. Now and then it slackened, only to return with greater force a few minutes later.

As the Miata rounded a curve, a migrant camp appeared on their left. It was a dusty hovel surrounded by a wire-mesh fence that made it look more like a prison camp. It seemed to be divided into two distinct sections—trailers and small concrete-block homes on one side and several low buildings on the other. He'd passed the place before but hadn't really noticed it until the night he and Bishop had gone flying. He remembered how the camp had appeared suddenly against the flatness, a glistening fairy tale of soft orange lights. But now, in daylight, it looked as grim as a prison camp. He watched it shrink in the rearview mirror, then vanish like a mirage.

"Are the fields around the ranch still producing?" McCleary asked.

Quin nodded. "Kate said they're just growing strawberries and green beans now, enough for a tax write-off. Jack was still getting his pickers from the camp, though. He never had much of a head for figures, so David does the financial end of it.''

"You think he's the type to send her that drawing and note?"

"Not D. L. Bishop, not someone who can do what he used to with music. Besides, Kate says they're just friends and he has more women in his life than he knows what to do with.''

Which didn't exonerate him from suspicion.

The road curved again and the Bishop ranch rose from the unrelieved flatness, a vision straight out of the country's heartland. The house and barn, enclosed by a faded picket fence, looked as if they'd been painted against the backdrop of bleached white sky. There was a plethora of trees in the yard, but the drought had taken a toll: leaves were browning, branches had snapped like toothpicks, the grass was checkered with patches of brown. On both sides of the house were huge trellises covered with bougainvillea vines blazing with red blossoms. They seemed to be the only plants flourishing in the heat.

The gate was open and parked in front of the house was a police cruiser. "Shit," Quin muttered. "If that's macho man Garrison, I might as well stay in the car.''

"What for? To him you're invisible, anyway.''

"Good point. Besides, we have more business being here than he does.''

"We do?''

"Sure. Kate gave us the key.''

A key didn't entitle them to admittance to a crime scene.

McCleary parked behind the cruiser. The heat and the wind struck them instantly and he felt as though he were in the middle of a Kansas prairie at high noon in August. Around them, branches rustled, leaves fluttered to the ground, bougainvillea blossoms swirled through the air like tiny UFOs. One end of a yellow police band was tied to a porch railing; the other end flapped around, victim of the wind or Garrison's whim. The screen door slammed open and shut, making an awful racket.

The place possessed a terrible vacancy, as though it had been uninhabited for years and the elements had rotted it from the ground up. Perhaps on some level, McCleary thought, the

79

house understood that something unspeakable had happened here and its essence had simply withdrawn, a soul taking leave of a body.

It spooked him.

The door opened as they reached it and Garrison, grinning from ear to ear, boomed, "Well, Mike, Mrs. McCleary. What brings y'all out here?" *Y'all* rolled off his tongue in a deeply southern drawl.

I could ask you the same thing, pal. "Kate asked us to pick up a few things," he lied.

"Uh-huh." He didn't open the door any wider, didn't invite them in, just stood there looking as guilty as a kid discovered with his hand in the family coffer.

"It won't take long."

He started to say something, but from inside the house a woman shouted, "Hey, Lou, could you help me with this stuff, *please*?"

Garrison's grin stretched like a rubber band, then popped. "Yeah, hold on a second." He stepped back, admitting them, and stabbed a thumb over his shoulder. "Stephanie Bishop wanted to get some things she'd stored in the attic." He gestured toward several suitcases and a trunk against the wall. "Old dishes and clothes. Seeing how she and Kate don't get along very well, I figured it'd be easier if I just brought her out here."

Maybe, maybe not, McCleary thought, but he was willing to give Garrison the benefit of the doubt. As an ex-cop, he could sympathize with Garrison's compromising position. His long-standing friendship with Bishop had put him smack in the middle of a family feud.

"I hope they're her things," Quin remarked.

"They certainly are," snapped the woman who appeared in the hall carrying cartons stacked to her chin.

She stood six feet and reminded McCleary of a pantomimist: very white skin, very red lips, very black hair that barely reached the tops of her ears. Her short shorts showed muscular calves and sinewy thighs, and her sleeveless T-shirt revealed slender arms with hillocks of muscles. She looked curiously asexual and could have been a man with marvelous bone structure masquerading as a woman.

"Stephanie Bishop, Mike and Quin McCleary," said Garrison in a weary voice, as though he wished he were anywhere but here.

"Nice to meet you. Would you mind helping me with this stuff, Lou?"

"Yeah, sure." He took one of the cartons she held and, on his way past them, said he'd be right back.

"Don't hurry back now, hear?" Quin murmured as the door shut behind them. "How do we know they aren't carting away evidence?"

"We don't." McCleary suggested she go upstairs and find some things of Kate's they could take with them to make their story look good. "I'll keep him busy down here. We can always come back and poke around once they've left."

He watched Garrison and Stephanie through the window, loading the suitcases and boxes into the trunk and backseat of the cruiser. At one point, they began to argue. He couldn't hear what was said, but it was obvious that Stephanie was furious, her hands moving around as his patted the air: right, okay, got it. There was more to it than Stephanie, sister of the deceased, and Garrison, family friend. But exactly what it entailed was anyone's guess.

Garrison returned to the house alone, sweat bright in the creases of his face. "We're going to shove off, Mike. You and your wife going to be much longer? I've got to lock up."

"Is the place still off limits?"

"Not technically. But the department's policy in murder-one cases is to keep the place sealed for at least a month if we can, just as a precaution."

"Then we'll lock up."

He didn't seem too happy about it, but nodded and attempted a grin. Then he hurried down the front steps, pausing long enough to tie the police band back into place. When McCleary went upstairs, he found Quin sitting on the water bed, examining several articles of clothing.

"You dreaming of shopping on Worth Avenue or what?" he asked.

She held up a silk robe. Light shone through the pair of holes that had been cut where Kate's breasts would have been. Then she poked her fist through the missing crotch of a pair of panties. "Either Jack had some fetishes even Kate didn't know about or whoever sent Kate the note and the drawing has been here."

"Is there anything else?"

"No. I went through the bureau and the closet."

"Let's check the place from top to bottom."

It took them an hour, but they didn't find anything else. None of the windows or doors had been jimmied. There were no broken windows. "Did you ask Kate who all had keys to the ranch?" he asked.

Quin was leaning against the doorway of the utility room, dipping her hand into a Baggie of Cheerios. "Yeah. The cops, the caretaker, her attorney. But Jack was a real freak about spare keys. That weekend we were here, when you guys were in town, Kate and I got locked out of the house. We got back in when she used a spare key taped to the inside of the rain gutter."

It was there, all right, held in place with a piece of electrical tape. McCleary pocketed it. "She needs to get the locks changed out here."

"Won't Garrison be surprised the next time he tries to use his key," Quin said with a laugh.

"You're jumping to conclusions about him."

"I don't think so." She slipped her sunglasses back on as they came out of the shadows at the side of the house. "He's guilty as hell of something. And if he's involved with Little Miss Twit, it makes him even guiltier."

"You think he's the perv?"

"Christ, Mac, for all we know, he could be jerking off in public parks at night. But I don't think Garrison is the point."

"Then who is?"

"Jack." She paused. "You know those *molas* we have in the living room?"

He nodded. Molas were stitched designs on cotton that were native to the San Blas islands in Panama. Bright, vividly colored threads were used on darker backgrounds and sometimes depicted mirror images of objects—parrots, for instance, or machetes. The concept was simple, but the patterns were so intricate, so marvelously complex, McCleary always felt that he was looking at something executed by M. C. Escher. Layers within layers, each with a story.

"What about them?"

"I'm beginning to think Jack's life was like a *mola*, Mac, and that the reasons he was killed are just as complex."

10

KATE SPENT MOST of her time at the center in a room they had dubbed Max. It wasn't a nickname or an acronym. It was simply short for maximum—as in efficiency, ease, information retrieval, computation—and aptly described the electronic equipment.

The centerpiece of this expensive collection was a computer that was hooked up with other near-death centers around the country. Most were as small as this one and associated with a university. A few were private operations run by psychiatrists or psychologists who, like Jack, had become fascinated with the field through patients who'd had NDEs.

By networking, they increased their data bank and were able to tap into cultural and racial variables that might not be otherwise available in their respective areas. The center in Berkeley, for example, had the largest data bank on Orientals who'd had NDEs. This center had the largest data base on Hispanics. Washington, D.C., knew everything there was to know about how blacks experienced near-death.

Over the years, Kate had struck up computer friendships with researchers whose goals were similar to hers. One of them was her counterpart at Berkeley, a man named Elliot Wise, who she always went to first when she had a question. And this afternoon, her question was simple.

She hooked up the modem, tapped in the code for Berkeley, then: ELLIOT, IT'S KATE. YOU THERE?

I LIVE HERE. WOLFE TOLD ME WHAT HAPPENED. SUFFICE TO SAY I'M SORRY AND I KNOW YOU'LL GET OUT OF YOUR PREDICAMENT. WHAT'S TODAY'S QUESTION?

YOU HAVE ANYTHING ON AN "ECSTASY" PHENOMENON THAT

NDEERS EXPERIENCE AS A RESULT OF BEING ALIVE AND NOT BECAUSE THEY'VE JUST FOUND OUT DEATH ISN'T THE END?

There was a lapse of several seconds. IT'S A FINE LINE, BUT I KNOW WHAT YOU'RE TALKING ABOUT. HAVE ANALYZED 300 CASES FOR THAT VERY THING AND FOUND THE PERCENTAGE IS SMALL. AROUND 6 PERCENT, ROUGHLY THE SAME AS THOSE WHO REPORT NEGATIVE EXPERIENCES. THIS WAS ALSO AN INTEREST OF JACK'S.

WHEN DID HE MENTION IT TO YOU?

ASK ME SOMETHING SIMPLE.

ROUGHLY.

There was a long pause. FOUR YEARS, GIVE OR TAKE. I THINK HE'D JUST LEFT PRIVATE PRACTICE.

No, that couldn't be right. Until Tom Lewis, she had never dealt with a patient who reported this kind of experience. YOU SURE ABOUT THE TIME?

YES.

WAS IT RELATED TO A SPECIFIC PATIENT HERE?

A WOMAN, BUT I DON'T RECALL HER NAME. I TOLD HIM I'D HEARD ABOUT THE ECSTASY PHENOMENON FROM OTHER RE-SEARCHERS BUT HADN'T STUDIED IT PERSONALLY. HE ASKED IF I KNEW OF ANY PHYSICISTS WHO WERE STUDYING NDES AND I GAVE HIM THE NAME OF A FORMER PATIENT WHO'D TAUGHT AT BERKELEY. RICHARD URUZO. HE'S NOW RETIRED IN YOUR AREA. YOU WANT AN ADDRESS?

DEFINITELY.

GIVE ME A FEW MINUTES. GOT SOMEONE ELSE HERE.

THANKS, ELLIOT.

SURE THING. I'LL TRY TO REMEMBER THE NAME OF THAT FEMALE PATIENT, TOO.

He signed off and she sat there, thinking. When Jack had first started at the center, he had brought some of his private patients with him. It seemed likely that the woman who had precipitated his question to Elliot Wise had probably been among them, otherwise she would have heard about the ec-stasy phenomenon. The woman's name was probably in one of the four-hundred-plus files on Jack's former patients that she'd dropped at the McClearys' office earlier. But if she'd been one of his NDE patients who he'd brought with him to the center, then her name would be on the computer here.

As Kate got up from the computer, Sammy Dayton strolled in, as tall and thin as the scarecrow in Oz. As usual, his clothes looked as if he'd slept in them: the fabric of his shirt puckered around the buttons, the legs of his jeans were too short, his socks puddled at his ankles. It was as if Sammy lived his entire existence in his head and couldn't be bothered with mundane details like pressed clothes.

But even his disheveled appearance didn't diminish the power of his presence for her. It was that little-girl feeling, she thought, the sense that Sammy, two years her junior, would wave his wand and make everything better.

"Have you entered any of that data on Lewis yet?" he asked, flipping through pages on a clipboard.

"I was just about to start."

"Well, here's what Ray and I collected from family and friends. He finished transcribing our notes last night." He looked up as he handed her the clipboard and frowned. It narrowed his eyes until they were just sharp pricks of blue light in his cheeks. "You look tired. And you're too thin."

Even his unsolicited opinions on her appearance were somewhat paternal, she thought, and irritated her. "I haven't been sleeping well."

Kate dropped the clipboard on the desk next to the computer and walked over to the coffeepot on the counter. She felt Sammy's eyes following her. "Why don't you take some time off, Kate?"

"I already did. When I was in jail."

"That's not the same thing."

She turned around. "Look, I don't want to take time off. This keeps me busy."

He ran a finger across his upper lip, looked down at his scruffy loafers, raised his eyes again. She knew immediately that she wasn't going to like what he was about to say. "There's been some talk among the trustees about suspending you until the trial decides things one way or another."

Funny, but this was one thing she hadn't even considered. "On what basis? This hasn't impaired my ability to work."

"It has to do with adverse publicity for the center, Katie, not your work. Since the story hit the papers, our referrals have fallen fifteen percent."

And referrals were part of what their annual budget was based on. It came down to money, of course. She was now a liability. "When is a decision going to be made?"

"I don't know. I hope I've convinced them to hold off for a while. People have short memories, Katie. Now that the story's dropped off the front pages, I think referrals will pick up again."

Until the trial. "What do *you* want me to do, Sammy?"

"I want you to stay. And I want you to put this stuff on Lewis in the computer and get more sleep and eat more."

She laughed. "Anything else?"

"Yeah. Ray and I are giving a seminar on death and dying to a group of nurses at St. Mary's Hospital a week from today. On the seventeenth. Come with us."

"Okay."

"Good." He smoothed a hand over his head, hesitated as if he were about to say something else, then left.

As she sat down at the computer again with her coffee, the screen scrolled. KATE, IT'S ELLIOT. YOU THERE?

WAITING PATIENTLY, she typed.

The address for Uruzo was in Boca Raton, an affluent suburb south of Palm Beach. THE ADDRESS IS A YEAR OLD. DON'T KNOW IF IT'S STILL CURRENT. SAME WITH PHONE NUMBER. ALSO, I WENT BACK THROUGH MY NOTES. THAT PATIENT'S NAME WAS PEARL HANLEY. HOPE THAT HELPS.

IT'S A START. THANKS SO MUCH.

LET ME KNOW WHAT HAPPENS.

WILL DO.

She initiated a global search through the files for Pearl Hanley. While she waited, she tried the number Elliot had given her for Richard Uruzo. A recording informed her that the number had been changed and was now unlisted. At least he was in Boca, she thought, and wondered how soon she could get away to drive down there.

The computer beeped, signaling the end of the search for Hanley. FILE NOT FOUND.

Either Jack hadn't treated Pearl Hanley here or, for some reason, he hadn't entered her name in the computer. But if she wasn't a patient, then why had he told Elliot Wise that she was?

Kate walked down the hall to Wolfe's office. It looked as if a tornado had touched down—papers and files strewn across the desk, books piled on chairs, memos spilling out of the wire basket at the corner. He was on the phone, leaning back in his chair, feet raised on an open drawer, and rolled his eyes when he saw her. *Marsha,* he mouthed.

"I'll come back."

He shook his head and gestured toward one of the chairs. Kate sat, lit a cigarette. Wolfe fished under the papers for an ashtray and passed it to her, nodding at whatever Marsha was saying. "Uh-huh, it's all my fault. Okay, whatever you say. I accept full blame. Now if you don't mind, I've got to get back to work." He slammed down the phone, fuming. "Can you believe her goddamn nerve? She actually accused *me* of stealing *her* towels. Christ, she's the one who moved out of *my* place. And what the hell would I want with a set of towels from Montgomery Ward?" He pulled out his pocket watch. "Twenty minutes of my time she wasted."

"You should have just hung up as soon as you heard her voice."

He snapped the watch shut and slipped it back into the pocket of his slacks. "With her, it's best to let her get things off her chest. Besides . . ." He grinned. "Her personality aberrations are fascinating."

"Jesus, Wolfie. You sit around analyzing all these women?"

"Just the ones who've obviously got big problems."

"Is that what you did with me?"

His smile faded and he sat back, gazing at her with a seriousness she hadn't anticipated. "It was different with you."

"It was?"

"Sure. I was in love with you." He shrugged. "So your personality aberrations were also my own."

Kate laughed. "Gee, thanks. I didn't realize my personality was warped."

"Only when it came to Jack."

"What the hell's that supposed to mean?"

"Nothing." He fussed with the things on his desk, straightening them. "I guess I'm just feeling resentful. Do you realize that if it weren't for Jack, we probably would have gotten married?" There was no sentimentality in his voice; he was just presenting a fact, as though they were discussing a patient.

"You wouldn't be in the position you're in now and I wouldn't be sitting here regretting every decision I've made since." He shook his head and started twisting the end of his mustache. "All these choices we make. At the time, we don't consider their long-range effects."

It was the first time he'd ever said this much about what had happened between them and Kate didn't quite know how to take it. So she changed the subject and asked if he remembered a patient named Pearl Hanley. Nope, he replied without hesitation. The name didn't ring any bells. Was he sure? she asked. Of course he was sure. He might be weak on faces, but he had a good memory for names.

Especially if they were women, she thought.

"Why?"

"Drive down to Boca with me and I'll tell you on the way."

"Now?"

"At five, when we knock off."

He glanced at the mess on his desk and she could almost hear him thinking that he never had enough time, the work was endless, he was ready to toss in the towel and become a janitor. To her surprise he said, "Screw it. Let's leave now. What's two hours, right? Sammy's always leaving early and coming in late. Let's go."

Boca Raton was a Spanish name that meant *mouth of the rat*, which was supposedly the shape of its shoreline. But even from the air Kate had never seen the resemblance.

It wasn't a town so much as a series of walled developments, little Jerichos that hid sprawling Spanish-style homes, manicured lawns, streets shaded by gracious old trees. Its numerous canals held yachts that were sometimes larger than the homes they were docked behind, and its roads seemed to have more expensive cars per capita than any city in South Florida except Palm Beach.

Years ago, Kate remembered seeing an ad for Boca in which it was called "the city where one out of every forty-three people is a millionaire." She suspected the present figure was about one in ten.

She turned off U.S. 1 onto Camino Gardens and saw the pink hotel, Boca's most famous landmark. Shaped like a silo, it was rose from the edge of the intracoastal canal, soft pink against the blue, blue sky.

Directly across from its front entrance was Royal Palm, one of Boca's more exclusive walled developments. Kate pulled up to the guardhouse and gave her name and phone number to the little man inside, who dutifully jotted it on a clipboard and asked who she was visiting. When she told him, she expected him to tell her Mr. Uruzo no longer lived here. Instead, he shook his head.

"About now, he's on the golf course, ma'am."

"Here?"

"No, ma'am, over at the hotel. Ask at the pro shop. They'll direct you to him."

There was another guardhouse at the entrance to the hotel. It, too, was inhabited by a little old man who took down her name, then asked who she was going to see and what room the person was in.

"He's just playing golf here."

He slipped a ticket with VISITOR on it under her windshield. "Valet parking's at the front, ma'am."

"I don't want to valet park."

"Sorry, ma'am. If you're visiting, you have to valet park."

"Some racket," Wolfe murmured as they drove past.

"Welcome to Boca, Wolfie."

Plants and trees flourished on the grounds, untouched by the drought, as if the hotel existed under an invisible dome that controlled the weather. Even the air smelled green. Inside, the lobby stretched forever eastward, large enough and wide enough to roller-skate in. It was like a small, elegant city with chandeliers instead of street lamps, roads of Mexican tile, and signs pointing the way to the newsstand, the hair salon, the swimming pool, the restaurant, this ballroom and that.

When Kate asked the man in the pro shop about Uruzo, he glanced at his watch. "About now, I'd say he's on the fourth hole. Take a golf cart. It's quicker."

Wolfe drove the cart the same way he did a car, fast and furiously, as though he owned the road. They sped down small hills, tore across greens, raced through a bed of flowers with Wolfe laughing and Kate gripping the sides of her seat. When they reached the fourth hole, Wolfe's hair looked as though he had stuck his finger in an electrical socket.

"They'll probably bill us for the flowers," Kate griped.

"I couldn't find the brakes."

"Sure." She looked at him and they both laughed.

Wolfe tilted his head toward an elderly gentleman who was kneeling on the green, measuring the distance between the hole and a golf ball with his club. "You think that's him?"

"Let's hope so. The way you drive, we wouldn't survive the trip to the next green."

They got out, waited until the man had finished his measurement, then Kate said, "Mr. Uruzo? Could we talk to you a minute?"

He lifted his head. Sunlight winked off his sunglasses and bleached the gray from his hair so that it was perfectly white. "Let me sink this little guy first." He glanced at the hole, then looked down, drew back the club, and smacked the ball. It rolled across the green and stopped at the lip of the hole. "I'll be go to hell," he muttered. "It stops an eighth of an inch short. You ever seen such a thing?"

"Happened to my dad all the time," Wolfe said.

Uruzo strolled over, limping slightly. "Happened to Palmer, too, in the . . ." He frowned, then shrugged. "Well, I can't remember. Do I know you two?"

"Not yet." She introduced herself and Wolfe. "Elliot Wise at Berkeley gave me your name. He said you might be able to help me out with something."

"Wise." Groping for a face to fit the name. "Oh, right. The ghoul. A lot of them are ghouls, you know, these people who study death." He dabbed at his damp forehead with a handkerchief. "Too bloody hot out here for me. You follow me to the clubhouse and we'll talk about death and ghouls over something cold." He limped off toward his golf cart.

"An aberrant personality with incipient memory loss," Wolfe whispered.

"Be nice, Ray."

Wolfe's opinion about the old man underwent a dramatic transformation, however, when his golf cart took off like a shot across the green, sailed around the edge of a sand pit, careened down a path, and stopped abruptly in front of the clubhouse. He was chuckling to himself as he got out. "So, what were we talking about?" he asked as they went inside.

"Ghouls," Wolfe replied.

"Ah, right. Elliot Wise. Actually, he's quite nice, but he does tend toward morbidity. Very intense most of the time, always digging, digging, digging for answers. He used to drive me crazy with his questions." They settled at a table next to the window and a waitress took their order. "You wanted to know about Elliot, right?"

"Not exactly," Kate said, and explained.

"Bishop, Bishop. That's *your* name, isn't it?"

"He was my husband."

If he caught the *was*, he gave no indication. "Describe him."

Uruzo closed his eyes and rubbed his temple as she talked. Before she was finished, his eyes flew open and he snapped his fingers. "The pilot. Sure, I remember. We had lunch here. We went flying. He's got that same intensity that Elliot does. Another ghoul."

"Do you recall what you talked about?"

He dismissed the question with a flick of his hand. "Death, what else."

The waitress brought their drinks. Uruzo savored his beer with the delight of a man whose doctor had forbidden him to drink alcohol. "Do you recall the specifics of your conversation?" Wolfe prodded.

"Certainly." He glanced at Wolfe, amused. "My memory is still quite good when I'm able to associate things." He rubbed his chin, frowning a little. It made his bushy brows fan out. "In this case, it's the flying. I remember Mr. Bishop saying that when he flew, he entered a euphoric state of mind that he likened to some components of the near-death experience. Have either of you ever had an NDE?"

Kate and Wolfe shook their heads.

"Too bad. Researching a phenomenon isn't quite the same thing as experiencing it."

Wolfe made a face. "I've got absolutely no interest in dying, Professor."

Uruzo laughed. "Can't say that I blame you. But my own

experience certainly changed the way I look at things. Changed my approach to physics, too." He sat forward, hands cupped around his mug of beer. "That euphoric state your husband experiences when he flies, Mrs. Bishop, is what I call quantum consciousness. Much of the research being conducted in quantum physics suggests the possibility of a fundamental unity that lies deeper than man's present view of reality. If this unity can be proven, man's ideas about the world he lives in will be shattered. I believe that one of the elements in this unity is a connection between certain wave forms and certain states of consciousness. In other words, that consciousness itself is some sort of quantum effect. Or that consciousness creates reality and not the other way around," he finished.

"Is that what you believe the near-death experience is?" Wolfe asked.

"Absolutely." He lit a pipe that he'd been filling with tobacco and puffed on it. Smoke drifted up around his face; sunlight streamed through it. For a few moments, he reminded her of some ancient tribal shaman imparting wisdom to younger members of the tribe. "I wouldn't have said that before my own experience, but I can't say otherwise now. If you believe in heaven and hell, then initially that's what you'll experience. If you believe there is nothing after death, then that's what you you initially experience. That's rather simplistic, but you get the idea.

"The euphoria associated with NDEs is rather simple," he said. "If you frighten a man badly enough, make him think he's about to die and then jerk the threat of death away from him, you trigger a euphoria unlike anything else. It's a combination of intense relief and an almost preternatural sense of what it means to be alive. It's a popular ruse in prison camps to get a man to talk. As effective as pain. And after that most men will do anything, admit to anything, just to stay alive."

It was dark when they left the hotel and the air was still humid and uncomfortably warm. Strings of Christmas lights climbed bushes and trees like luminous snakes dancing to some snake charmer's flute. Kate guessed the decorations had gone up after Thanksgiving, as they did almost everywhere in South Florida. Maybe this Christmas she would take the *Jungle Queen* down the intracoastal to enjoy the lavish display of lights in the homes along the canal. It was one of those tourist trips that Jack had refused to take, along with the airboat rides in Loxahatchee, Disney World, Busch Gardens, and most of the other tourist trips. She didn't know why she should think of this now, as she and Wolfe were speeding north on the interstate, but there it was, a memory as bright as the stars popping out against the black skin of the sky.

"What now?" Wolfe asked, as though she had all the answers.

"I don't know."

"I didn't mean about Jack. I mean in general."

"Home, I guess. Then I'll head over to the McClearys' and we'll go through Jack's files."

"You want some help?"

"It's going to be a late night. You won't get your usual eight hours."

He laughed. It was an odd sound: uneven, like hiccups. "How come you make that sound like *my* personality aberration?"

"Just giving you fair warning."

"I wasn't *that* bad when we were together."

"No. You were worse. You were like Quin gets when she doesn't get to eat. But I'd love some help."

"Drop me at home and I'll meet you over there and work until midnight or one. How's that?"

"Great."

He turned his face toward the window and was silent for a long time. This, she knew, was the brooding Wolfe who turned an event over and over again in his mind, scrutinizing it from every conceivable angle until he had drawn a conclusion. She had found it maddening when they were lovers, but it was his strength as a researcher.

"Just say it, will you?" she finally blurted out.

"You think it could ever be the same with us again?"

"Do you?"

"I asked first."

"I guess it depends."

"On what?"

"On whether I go to jail."

The words hung there, huge and ugly.

11

1.

BISHOP'S MEDICAL RECORDS rose from the living-room rug in neat stacks like a child's building blocks. Four hundred and fifteen files, Quin thought, but who was counting?

The outside of each file bore the person's name and the year he or she had become a patient. It had taken her, McCleary, Kate, and Wolfe two hours just to separate the records by years and to sort NDE patients from the others. Pearl Hanley's name wasn't among them. So they eliminated everything before 1986, the last year of Bishop's private practice and when he'd first mentioned Pearl Hanley to the Berkeley researcher. This left a hundred and thirty files.

Now they were going through their respective stacks, looking for near-death patients and anything on the Hanley woman. It was possible, Quin thought, that her file had gotten mixed up with someone else's when Bishop had packed them or that she was filed under a different name—her maiden name, her married name, an alias—no telling. Or perhaps she had begun as a regular patient and was in the enormous pile they'd eliminated at the beginning.

By midnight they'd run across six NDE patients, but none was Pearl Hanley, so Quin tackled the pre-1986 files. It became apparent that in the earlier years of his private practice Jack had treated an astonishing range of disorders—everything from insomnia to sexual dysfunctions. But for the last two and a half years of his practice, the focus had narrowed considerably. The majority of his cases seemed to involve sexual problems of one kind or another. The socialite who was frigid, the high-powered businessman who couldn't maintain an erection, the promiscuous seventeen-year-old.

It reminded her that she still hadn't told Kate about Fargo's remark concerning wild parties at the ranch. She decided she wouldn't say anything until she or McCleary had substantiated the statement. She hated to withhold from Kate, but why mention it if it might not be true?

The twelfth file she opened was on a patient named Edward Burrows. He and his wife, Pearl Hanley, had consulted Jack about their marital problems in 1984. In late 1985, shortly before they were divorced, Pearl had ingested a handful of Valium and nearly died before she reached the hospital. Her near-death experience was recorded at length in the records, and it sounded like a nightmare. Bishop had noted that her description of the euphoria she had felt when she realized she hadn't died was "the most curious thing I've yet observed in any NDE patient."

Although her therapy continued into 1986, Bishop had never made up a separate file on her and his notes had become increasingly shorter. *Mrs. B. disappointed by divorce settlement. Mrs. B. relates prolonged episodes of insomnia, Valium prescribed. Mrs. B. promoted to V.P. at Beach National.* His final note was short and cryptic: *Pearl understands.*

That was it. Nothing to indicate whether her therapy had been discontinued or she had just quit going or what. Quin went back through the file, certain the pages were out of order. They weren't. When she announced that she'd found Pearl, Kate's face was perfectly blank. It was as if she sensed that Pearl Hanley Burrows would offer up secrets she might be happier not knowing.

There were always points of no return in an investigation, Quin thought, junctures where event A would lead to B as inevitably as the sun rose. And this, she knew, was such a juncture.

"Mac?" she whispered. "You asleep?"

"I almost was." He rolled onto his back. "What time is it?"

"Ten after four."

"Haven't you gone to sleep?"

"No. The baby has the hiccups. Give me your honest opinion about Jack."

He groaned and pulled the sheet up around his neck. "Why do we always have these conversations in the middle of the night?"

"C'mon, tell me. I want a man's opinion."

"Since when have you ever lacked for opinions?"

"Indulge me."

He sat forward, fluffed the pillows up against the headboard, and leaned back into them, yawning. "Jack. Okay, let's see. During that first year he and Kate were married, when we were seeing more of them, Jack and I were more or less forced to get along because you and Kate were always taking off."

Funny, she didn't remember that. "Taking off where?"

"Shopping, for lunch, whatever. So there were Jack and I, sitting out by the pool and trying to be companionable. The only things we had in common were art and movies, I think."

"Did he ever talk about Kate?"

"Not much."

"Did you ever talk about me?"

"Not much."

"Why not? Kate and I talked about you two."

"Men aren't like women in that respect."

Ah, yes. This was a familiar tune. She poked him in the ribs. "So that means I know more about Jack and Kate's sex life than you do."

He laughed. "Probably."

"What else do you know about him?"

He thought for a moment. "Jack used to hunt as a kid."

"Hunt what?"

"Birds, squirrels, alligators. His old man got him into it."

"Kate never told me that."

"He probably never told her since she feels the same about hunting as you do."

"You think he was unfaithful to her?'

It was the wrong question to ask, an old bone in their marriage. In the brief silence, Quin heard echoes of Sylvia Callahan, a woman with whom McCleary had been involved before Quin had entered his life. Their affair has resumed several years ago during a homicide investigation and Quin still felt deeply unsettled by the whole thing, even though Sylvia was now dead.

"Yes," he said finally.

"Why?"

"He implied it. At the time, I didn't realize that was what he was saying, but it makes a weird kind of sense now."

McCleary couldn't remember Jack's exact words, only his remark that he wished Kate weren't so straight sexually. So monogamous.

"Do you ever feel that way about me?" She hated how small and lost her voice sounded in the dark and wished she hadn't asked.

"No." McCleary sank deeper into the pillows and turned on his side, lifting up on an elbow. His hand rested lightly against her belly. "Callahan's dead, Quin. You think about her more than I ever did."

"Well, forgive me if I can't quite figure out why you had to resume a relationship that had ended before you and I ever met."

"Christ, Quin. Is Callahan always going to be an issue with us?"

"Her name was *Sylvia*."

She threw back the covers, rolled onto her side, lifted herself up, swung her legs over the edge of the bed, irritated that she couldn't move more quickly. She pushed to her feet and waddled out of the room and down the hall to the bathroom. She ran the water and sat on the side of the tub while it filled, soaking her swollen feet, feeling miserable and fat and ugly. She cried a little and talked to the baby.

Quin promised her daughter that things would be different for her. She wouldn't have to contend with the kind of peer pressure that made her wear flats so she wouldn't look taller than every boy in her ninth-grade class. She wouldn't have to wrap her hair on a beer can every night to straighten it because straight hair was in. She wouldn't have to stuff her trainer bra with toilet paper. She would never be made to feel too tall, too short, too thin, too fat, too anything at all. Her insecurities, if they existed, would be temporary landmarks in adolescent rites of passage. They wouldn't stick around and muddy up the rest of her life. She also promised Baby McCleary that she would have a name before she was born.

When Quin crawled into bed a long time later, McCleary's back was to her and she heard the soft, solitary song of a bird.

2.

Clicker moved restlessly around the darkroom, waiting for the photographs to dry.

They were pressed down against a circular metal drum and covered by a piece of taut canvas. The drum rotated slowly, its heat distributed uniformly across the metal surface. It dried the prints in a quarter of the time it would take if he hung them up and also kept them from wrinkling. It was what the pros used, Jack had said the first time he'd seen it, as necessary as a camera.

When the bell on the timer sounded, Clicker turned off the machine and lifted the canvas top. The photos slipped to the counter, warm as toast, wrinkle free, perfect. Six different shots of Pearl in black and white, her face clearly visible. He snapped on a pair of rubber gloves, fanned the photos out against the counter, and picked the best one. He slipped it into an envelope that was already stamped and addressed to Kate. He sealed it, slapped extra tape across it, set it aside. He would deliver it himself tomorrow.

This, too, was one of the rules. If he was going to clean up Jack's mistakes, after all, he had to be fair about it. Fairness was a virtue, as his mother used to say, not that *she* knew a damn thing about fairness.

He tidied up the darkroom, then stashed the extra photos in a box hidden behind a panel in the cabinets under the counter. He was tempted to linger over the other pictures inside, the incriminating pictures, but there wasn't time. Tonight he was a busy, busy man with a tight schedule to keep.

Clicker locked the darkroom and went into the bedroom for his slingshot. He slipped it inside his windbreaker with a couple of the nice-sized rocks he'd found out at the ranch. As backup he brought along the 9-millimeter Walther. Even on cleanup duty a man couldn't be too careful. Especially on *this* cleanup duty.

The last thing he picked up was the tiny squeeze bottle. Feed your head, as Grace Slick used to say. Yes siree, old Grace sure knew what she was talking about.

He'd driven halfway down the block before he realized he wasn't wearing his black canvas shoes. He swung into a U-turn and raced back to the house. Some people carried a rabbit's foot or a lucky coin; he wore the canvas shoes. He'd owned them for years, had worn them the night he killed Jack, wore them on the Death Flats, and he would wear them tonight with Pearl.

He drove onto the interstate and headed north to Jupiter, Burt Reynolds country. He set the cruise control at 55. He wasn't going to risk getting pulled over for speeding, not with a piece in his windbreaker and the squeeze bottle in his shirt pocket, whispering to him, teasing him, a mushroom begging to be sampled.

Feed your head.

But Clicker knew the value of discipline and managed to keep the bottle in his pocket for another ten minutes, until he saw the sign for the Jupiter turnoff. Then he stuck the tip of the nozzle into his nostril. His body seemed to feel the hot spurt before he'd even squeezed the bottle. Jack had told him it would be like this sometimes, nerves and glands primed through habit to anticipate, salivating like well-trained dogs. But he knew it was more than what Jack had said, more than mere habituation. He knew that under the drug's influence, his central nervous system became a conduit through which the future spoke to the present.

He squeezed the bottle only once. A tiny squeeze, hardly a squeeze at all. The cool spray zipped through the tissues of his nose and swept up, up through his sinuses and exploded in his brain. He gasped as the pleasure struck him, hands hooked like claws over the steering wheel, his erection straining against his jeans. Blood roared in his head. Fire burned in the space between his cells, his molecules.

Then he blinked and he was only a man in a car, speeding along a highway toward the release and perfection of his need.

He blinked again and he was in the field a block from Pearl's house. Another blink and he was striding through the field, the tall grasses rustling with his movements. An owl hooted in the silence. The breeze carried the rich salt scent of the sea.

There were only three houses on this street and Pearl's place was at the very end, a solitary A-frame shrouded in sea grape trees and pines. It wasn't the mansion she had been accustomed to when she was married to Burrows, but it wasn't poverty either.

He started up the driveway, his killing shoes crunching over the wood chips that blanketed it. Starlight filtered through the integument of branches overhead. The breeze skipped through the tall plants in the yard. Crickets cried for rain.

The lights were on and the blinds were up; pretty Pearl was suffering from insomnia again. There she was, curled on the couch, reading. He wondered if she missed Jack. Probably not. Women like Pearl had hearts of ice. They played out the hand that had been dealt them, cheating when they could, manipulating the game to their own best advantage.

He crept past her silver Porsche in the carport, spoils of her divorce settlement, and knocked at the side door. Her face appeared in the square of glass, dark eyes widening with surprise, that lovely mouth swinging into a cool smile, her black hair loose around her shoulders. She was almost as beautiful as Kate.

She unfastened the chain and opened the door. That face, that long white neck, that tiny wisp of a waist, those legs. Even her bare feet were lovely. She was wearing a silk kimono that ended at mid-thigh. It was cut so low in front, he could see the swells of her breasts. "Little late for a visit, isn't it, hon?"

Her voice always shocked him. It should have been soft and musical, as her looks implied. But it was hoarse and ordinary. "Just checking in. I hadn't heard from you."

She shrugged, scratched at her right calf with the toes of her left foot, and walked away from the door. "Nothing to say. Besides, we've been real busy at work. You want something to drink?"

Clicker shut the door and turned the lock in the knob. His temple throbbed. "A cold beer."

"I couldn't sleep," she said on her way into the kitchen. "Every time I closed my eyes, I thought I felt Jack around." Her laughter was a nervous thrill. "Silly, I guess. But deep down, I think he'll get in touch with one of us."

A note from the beyond, a call from the graveyard, Jack haunting them. Right.

Clicker settled on the sectional couch and glanced at the book she'd been reading. *The Evidence for Spirit Communication.* "No wonder you can't sleep, reading shit like this."

She handed him the beer, twisted the cap off her own, and lowered herself to the couch, legs folded beneath her. "It's not shit. The author presents twenty *very* convincing cases."

Clicker pulled out the squeeze bottle and held it up. Her eyes fixed on it, bright and feverish with a need that transformed her face. "Sure. Why not. Why the hell not. Mine's almost gone."

Her hands moved impatiently over her kimono, smoothing wrinkles, playing with the sash at her waist, her eyes never straying from the squeeze bottle. She watched as he spun the cap. "Have the police been in touch with you?" he asked.

"Why would they be in touch with me? They already charged Kate."

"You think she killed him?"

She shrugged, interested only in the drug now, and reached for the bottle. Clicker laughed and held it out of her reach. "Tip your head back. I'll do it."

He squirted a little into each of her nostrils. She made a soft, almost helpless sound as the liquid burned a path to her brain. Her breathing quickened, her hands clenched into fists in her lap, her legs slipped out from under her, and she closed her eyes, abandoning herself to sensation.

Clicker treated himself to another squirt, more generous this time. It lit up the inside of his head. The room began to pulse, colors vibrated, her eyes connected with his, her face glowing like a pumpkin, exposing retes of tiny capillaries and veins. Her eyes were dark wax melting into green. Something flowed between them that he couldn't describe. It was invisible, tasteless, and yet it possessed weight, shape, reality, and pushed up against him, a cat in heat.

This was the long, smooth edge of the libido in overdrive, spinning its illusions of beauty and communion. He didn't know what it was to Pearl, maybe nothing more than the anticipation of a good fuck with just the two of them this time. No Jack.

Sorry, Jack.

She moved up against him, whispering that she wanted to go for a swim, would he like that? Her hands were already working at the kimono sash, unknotting it, and now she was standing, smiling in that way she always did on the flats, crooking a finger at him, laughing. Then she was leaning over him, nibbling, whispering, asking why he wasn't wearing that delicious cologne he had when it was the three of them. Her hand unzipped his slacks, reached inside.

Pines, beach, starlight, he and Pearl in a field of sea oats on an old towel: These were the details Clicker remembered later.

Everything else was a blur of sentience, a river of pleasure in which he was submerged, drowning, dying. At the moment of his death, he became this river. He leaped the boundaries of his own flesh and rushed along the grassy banks of a field in another place, another time, another universe. He wasn't aware of specifics, like the shape of a breast or the taste of her mouth. The details were smaller, minute, fleeting: the color of freckles blended with the texture of a hair or the width of a single pore. He shrank and dived inside the pore. He swam through blood, fluids, a cell. The cell expanded, then burst through a membrane of skin and sprang into the sky where it glowed like a moon. He became the stars. His essence thinned out, narrowed like a bullet, and he shot through the music of space.

Her voice reached for him in the dark, in the odor of water and salt. "Did you kill him?"

The rules, he thought. Remember the rules. "No."

She lifted up, her face dark above his, her hair falling around them like rain. "You can't lie worth a damn, hon, not to me, not now. Did you like it?"

"Like what?"

"Killing him. That's what we're talking about, isn't it?"

Under his head, where his clothes were folded, he felt the shape of the slingshot. The rocks. The dead were never dead, he thought, but they couldn't spill their secrets. So the rules didn't matter with Pearl. He shrugged; let her decide what it meant.

"I take it that's a yes," she said.

"Yes."

"Why'd you do it?"

Because Jack had gone too far on the flats. Because of Kate. Because.

"Okay, let me put it this way." Pearl sat up, hugging her legs. His finger slid along the length of her spine, over tiny ridges like steps. "Did you enjoy it?"

"Yes."

"Because it was Jack or just because?"

"I don't know."

"They'll find out, hon. Someone will piece it together."

"Never."

She laughed, shifted around, lowered her head to his groin. A spinning red vortex filled his head, sparks shooting off it. His bones turned to rubber, his organs dissolved and re-formed, molecules and particles whirring, spinning apart, congealing again. He was being re-created.

His eyes snapped open just as the moon tilted to the right and slid out of the sky. It landed inches from his head and bounced toward the water, a luminous beach ball. Stars rained down around it. He reached out to catch them and they slipped through his fingers like sand. He started to laugh and Pearl lifted her head and asked what was so funny and he told her the moon had just tumbled from the sky and stars glistened in her hair.

She shook her head. Stars flew from her hair like Tinkerbell's magic dust and trailed behind her as she ran toward the water.

Clicker sat up, dug under his clothes for the slingshot, the rocks. Two chances, that was fair. He fit the smaller stone into the slingshot and thought of the squirrel, that nasty fucker infested with Okeechobee fleas. And when Pearl stood still at the edge of the water, he let the stone fly.

It struck her in the back of the head. He heard the sound that escaped her as her knees crumpled, as her hand flew up, as she stumbled. Then she was on her hands and knees in the sand, moaning, shaking her head like an enraged bull with lances sticking out of its spine. Not good enough, fuck, it wasn't good enough. She had to be dead, not crippled. He grabbed the remaining stone and ran toward her. She rocked back onto her knees and reared up, a dog doing tricks. Her mouth opened to shout for help, to call his name, he didn't know which, it didn't matter.

The second rock sped away from him, flying through sea spray and falling stars in a perfect arc. When it slammed into her mouth, the fit was perfect. He ran toward her. She grappled in the sand, sucked for air; her hands clawed at her throat.

He felt her terror, her agony, and the moment when death overtook her like a locomotive, releasing her. For a split second, the drug allowed him to experience her release, her soul hissing from her, an invisible puff of smoke. She toppled facedown in the sand. Her limbs didn't twitch as the squirrel's had. A wave broke just beyond her, its foam hissing, bubbling, finally dissolving. Strands of seaweed stuck to her black hair. A crab burrowed up from the sand inches from her hand, hesitated, then darted sideways and grabbed at her finger. Clicker smashed it with his fist.

He grasped her hands and pulled her through the sand to the sea oats. He pulled on his clothes, slipped the slingshot into the back pocket, then wrapped Pearl up in the towel like a mummy. A few tendrils of her hair had escaped and curled over the towel. He plucked them out and put them in his wallet. A memento no one would miss. It was within the scope of the rules.

He leaned over her, waiting to feel her presence, hoping he would, disappointed when he didn't. He eased the towel down away from her eyes and, touching them gently, shut them. He hurried back to the house, wiped off everything he remembered touching, and took the beer bottle with him when he left.

As he drove toward Kate's to deliver the envelope, he thought about the sun coming up, about someone—perhaps a neighbor out for his morning constitutional—strolling the beach and discovering the body. It thrilled him.

12

1.

KATE HAD ENVISIONED what she would do, what she would say, what Pearl Hanley would do and say. She had stood in front of the mirror and rehearsed her words out loud. She had practiced keeping her face utterly expressionless, a blank slate on to which Pearl could project whatever she wanted.

But as she parked down the street from the Beach National Bank, her courage deserted her. She began to sweat. To shiver. Let Quin do this, she thought. But she needed to see this woman, speak to her, understand what Jack had seen in her. As she got out of the Jeep, her bones seemed too brittle to support her weight.

The sun struck her in the face, the sidewalk quivered, the shops blurred. She felt as though she were moving through the thick, syrupy air in a dream. She stopped in front of the bank, her blouse sticking to her skin, her hair curling damply against the back of her neck. Her palms were perspiring. Her body seemed to be losing moisture at an alarming rate and she wondered if, when she walked inside, she would simply crumble and turn to dust.

It was ten A.M. Pearl would be here by now, inside the cool interior, at a desk, chatting with a customer, perhaps sipping coffee. She would have soft, pale skin, a body of sleek, graceful lines, a face that drew second glances on the street. Kate's image of her had been culled from the things Jack hadn't said in his notes, from the details so meticulously omitted. And from these same omissions she knew Pearl and Jack had been lovers, that it had started after her near-death experience, and had still been going on when Jack was killed.

It explained their bickering, the weekends he supposedly

had gone to the ranch alone, explained the emotional absence between them for which she's always blamed herself. She wondered if David knew. Or Stephanie. Or Wolfe and Sammy.

Inside, she thought. Push the door and go inside.

The cool air shocked her and for seconds she just stood there, her heart thudding, the room blurring, her muscles shrieking for her to flee. She forced herself to walk over to a young man at one of the desks to her right, "Excuse me. Is Ms. Hanley in?"

"No, I haven't seen her today." Smiling. "Is there something I can help you with?"

"I really need to see Ms. Hanley. Do you have any idea when she'll be in?"

Still smiling. "I sure don't."

"Could you ask someone?"

"Oh." As though the idea had never occurred to him. "Sure. I'll be right back."

He got up and walked over to one of the larger desks at the window, where an older woman in a bright red suit was talking with a black man whose back was to Kate. The young man interrupted them. The three of them glanced toward her, conferred, then the black man stood and strode across the room toward her.

He was about Quin's height, five ten, with a chest the size of Clint Eastwood's, sideburns fading to white, and eyes so dark they were as nearly as black as his skin. His khaki slacks, short-sleeved shirt, and running shoes told her he was not a bank employee.

"Mrs. Bishop?"

How does he know my name? "Uh, yes."

"I'm Detective Eastman, ma'am, with IAD."

"With what?"

"Internal Affairs Division, Palm Beach County Sheriff's Department. Could we step outside for a minute?"

"For what?"

"I'd like to ask you a couple of questions, ma'am."

"About what?"

"Pearl Hanley."

"Yes, but—"

"Please, ma'am. This won't take long." He touched her arm and tilted his head toward an exit sign to his left. "We'll go out that way."

They emerged in an alley behind the bank, where a 1954 Cadillac was parked. Eastman leaned against it. "Where were you between midnight and three A.M. this morning, Mrs. Bishop?"

Panic. Midnight and three. She couldn't remember. She was suddenly back at the ranch the morning after Jack had been killed, sitting there in the hot sun as Garrison fired questions at her.

"Mrs. Bishop?"

"I was with friends."

"Which friends, Mrs. Bishop?"

"The McClearys. I . . . look, am I being accused of something? What's going on? I don't even know Pearl Hanley."

"And who are the McClearys?"

"Private detectives I've hired." She ticked off their office number, home number, address. "We were going through my husband's old medical records and found Ms. Hanley's file among them. I wanted to talk to her."

"About what, Mrs. Bishop?"

"About whether she was having an affair with my husband, Detective Eastman. About whether she killed him. About whatever the hell she knows."

His expression changed, but she didn't know what it meant. He shut the notepad in which he'd jotted the information she'd given him and said, "Wait right here and I'll be back in a minute."

When he returned, he informed her that Quin McCleary had confirmed her story, and opened the passenger door for her. "C'mon, I'd like to show you something."

She stayed where she was. "I'm not going anywhere until you tell me what's going on."

He was already on the other side of the car and regarded her across the roof as though she were a somewhat exotic and very curious bug. "Pearl Hanley was murdered between midnight and three this morning. Now, would you please get into the car, Mrs. Bishop?''

2.

When McCleary had lived in Dade County, it seemed to take him all day just to drive from one end to the other because of the traffic. But this morning the interstate whisked him out of Palm Beach County in twenty minutes and to the outskirts of Indian River County in a little over an hour. A breeze compared to Dade.

This was Florida's treasure coast, an area that ran roughly from Fort Pierce to Cocoa Beach. It was smaller than Palm Beach County and had only one main city, Vero Beach, and a number of small towns. Vero was renowned for two things— as the spring training camp for the L.A. Dodgers and as the home base for Piper Aircraft, which had their main plant here. It occupied the west side of the airport. To the south were the terminal, tie-down areas, gas pumps, and half a dozen flight services that offered everything from ground school to sightseeing tours of the area.

At one of the flight services, McCleary was directed to a hangar on the west side of the airport next to the Piper plant. He found it easily enough, an old hangar the elements had beaten down, its doors thrown open to the warm breeze.

Inside were dozens of planes in some stage of repair. Some were missing doors, others had only one wing or no tail or crumpled propellers. Willie Nelson's voice exploded from an unseen radio and reverberated against the walls, masking the sounds of hammering and drilling coming from two men who were tearing apart an engine. A man who looked like an aging hippie sauntered out of a small office and shouted, ''Help you with something?''

''I'm looking for Wayne Shepard.''

''I'm Shepard.'' He cupped his hands around his mouth. ''Hey, Joe, turn off that noise!''

Willie Nelson's voice went down a few decibels. Shepard stuck a finger in his ear and moved it rapidly. ''Goddamn country-western stuff's going to make me deaf. C'mon into the office. I didn't catch your name.''

"McCleary. Mike McCleary."

The office could have been Fargo's—just as messy, just as smoky. Shepard lit a Marlboro and leaned back in his metal chair until it touched the wall. "What can I do you for, Mr. McCleary?"

"I understand you know about some wild parties that took place out at the Bishop ranch."

Smoke drifted through Shepard's teeth. "Whose ranch?"

McCleary pulled out the photograph Fargo had given him and stabbed his finger at Bishop. "This man's ranch."

Shepard picked up the picture, puffed on his cigarette, dropped the photo on the desk. "We were in a flying club. I don't know anything about any parties."

"That's not what Roy Fargo says."

He came forward, dark eyes skewing against the smoke. "You a cop?"

"Private detective. Hired by Kate Bishop."

"Maybe if she'd done better by her old man, you wouldn't be here, huh, McCleary."

"Look, all I want to know about is the parties. Who was there, what went on."

"I didn't say nothing about parties, man, you did." He stabbed out his cigarette, pulled a toothpick from his pocket, poked it between his teeth. "So don't go putting words in my mouth."

"Fargo's willing to testify," McCleary lied. "That means you'll get subpoenaed as well. You either tell me or you tell the court."

"I think you'd better leave, man, before I lose my temper." Shepard stood, still working the toothpick between his teeth. He wasn't as tall as McCleary, but he outweighed him by forty pounds. "I got nothing to say to you or any goddamn court. What I do with my time is *my* business. Got it?"

His fingers sank into McCleary's chest and he leaned into his face, his breath stinking of smoke, his dark eyes laughing. McCleary's patience snapped. He grabbed Shepard's wrist, bent it back, saw a punch coming and twisted, deflecting it to his side. Then he released Shepard's wrist and punched him in the gut. He stumbled back, coughing, clutching his arms against him, and crashed into a filing cabinet against the far wall. He slumped to the floor. McCleary grabbed the metal chair from behind the desk and, before he could get up, dropped it over Shepard and straddled it. The upper, curved part of the chair was jammed under Shepard's throat and the lower edge cut across his stomach, trapping his arms.

"Jesus," he gasped. "Can't breathe."

"All you have to do, Shepard, is tell me about the parties. Who was there, what happened, how many parties there were."

"F'you."

"Yeah, you, too, pal." McCleary leaned into the upper part of the chair; Shepard's eyes widened. "I got all day."

He groaned, squeezed his eyes shut, tried to buck and throw McCleary off. When he realized it was futile and that his air was diminishing by the second, he hissed, "Couple times."

"What was that, Shepard?" McCleary let up a bit on the pressure. "Can't quite hear you."

He coughed. "Only went to a couple."

"Give me names, Shepard."

"Dunno."

McCleary applied pressure again. Shepard wheezed. "Okay, okay."

He eased up again on the pressure and this time Shepard talked fast. "Palm Beach people, friends of Jack's, dunno who they all were, remember a woman named Pearl and a cop named Garrison and Jack's brother was there, playing music, man, and that's all I know, I swear."

"Who else?"

"Dunno, man. Really."

"What happened at these parties?"

"Lemme up, man, just lemme up and I'll tell you."

McCleary let him up and Shepard, rubbing his throat and coughing, made good on his word. He attended three parties last spring, he couldn't remember the exact dates, but it was always when Jack was at the ranch without Kate. There were usually about twenty people, some from Palm Beach and others from the communities around Lake Okeechobee, all of them swingers in fast crowds, as Shepard put it. The orgy room upstairs had nothing but pillows in it, with soft lights and music and a bowl of condoms at the door. Coke and grass were usually available, but never in large quantities. Shepard claimed to have seen Garrison and Pearl the three times he'd attended, Stephanie Bishop twice, and David Bishop only once, the night he and a band provided live entertainment. He stopped going because he thought sooner or later someone was going to find out and the place would be raided. Shortly after that the flying club broke apart and he never saw Jack again.

McCleary asked if Fargo or Frank Abalonee, the other member of the flying club, ever attended. No way, Shepard said. Fargo was married with kids and Abalonee was too straight. But he had the impression that Abalonee knew about the parties. Was the ranch caretaker ever there? McCleary asked. He didn't know. The only people he saw who weren't guests were a couple of big dudes who kept watch outside.

"Did you know Garrison was a cop?"

"Only after Jack was killed, when I read about it in the paper. That's all I know, man." He was leaning against the wall, still rubbing his throat. "So if you don't mind, I got to get back to work."

"Thanks for your time." McCleary grinned. "Hope your larynx recovers." Shepard slammed the door as McCleary stepped back into the noisy hangar. The last McCleary saw of him, he was on the phone, probably with Fargo. So much for his cover as a prospective buyer for Bishop's Bonanza, he thought.

He drove back to the terminal and called the house. He felt guilty about leaving this morning before Quin was up, before he could apologize for last night or tell her where he was going. He had heard her come to bed at the crack of dawn and figured she was still sleeping. But when she didn't answer, he hung up and phoned the office.

"St. James and McCleary."

"It's me."

"Hi, me." Her voice was neutral, which meant she wasn't sure who was at fault for last night's tiff.

"I figured you'd still be asleep."

"A Detective Eastman from Internal Affairs woke me,

checking on Kate's whereabouts last night. Pearl Hanley's turned up dead.''

Jesus. ''What's IAD doing on a homicide?''

''I don't know. I didn't ask. He wanted to know when he could meet with us. Since I didn't know where you were or when you'd be back . . .'' An accusatory tone had crept into her voice now. ''I told him this evening. He suggested a place called the Hollywood Cafe in Lantana. Where are you, anyway?''

''Vero.''

''You find Shepard?''

''Yes. He verified the parties. I'll tell you about it when I get back. And, Quin, I'm sorry about last night.''

''It's my fault.'' Practically whispering. ''I feel big and ugly all the time.''

He saw her suddenly and clearly in his head, and told her she had never looked lovelier to him. She laughed, a soft, delighted sound. ''Sure, Rodin's woman. See you later.''

''Love you,'' he said, and hung up.

3.

Jupiter: like the planet.

It was the only thing Kate could think of as Eastman pulled his aging Caddy up to the police blockade in front of the A-frame house. There were cops in the driveway, cops combing the fields on either side of the house, cops talking with a clutch of reporters.

Kate averted her face, certain some of the reporters were the same ones who had left messages on her machine, who had congregated outside the sheriff's station the morning of her release. Eastman noticed and touched her elbow, guiding her away from them, toward the driveway. Neither of them spoke.

The silver Porsche in the driveway was identical to Jack's, the same year and model, a $60,000 Carrera, except that his was black. And inside the house she noticed Jack's touches—the wicker couch with cushions in the identical Southwest pattern in their bedroom, the Southwest throw rug on the pine floor. On the walls were Southwest tiles of adobe huts and

113

Indian women done by the same artist who had painted the acrylic that hung in their bedroom. Mullan. She felt a peculiar vacancy in her chest, a sense of unreality. It was as if she had just walked into Jack's other life.

"Why did you bring me here, Detective Eastman?"

"Fitz."

Fitz, Bitz, Litz, she didn't give a good goddamn what this man's first name was. She didn't want to be on a first-name basis with him. He was a cop, and right now she was sour on cops. "Why?" she repeated.

"In here."

As she followed him toward the back of the house, they passed several men engaged in tasks she knew were related to forensics, but not like anything that had been done at the ranch after Jack was killed. She stopped, watching them. Eastman also stopped.

"They're state forensics people," Eastman said. "They've already photographed and charted every corner in this house and have used both chemicals and powders to lift whatever fingerprints are in here. Later," he explained, "they'll darken the house and shine a Luma-lite around. Its beam highlights body fluids, fibers, and fingerprints. They also have an argon ion laser, a portable model about the size of a small camera box, which throws a six-inch beam that can detect fingerprints that might be impossible to find otherwise. The larger model will be used to lift prints off Ms. Hanley's body, if there are any."

"Why wasn't this done for Jack?"

"Because you were charged with the murder, Mrs. Bishop. They thought it was an open-and-shut case. I've also got a criminal psychologist working on a profile of this guy. None of that information, by the way, will be in the press." He touched her elbow, guiding her into the bedroom.

Pine furniture, a canopy bed, a Southwest bedspread that matched the cushions on the chairs, and a throw rug. The sliding glass doors opened onto a deck that overlooked the ocean. The room of a woman alone.

Eastman opened the top drawer of the dresser and brought out a framed photograph, which he passed to her. Jack and

114

Pearl. They were laughing, her head thrown back, as though he had just told a rowdy joke, his arm around her shoulders, her arm at his waist, red nails visible against his belt. Kate's heart seized up, she felt tears building at the backs of her eyes.

Eastman gave her a chance to speak. When she didn't, he said, "On the basis of this photograph alone, Mrs. Bishop, the press can nail you so badly you'd never get a fair trial in the state of Florida, much less in Palm Beach county."

"I have an alibi." Her voice sounded hoarse and weak.

"Yes, from a woman who was your college roommate and who also happens to be the detective you hired."

She didn't say anything and Eastman strode across the room and stopped in front of the sliding glass doors, hands in his pockets, and gazed out. Sunlight illuminated his profile and for the first time she noticed that he had strong features, all bold lines and sharp edges. She sensed, suddenly, that he was not at all like Garrison.

"Normally, I don't have a problem with prosecutors. But in this case I do. In this case he's a son of a bitch from an old Palm Beach family who is going to seize on this piece of evidence and find fifty other pieces of evidence to support it. Then he's going to weave it all into a very convincing story about how you shot your husband because he was having an affair with Pearl Hanley and then you killed her and your college roommate covered up for you."

"I didn't kill anyone."

"I believe you."

She couldn't have been more shocked if Eastman had confessed to killing Pearl himself. "You do?"

He turned. "But what I believe isn't going to matter without proof, Mrs. Bishop."

"Forgive me if I'm being cynical, but just what the hell is it that makes you different from ninety-nine percent of the people in your department and in this county who happen to think I'm guilty?"

"Garrison," he said.

13

Miguel the mechanic tapped two fingers against his watch. *"Media hora mas, señora."* Another half hour.

Quin was standing outside the garage near the office, the noonday sun beating against her back, Baby McCleary doing cartwheels inside her. "That's what you told me an hour ago when I called. I had to take a taxi down here."

"I did not tell you that, *señora*."

"Someone here did."

He threw out his arms, gesturing toward the cars lined up in front of the two stalls. "Please, *señora*, we have many cars besides yours, no? It will not be much longer."

"But suppose it needs a part? That could take a couple of hours to get and install." Or days, it could even take days, and then she'd be stuck without a car, the kiss of death in South Florida.

"If you had a newer car, *señora*, you would not have to come to the garage."

Swell. Now he was going to try to sell her one of the junkers parked in the adjacent lot. "I'll be back later this afternoon." She would have McCleary drive her over when he returned to the office. "You think it'll be ready by four?"

"Absolutamente, señora. No problema."

No problem: that usually meant the opposite. She envisioned her Toyota coming back with a dozen new parts that didn't need replacing and the things that were wrong with it still screaming for repair.

The office was at least two miles from here and it would probably take a cab an hour to arrive. Best to walk to the Esplanade on Worth Avenue, where taxis were plentiful, and grab one there. She started out at a swift clip, but that didn't last long. It was too hot and her feet were swollen again. She thought about the Toyota with its 85,000 miles on it, held together with a spit and a prayer, breaking down on I-95. Things happened to women in South Florida whose cars broke down on the interstate. And they happened in Palm Beach County almost as often as they did in Dade.

A new car was definitely in order.

McCleary, the voice of reason, would tell her she was fretting about something that might never happen. But he wasn't pregnant. He could still bend over to tie his shoes. She would be hard-pressed at this point to defend herself against a poodle.

She'd fretted over such things before she'd gotten pregnant. But that was different. Since her fourth month, when her bulk had begun to noticeably restrict her ability to accomplish ordinary tasks, her imagination had been running wild.

But the brown Firebird that had been tailing her for the last two blocks wasn't imagination, now was it. It was right back there, as solid as she was, bigger than she was, taking up space just like she was. If she stole another look behind, she would see it moving slowly up the street, a giant brown beetle, close but not too close, and inside would be her old buddy from Lake Mangonia, the hulk who had attached an electronic bug to the underside of her car.

She picked up her pace, wishing it weren't so bloody hot, that she weren't so large, that she didn't waddle. In minutes her shirt was stuck to her back, beads of sweat rolled down the sides of her face. She turned onto Worth Avenue, shopper's paradise, and headed toward the Esplanade. Plenty of nooks and shops to vanish into there.

If it came to that.

Which it wouldn't.

She looked back.

The Firebird was turning, the sun struck the windshield just right, and she saw two shapes inside. The car rolled on through the heat, light glinting now from its shiny hood.

Quickly. Through the arch. Into the courtyard.

Like Alice, she passed into the rarefied air of another world.

The Esplanade, with its fountain spewing arches of water and its shaded stone path, reminded her of a European village. The women all looked as if they might be somebody, a Rockefeller, a Trump, a Kennedy, Yoko Ono in disguise. They wore huge sunglasses, high heels, bright red lipstick. Their wide-brim hats bobbed in the hot air like cut flowers in water. Poodles and Pekineses with bows and obnoxious barks snuggled in arms adorned with gold and designer watches whose names Quin couldn't pronounce.

"Excuse me, excuse me," she murmured, bumping into silk, leather, passing through the slipstream of perfume that tickled her nostrils.

She looked back, scanning the crowd for God knew what, and spotted the two men. She recognized the hulk from the lake; the man with him was his clone: reflective shades, ties, suits, jackets that probably hid weapons. Why else would anyone wear a jacket in ninety-three-degree heat? And hey, running shoes, nice touch.

She knew they knew she'd picked them out as occupants of the Firebird because they were suddenly darting this way and that to avoid bumping into shoppers. Her head snapped right, left, right again as she sought a store to dash into. But the problem with a store, any store, was that she would be trapped. The men would wait around outside until she emerged. She needed stairs, a back door, a hole in the ground that would open up and swallow her.

The stairs that led to the second floor of shops were just ahead. But the men were going to reach her before she reached the stairs. It was possible they just wanted to chat, to ask a few friendly questions about Jack or Kate. Maybe she had some unpaid parking tickets she didn't know about and these were the boys the city sent to collect. Maybe they were feds and she was breaking a law by not sticking around. Fifty million maybes. She was sick to death of maybes. The only thing she knew for sure was that she had absolutely no interest in finding out what they wanted or who they were. But in a minute she wasn't going to have a choice.

Quin broke into a run, her belly bouncing like a bag of potatoes, and charged into a woman in front of her who was weighed down with packages and tugging a reluctant poodle along on a leash. Bags and boxes tumbled from her arms. The poodle raced around in circles, yipping madly, its leash wrapping like ribbon at the woman's legs.

In seconds, the promenade was an obstacle course of chaos. The woman stumbled forward, trying to grab the leash, the dog, her hat, her packages. She fell to her knees. The poodle got loose and ran around in a frenzy, barking and growling. Quin flew on, silently apologizing to the woman for ruining her shopping spree.

She reached the top of the stairs, winded. It hurt to draw a breath. Baby McCleary kicked, protesting the exertion. The men weren't far behind her, giants on an urgent mission. She ran into a tearoom, where the aromas wafting from the bakery pursued her into the ladies' room. She slammed the door shut.

A hefty black woman in a uniform was seated on a stool next to the sink and glanced up from the book she was reading. Quin guessed she looked utterly frightful, because the expression on the woman's face made it abundantly clear that she was not someone to fuck with, if that was what Quin had in mind.

"Two men." Quin sucked air in through her teeth. "Out there. My ex. You haven't seen me."

The woman grinned; her teeth lined up in her mouth like a gang of thugs in white tuxedos. She knew all about exes—husbands, boyfriends, take your pick. She swiveled on her stool and kicked open a metal cabinet beneath the sink.

"You fit in there, lady?"

She would make herself fit.

Quin crouched and backed into the tiny space, squeezing her arms tightly at her sides, pulling her neck down like a chicken's. Her knees cracked. Baby McCleary rolled through her noisy amniotic world, tiny fists punching the walls of Quin's womb. The metal door clicked shut. The dark closed around her, a fist. She was sealed in, an astronaut in a space capsule, and she didn't like it.

The pressure on her bladder was excruciating. Her stomach rumbled with hunger. Her breath rattled in her chest. She stared at the hands on the face of her watch, counting off seconds, minutes.

At two minutes and sixteen seconds, she heard the woman say, " 'Scuse me, boys. But the men's room be next door.''

The voice of the man who spoke was muffled. Quin pressed her face into her hands, sweat streaming from her pores, her need for fresh air and light so extreme, she nearly screamed.

"Sonny, I don't care if you be an angel from God's green acre. Ain't decent, you bein' in here, and no, I ain't seen no pregnant lady. So if you don't mind, you just be movin' on. . . .''

Don't sneeze, burp, fart, grind your teeth. Play dead, Quin thought, and waited.

When the door finally opened, she popped out, a jack-in-the-box, an overdone cookie. "There was some ladies in here and I wanted to wait for them to leave 'fore I opened the door.'' The woman helped Quin to her feet. "You okay?''

"Yes, thanks.'' A lie. She jerked some towels from the dispenser, ran them under the faucet, pressed them to her face. It helped.

"Your old man's got himself some badass friends.''

"I know.''

"Said they was undercover po-leese.''

"Yeah, and I'm Joan Rivers.'' Quin wadded up the towels, tossed them in the basket. "I really appreciate your help.''

"You best be takin' it easy, honey. Don't want to go tirin' yourself out 'fore the baby's born.''

She was anxious to leave. "Is there a back door to this place?''

"You bet. C'mon. I'll take you just in case them boys don't have a lick of sense and be waitin' out there.''

Quin hoped she didn't run into the woman with the poodle downstairs.

A hot bath. A mammoth meal. Silence. Nothing too complex in that list of needs, Quin thought. But the prosaic seemed as unattainable at the moment as the riddle of Schrödinger's cat.

She was standing in front of the kitchen sink at the office, satisfying her hunger with a fat, juicy mango that had cost her two bucks at Publix. Out of season in Florida, this one hailed from Mexico. When she'd polished it off, she set the seed on a paper towel to dry out. She would plant it at the side of the house, she decided. And maybe in five years it would be large enough to bear fruit and shade the house from the morning sun.

Five years. Her daughter would be in kindergarten. She would be forty-five years old. One of her cats would probably be dead from old age. And would she still be fleeing from bouncer types in Firebirds? Would murder still dominate her life?

She wiped her mouth and hands with a wet towel and padded through the hall, certain now that she needed a new life, a simpler life, a life where events could be connected by straight lines and one-word answers.

But if she had wanted that kind of life, she thought, she shouldn't have married McCleary.

She sank into the chair at the front desk, wishing the phone would ring and the person on the other end would need something simple. A straightforward surveillance case. An insurance investigation. A missing pet.

Instead, the bell over the front door jingled and a very tall, very slender man with a balding head and intense blue eyes strolled in. His clothes were so wrinkled, they seemed to ripple down his body in waves. But his smile was bright and quick, and when he spoke, his voice possessed the same mesmerizing quality as his eyes.

"You must be Quin."

She nodded and pressed her palms to the desk, pushing herself up. "And you're . . ." But she knew. She knew from Kate's description and from McCleary's. "Sammy Dayton. It's a real pleasure to meet you."

"I feel like I know you," he said as they shook hands. His grip was firm, confident, just as she'd expected. "Kate's talked about you for years."

She was so delighted to have company, she overdid the hostess routine. Coffee? Something cold to drink? No, no, he said, patting the air with his mammoth hands. Although he

121

sat in the chair, he remained at the edge of it, poised for flight. "I was in the neighborhood and just wanted to invite you and Mike to a near-death workshop we're giving on the seventeenth. Is he around?"

"He won't be back until later this afternoon."

"He had a lot of questions about what we did at the center and I thought the seminar might answer some of them." As he told her where and when it would be, one of his hands slid over his balding head. "I hope you can both come."

"We'll certainly try, thanks." She started to ask him if Kate had gotten to the center yet but realized that might entail an explanation about Eastman's call and Pearl Hanley's murder. If Kate wanted to tell him all that, fine, but it wasn't her place to do so. "How long a seminar is it?"

"One to four. We just cover the basics on death and dying and leave time for a question-and-answer period at the end."

"I've got a question," she said, sitting back. "It's something I always forget to ask Kate. Has the center ever studied any NDEs that happened during labor and delivery?"

McCleary, if he'd been there, would have laughed and called her an alarmist. Dayton, however, took her seriously, and she liked him for it, even though she sensed it was nothing personal, that he took all questions about NDEs seriously.

"We had one a couple of years ago. It happened during an emergency C-section. The woman died for one minute and eighteen seconds. She later related everything that had taken place in the delivery room during that time—this nurse shouting at that nurse, the OB lifting her son from her womb, a nurse suctioning the baby's mouth, putting drops into his eyes, the sound of that first miraculous cry. That's the only instance I remember."

"Well, that's a relief."

He laughed and leaned toward her, those blue eyes reaching down inside her. "But I've listened to plenty of stories about labors and deliveries, and my personal feeling is that there're certain points, like during transition, when the experience is very similar to an NDE."

Transition: that was when you promptly forgot everything you'd been taught in Lamaze and begged for an epidural, a

122

massive dose of Demerol, oblivion. Yes. She'd heard her share of stories about transition and hoped she was mentally absent for her own. "Similar in what way?"

Dayton grew pensive again, considering the question carefully. Some women, he said, felt as though they detached from their bodies. Others claimed they communicated with dead relatives. Sometimes, women in transition reported hearing celestial music or seeing and hearing things they couldn't later explain. "Pain is often a catalyst for an altered state of consciousness, so the similarities aren't that surprising. It's one area where more research should be done."

So transition would be a little death, she thought. Like orgasm.

Before she could comment, the phone rang and Dayton stood. "I've got to run. It's nice to finally connect a face with the name. Hope to see you at the workshop."

As she picked up the receiver, she followed Dayton's bald head bobbing above the crowd of pedestrians. "St. James and—"

"Quin, it's me. Kate." She sounded hurried or frantic, Quin couldn't tell which. "Can you get over here?"

"I don't have my car. It's at the garage. Where are you?"

"I just got home. I . . . Look, I'll be over there in five minutes."

Before she could say anything, Kate had disconnected.

Less than five minutes later, Quin heard a shriek of tires in the alley and went back to the rear door to let Kate in. She was as tight as a spring, her black hair combed by the wind, her leather bag snug at her side as if for protection. In her hand was a manila envelope, which she thrust at Quin as though she couldn't get rid of it fast enough.

"This was in my mailbox." She stabbed a finger at the return address. *J. Smith, 600 NW 19 Street, Fort Lauderdale.* "There is no J. Smith at this address in Lauderdale. It's the clubhouse for a development called the Tennis Club."

"Okay, okay, just calm down, Katie."

"*Don't* tell me to calm down, Quin. I've been calm too goddamn long. That's the problem."

Quin opened the envelope. Inside was a packet of 8×10

black-and-white photographs. The top picture was of a pretty brunette affecting a Marilyn Monroe pose, playing to the camera with her eyes, her smile, the angle of her head.

"That's Pearl Hanley," Kate said.

Quin looked up at her. "You sure?"

"Of course I'm sure."

The other two photos were of her and McCleary strolling on the sidewalk right outside the office. She knew the picture had been taken last week, because she was wearing one of her secondhand maternity outfits, which she wore only when everything else was in the laundry. The length of the shadows on the sidewalk told her it was morning, fairly early.

"He dropped it in my mailbox last night or early this morning," Kate said. She was sitting at the kitchen table now, lighting a cigarette. "I don't want you and Mac working on this anymore, Quin. It's too risky."

"Don't be ridiculous. We're making some headway."

Her expression settled like concrete. "*Pearl's dead.* You're in jeopardy as long as you're working for me, so I'm firing you."

"Fine, fire us. But it's not going to make any difference. We started this and we're going to finish it."

Kate's hazel eyes blazed with fury, and when she spoke, she was nearly shouting. "It's *my* life and I don't want you and Mac in it. That's it. That's all there is to it." She got up, swung her purse over her shoulder, headed for the door. Quin caught her arm.

"Kate, please . . ."

She jerked her arm free and spun around. Her mouth opened, and when nothing came out, her face suddenly crumpled and she began to cry. Quin held her but didn't say that things were going to be okay, that she would get through this, that her life would be her own again. They had known each other too long for platitudes—or for secrets.

When she'd gained control of herself again, Quin sat her down and told her about the parties at the ranch.

14

1.

EVER SINCE SONNY Crockett had hit prime time, cops rarely looked like cops anymore, McCleary thought. Lou Garrison was an exception, but Fitz Eastman was not. He could have passed for a pro basketball player.

Born and raised in Liberty City, site of Miami's worst race riots, Eastman had been in law enforcement for nearly twenty years, with the last twelve spent in Internal Affairs. McCleary pegged him to be in his late forties and liked him immediately. He was forthright, with a brisk economy of speech that suggested he had neither the time nor the inclination to debate his stance in the Bishop case. He believed Kate had been framed, Garrison was behind it, and if the four of them worked together, they could prove it.

He'd been investigating Garrison, he said, for more than two years. "It started before then, with a coke bust at a marina in the northern part of the county. A cop was shot and Lou answered the distress call. Two of the guys involved were from my old neighborhood in Liberty City. They figured I might be able to cut them some slack, we being from the same streets and all, so they were real generous with information. They claimed they were transporting eighteen keys of coke, but only sixteen keys were turned over to the department, so somewhere between the marina and the station two keys had apparently vanished.

"When I questioned Garrison and the rookie, they stuck to their original figure. But I think the rookie was so grateful to Garrison for saving his ass, he would've lied to his mother. That's when my suspicions started. No way I could prove anything, though, on the word of a pair of would-be cop killers.''

After that, Eastman began keeping close tabs on Garrison. It wasn't easy to do because Garrison had been around a long time and had a network of good-ole-boy snitches that seemed to exist at every level of law enforcement in the county. "Also, I'm black and he's white and this is still the south."

"Is that the only instance?" McCleary asked.

"Christ, no." There had been other stories—intimidation of parolees, Garrison's presence at drug busts that didn't involve homicide—but nothing Eastman had been able to substantiate and no outright infractions. Garrison always stayed just inside acceptable parameters. "I was out of town when Mr. Bishop was killed, but once I got back and reviewed what had happened, it smelled bad. And with Pearl's murder, it smells worse."

Her autopsy revealed rather large amounts of androgen in her bloodstream, the same substance that had shown up in Bishop, as well as traces of LSD, peyote, and cocaine. Eastman speculated that the substances were in liquid form and used nasally. The coroner said Pearl had recently had intercourse, but there was no semen. "One of my boys turned up an empty condom packet in her bathroom wastebasket. There was also a six-pack of beer in the fridge with two bottles gone, but we found only one of the bottles, with her prints on it. My point," he said, sitting forward, "is that our boy got careless."

"You mean Garrison," Quin said.

"I'm not saying Garrison killed Jack or the Hanley woman. But he's involved somehow and this is all connected to something else."

The waitress arrived with their dinner order, cutting the conversation short. Kate, seated next to Eastman here on the porch of the Hollywood Cafe in Lantana, hadn't said much on the ride down or since they'd arrived. Not surprising. It was bad enough to lose someone you loved, worse still to lose that person to murder, McCleary thought. But it was unthinkable to then discover that the man you were married to had lived a life steeped in duplicity and that you were only one part of a much larger and not very pretty picture.

When the waitress had left, Quin pointed out that their suspicions about Garrison didn't mitigate the fact that Kate's snub-nosed .38 was the murder weapon. Or that she and Jack were the only people at the ranch the weekend he was killed. Or that Pearl's relationship to Jack and her murder were going to provide the prosecutor with additional ammunition. Eastman agreed.

"But the state attorney's office hasn't arrested Kate for the murder."

"Not yet," Kate murmured.

"It won't happen as long as the McClearys stick by their story."

"It isn't a question of *sticking* to it," Quin said. "It's the truth."

Eastman smiled and help up his hands. "Hey, I'm on your side. All I'm saying is that if it goes to trial, the connection between Jack and Pearl is going to come up."

"So what do you suggest?" Kate asked.

Eastman's plan was simple: a twenty-four-hour tail on Garrison; a continuous exchange of information among the four of them; following up every lead, however remote; and a close scrutiny of everything Bishop was involved in. "Which is going to fall primarily on you, Kate. You know more about near-death than any of us. The answer to what your husband was into is somewhere in that center."

Thunder rumbled in the distance when they left the restaurant a while later. Clouds had sailed across the stars and wrapped around the bottom of the pale, slivered moon. McCleary smelled rain in the air as he walked Eastman to his aging Caddy. "What're the chances of the state crime lab coming up with something, like a fingerprint?"

Eastman rocked his hand. "Hell, you were a cop, Mike. You know as well as I do that if she'd been killed in the house, we'd be looking at better odds."

"And the photos?" McCleary gestured toward the envelope in Eastman's hand. "What do you make of those?"

"Probably the same thing you do. Pearl's dead because she knew something about Bishop and his killer and because she was in the way. You and your wife are in the way." He paused. "If I were you, I'd send Quin packing."

Right. He had about as much of a chance of convincing Quin to leave town as he did of winning the lottery. In fact, the odds of winning the lottery were probably better. "You don't know Quin."

"Then I'd be damn sure she's got a weapon and isn't afraid to use it. The same goes for you, my friend."

A crack of thunder punctuated his warning, then a bolt of lightning cut a jagged path across the black sky and turned the air a pale, pulsing blue. "We'll be in touch." Eastman slipped behind the wheel of the Caddy and drove away.

2.

In the dream, Kate was in a garden with Tom Lewis, the snakebite victim. He was parting the low branches of the tree he'd been pruning when he'd been bitten, explaining where he'd been standing, where the snake had been, how it had happened.

Kate leaned in for a closer look and there was the snake, coiled like a rusty spring against the branch, so still it looked as if it had grown into the bark. But something was wrong; it wore Jack's face, those same intense eyes, that same stubborn jaw, and when it opened its mouth, its tongue hissed out, a dark ribbon as sharp as a blade, and it spoke in Jack's voice. "Schrödinger's cat, Katie," then it sank its fangs into the back of her hand.

She screamed and shook her hand, trying to get it off, but the snake clung, its fangs sinking deeper and deeper until they tore through her palm. She smashed her hand against the trunk, squashing the snake's head, and the fangs turned to dust. As she ran out of the garden, Lewis shouting something behind her, the landscape shifted like sand under her feet and walls grew up around her and the light changed.

Awake, she was awake, she was sure of it, she pinched herself and felt it and realized she was in the doorway of the bedroom watching Jack and Pearl Hanley making love. Her skin was the color of ivory, her legs were bent, Jack's hands covered her knees as he pumped away inside her. He turned his head slowly and said, "Go away, Katie. This doesn't concern you."

128

Pearl lifted up on an elbow, her black hair wild around her face, her lips drawing away from her teeth in a parody of a smile. Kate raised her arms, shocked to see that she was gripping a gun, that her finger was squeezing back on the trigger. Pearl's face blew up in an explosion of blood and bone and then Lieutenant Garrison appeared, shaking his finger at her as if she were a small child. "No, no, bad girl," he said, and Jack laughed and snatched up the phone when it rang and held it out to Katie.

"It's for you." Then he turned back to Pearl with the shattered face, Pearl who was dead, and rode the corpse to his own completion.

Kate bolted out of the dream. A breeze blew through the open windows and a light, warm rain was falling outside. The milky light rested against her cheek like a mother's hand. It was morning. But the dream was stuck in the room with her, she could smell blood, Pearl's blood, and she could still hear Garrison's voice. Instead of bad girl, he was saying, "Mrs. Bishop?"

She glanced at the clock; the hands stood at seven. She shrugged on her robe, went to the window. Garrison stood on the porch steps in a red rain slicker, peering up at her, his face as innocent as a cherub's. "A little early for house calls, isn't it, Lieutenant?"

He held up a brown paper bag. "Our property sergeant ran across those missing things of yours. Just dropping them off, ma'am."

She wanted, suddenly, to look into his face, to see his eyes, to measure, if she could, the depth of his malignancy. "I'll be down in a minute."

When she backed away from the window, her gaze paused on the gun McCleary had given her last night when he and Quin had dropped her off. A GLT .380, an automatic with six shots to the clip. She touched it, drew her hand back. When she was dressed, she slipped it inside the waistband of her jeans, her blouse covering it.

No sense in taking a chance.

He smiled pleasantly when she opened the door, a smile

129

she recognized from those weekend parties here at the house, his social smile. She didn't return it.

"Where were these things, anyway?"

"They got mixed up with someone else's. It happens sometimes."

Sure it does.

"Real sorry about the inconvenience."

Yeah, you look sorry.

"You might want to check to make sure everything's there."

He handed her the bag and she looked inside. An extra set of keys that had been zipped into a compartment in her purse, a wad of photographs still in their vinyl pockets, a Parker pen-and-pencil set Jack had given her. "I guess it's all here."

"Then could you sign off on this, Mrs. Bishop?"

Always, they had been *Mrs. Bishop* and *Lieutenant.* "Okay."

He passed her a form with the Palm Beach County sheriff's department name and address at the top. Under it was: PROPERTY RELEASE. He asked her to date it, too.

She did, then added a note that the things had been returned after her release, personally delivered by Lieutenant Garrison due to a mix-up in the property room. "Just for the record."

Garrison ran a finger under his nose, which shot out from his face like a boomerang. "That really wasn't necessary, Mrs. Bishop."

"Oh, I think it was, given the circumstances."

He looked at her, rain pouring off the roof behind him in a transparent wall. "Excuse me?" Polite as you please, brows fanning together in a frown.

"The circumstances. You know. Our being adversaries, Lieutenant."

His mouth twitched, almost making it into a smile. "Oh. That." His shoulders moved around under his slicker, as though it were too tight on him. "I suppose you've heard about the murder of one of Jack's ex-patients. Up at Jupiter?"

She wondered how he'd known Pearl was an ex-patient. "It was on the late news last night."

Softly, so softly she wasn't even sure she heard him right,

130

he said, "Watch your step, Mrs. Bishop," then he trotted down the steps and out into the rain to his car.

Kate stood there a moment, hating him, wondering if Eastman had put a tail on him yet. Probably not. The bureaucratic machine never worked that quickly. She darted back into the house and grabbed her purse and car keys from the counter. She jerked her raincoat off the hook in the hallway closet, scooped up her gardening moccasins from the porch, and raced across the driveway to the Cherokee.

The red Jeep wasn't an inconspicuous vehicle, but Garrison wasn't expecting to see her. This emotional tunnel vision was like an NDE that deviated from the usual pattern because the individual had strong beliefs about what death was. The man who believed, for instance, that there was nothing after death was likely to experience that nothingness upon dying. Heaven and angels were often experienced by individuals who believed in them. And since Garrison believed he had left her back on her porch and that it probably wouldn't occur to her to follow him, he wouldn't be looking for her in his rearview mirror.

He headed south on Ocean Drive past Mar-de-Lago, Trump's slumbering palace, past mansions that belonged to people Jack had known, then turned off on a shaded side street. Kate's heart did a funny little number in her chest. She knew his destination, Christ, she knew.

She went around the block and parked the Cherokee in a supermarket lot three streets south of Stephanie's house. Then she hoofed it back, the rain coming down harder, as if to spite her. But she didn't mind. The raincoat kept her dry and her moccasins were impervious to everything. Besides, for a peek at Garrison's business with Stephanie, she would trek through worse than this.

The neighborhood was ideal for Jack's sister, affluent but not extravagant. She had a Palm Beach address, she could hobnob when it suited her, but she didn't have the overhead of an estate.

Except for her Corvette and her huge collection of clothes, she was not much of a spender. Whatever jewelry she owned had come from her mother. She rarely traveled or entertained. Her money went back into her gym and into whatever the latest

131

health craze was. Herbs, macrobiotic foods, teas, vegetarian—every month it was something different.

Kate cut through a front yard four houses down from Stephanie's and peered around the end of a hibiscus hedge. Garrison's Plymouth was at the curb in front of her place, a beached gray whale.

She walked briskly toward the house. In case a local busybody was anxiously scanning the road for the neighborhood crime watch, Kate affected that Palm Beach posture that made it clear she had every right to be where she was. It was not something she had ever perfected, but she had it down well enough to pass for someone's sister or guest. Appearance was everything in this town.

Two more houses. Then what? Stroll through the gate and up to the front door and ring the bell? Peer through the windows? Go in the back past the pool? Whatever she decided, the point was that the old Kate never would have gotten this far. This was the sort of prank Quin had always been good at, Quin who was paranoid but basically fearless, even if she didn't believe it herself.

At the gate, she hesitated. Rain drummed the back of her head. Do it, she thought, and lifted the latch. She started through the trees to the front door, heard laughter, and veered toward it, around the side of the house.

Her footsteps were cushioned by ferns and ivy that blanketed the ground. Hedges stood between her and the next house. She couldn't be seen or heard, but for all she knew security cameras were hidden at the periphery of the house, under the eaves, and right this minute Stephanie and Garrison were having a good chuckle as they watched her on the swimming-pool monitor.

Now she could see the screen that covered the pool and the patio. Plants pressed up against the inside of it, Stephanie's little rain forest. The pool and the patio area had been a big hit with the Palm Beach ladies the one time Kate had been here for Stephanie's annual event, a fashion show put on by a Worth Avenue shop. She remembered how the ladies had tossed silver dollars into the wishing fountain, had sipped tea from the top of the small bridge that arched over the pool, had oohed and aahed over the exotic plants.

Kate crept closer.

The laughter had stopped, but the murmur of voices blended with the noise of the rain. She backed up to the wall, slid down into a crouch, waited. Minutes ticked by, then there was a lot of splashing and Stephanie moaned, "Oh, God, babe, harder, harder . . ."

Babe: make me gag, Stephanie.

Kate dropped to her hands and knees, flattened out against the ivy and ferns, burrowed through them like a snake toward the screen. She wanted to see. Had to. Her husband's sister and the bastard who'd arrested her.

Kate lifted her head from the loamy scent of earth and plants. The view through the screen wasn't great, but it was good enough. They were in the shallow end, near the bridge. Stephanie was pressed back against the steps, hands gripping the railing above her. Her breasts were nothing but pinheads on a hard surface of tanned flesh. Her head was thrown back, her thighs were throw open, Garrison's head bowed between them.

One of his hands was under her, supporting her. The other moved hard and fast between her legs, a piston, and kept up its momentum even when he lifted his head, when he said, "You close, Steph? You close?"

Her eyes were squeezed shut, she ground her hips, she rolled her lips together, then she emitted a shriek only partially muffled by her hand. As if on cue, Garrison's hands closed at her waist, spun her around, and pushed her down against the steps. She raised her buttocks, gleaming wet pearls, and he slammed into her.

Like the drawing. *You're going to love it when I do this to you.*

Kate pressed her face down into the ferns, the ivy, back into the clean, pure scent of the earth. Memories surfaced of Garrison hoisting his slacks and reciting her rights the day he arrested her, of Stephanie demanding that she not attend Jack's funeral. With these resurrected memories came a terrible regret—not for Jack, not for the life she'd had, but for what she had lost in the years she had known him and for what might have been if she had never met him.

She pushed away from the screen, then got up, brushing the leaves and the twigs from her raincoat, Stephanie's groans and Garrison's grunts pursuing her.

She ended up in front of David's house, the Cherokee's engine ticking importantly in the silence, the rain pouring over the windshield, her fingers gripping the steering wheel so tightly they began to ache. David, her friend, her ally, who had provided "musical entertainment" at the ranch orgies and never told her.

She knocked, rang the bell, no one answered. The door was unlocked and she walked in. The marionettes against the wall watched her, especially Princess Leia with the spooky blue eyes. Kate looked away from her and went over to the old RCA TV. The top of it was crowded with photos in cheap plastic frames of the Bishop family, pictures David had taken. They were the sort of thing you'd find on a coffee table or mantel in the home of someone's grandparents. The elder Bishops, Jack and Stephanie, aunts and uncles and cousins, David's ex-wife, Stephanie's ex-husband, David's two kids, herself.

Does anyone you know dabble in photography? Eastman's voice.

"David? It's Kate."

The door to his den opened and he poked his head out, his hand covering the mouthpiece of the receiver. "Katie. Give me a second. I'm on the phone."

The door shut again. She slipped off her wet moccasins, shucked her raincoat, padded silently across the room to the door. A voyeur, she thought. That was what she'd become. Peeping through patio screens, listening at closed doors, waiting, hoping, everyone she knew now riddled with suspicion and consumed with motives. But she didn't move away from the door.

". . . you'd be selling fourteen points higher than when you bought, Jerry. I think it'd be a smart move."

134

A bubble of laughter slipped up her throat. He was talking to a client, that was all.

". . . right. Call me back in about fifteen minutes."

Kate hurried across the room and David shuffled out a moment later, tugging the tiny gold hoop earring in his right ear, his eyes bright with delight at seeing her. "What a terrific surprise. You have the day off?"

"I'll be going in later. Sammy doesn't get too uptight about when we put in hours, as long as we put them in."

"Coffee's on. You want a mug? It's Cuban," he added, knowing how much she liked her coffee strong.

"Sounds good."

Easy talk, like old times, as though Jack had never died.

He returned with two mugs of coffee and they settled near the window, close to the marionettes and puppets, those little beings who had filled the void when he had ditched his musical career. The rain danced against the jalousies of the open windows, the ceiling fan turned slowly, monotonously, and Princess Leia watched, listened.

David was chatting about the Christmas benefit that was coming up and she nodded and sipped at her coffee and when she couldn't stand it anymore, she blurted out, "Tell me about the orgies at the ranch, David. And about Pearl Hanley."

He looked as though she'd struck him. It was Leia who spoke in a voice that belonged to the elder Mrs. Bishop. "Jackie boy was bad and now he's dead and you'd be happier leaving it all alone, Kate."

She leaped up, grabbed Leia off the shelf, threw open the lid of the cedar chest against the wall, and stuffed her inside. "*You* talk to me. When did the parties start?"

He rubbed a hand over his handsome face, sat forward, back again. "Before you met him." The parties had started small, six or eight people, a Palm Beach crowd into fast living and kinky kicks. Over the years, the numbers burgeoned into fifteen, twenty, sometimes as many as thirty people. "When you two got married, they stopped for a while. Then, about the same time those weekend bashes started up, so did the parties at the ranch."

"Where the hell was I?"

"Sometimes you were working Friday or Saturday nights. Sometimes Jack told you he had to drive out to the ranch to check on the fields or that he and I were going to go hunting. I don't know. You tell *me* where you were. How you couldn't have known."

It was that blind spot again, she thought. She had never expected something like this of Jack, so she hadn't seen it. Emotional myopia. "And Pearl?"

He shrugged. "She and her husband were in marriage counseling. They had an open marriage and Burrows was discovering that he didn't much like it. The counseling didn't work, they separated, Pearl started going to the ranch parties. She tried to commit suicide when . . ."

"I know that part. That was before I came along." Her hands trembled with fury when she raised the mug of coffee to her mouth. She set it down and kept her hands clasped in her lap, trapping them there. "How often was he seeing her when he and I were married?"

"Aw, Christ, Katie. I don't know. Once a week, maybe once every couple of weeks, not a lot. Even before he met you, Pearl was seeing other people, she wouldn't commit to Jack. It seemed that the only time she bothered with him was when she was depressed or needed something."

"And she was still his patient?"

"Yes. Before he met you, before her suicide attempt, she was just a patient. But the near-death thing was the turning point somehow. Jack wanted to marry her, Pearl refused, and they split for a while, until right after you two got married. It was like, I don't know, like once he was taken, that was when she wanted him most."

Kate stared at her hands, bloodless now, as colorless as dry leaves. "You could have told me." She whispered it, cleared her throat, raised her eyes. "You could have at least *implied* it."

His face tightened then, his eyes pulling together, the corners of his mouth drawing in. "He was my brother, Katie. I may not have liked everything he did or condoned it, but it wasn't my place to tell you what he was doing."

"Garrison was at those parties."

136

He nodded.

"He *arrested* me, David. It's possible he killed Jack because Jack was blackmailing him about the parties."

Another nod.

"Say something, dammit," she shouted.

"What can I possibly say?"

"He's fucking Stephanie. If the house is sold, she gets nearly four million dollars. Part of that would be Garrison's if they got married."

His eyes sought hers and spoke to the friendship that had existed between them. "And I'd get the other half of that money." Then, more softly: "Does that make me a suspect, too, Katie?"

Yes. No. "I don't know." She stood, looked at him, shook her head. "I just don't know." She slipped on her moccasins, grabbed her raincoat, and left.

Behind her, in a soft, wistful voice that was Jack's, Princess Leia the marionette called, "Kaaa-tie, come back, Kaaa-tie, forgive me, Katie, forgive me for being mean."

She walked on without looking back.

15

1.

FOR QUIN, THE trip to Fort Lauderdale on the morning of the fourteenth was more than just an excursion to buy a crib. It was a respite from murder, from death and near-death, a chance to do something with McCleary that was not work-related.

Not once during the drive south did either of them mention Jack or Kate or Eastman or any of it. They talked, instead, of small, personal things. Wallpaper for the baby's room, whether to screen in the back porch when they had the money, the berm they would have in the front yard, who wanted what for Christmas.

McCleary, naturally, had brought along the file of articles he'd collected on cribs. He'd compiled dozens of similar files on infant seats, walkers, strollers, the pros and cons of cloth and disposable diapers, traveling with infants. This compulsive aggregate of information, she knew, made him feel like a participant in the pregnancy, and hell, if it had been left for her to do, it wouldn't have gotten done. He was the scribe of the family.

Baby Love was a discount warehouse on Highway 441 that sold anything and everything related to babies and children. There were things inside she'd never even imagined: bottles shaped like pretzels that were easy for an infant to grasp; Ninja Turtle night lights; Ewok teddy bears from *Star Wars*; mobiles strung with Disney characters; booklets on colic, on potty training, on what solids to feed the baby and when. It was an entire world of merchandising magic and she wasn't immune.

She grabbed a shopping cart from the row next to the wall and McCleary groaned and reminded her they were here to buy a crib, that was all. She said it was more than sixty miles down here and back and why not take advantage of the sales while they were here? He didn't argue. They wheeled the cart up and down aisles, in and out of rooms, picking from here, there. The cart was nearly filled by the time they reached the cribs.

McCleary moved among them, the informed consumer. This one didn't have the right kind of railings; that one didn't have a plastic strip across the railing for when the baby was teething; this one here would be too easy to get out of. They settled, finally, on a crib that cost two hundred and fifty dollars, then had to shop for a mattress, bumpers, padding.

They left Baby Love as most prospective parents did, about six hundred dollars poorer, all of it on credit cards.

At home again, Quin fixed an early lunch, which they ate in the nursery while McCleary struggled through the booklet of directions, the crib's unassembled parts spread out all over the floor. The three cats crowded around to see what the fuss was. Merlin, the black cat and the oldest, kept burrowing under the mattress while Hepburn, the Persian, tried to curl up on top of it. Tracy, the calico, was more interested in Quin's tuna sandwich and batted at it, hoping to snare a bit when he thought she wasn't looking.

McCleary managed to assemble one side of the crib, only to realize he had screwed the bolts into the wrong places and had to remove them and start over again. Quin suggested they leave the task until tonight. McCleary wouldn't hear of it. He had started the goddamn thing and now he was going to finish it.

Three hours later he did.

It stood there, lovely and simple, beneath a rainbow-colored hammock they had bought in a market in Caracas years ago. A Minnie Mouse clock that Quin's sister had sent them was on the opposite wall, ticking quietly, marking off minutes and days and weeks until the baby's birth. A diaper changer occupied a spot at the sliding glass doors that opened into an atrium. At the foot of it was a diaper pail. They had picked up the bureau at a garage sale and McCleary was in the process of refinishing it. At the moment, it was three different colors, but in her mind's eye she saw only the finished product.

"She's real now, Quin," McCleary said, sitting on the floor with his legs folded Indian-style.

"I always wonder what she'll look like."

"Your eyes." As though he'd seen her.

"Your mouth," She had her visions, too.

"Whose nose?"

They looked at each other and laughed, and he leaned toward her and kissed her.

For long moments, her entire being was nothing but the pressure of his mouth against hers, his cool tongue slipping along her lower lip, curling around her tongue, speaking to her. Then it was his hands, unfastening the buttons on her blouse, working her skirt down over her hips, sliding a baby pillow under her head. Her stomach rose between them, an impossible mountain, but he paid homage to it, his mouth slipping over it, his hands defining it.

They had learned to be innovative. It was best with her on her side, McCleary behind her, their bodies curved together like spoons, his hands at her breasts, her stomach, between her thighs. In the beginning, he had worried about the baby, that he would hurt her somehow, and it had impeded their lovemaking. But that fear had proved groundless and now, nearing her seventh month, he knew how to touch her, to arouse her, to bring her to the edge and hold her there.

His finger eased into her from behind, then out and in again, seeking that perfect rhythm, the rhythm of heartbeats and blood rushing through veins. He lifted up and she turned her head, her mouth opening against his, hungry for his. His other hand slipped over her throat, her breasts, reading her like a blind man, then his mouth followed, and Quin shifted onto her back, her feet sliding up against the rug until her legs were bent at the knees.

Light seeped through the Levolor blinds, falling in ribbons across one side of his face. For an instant, it changed the color of his eyes. They were no longer the hue of smoke in a woods on a cold day; they were as clear and transparent as water and she could see herself in them. He rubbed his cheek against her tummy, his beard tickling her, his hands holding her at the hips, his mouth in a hot glide down the center of her.

His tongue slipped over her, into her, around her, savoring her. Then it was his finger again, the pressure of his thumb, stopping, moving, pausing again. Her skin was slick, her breath had swelled like a tumor in her chest, her cells were coming undone, his finger was still inside her, a part of her, a pressure that held her suspended at the electric edge.

Then it started all over, his mouth, his hands, playing her like an instrument until she began to shudder, to moan, to whisper, urging him inside. He turned her on her side, entering her from behind, and when he came, the baby suddenly kicked, and she laughed and so did he.

"She's spying on us," he whispered.

"Listening to us."

"Suppose she remembers it?"

"Impossible."

"But she might."

"Talk to her."

He slipped out of her and Quin rolled onto her back and McCleary put his mouth to her stomach, hands cupped at the sides of his face. Then he looked up. "What do I say?"

"Whatever you want."

"It's Daddy, hey, this is your daddy. We just put up your crib."

Their daughter rolled and kicked. McCleary drummed his fingers against her stomach, and a moment later the baby responded with two quick punches, then hiccuped and went still.

Beaming, he said, "I think she recognizes my voice."

Quin stood in front of the full-length mirror in the bedroom, her hair wet from the shower, the button on her slacks straining. She wondered how much weight she'd gained since her last doctor's appointment. Thirty was the limit for the entire pregnancy and last month she was at twenty-eight.

McCleary came up behind her, rested his hands on her shoulders and his chin on the top of her head.

"What?" Her eyes met his in the mirror.

"Don't get mad, okay?"

"Mad at what?"

"I think it'd be a good idea if you stayed with Bean for a while. Or your folks. The—"

Her eyes snapped from his face. "Forget it."

"Yeah, that's what I thought you'd say." And he moved back across the room, away from her.

She went into the bathroom to dry her hair. McCleary appeared in the doorway before she'd finished. "I've got an appointment with the caretaker at the ranch this afternoon. You mind manning the phones?"

"I was going to meet Kate at the center later this afternoon. I'll leave the machine on."

He nodded, started to duck out again, but she said, "Whose idea was it for me to skip town? Yours or Eastman's?"

"Eastman suggested it; I'd already been thinking it."

"Your photograph was in that envelope, too, Mac."

"But I'm not pregnant."

"That doesn't make me handicapped, you know."

He sighed, rolled his eyes. "Hey, I don't want to get into an argument where I'm accused of being a sexist pig."

"I've never called you a sexist pig."

"That's true. I think your words have been macho ex-cop or something to that effect."

"Is it my imagination or do we always argue after we make love?"

"I'm not arguing."

"Yeah, I'm standing here arguing by myself."

He grinned, planted a kiss on top of her still-damp hair. "That's right. Take your gun when you leave, and see you tonight."

Swell. She turned on the dryer and brushed furiously at her hair, annoyed that he'd had the final word, that he really hadn't answered her question, that he'd implied *she* was a nut who carried on arguments in his absence.

Quin turned off the dryer, dropped it on the counter, waddled toward the front of the house. She threw open the utility-room door that led to the garage. McCleary was just backing out and stopped when he saw her. He lowered his window as she approached the Miata.

"If you were pregnant, I wouldn't suggest that *you* leave town."

"Christ, Quin, drop it, will you? It was only a suggestion."

"That may be how it started out, but that's not how it ended up. Once I said forget it, all those walls went up."

"What walls? What the hell're you talking about?"

The walls, emotional walls. "Oh, never mind."

"Fine."

And with that he backed out of the driveway and into the rain and didn't look back. She stood there with her damp hair, in her tight slacks, began to cry, stopped crying, watched the rain dancing through the empty street. She longed to be thin again, sane again, and wondered how a day that had started so well had plunged so quickly into blackness.

2.

The rain let up before McCleary reached Belle Glade, and by the time he pulled into the ranch, the sun was shining. The damp trees glistened, the air steamed, and the dirt driveway was a river of mud.

A battered pickup was parked in front of the house and the caretaker, Eduardo Iglesia, was sitting in an old rocker on the porch, smoking. McCleary greeted him in Spanish and he smiled and dropped his cigarette as he stood. He was short and thin, with a Boston Blackie mustache and liquid eyes the same deep copper as his skin. *"Mucho gusto,"* he said as they shook hands. In Spanish he asked if McCleary preferred to sit out here on the porch or inside. Here was fine.

"What would you like to know, *señor*?" Iglesia had a thick accent and spoke slowly, enunciating his words carefully. "I already tell what happened to the police."

"I'd like to hear it directly from you."

Iglesia lit another cigarette and related basically the same story Garrison had told McCleary. "Mrs. Bishop says you don't come out to the house every day, right?"

"No, *señor*. I come once, maybe two times a week to check on everything and my wife she is here once to clean. Most days I am in the fields, supervising the picking."

"And you don't usually work on weekends, do you?"

His eyes turned bright with fear as he realized where McCleary was headed. "No."

"Then what prompted you to stop by here at five-thirty on a Saturday the morning you found Mrs. Bishop?"

He squeezed the end of his cigarette, gazed out at the empty, muddy driveway, then dropped the cigarette to the floor and crushed it with the heel of his boot. "I cannot answer your question, *señor*. I am sorry."

"Can't or won't?" McCleary asked.

Iglesia stood, started down the steps, stopped when McCleary asked him in Spanish what he was afraid of. "You do not understand, *señor*."

"Help me to understand."

"I cannot."

"Do you want Mrs. Bishop to go to prison?"

He grasped the railing, shook his head. "No, no, of course not. She is a nice woman, a good woman. She always gives Isabel, my wife, extra money when she cleans, she asks after my children, she sends a doctor when one of the children is ill. But . . ."

"Do you have a green card?"

"Sí, claro, señor."

"And your wife? Does she have a card?"

He swallowed, rubbed a hand over his face. Quietly: "No. *Señor* Bishop . . . he was helping us to get a card for Isabel."

"In return for what, Eduardo?"

Something terrible happened to his face. His features sagged as if beneath the weight of his terrible secret and he sank to the step, weeping softly into his hands. McCleary was shocked into muteness. Then he got up and sat on the step beside Iglesia.

"Whatever you tell me will be kept in the strictest confidence. I promise you."

"No *policía*?"

"No. You have my word."

He rubbed his nose with his sleeve and began to talk. On the Wednesday before Thanksgiving, he said, Bishop had called him. "He says me and Isabel should come to the ranch Saturday morning to, how do you say, *arreglar*?"

144

"Fix up."

"Straighten up. That is the word. We should straighten up. After some parties we *limpiar*, clean up, late in the afternoon. After others we are only supposed to *straighten*, which means me or Isabel come very early and do not have to bring food the day of the party. Always after the parties when we *straighten*, we arrive at five-thirty or six. That is why I came and found the *señora* on Saturday morning."

When the plane's oil-pressure problem had made it impossible for Bishop to fly Kate back into town, McCleary thought, he'd apparently forgotten to inform Iglesia there had been a change in plans. "What happens at the parties where you bring food and only clean the next day?"

Iglesia shifted on the step, lit another cigarette. "Isabel buys food and we come to the house to prepare it and make sure the air-conditioner is on, so that it is cold inside when the *señor* arrives. Sometimes he asks me to come back to park cars. He pays me much money for this."

"You know what goes on at these parties?"

He looked uncomfortable now. "*Sí*. But the *señor* and I we do not speak of it. We pretend I do not know that the *señora* never comes, that I do not know what happens in the big room upstairs."

"The morning Lieutenant Garrison showed up here, did he tell you not to mention these parties to anyone?"

His voice was nearly inaudible. "*Sí.*"

"He knows your wife doesn't have a green card."

He nodded, inhaled deeply from his cigarette, then flicked it away from him. It arced through the hot sunlight and landed in a puddle, where it hissed.

"How long have you known about these parties?"

"Many years. Six, seven."

"What about these other parties. Where you only *straighten* up afterward?"

"These were not parties," Iglesia said. "Only men come, in two planes. One plane it is the *señor*'s, the other it has high wings and balloons around the wheels."

"You mean pontoons."

He snapped his fingers. "*Sí*, pontoons. That is the word. A plane for the water, but this plane can also be for the land. I have seen it as both. When it is for water, it comes down over there."

"On Lake Okeechobee?"

"No, no. There is a small lake near the fields. A long, skinny lake. Maybe they sometimes leave on this plane, but the times I watch, they leave in the *señor*'s plane and do not come back until it is almost light. I do not know where they go."

"How many men?"

"Five, six, maybe seven. I do not see their faces, *señor*."

"How do you know about this? Are you at the house?"

He shook his head. Two years ago, on a hot night in August, he'd driven over to the ranch to turn on the air-conditioning. The Bishops were supposed to arrive the next morning and he knew Bishop would want the house cool. He was inside when he heard the plane and was surprised Bishop had already arrived. He went out to say hello, but Bishop got angry with him for being there. Iglesia explained why he'd come and Bishop said fine, fine, he was doing a good job, but he could leave now.

"While I drive away, I see men coming out of the plane and I watch the lights of another plane coming down. Later, I go back and wait in the barn and see the men come from the house. They laugh and slap each other on the back. They get into the *señor*'s plane and fly away."

"Why did you hide in the barn?"

"I was curious, *señor*. And I think to myself . . ." He tapped his temple. "The more I know, the safer Isabel and me are."

"Did you ever see the numbers on the seaplane?"

"No."

"What color was it?"

"Black."

"You're sure?"

"*Sí*. Black. There is a picture on the side. A monster in white. It has the head of an eagle and the body of a lion."

A griffin. "Was that the only time you saw it?"

"No." He had hidden twice after that night and each time,

after a few days had gone by, he heard "things" and didn't know what to think.

"What kind of things?" McCleary asked.

"Rumors," he replied. "Stories."

"From whom?"

"Workers at the camp."

"The migrant camp?"

"*Sí.*" He had friends at the camp and he also heard stories from the migrants who worked Bishop's fields. "You see, *señor*, many workers come here for a better life and find a life that is more bad than before. But I hear that some men they are paid much money for other jobs. Special jobs in Orlando or Miami. So they leave the camp and not come back. I figure out that these men leave on the same days the men in the plane come to the ranch."

"Who oversees the camp?"

"Arturo Cordoba. The *jefe*. He likes workers who do not have green cards. He can pay less money. They depend more on him, you understand?"

Loud and clear. "So he arranges these special jobs?"

"I think so."

"Then you know of three men who haven't come back?"

"Six, *señor*. These men do not have families, but they have friends, no? And the friends not get letters or phone calls."

"Do any of them have girlfriends?"

He nodded.

"Would they talk to me?"

"No, no, *señor*. They are afraid."

"I'm not going to turn anyone in, Eduardo. I want to help Mrs. Bishop."

He thought about it. "I will talk to them, *señor*, but I cannot promise."

"I understand. I'll call you in a couple of days. Or you can call me." He scribbled his home and work numbers on a scrap of paper. "I'll meet them wherever it's convenient for them. No one needs to know."

As McCleary drove out of the ranch, Iglesia was still seated on the step, smoking, gazing after him.

16

1.

IT WAS NEARLY four when Quin arrived on campus and the TGIF rush toward the weekend was already on.

Umbrellas grew from the wet streets like colorful, exotic mushrooms as students flocked across the street to the off-campus bars. Cars pulled away from buildings, faculty members hurried toward the employee parking lots. It brought back memories of her own college years.

Despite all the social unrest during the sixties, that time in her life now seemed marvelously uncomplicated. Everything was an adventure. It was no big deal to drive to Washington, D.C., on a Friday, arrive on time for a peace march on Saturday, crash that night on someone's floor, then get up after two hours of sleep and drive back to Florida for classes on Monday. If there was a concert in Atlanta in the middle of the week that they wanted to attend, then eight or ten of them would pile into Kate's rickety old van and go. Nothing stopped them. The point was to experience as much as they could in any way they could. They accumulated memories with astonishing urgency, almost as though none of them believed they would ever see thirty.

Now here they were at forty, she thought. Of the group she and Kate had known best during those years, four had died in Vietnam, three had overdosed on drugs, two had committed suicide, one had died of AIDS. The other twenty were scattered across the country, most of them married with kids. They practiced law, wrote books, taught school, sold commodities and insurance, and ran for public office. A few of them kept in touch for all of them, passing along bits of news and gossip in annual Christmas cards.

She felt a brief stab of nostalgia for those years but considered herself fortunate to be where she was, doing what she was. She wished that Kate had been as lucky.

The center was as quiet as a tomb inside. The receptionist had already left for the day and Wolfe was alone in the lab, hunched over a typewriter at one of the desks. He was scratching his head with the end of a pen, and from where Quin stood it looked like an old bone sticking up from his curly dark hair. He peered at her over the rims of his Ben Franklin specs.

"Hey, Quin, you're an ex-English teacher. Its misogamist spelled with *i* or *y*?"

"*I.*"

"Shit. Where's the Wite-Out." He lifted papers, opened drawers, checked the floor.

"Here, Wolfie," The bottle was on a stack of papers on the chairs, and as she picked it up, the papers sprang out and spilled to the floor. She and Wolfe crouched at the same time to retrieve them. "Who's the misogamist, anyway? You?"

She laughed as she said it, but Wolfe wasn't amused. "I would've married her in a heartbeat, Quin. But Jack happened."

As though Bishop were an event.

"So she met him, so what." The smell of his after-shave tickled her nostrils and she rubbed her nose. "You were still seeing her then. You didn't have to just give up, Ray."

He poked his glasses back onto the bridge of his nose. The lenses made his gray eyes seemed huge. "You don't know how he was, Quin. When he wanted something, he went after it with a vengeance. And he wanted Kate badly. I couldn't compete with him."

She heard the bitterness in his voice and thought of triangles, the old story of love betrayed, love lost, and revenge. Murder had been committed for less. But Wolfe wasn't the type, was he?

"She tell you about following Garrison the other day?" he asked.

"Yes."

"Someone needs to take that fucker out of commission." He stood and jerked a thumb over his shoulder. "She's cleaning out Jack's office."

"Thanks, Wolfie."

The door to Jack's office stood ajar, but Kate wasn't inside. Cardboard boxes were scattered around, drawers lolled from the desk like discolored tongues, the walls were bare, books had been pulled from the shelves. A framed Southwest painting by one of Jack's favorite artists stood against the wall; a jagged crack in the glass split the image in two.

Quin sat in the comfortable leather chair behind the desk and sighed as she freed her swollen feet from her shoes. She ran her fingers over the laptop computer, admiring it, wondering how much it had cost. A pair of hard-disk laptops were at the top of her and McCleary's wish list. But like the other items on the list, laptops would have to wait until their finances improved, after the baby was born.

She turned it on and, at the C prompt, typed in DIR for directory. There were four programs but only one file, containing a breakdown of the center's budget for the year. Too bad.

Swiveling in the chair, she gazed out the window at the view Jack had seen for the last several years of his life. Bottlebrush trees with their oblong, furry red blossoms, dracenas whose long, slender leaves dripped water, giant philodendrons. Beyond them lay a stretch of green that ended at the science building. Leaden clouds scudded the curve of sky above the plants.

In the window was a long box that contained impatiens, all but one shriveled from neglect and as dead as Jack was. Quin plucked dry leaves from the lone survivor, a pretty thing with violet blossoms. It came loose from the dirt and as she stuck her fingers down deeply into the soil to replant it, she felt something and dug it out.

It was a three-and-a-half-inch square computer disk wrapped inside a plastic Baggie. Smiling to herself, Quin brushed the soil from the bag, removed the disk, slipped it into the drive. She changed the C prompt to A, typed in DIR:

MOLE	CLICKER
ACE	GRIFFIN
NOVEMBER	NABISCO

"What the hell." She brought the cursor even with MOLE, hit ENTER. The screen scrolled, then the computer informed her she couldn't access the file on the A drive. She copied the file to the C drive, hit ENTER again. The laptop beeped and flashed: FILE NOT FOUND.

But she'd copied it to the C drive, it had to be there. She requested a global search on MOLE, which would also scan any files that might be hidden. The computer hummed and clicked, the screen blanked, and lit up again. MOLE: ENTER PASSWORD.

A hidden file. And no telling what kind of password Bishop had cooked up. Rather than trying to second-guess him right now, she copied the next file, ACE, from the disk to the hard drive and went through the global search again. The results were the same. A request for a password.

She ran a global search on the hard drive to see if any of the other files were on it. They weren't. Maybe they never had been. Or maybe Jack had deleted them when he'd transferred them to the soft disk.

"Quin, hello." Dayton stepped into the room, his palm already moving back over his balding head, as if it were his equivalent to a wave or a handshake. "This is a nice surprise."

"Ray said Kate was in here, but she must've gone to the restroom. I started admiring the laptop and couldn't resist." She was overexplaining, but she couldn't help it. She felt vaguely guilty, as though she'd been caught doing something sneaky. "Was it Jack's?"

"The center's. We have a couple that are battery-powered, our summer backups to get us through electrical outages during thunderstorms. It's got some terrific features."

He came toward her and Quin quickly cleared the screen, popped out the disk, and set it aside, hoping he wouldn't pick it up. He didn't. He stood behind her and reached over her shoulders, playing the keys. Hairs sprouted from the backs of his fingers, little black weeds. His skin smelled faintly of soap. She felt his breath against the top of her hair as he showed her the neat tricks the computer could do. Quin wished he would move back, away from her. His proximity was disquieting, a violation of her personal space. When she scooted the chair forward, the edge of the desk pressed against her stomach. It didn't hurt, but it was uncomfortable.

"Excuse me," she said, pushing back. "It's a little crowded here."

"Oh, sorry." He stepped to the side and finished demonstrating how the musical composition program worked. It was Greek to her. She knew her ignorance showed on her face and that he saw it. He kept turning those strangely compelling blue eyes on her, and if she hadn't known better, she would have thought that he was coming on to her.

"Hey, here you are. I was beginning to wonder what happened to you," said Kate. She was carrying a couple of cardboard boxes, which she dropped on the floor with the others. "I thought you'd left, Sammy."

"I was on my way out when I got a call from one of the trustees." He hesitated and glanced at Quin, apparently uncertain whether he could speak freely in front of her.

"It's okay," Kate said. "Quin knows what's going on. I'm suspended, right?"

His palm traveled over his head again. "No, he called to tell me they're going to meet this weekend and you'll be one of the things they're discussing."

She shrugged, knelt down, and fitted a stack of books inside one of the boxes. "Well, I don't have to be psychic to know how *that's* going to turn out. Maybe I ought to be cleaning my own office."

"Don't jump to conclusions," Dayton replied. "Sometimes these turkeys surprise even themselves. And whatever you do, don't spend your weekend worrying about it." Then he bent and bussed her on top of her head. "Nice seeing you again, Quin."

He left and Kate remained where she was, her hands busy filling cartons. "I don't need this goddamn job," she muttered.

"Hey, it's their loss, if that's what it comes to." Quin slipped the disk into her bag. "You want some help?"

"You're not supposed to lift stuff."

She groaned. "God, you sound like Mac." She got down on the floor. "Did Jack have a computer at home?"

"No. He kept talking about buying one, but he never got around to it. Why?"

"Just wondering."

"You heard anything from Fitz?"

"Not yet. You?"

"I called him after following Garrison."

"What'd he say?"

"That I shouldn't pull a fool stunt like that again. He's got a tail on Garrison now. He was also real interested in the veiled threat he made." She sat back on her heels, hooked a strand of hair behind her ear. The late-afternoon light struck her face in such a way that she looked prettier than she had in days, more like the old Kate before Jack's murder. "Tell me the truth, Quin. You think I have a prayer?"

Quin squeezed her hand. "Better than that. Don't be morbid. C'mon, let's go get a drink and have dinner or something. Leave this mess."

Kate took a look around, then flashed that quick, brilliant smile and got to her feet. She held out a hand, Quin grasped it, Kate pulled her up.

"Jesus, to be thin again."

"And free," Kate said softly.

2.

There was no wind at the Belle Glade airport this time and McCleary found the stillness disconcerting. Heat poured over the tarmac and field, baking the ground, quivering inches above the asphalt so that it looked like something living. There was no evidence of the earlier rain; the heat had sucked the moisture into itself with the voracity of a thirst-driven beast.

There was more activity out here today—planes circling, taking off, landing—and business at Fargo Flights appeared to have picked up. A woman in an orange flight suit was behind the desk, a pretty little thing with a pixie haircut. She said Roy was up with a student right now, but could she help him with anything?

"I need some information on seaplanes. Well, actually, on regular airplanes that can also be seaplanes."

She smiled and leaned into the counter. "You mean a plane with landing gear equipped with floats."

"Yeah, I guess that's what I mean."

"What about it?"

"Is there any particular model that's commonly fitted with floats?"

"Most airplanes can be fitted with floats. But around here the Citabria is a big favorite because it's good for the lakes and the Everglades."

"Is it a high-wing, single-engine plane?"

"Yup, sure is. Let me show you a picture." She went through a stack of magazines at one end of the counter, brought one of them back over, flipped it open. "Here you go. The landing gear facilitates quick and easy changeover so that most owners do their own. There's wraparound visibility, a twenty-four-inch cockpit that makes it incredibly roomy, a hundred-pound baggage compartment, thirty-six-gallon wing tanks, and lift-off with one man aboard is in about eleven seconds at slightly over fifty miles an hour."

"Sounds like you fly these."

She laughed. "My dad owned one. It's what I learned to fly in. It's a terrific plane."

"Could you fit six men in one of these?"

"Not legally. The weight limits would probably be okay, though, if the backseats were out and there wasn't any luggage and the fuel wasn't at the max. You looking to buy one?"

"No, I'm trying to find one." He gave her Iglesia's description of the plane he'd seen.

"Black with a griffin on it." She frowned, thinking, then shook her head. "Not around here. At least not that I've seen. But I'm only filling in today. Roy's regular guy is out sick. I live in Vero. You oughta stick around and ask Roy, though. If there's a black Citabria with a griffin on it anywhere from Dade north to Indian River, he'll know about it."

"Thanks. I will. Could I have this picture?"

"Sure thing."

She tore it out of the magazine. He folded it and slipped it into his pocket. "You've been a big help. I appreciate it."

Fargo showed up twenty minutes later, striding across the

tarmac with a teenager dressed as though she were color blind. Lime-green T-shirt, red nylon gym shorts, blue high-topped sneakers with pink socks. But with her body it wouldn't have mattered if she'd had painted skin. As they neared the terminal, she veered off toward the parking lot with a wave.

Fargo gazed after her; McCleary knew a lustful smile when he saw one. But the smile vanished like yesterday's paycheck when he saw McCleary.

He marched right over, sunburned arms swinging at his sides, and flipped his shades onto the top of his head. His eyes shrank to dark points of light in his ruddy cheeks. "I don't appreciate being lied to, McCleary."

Wayne Shepard, he thought. "You aren't getting any gold stars for honesty, either. You knew more about those parties at the ranch than you were saying."

"You weren't inquiring about the parties." He pulled a Baggie of cookies from his pocket and dug his hand inside. He bit into one with a vengeance. "If I remember correctly."

"And that's not why I'm here now. I need to know who owns a black Citabria with a griffin on it that's sometimes converted to a seaplane."

McCleary sprang it on him and Fargo flinched, as if from a sudden, sharp twitch in his side. "No such plane around here." The answer was too quick. "Least not that I know of."

"Thanks for your time, Mr. Fargo."

He drove back to the ranch and showed Eduardo Iglesia the picture of the Citabria. He was sure it was the plane he'd seen.

3.

The campus seemed small and tight at night, especially on a Friday, Kate thought, like a room with only one tiny window and a locked door. It was late, hardly anyone was out, and the street lamps were as dim as flashlights, casting pale circles of light that didn't even reach the curb. She was grateful that she wasn't alone in the Cherokee, that Quin and Wolfe were crammed in the front seat with her, as raucous as a couple of sailors on shore leave.

They had gone to a bar near campus, where she and Wolfe had shared a pitcher of beer and Quin had consumed Perriers.

Then she'd driven everyone to dinner at an Italian restaurant in North Palm Beach, a place she had never been with Jack, had never been at all. That was important. Finding her own spots, creating her own history separate from her life with him.

Now, as she swung into the center's lot to let them off at their own cars, she experienced a certain dread at the prospect of going home. The house was too big for her, the rooms were haunted with her memories of Jack, she heard noises when she closed her eyes at night. But to capitulate to the fear of being alone there seemed to allow Jack's killer too much power over her life, and too many people already held power over her.

"You sure you don't want to spend the night?" Quin asked as she got out.

"Yeah, I'm sure. But thanks. See you at the memorial service tomorrow, Quin."

Quin said good night to Wolfe, then climbed down and moved slowly to her car. "You sure you're okay in that house?" Wolfe asked, touching Kate's shoulder.

"Mac gave me a gun."

"You know how to use it?"

"Yes, Wolfie, I know how to use it." She poked him in the ribs. "It's past your bedtime, isn't it?"

"Not quite yet." His mouth swung into a comic grin and they laughed.

Old times, she thought, and suddenly remembered how Wolfe's mouth had tasted, of how its shape had changed against hers, of that mouth against her skin in her life before Jack. She was sure the memory radiated from her like an odor because the air between them grew suddenly tight, still, warm.

His hand moved from her shoulder to her hair and he leaned toward her, kissing her on the mouth. A shy, hesitant, innocent kiss, until her arms went around him. Then his mouth opened against hers and she pressed up against him. It felt so good to be held, to inhale the familiar scent of his skin, to feel the shape of his hand against her thigh.

"Jesus, Katie. I've missed you so much," he whispered, his mouth against her neck.

She squeezed her eyes shut, wanting to love him again, to find the years they had lost to Jack, but it was too soon, she had nothing to offer him except trouble. And yet she didn't pull away when he kissed her again. She didn't stop his hand as it slipped under her skirt, warm against her thigh.

She shifted, adjusting her leg so it rested against his, inviting him, admitting him, grateful it was dark, that the lot was deserted, that the campus was practically a ghost town. His thumb and forefinger slipped under the leg band of her panties and he asked if she remembered that time in his car at the drive-in, the two of them like this, the gear shift in the way. She laughed yes, yes of course she remembered, way back in the beginning, the night they became lovers.

But tonight was not then, tonight she was dry and it hurt when his finger tried to climb inside her. It's okay, Wolfe whispered, relax, it felt good just to hold her, it had been so long. He touched her differently then, quick, teasing strokes, and his mouth was at her throat, her hands were in his hair, at the sides of his face, reading the bones and skin as though she were blind.

She inhaled the musk scent of his skin, that cologne she'd bought him years ago, a scent that struck other memories, freeing them, freeing her. She moved up against him and his finger eased into her, slow, deep, as if to get lost inside her, to turn her inside out. Her breath hitched in her chest and she clung to him, and he whispered to her, arousing her with his words, with the texture of his voice, and suddenly everything was in the way. Her clothes, the steering wheel, there wasn't enough room, his finger was driving her, she was going to come.

Moments, that's all it was, moments in which it seemed she hadn't been touched for years, for centuries, not like this, as though it mattered. She fumbled for his zipper to free him, but Jack's face took shape behind her eyes, inside her eyes, spreading across her inner vision like smoke; Jack laughing, Jack touching her, Jack with his scarves, his dark pleasures. Jack, killed four weeks ago tonight.

"Please." Her fingers closed over his arm. "No." She pushed him gently away, feeling like a fool, like a thirteen-year-old tease in the backseat of her daddy's car. "It's too soon, Wolfie."

He moved away from her, adjusting his clothing, neither of them speaking. The windows were fogged. She ached all over inside.

"When this is over, I'd like for things between us to work again, Katie. Do you think we could try?"

"I hope so." It was the most she could offer, but it was enough for him.

He touched her chin, kissed her quickly on the mouth again. "I'll follow you out of the lot. Call if you need anything and I'll pick you up for the funeral at two tomorrow."

He followed her in his snappy blue MG to the bridge for Palm Beach, then swung into a U-turn and headed back into town. She drove over the bridge, but instead of turning south on Ocean Drive, Kate went north. She had no particular destination in mind; she simply wanted to drive, that was all.

Her window was down, the warm night air blew through the car, she popped in her now worn *Distant Horseman* tape, and her mind went elsewhere. Forty minutes later she was on Pearl Hanley's street. The police band was gone, the street was empty of cars, there was only the moon directly in front of her a solitary, watchful eye.

She killed the headlights and pulled far enough into the drive so the car wouldn't be seen. She took a penlight from the glove compartment, swung her purse over her shoulder, slipped the keys from the ignition.

Hello, Pearl. Tell me what you know.

She walked around to the back of the house, found an unlocked window, and climbed inside.

17

1.

CLICKER WALKED UP the beach with his black canvas shoes in his hand. At night, with the long, curved stretch of sand deserted like this, he loved the sea. He loved its rhythms, its song, its presence. Like the night, the sea had stories to tell if you knew how to listen.

But tonight a buzzing in his right ear kept intruding. He knew what it was. Jack. Jack was whispering to him, urging him to remember, as though remembering would make him account for his sin.

He had not gone to the ranch that night with the intention of killing Jack. He had gone there to talk. And yet he had carried Kate's .38, carried it next to his heart like a kid in the army with a photo of his wife.

Jack was on the porch when he arrived, a big man even when he was sitting and solid as a house. His feet were resting on the railing, crossed at the ankles, his rancher pose. The wind was just beginning to rise, stirring the trees around the house, but it didn't seem to touch Jack. That's how it was with him. His dark side was untouched by anything, even Kate.

He raised his beer in greeting. "Must be my night for visitors."

"So where are they all?"

"Probably in Belle Glade by now getting drunk. Or partying out there on the flats." He chuckled, but Clicker didn't. "I can see your sense of humor deserted you on the drive out here."

"Something like that."

"What's the problem?"

"We need to talk."

He downed the last of his beer and crushed the can. "Sounds serious."

"It is. It's got to stop."

"What does?"

"The flats."

Jack sat forward, his long arms reaching out until his palms touched his knees. Moonlight washed across his face and crouched in the pockets of his eyes, making him look like the predator he was. "Is that coming just from you or are you speaking for the others, Click?"

"I don't know about the others."

The lines in Jack's face all seem to move at once, twitching against the wind. This weird, shifting topography of bones and flesh disoriented Clicker, made him dizzy, and he looked away.

"This has more to do with Kate than the flats, doesn't it?"

"I didn't say anything about Kate."

"You don't have to. I've seen the way you look at her."

"Whatever you've seen, Jack, is in *your* head, not mine. I only came here to say that things on the flats have gone too far. It was fine when it was just you and me, but you shouldn't have brought Pearl into it. Or the others."

"No one's twisting your arm. Don't come. I don't give a shit one way or the other."

"Then the others will think I'm another Abalonee."

Jack stood then, his hands on his hips, gazing out at the darkness. The wind combed his hair back and he looked as regal as a god, like some mythical being conjured from the depths of space. He frowned; he didn't like to be reminded of Abalonee. "Frank's my mistake. I misjudged him."

"A lot of good that's going to do us if he talks."

"He's not going to talk. He has too much to lose. You want a brew?"

"I want to settle this."

"It's settled. Don't go out to the flats. See how simple that was?" He smiled. "Be right back. I need another beer."

Just like that, Jack had dismissed him as though he were a hired hand, one of the lackeys who worked his fields, and Clicker literally saw red. It filled his eyes like blood and whipped through him, a hot, violent tide, and when Jack turned

160

to go inside, when the screen door was open and he had one foot in the house, Clicker pulled the .38 from his windbreaker.

He fired. Missed. Fired again and again and again. Jack toppled into the front room. The wind slammed the screen door shut. Seconds ticked by. Clicker didn't move, didn't breathe.

Then the air swooshed from his lungs, he moved toward the door, the gun still in his hand. Jack was sprawled facedown on the floor, not a god at all, just a graceless creature of flesh and bone and blood. The air stank of blood, blood was spreading across the back of his shirt, pooling on the floor. Clicker's knees cracked as he crouched beside him. He didn't want to touch him but couldn't stand the way Jack's eyes were looking at him. He shut them, then saw the bulge in Jack's pocket and laughed. Sly fucker, sitting out there on the porch in the dark, getting high or about to.

Clicker slipped the little squeeze bottle out. Spun the cap. Jammed the nozzle into his nostril. Squeezed hard. The drug exploded in his skull, a wave of panic slammed into him, and all he wanted was to get away. His damp fingers jerked across Jack's neck, seeking a pulse. He couldn't find one. No pulse sweet Christ the wicked god was dead goodbye goodbye goodbye.

He tore toward the door.

Outside, he frantically wiped the door and the gun and the railing, and oh God, how he wiped, up and down, over and over again. He hurled the gun into the house, then hurried out back to cut the wires, to make it look like something it wasn't.

And the entire time Jack had still been alive and Kate had been in the attic. Hidden. Waiting. Terrified.

Kate.

Now he could see Pearl's house and the dune of sea oats where he had left her body. It was against the rules to go back, but he needed to. He needed to walk through the spaces she had lived in, to breathe air she had breathed, needed to be sure he hadn't left something of himself behind. It seemed that he had, something small, insignificant, something the cops might or might not notice.

He saw the deck outside her bedroom, the sliding glass

doors, the windows. For an instant, he thought he glimpsed a wink of light, maybe the reflection of moonlight on water, he wasn't sure. He dropped to his knees, listening. Crickets, frogs, the noise of waves breaking on the sand.

Then his ears began to buzz again, louder this time, more insistent. He jammed his finger into his ear and moved it rapidly. The buzzing receded. He got up, averted his eyes when he passed the spot where he'd left Pearl. He'd done her a favor, after all, she was with Jack now, who'd always been her favorite. The two of them were probably up to no good. He could almost see them, beings of ectoplasmic lace who haunted innocents on darkened roads and danced to music the living would never hear. Maybe they had met his mother, sure, they were one of a kind, those three.

He moved on toward Pearl's house.

2.

Kate sat at the foot of the bed where Pearl had slept, where Jack had probably slept, and rubbed hard at the knot in her chest. She wondered what she could have done differently. Had she loved him enough? Expressed that love often enough? Had she nagged him? Made unreasonable demands? Why had he married her?

Her penlight skipped through the dark, touching down on the dresser, the closet where Pearl's clothes still hung, the nightstand, the Southwest rugs, the pair of Mullan paintings on the wall. She thought of the photograph of Jack and Pearl, the picture Eastman had shown her here in Pearl's room. She saw it brightly in her mind's eye, Jack and Pearl and, behind them, the old fire tower on the Death Flats.

It was a miserable stretch of land that lay twenty miles south of the ranch as the crow flew. The road was dirt, the sky was always colorless, burned white by the sun, except at sunset, when colors filled it. The only things out there were mangroves that marked the boundary of the flats, a scattering of palms, the fire tower, an abandoned airfield and a few old huts the army had left behind. Its desolation, its rawness, its alien air, had fascinated Jack.

She set the penlight down and took the gun from her purse.

She held it in her hand, ran her fingers over the cool, smooth barrel. Such power. She snapped out the ammunition clip: her finger squeezed back on the trigger. The click it made echoed in the room's stillness, disturbing the air that Pearl had breathed, that Jack had breathed, their molecules mingling like spit in water.

Goodbye bullets, she thought, and ejected them. They lay around her on the quilt like the petals of a flower that some woman had picked while making a wish. *He loves me, he loves me not.* . . .

She chose one that lay in the slender beam of light and slipped it back into the clip, snapped the clip back into the gun.

She ran her tongue over the barrel, loving the shape of it, the texture, the ineffable *reality* of the thing. She stuck the barrel in her mouth, sucked on the end of it, let her teeth touch it. She thought of Jack whom she had loved and married and promised until death do us part Jesus God how could he, and her finger eased back on the trigger and tears burned the corners of her eyes and she promised what she would do if she lived.

Her head filled with air like a balloon and she seemed to float away, up toward the blue canopy of the bed, up into the illusion of sky, up, up into the dark tunnel with the promise of light at the end. But the gun made a weird, hollow noise and she felt the deception against her tongue, that thickness of life. Tears spilled on her cheeks, her wrists ached. She squeezed her eyes shut in relief or disappointment, she didn't know which, and slipped the gun from her mouth.

She suddenly sensed something behind her, on the deck, and twisted, shining the penlight at the glass. Its beam was too weak and thin to penetrate the dark, but she glimpsed a flicker of movement, a shape, a man—she was sure it was a man—and she panicked. Her arm jerked up just as it had in her dream of Pearl, of Pearl and Jack, and she fired, the explosion deafening her.

Cracks spread through the glass door, a spiderweb of cracks, then it shattered and glass rained into the room, out onto the deck, tinkling like wind chimes as they struck. She grabbed her purse, the loose bullets spilling to the floor, and leaped from the bedroom, blind with fear. She stumbled over something in the hall, caught herself, and ran on, the man behind her, his footfalls like a giant's feet, fee, fie, foe, fum . . .

She knocked things aside to slow him down. A chair, a lamp, a vase, a table. But the house now seemed huge, a cavern with a dozen rooms, all of them riddled with hazards that rose from the dark to trick her, grab at her, immobilize her. She passed in and out of moonlight that streamed through cracks in the blinds, the curtains, and made it to the front door. She struggled with the dead bolt, couldn't get it open, couldn't remember if she'd seen another door when she was here with Eastman.

Stairs.

She spun and flew up the staircase, one hand slapping the railing, the other still gripping the useless gun, panic a hot whip at her back. Ribbons of light fell unevenly across the floor, enough to see that she was in the loft. Desk in the corner, bed against the wall, porch doors in front of her, bathroom to her right. She ran into it, yanked the door shut, turned the lock in the knob. Kate backed up to the wall, sucking air in through her teeth, hands tight against her chest, eyes darting around. Sunken tub with the jut of a window beyond it, double sinks, a huge linen closet. But no other exit.

She heard him on the stairs, knew that the door wouldn't hold him for long, that she couldn't just stand here. To the window. It was just a decorative pane of glass, wouldn't open, had never opened.

Now he was in the loft. He didn't shout, speak, didn't say a word. He couldn't; she would recognize his voice. But he slammed his body against the door and she felt the reverberation to her toes. He rattled the knob, then hurled his body against the door again, breathing furiously, snorting like a bull.

Kate threw open the door of the linen closet. It was huge. Shelves of towels climbed to the ceiling on her left, shelves of sheets rose on the right. But level with her hip was the yawning mouth of a laundry chute, barely wide enough for her to fit into. If it narrowed halfway down, she would be stuck, he would catch her, she would die. But she would die if she didn't try.

She whipped off her shoes, shoved them into her purse with the gun, zipped it shut, threw the purse down first. It struck something at the bottom. Okay, do it, do it now. She grabbed

164

hold of the shelf, balancing as she lifted her left leg into the chute, then the other, so she was now perched at the lip of the opening. A protruding nail, a sliver of cracked metal, and she would be sliced to bits.

But when he slammed into the door again, she heard the wood crack and let go. She slid down, down, her arms extended over her head, the chute curving. Her skirt hiked up, her blouse bunched, her spine and the backs of her legs scraped against the metal, slowing her down. She had a momentary vision of herself stuck in this tube, unable to go down or up, and the man would be below her, reaching inside, trying to grab her feet. She imagined the metal walls closing in on her, squeezing her to death, and suddenly she couldn't breathe, the blackness licked at her, she couldn't hear anything, she didn't seem to be moving at all.

Then the chute spit her out. She landed in a pile of clothes, her breath exploded from her chest, her skin stung in half a dozen places, but she was alive, dear God, alive. Her hands slapped through the clothes for her purse. She found it and lifted onto her knees, not trusting herself to stand. She was too dizzy; the darkness disoriented her.

Door. There had to be a door. Most utility rooms in Florida had one that opened into the garage or to the side of the house. But the air was the color of pitch. She stood, heart pounding, palms slick with sweat, eyes sweeping through the blackness for a sliver of light. There, right there, on her left.

Distantly, she heard him at the bathroom door upstairs. In seconds, he would break through, see the chute, and race down the stairs. She moved forward, hands in front of her, seeking something, anything, she could hold on to. She found the edge of a sink. A washer or a dryer. The crack of light was so dim and pale that it was merely a suggestion of light, a tease, level with her feet. She groped for a door knob, nearly wept when her hands touched it, but held them still, listening for the man before she turned it.

She heard him upstairs.

Go. The door opened a crack before the chain stopped it. Her hands shook as she unfastened it, then she fell out into the smell of sea and salt and night and raced around the side of the house toward the Cherokee.

But the door was locked. Habit, all these years of locking the door without thinking about it. Frantic, she dug for her keys, couldn't find them, realizing they must have fallen out onto Pearl's bed. Or onto her bathroom floor. She ran to the back of the Jeep, felt along the inside of the bumper where she kept the spare. There, the little magnetic box. Hurry, Christ, hurry. The lid was stiff, she couldn't slide the damn thing back, oh, please, please . . .

The lid gave.

The key fell out.

She grabbed it off the ground, ran to the door, jammed it in the lock, hurled open the door, and threw herself inside. The engine roared. Kate slammed the Cherokee into reverse and squealed out of the driveway, tires spitting wood chips, pebbles, dirt.

3.

Just as the lock on the bathroom door surrendered to his relentless assault, Clicker heard the car. *Her* car.

Fury sprang from his pores. The buzzing in his head tightened to a whine, then exploded in the shriek of a hundred saws echoing in the cage of his skull. He slapped his hands over his ears. The noise drove him to his knees, where he groveled, shaking his head, whimpering like an injured mutt. The pain, oh, Christ, the pain, white-hot needles digging through his ears to his brain.

He passed out briefly and came to on his back on Pearl's bathroom floor, something sharp sticking into his back, his head throbbing. But the shrieks were gone and in their place was a long, hot silence, an absence of anything human. He rolled onto his side, felt behind him, sat up with a set of keys in his hands.

Kate's keys.

He started to laugh, got to his feet, and trotted down the stairs, through the hall, his shoes crunching over the broken glass. Then he was running down the beach again, her keys tight in his hand.

4.

Kate ended up at the Holiday Inn on Delray Beach, where she checked into a room on the third floor, facing the ocean. The locks were probably secure, even though they weren't computerized. But she jammed the back of a chair under the door knob so if someone came in the chair would topple, alerting her. She still didn't sleep well.

She came to in fits and starts all night, like a worn engine with loose pistons and faulty gaskets. She checked the chair, the locks, then stood for a while at the window and watched the street, wondering what kind of car he drove, where he was right now, what he was thinking.

She could feel him out there in the dark. She was connected to him. He'd created the connection with his drawing, his note, his calls, by desecrating her clothes at the ranch, created it in a hundred small and different ways, and now he was jerking on the invisible cord that bound them, jerking and laughing, reminding her that he still held the power.

Kate stepped quickly away from the window, her heart racing, and looked frantically around the room. If he found her, if he got into the room, she would— What? Just what the hell would she do? Hide under the bed? Scream? Hurl herself out the window?

Weapon. She dug the gun from her purse, turned it over and over in her hand. Useless. Its bullets were scattered all over the floor in Pearl's bedroom. She swept through the room looking for something she could use as a weapon. The phone, if she hurled it and struck him in the head; a pair of manicure scissors, if he was close enough and she could sink the blade into his eyes; a complimentary bottle of wine on the bar. Yes, perfect.

Kate got back into the bed with it and lay there, fingers gripping the neck, eyes fixed on the door. I'll hear him, she thought, and I'll kill him.

She fell asleep clutching the bottle and dreamed she was running, that he was behind her, gaining on her, that he shouted to her in Jack's voice, that his laughter was Jack's. She bolted upright in bed, eyes darting through the pale light, pausing finally on the wine bottle on the rug. The room was still and cool, the chair was in place. She was alone.

Kate listened at the door, heard nothing, went to the window. Faint ribbons of light crossed the horizon like luminous stitches. Waves broke on the beach. A few cars whispered by. The world was the same, but she was not.

She showered, put on yesterday's clothes, then went downstairs and ordered breakfast in the coffee shop. She sat with her back to a wall, where she could see the door, the windows. She didn't eat much, but the four cups of black coffee she drank revived her.

At eight on the button, she called a West Palm Beach security company and explained what she wanted. No one would be able to get to her house before Tuesday. That wasn't soon enough, she said, and hung up and called another company.

When she started to get the same runaround, she informed the woman on the other end that there were forty-two windows and eight doors in the house and all needed locks. She said she wanted the best security system on the market, she didn't care how much it cost, but it had to be done today. The woman sighed as though she heard this routine every day, promised she would see what she could do, and asked for Kate's address. When she gave it, the woman's tune suddenly changed. Someone would be at her home at ten.

Oceanside in Palm Beach was a Houdini wand.

Kate drove to a gun shop downtown and bought six magazines for the GLT .380 and twenty boxes of bullets, fifty to a box. She paid for a booth and targets in the shooting gallery. Inside, she loaded the magazines she'd purchased and the one already in the gun. Forty-two shots at her fingertips.

The man at the desk had given her two kinds of targets: a bull's-eye and a silhouette of the human body. She attached the silhouette to the pulley and reeled it out fifty feet. Head? Chest? Balls? Chest, she decided. It would be easier to hit.

She emptied three magazines and started on a fourth before she struck the heart, bright red and shaped like a valentine. By the time she had gone through three boxes of bullets, she could hit the heart at a distance of seventy-five feet.

It was a good beginning.

18

1.

THE BREAKERS HOTEL & Club was like ancient Rome, Quin thought. All roads in Palm Beach eventually led there—if not literally, then certainly figuratively. It was a sprawling, extravagant resort on a hundred and forty acres in the heart of Palm Beach, both a landmark and a symbol of what the city was about, the kind of place where you were expected to wear a coat and tie to the bathroom.

The hotel was a pink palace at the lip of the Atlantic. It had five hundred and twenty-eight rooms, two eighteen-hole golf courses, an oceanfront heated fresh water swimming pool, a half mile of private beach, nineteen tennis courts, and an activities center. During the tourist season the cost of rooms ranged from two hundred and sixty dollars to eight hundred dollars a day.

Loose change to the guests who stayed here.

The original Breakers was built in 1896 from Dade County pine lumber—a touch of irony she appreciated, since pine trees were now as scarce in Dade County as the open land they'd once filled. The hotel was financed by railroad magnate Henry Flagler, who wanted to have a so-called proper hotel in Florida. In those days it was known as the Palm Beach Inn, had two hundred rooms, and was bright yellow, Flagler's favorite color. It was renamed in 1901.

All of these facts had come to Quin via Harold Javitt, the friendly neighborhood baker. But his favorite story about the Breakers was what had happened to it on an ordinary afternoon in 1925.

Marjorie Merriweather Post was at the front desk chatting with actress Billie Burke when someone ran up, shouting about a fire raging out of control in one of the guest rooms. The flames, fanned by a strong southeasterly wind, quickly consumed the hotel and by midafternoon much of the island was on fire. Martial law was declared and the National Guard was called in to patrol the streets. By dark, there was nothing but a pile of burning rubble where the Breakers had once stood. A fitting place, she mused, for a post–memorial service brunch for Jack Bishop.

Quin parked the Toyota in a visitor's spot. It was one of the saddest-looking cars around, a pauper among kings—Porsches, Mercedeses, BMWs, a Rolls, an Excelsior with gold-rim tires. The heat was relieved somewhat by a breeze blowing in from the ocean, but she was still uncomfortable. Her feet, sheathed in stockings and jammed into a pair of navy pumps, were already swelling. The fabric of her dress, a navy-blue and white number that was one of the prettier maternity outfits she'd found, was sticking to the backs of her legs and made her stomach itch.

She detested going to any function alone, especially big affairs like this. But Kate had hitched a ride with Wolfe and McCleary was with Eastman today, the two of them combing through Pearl Hanley's home for leads. Later, he would be at the migrant camp talking with Arturo Cordoba. It was just as well. She wouldn't be able to pressure Kate any more than she had over the phone this morning about moving in with them for a while. And she wouldn't have a chance to pick at McCleary for pulling out of the driveway as he had yesterday in the middle of an argument. A detail he had conveniently ignored last night.

Quin cut through the lobby, splendid with its marble floors and chandeliers and antiques. She paused at a handcarved Louis XVI desk and chairs and at a gallery of sepia photographs depicting the history of the hotel. Then she turned down a hallway wide enough for a pair of elephants and followed signs to the clubhouse.

Thanks to Stephanie, the brunch had become an *event*. There were at least two hundred people in the clubhouse, a tremendous room with glass walls that faced the ocean. Those present included such luminaries as the mayor, the local congressman, the gossip columnist for the *Palm Beach Post*, and of course a slice of Palm Beach's upper crust. Their voices, the scents of their perfumes and after-shaves, the rustling of their expensive clothes, filled the room with a life of its own.

Quin stood at the periphery of the crowd, feeling large and conspicuous and out of place. She spotted the buffet table on the other side of the room heaped with enough food to feed a third-world country for a day. Food was something she could relate to, and she made her way toward it, hoping no one would notice if she ate and split. She was desperately in need of sleep. She and McCleary had stayed up late last night trying to access the files on the disk she'd taken from Bishop's office at the center, and right about now she felt as strung out as a junkie.

The table was a smorgasbord of color: dips as white as whipped cream, plums the same shade as Liz Taylor's eyes, sliced kiwis like glimmering emeralds, salmon pinker than coral, black breads and brown, caviar and oysters and ten different kinds of cheese. And she hadn't even reached the main dishes yet.

An elderly black man in a stiff white uniform served her entrée, a seafood casserole with plumes of steam wafting from it. She stood in what she hoped was an inconspicuous spot against the wall, wishing she could sit down or go barefoot or both. She picked at her food and surveyed the crowd, noting who stood where and with whom.

Kate and Wolfe were talking to Sammy Dayton, who was as nervous as a mosquito. He twitched and fussed in his suit, which actually looked as though it had been pressed, and kept smoothing a palm over his bald head, moving whenever the crowd pushed up behind him.

Garrison was with Stephanie Bishop near the fountain. She wore an elegantly plain black dress, a heavy gold choker, spiked black heels. Her hair had a ton of mousse on it that kept it swept back from her face. She seemed curiously androgynous.

David Bishop weaved through the crowd with drinks in hand. His tie was a luminous orange, shaped like a Popsicle. When the gossip columnist moved in on him, he looked a little panicked, as if he wanted to be anywhere but here. She knew the feeling. But even the columnist would be preferable to the dork who'd attached himself to Quin a few minutes ago. He seemed familiar, but she couldn't place his face. Thin and pale, he wore black-frame glasses that gave him an oddly studious appearance. He was chattering nonstop about Jack, about his friendship with Jack, that they had gone to high school and Dartmouth together. Every high school in the country, she thought, had a guy like this one, the class brain, the valedictorian, the kid befriended for his homework papers, his test answers.

She just stood there nodding, hoping he would get the hint and go away. But he clung to her like a hangover. She finally introduced herself to find out his name, what the hell.

"Abalonee, Frank Abalonee, it rhymes with baloney." He yukked, poked at his glasses.

The elusive Abalonee, mystery man in the flying club photograph. No wonder he'd looked familiar. "You and Jack were in a flying club together."

"Uh, yeah, that's right." Another yuk. "Just for a while. Things broke up, no one had any time. I still try to fly once a week or so, but don't always get around to it."

"I guess Garrison was in your class, too, right? With you and Jack?"

"Garrison?" He blinked fast.

"You know, Lt. Garrison, the man who arrested Kate for Jack's murder."

"Oh. Lou. Sure. Sure, I know Lou. Not well." He stared at his plate, his lips barely moving, like a ventriloquist's. "I know Kate hired you and your husband, Mrs. McCleary. I have something Jack gave me that may help you out. It's a key to a locker Jack rented at the Amtrak station in West Palm. Here, take it."

He held a rolled linen napkin at the side of his plate and stabbed it toward her, a spy passing secrets. When she didn't reach for it, he hissed, *"Take it."*

She was slightly buzzed from what she'd been drinking, beer and cranberry juice and lime, the first booze she'd had since she'd gotten pregnant, and couldn't reply as quickly as she wanted to. "When did Jack give you the key, Mr. Abalonee?"

"A week before he was killed."

"Why?"

"Look, I don't want to get involved. I can't afford to, you understand? Just take the napkin."

"Involved in what?"

His eyes met hers, melted into hers, and she felt the acuteness of his fear. "It's not safe to talk here. Just take the goddamn thing."

"I'd like to talk to you in private, Mr. Abalonee. Wherever it would be best with you."

"All I've got to say is in the napkin. Take it."

She did, dabbed her mouth with it, and he turned and walked off.

2.

McCleary and Eastman spent several hours combing through the mess at Pearl Hanley's, labeling the items they would take and listing them for her next of kin. They found little of interest. Pearl had not been a pack rat. Whatever secrets she'd had, she'd taken with her.

For part of the time the local forensics crew was there, poking around, dusting for prints, sweeping up the glass to examine later for blood, hairs, threads of fabric. Nothing was too small or too minute. After all, fibers from a ski mask helped to convict Ted Bundy.

Eastman didn't say much. He wasn't a man who talked just to break up the silence. But he did remark that Garrison supposedly hadn't left his place once he'd gotten home last night. The way he said this, though, implied that Garrison probably suspected he was being tailed and knew all the tricks in the book for shaking a tail if he wanted to leave the house badly enough.

When they were upstairs, examining the ruined bathroom door, Eastman asked if McCleary thought the man was large.

"A guy doesn't have to be large to do damage like this. He's only got to be mad."

Eastman grinned. "You and the shrink agree."

"Which shrink?"

He pulled some folded sheets from his pocket. "I got the psyche profile on this guy before I came over here. That's a copy. You can keep it."

McCleary sat at the rolltop desk and unfolded the sheets:

PSYCHOLOGICAL PROFILE
(Re: Jack Bishop
Pearl Hanley)

Despite the variation in weapons in these two homicides, there are notable similarities in the MOs: 1) victims killed at night, in or near their homes; 2) lived in sparsely populated areas; 3) no sign of a struggle; 4) their eyes were shut when found; 5) something was done to the house or the body after the killings; 6) no clear fingerprints found at the scene.

Ms. Hanley's murder is especially interesting. Evidence indicates sexual intercourse shortly before she died, yet no semen was found. Two bottles of beer were missing from the six-pack in her refrigerator, yet only one empty bottle was discovered. An empty condom pack was found in her wastebasket. No evidence of forced entry into the house.

All of these details point to a highly organized and bright individual who knew his victims well and who his victims trusted. He prides himself on being in control. He plans his moves and acts accordingly. If a random element intrudes on his plan, he uses it to his advantage. It is unlikely that he panics easily.

If and when he experiences fear, it doesn't overcome him. He still remembers to attend to details—cutting phone lines, for instance, taking his empty beer bottle with him, wrapping his victim in a towel.

But the violence of the assault on Ms. Hanley indicates a man who seethes, broods, and explodes for no apparent reason. When in the grips of such an explosion, he is likely to become careless about details—i.e., forgetting

174

the empty condom packet, failing to count the beers that were in the refrigerator.

Given the care with which he wrapped Ms. Hanley's body and their sexual tryst before he killed her, it's likely that he took something of hers with him. Maybe a piece of jewelry or even something as insignificant as a fingernail or a strand of hair.

The photographs left in Mrs. Bishop's mailbox the day after the murder indicate several things: 1) gloating over his cleverness; 2) ego gratification; 3) assertion of his power and control over Mrs. Bishop.

As for the other photographs, I strongly believe he has targeted the McClearys, who he sees as impediments in his attainment of his goal. He included them to show you his sense of fair play—i.e., since Ms. Hanley was already dead when the photos were received, these balance the books, a clear warning.

The deliberateness he has demonstrated, the precision, the cunning, point to a methodical individual, a loner. Unmarried, perhaps divorced, unable to sustain a relationship for an extended period of time. This type is often motivated by a sense of mission that may spill over into his personal and professional life. But chances are he looks and acts and dresses normally. He may have some obvious quirks, but nothing to make him blatantly suspicious.

Just a comment on the calls to Mrs. Bishop, the obscene drawing and note. Calls of this type usually cease once an answering machine is used; the caller rarely goes on to send things through the mail. But the fact that this man has, combined with the brutal assault on Ms. Hanley, suggests fear and hatred of the mother, perhaps due to child abuse. By terrorizing Mrs. Bishop, he is acting out suppressed aggression against his mother.

Age: 30–45.

Hobbies: Anything a man can do best alone or with one other person.

Education: Difficult to pinpoint. But he doesn't work

well under close supervision. He needs to think he's calling his own shots.

Suggestions: This guy enjoys reading about himself in the media; it feeds his sense of power. So downplay the investigations. Pressure him. Lure him out. Bait him. Set a trap. But don't count on guilt or remorse tripping him up. Men on a mission rarely have a conscience. They play by their own rules.

McCleary folded the sheets, pinching them between his thumb and forefinger, creasing them. "Pressure him how? Bait him how?"

"I don't know yet. That's what we have to figure out."

3.

Quin unrolled the napkin. A small metal key, cool as a peach, dropped into her palm. It had a 23 engraved on it. She slipped it into a zippered compartment in her purse and started toward the buffet table for a refill. Halfway there she ran into Dave Bishop.

"You look like you can't wait to get out of here," he said.

Quin laughed. "It's that obvious, huh?"

"Only to people who feel the same way." He tugged on the tiny gold hoop in his ear as his eyes skipped around the room. "My sister's known for excesses, but I think she actually put together something Jack would have liked. The flair, the drama, the bullshit." He pulled a little puppet from his coat pocket and fit it on his index finger. It was a miniature Indiana Jones, replete with bullwhip and fedora and a face that bore a faint resemblance to Harrison Ford. "You have anything to say about it, Indy?"

In Harrison Ford's voice, Jones replied: "Take it from me, Dave. Jack would have liked it."

Quin laughed, delighted. "He's wonderful."

Jones tipped his fedora, said, "I bet Frankie talked your ear off."

"I got the poop on everything from high school to Dartmouth."

Bishop put Jones away. "You wouldn't know it to look at

him, but he's a venture capitalist who's never yet made a wrong investment. Or if he has, none of us knows about it.''

"Were he and Jack still friends?"

"Just when it came to flying. Other than that, not really."

Yet Jack had entrusted Abalonee with a key to something. That presented several possibilities: that Abalonee was lying; that Bishop was lying; that Abalonee was already involved which was why he said he didn't want to get involved; that Bishop didn't know who his brother's friends were; that the key was unimportant.

She didn't have a chance to dwell on it, though, because Garrison and Stephanie Bishop joined them. Compared to the day at the ranch, when she had hardly spoken to Quin, she was as effusive as a car salesman. Had Quin gotten enough to eat? Had she met everyone? When was her baby due? Was she exercising during her pregnancy?

"A friend of mine owns this marvelous little health store just off Worth Avenue and she carries *all* kinds of vitamins and herbs for pregnant women. You ought to drop in. Tell her I sent you.'' She flashed a magnanimous smile, then leaned forward, her chocolate eyes widening with commiseration. "It must be tough working through the pregnancy, though. I admire you for it."

"I have my days."

Garrison guffawed; he sounded like a parrot with laryngitis. "Well, I think it's terrific you're out there pitching, Mrs. McCleary."

"Christ, Lou, she's pregnant, not disabled," said Bishop, as though he were an expert on the subject.

Garrison shrugged and launched into a story about his sister's pregnancy. Stephanie yawned, glanced around, and walked off in the middle of the story. It obviously irked him, and a few moments later, he muttered something about the buffet table and left.

Bishop stared after him, an obscenity written all over his face. Then he excused himself and Quin was alone again, with an empty plate in one hand and an empty glass in the other. She set everything down on a nearby table and headed for the door.

Outside, she walked over to the railing and gazed down at the beach. A wind had kicked up, whipping the waves into white froth, bending the palm trees until they were curved like plants seeking light. The afternoon sun streamed down with the thickness of honey, pooling over umbrellas and across the lotion-slick bodies of the diehard sun worshippers.

The bodies, naturally, all seemed to belong to women who were thin, lithe, with tummies as flat as glass and boobs too perfect to be real. Soon, she thought. Today was December fifteenth; the baby was due February seventeenth. Two months and two days. Maybe the baby would come early. But suppose she was late? Suppose she was one of those rarities, a ten-month baby?

She would lose her mind, that's what.

Someone came up behind her and she glanced around. "Hi. Sammy."

His long shadow fell over her. "I'm with you. Fresh air." He stopped next to her, fingers curling over the railing as he took a deep breath and exhaled. "Jesus, it smells good. No perfume."

Quin laughed. "No after-shave."

He looked at her with those weird blue eyes of his, eyes that made her squirm even out here, in the open, with the sea at her feet. "I hate crowds."

"I hate being big."

"At least that's temporary."

"In theory."

"You'll see. As soon as the baby's born, you'll lose fifteen pounds like that." He snapped his fingers, another male expert on pregnancy. "It's all water."

Not really, guy.

Then he pulled out a fat joint and lit it and inhaled with the relish of a man who needed a high. It surprised her—not that he smoked, but that he was smoking here, on the boardwalk between the Breakers Hotel and the clubhouse, in plain sight of everyone. If anyone had been around.

He offered it to her; she shook her head. "You don't smoke?" He sounded surprised.

"Not since I got pregnant."

"Oh. Right. Everything crosses the placenta, I guess."

"Just about."

"Not too long after my NDE eighteen years ago," he said, "I went through a period where I experimented heavily with drugs. My Huxley period." He laughed.

"Huxley's trip on mescaline as he was dying?"

"Yes." He seemed pleased that she'd guessed. He said that in Huxley's descriptions, he recognized some of the same motifs and patterns that he'd encountered in his own experience. "I was curious whether it was the mescaline or Huxley's proximity to death that had triggered them, so I decided to find out for myself by ingesting three peyote buttons. They made me violently ill and I spent the entire time in bed, hallucinating like crazy and throwing up in a mop pail."

After that, he tried a little of everything—speed, downers, grass, smack, pain killers, acid, mescaline, coke. "Hallucinogenics came the closest to producing the same effects. And once in a great while, so does sex."

"Orgasm as a little death."

He laughed. "I never thought of it exactly in those words, but yeah, I guess that describes it." He took one more hit off the joint, then twisted the end against the railing, putting it out but not squashing it. "Anyway. I don't know how the hell I got started on that. Guess I'd better go back in. You coming?"

"I've got to run some errands." It wasn't an outright lie; she could almost feel the weight of Abalonee's key in her purse. "Tell Kate I'll call her later."

"Will do." His palm slipped over his bald head. "Drive carefully. A lot of nuts out there."

He walked back to the clubhouse, his gait quick and self-assured. She wondered how she could have thought he'd come on to her yesterday in Jack's office. She'd obviously imagined it and that bothered her more than if she'd been right. If she was looking to other men to find her attractive, then her self-image was in worse shape than she'd realized and so was her relationship with McCleary.

Christ, but it was a depressing thought.

19

1.

MCCLEARY TURNED OFF the highway onto a dirt road paralleling the fence that separated the migrant camp from the rest of the world. A thicket of pines rose to his right, but otherwise the land was nearly as denuded as the moon.

For a quarter of a mile, there was nothing but an asphalt parking lot on his left that rivaled K mart for lack of imagination. Then the administration building appeared, shaped like a loaf of French bread. Around it languished scrubby palmetto palms that were dying of thirst and a handful of banana trees with brown leaves. The empty spaces in between were filled with gravel.

The road ended where the building did and the fence extended some six or eight feet beyond it. A hibiscus hedge blocked his view of the back of the fence. Oriented now, he made a U-turn and headed back to the front, where the parking lot was. The man in the guardhouse didn't look up as he approached; the gate was open, so he drove on through.

Half a dozen buses stood in the lot, old things with nicks and bumps in the sides. There were twice as many golf carts, which he supposed were used to ferry employees back and forth between here and the living area to the east. These were parked on the right side. On the fence to his left was a sign that said VISITARS PARKING. Proper spelling wasn't high on the list of priorities around here.

He nosed the Miata into a space. From the glove compartment he retrieved a black eye patch he'd purchased at the optometry department at Sears. He fitted it over his right eye, then scrutinized himself in the rearview mirror with his left.

Not bad. Depending on his expression, the patch could make him look either sinister or dignified.

He adjusted his tie, hating the damn thing, spoke a few words to himself in a passable southern drawl. He was now Jim Davis, grove owner from Indian River County whose tangelo crop needed picking before Christmas.

The administration building was as bleak inside as out. The lobby was cramped and dingy, with tiny windows and a vinyl floor tracked with dirt. Men and women with black hair and eyes occupied the rows of metal chair. Some of the women had small children with them and all of them seemed to be whining. The air was thick and warm and stank of desperation.

At the front desk, two women were processing applications. One was arguing loudly in Spanish with a young man in a dirty shirt and torn jeans. Next to him was an even younger woman with an infant in her arms and two other kids younger than five clinging to her skirt.

"Permiso," McCleary said to the woman who wasn't arguing. *"El Señor Cordoba se encuentra?"* He concentrated on keeping his Spanish Americanized—no crisp *r*'s, a slow roll on vowels.

The woman looked up, her vapid eyes flicking from his face to his clothes, his watch, his eye patch. In seconds she'd assessed him as a rich gringo and smiled pleasantly. *"Su nombre, por favor?"*

"Davis, Jim Davis. Mah appointment's at four."

She punched out a number on the phone, spoke too softly for McCleary to hear, then hung up, smiling again. "Come with me, please. I will take you to *Señor* Cordoba."

The *jefe*'s office fell into the major tacky category: a painting of Christ's bleeding heart on black velvet; a Pepsi sign over the doorway, the likes of which could be found in every *cantina* in Mexico; a floor lamp that was definitely phallic; a large glass ashtray with Acapulco Hilton on it. To one side of the desk was a photo of a man he presumed was Cordoba with his wife and three daughters. It was in a weird ceramic frame that looked as if it had been fired by a *campesinos* high on grass.

The *jefe* himself fit the room like a shoe: a plump cigar smoker with curly black hair slicked back with something that smelled suspiciously like salad dressing. He smiled too much, a clenched-teeth smile, as though it hurt his facial muscles.

"*Señor, mucho gusto,*" he boomed, proffering a dimpled hand and pumping McCleary's arm. "Please, make yourself comfortable." Would the *señor* like a *cafecito*? Something cold to drink? No? Ah, well, then. "How may I help you? I am at your service."

"You were recommended to me by Jack Bishop, *Señor* Cordoba."

"A fine gentleman. We did business for many years. So tragic, what happened." He tapped his cigar against the edge of the Hilton ashtray, knocking off an ash the size of a ping-pong ball. "You are a grove owner?"

"In Indian River County. Do y'all provide workers that far north?"

"Yes, yes, of course." He waved the cigar around. "That is no problem. We cover Vero Beach to Miami. How many workers do you need? For what kind of crop?"

"About sixty. Mah tangelo crop this year is larger than Ah expected and Ah'd like the fruit on the market by Christmas."

Cordoba's eyes beamed with dollar signs at the mention of sixty men. "Very good, *señor*. I have a list of our fees right here." Out came a drawer. He rummaged inside it, frowned, opened another drawer. "My brochures are gone. Please excuse me one moment, *señor*."

When Cordoba had left, McCleary's eyes prowled the room and paused on a square of carpeting under the desk's kneehole. Compared to the rug in the rest of the room, it was conspicuously new. He dug at it with the tip of his shoe, working back a corner, and exposing a square of scuffed vinyl as rippled as sand.

Maybe nothing but what it appeared to be. But he filed that bit of information in the back of his head. Cordoba returned shortly with a stack of brochures and handed McCleary one. Then he launched into a sales pitch that was supposed to convince him the exorbitant fees were worth it. McCleary asked a few questions, said he'd be in touch in a few days. Cordoba's irritating grin shortened; he was disappointed the deal hadn't been consummated.

182

"If you have any special needs, *Señor* Davis, we can include them in the fee. We work in whatever way we can with our clients."

McCleary seized on something the caretaker at the Bishop ranch had told him. "Uh, yes, Mr. Bishop mentioned you provided workers for special projects."

A predatory gleam curled through Cordoba's eyes, but his voice was soft with caution. "Did he tell you how we work with such a project?"

"Yes," McCleary lied, and took a stab in the dark. "Ah understand it's not included in the regular fee."

"That is correct, *señor*."

"How much additional money would it require?"

"It depends. *Señor* Bishop paid five thousand for such a project."

"Ah see."

"He was quite satisfied. I take care of everything."

Since McCleary didn't have any idea what was actually being discussed, he backed off. He didn't want to blow it. "Ah'll be in touch, *Señor* Cordoba."

2.

Like so many cities in South Florida, Quin thought, West Palm Beach had expanded from the ocean to the Everglades. As new housing mushroomed overnight, so did new malls, new shopping centers, new grocery stores and restaurants, until there was no reason for people to venture downtown anymore. Shops went bankrupt. Restaurants closed. Businesses that survived moved west.

Now the city had big plans to revitalize the area with a beautification project that would cost untold millions and be underway well into the next century. In the meantime, the center of West Palm resembled a postholocaust city.

She wandered up and down streets in search of the Amtrak station. Old buildings rotted in the afternoon light. Potholes were slowly claiming the roads. Clumps of grass pushed up through cracks in the concrete. Crime, she knew, was at an all-time high in these neighborhoods and she wasn't particularly enthused about being here alone. Her pregnancy was as good as a neon sign that flashed EASY MARK, and as she hurried from the parking lot to the Amtrak terminal, she kept her purse snug at her side. Her Browning BDA was inside, a thirteen-shot automatic. It wouldn't do much against most of the automatic weapons in vogue with the drug boys these days, but it would make a potential mugger think twice.

The station itself was just another canker sore in an already blighted landscape. Its bricks were faded and crumbling, its floor was scuffed and dull, the air reeked of despair. It wasn't very crowded—a handful of people lined up at the ticket window, a dozen or so in the coffee shop, the usual assortment of bored employees and derelicts.

The lockers stood against a wall between the restrooms in an unlit alcove that smelled unclean. Locker 23 was at the end of the third row from the bottom and the key Abalonee had given her fit. Her speculations about what the locker held had ranged from the outrageous to the mundane. A body. The secret of life after death. Incriminating photos of participants at the orgies. A pair of bedroom slippers.

But when she opened the door, the only things inside were a dark plastic jug without a label and a small squeeze bottle with *Murine* on the front of it. She dropped the smaller bottle into her purse, pulled out the jug, carried it into the restroom. She spun off the top. The liquid was the color of urine and odorless. The stuff in the squeeze bottle was the same.

Now wouldn't that be a fine joke on Abalonee. His Dartmouth buddy had pissed in a jug, stashed it in a train station locker, then entrusted him with the key. No telling what he thought he'd been guarding—the secret of the universe, cash, jewels. Very funny, Jack.

Anxious to get back to her car, Quin tucked the jug under her arm and hurried out. Between her and the hallway stood one of the men from the Firebird. In a suit. Wearing his running shoes. With his shades on. She didn't want to guess what this guy would do if she pulled out her Browning.

"Hi," she said.

"I'll take that jug, ma'am."

Ma'am. So polite. He must have gone to the same school of impeccable manners as Garrison. "This old thing?"

"That's right, ma'am. Just set it right there on the floor in front of you."

And then run like hell, she thought. But she could never outrun him. Prepregnancy, maybe, but not now. "Sure thing." She set it down, glad she had stuck the smaller bottle into her purse. "There." She stepped back, arms lifted, palms showing. *See, guy? Empty, no gun, no knife, just me and my big belly.*

Quin kept stepping back as the gorilla moved forward, their eyes locked, each waiting for the other to do something unexpected. Something stupid. She stopped when her back touched the door of the women's room, her heart slamming around in her chest. If she pushed into the restroom, she would be cornered. So what? She was armed. But he might be a faster shot and she, no doubt, would be an easy target. She stood her ground.

"Just want to give you a piece of advice, ma'am." He picked up the jug, cradled it in his arm. "I woulda given it to you sooner, but you never gave me the chance."

"I don't read minds."

His smile widened as he inched toward her and slipped open his jacket, showing her his holstered automatic. "Bet you're reading my mind real clear now."

She didn't say anything. Her head raced, seizing plans, discarding them.

"I got nothing against you personally, ma'am. So I want you to listen real good to the advice I'm going to give you."

Her throat was dry and tight; she managed to nod. He was less than a foot from her now and she could see herself in the dark lenses of his glasses, a bimbo with her hands folded protectively across her stomach. Then her eyes dropped to the width of his chest, the size of his hands, his feet, and she had to look up as he stopped a few inches in front of her and fixed a palm on one side of her, trapping her between his body and a bulging arm.

"Don't fuck with the Bishop case if you want to live long enough to have your kid. And pass that bit of advice on to your old man. Okay? Can you do that for me, ma'am?"

"Sure." She whispered it. Then she slammed her knee into his groin and pressed back hard into the door.

It swung inward, swung fast, swung as he gasped, as he stumbled sideways, clutching himself. The jug slipped from his arm and rolled across the floor. She lurched away from him, but she wasn't quick enough, he was already hauling himself up, lunging into the hall after her. Quin stooped with a dexterity that astonished her, grabbed the fallen jug, spun, hurled it at him. It struck him in the face, knocking him back into the wall.

She tore through the station, her hand digging into her purse for her keys, her gun, her belly bouncing up and down, her breath growing short, a stitch burning in her side. Out the doors. Into the parking lot. Not much farther.

She nearly collapsed when she reached the Toyota. Her hand shook when she unlocked the door. Then she was inside, locking the doors, sliding the key into the ignition, praying the car wouldn't suddenly develop a new problem. But it turned over with an almost conscious ease, as though at some elemental level it understood the urgency. Quin slammed the gear shift into reverse and peeled out of the lot.

She careened into the street and didn't look back.

3.

The sky was alive with stars that hurled through the blackness of space in a blur of light as fuzzy as angel hair. All that punch, Kate thought. Glass after glass as she'd chatted with this person, laughed with that person, determined to stick around until the last guest had left.

She'd done it, too, and then she'd asked Wolfe to drop her at home, had packed a bag, gotten into the Cherokee, and fled. She'd driven aimlessly until she'd ended up here, at the cemetery, where everything eventually ended. Six feet under, in a crypt, as a handful of dust, what was the difference?

Kate parked the Cherokee in front of the Bishop family crypt, climbed down, leaned against the Jeep to steady herself. She scanned the moonless sky for Orion and spotted it in the blur, bright as a newly minted dime. Jack's favorite star. She waited for it to tell her something, to reveal something, but it had no secrets to share, at least not with her. All she heard were crickets, their cries crackling through the humid air like static electricity. In the starlight, within the narrow field of her vision, in the haze of all she'd imbibed, the marble crypt looked like the Trump Tower in a town of one-story buildings. If she glanced to the right or the left, she would see other crypts that were gaudier, larger, sublime. But they didn't exist for her right now. There was only this crypt, occupied by Jack, his parents, his grandparents.

There was space for David and Stephanie inside, but not for her. This was strictly a family affair. The family that's buried together, goes through eternity together, Jack's mother had once said to her. She'd laughed when she said it, but Kate knew it was what she believed. Old lady Bishop, who'd died in a nursing home shortly after she and Jack had married, had been placed inside the crypt with some of her favorite things. Her wedding ring, an emerald brooch, a set of Wedgwood china. A mummy with her gold.

Old lady Bishop sipping tea on the other side.

Jack was buried in a pair of jeans and a workshirt, as he'd stipulated in his will. No coat and tie for Jacky boy, nope, of course not, and no, he wasn't wearing his wedding ring. Stephanie had taken that and given it to Kate. Nice of her. It rested in a zippered compartment in her purse with the fat joint Sammy had slipped to her before he'd left.

Smoke it, he'd said. You'll feel better.

Better than what? Than last night? Last week? Last month? Who cared. She lit it. Drew the sweet smoke deeply into her lungs, held it, coughed. She walked over to the crypt, the soft grass cushioning her footsteps. She let her fingers slide over the engraved letters above the door. The marble was cool, damp from the humidity; the air around it smelled of flowers.

"So what's it like, Jack?" she whispered. "Cold? Dark? Scary? Boring? What? C'mon, you can tell me." She pressed her cheek to the marble, a dot floating across the inside of her lid like the bouncing ball in the old-time sing-a-longs. "Got nothing to say, Jack? C'mon, haunt me. Brush up against me. Breathe on my neck. Convince me there's something, that it isn't just hallucinations."

A breeze rustled the flowers around the crypt.

"Tell me about the tunnel, the goddamn light, the wonderful music, the beings. Tell me about God, Jack."

The crickets cried louder.

"Tell me about Pearl."

She stood there, smoking, waiting. Then she spat at the crypt. "You took nearly four years of my life," she whispered. "And for what?"

Kate dropped what was left of the joint and walked back to the Cherokee. She sat behind the steering wheel, wondering where she should go. Home was safe now, wasn't it? New locks on the doors and windows, a nine-thousand-dollar security system, the mansion sealed up like Fort Knox. Safe, yes, but she would feel like a prisoner inside it.

She could spend the night with the McClearys, but she didn't want to impose on them. Wolfe had offered his spare bedroom, but if she went there they would sleep together, and right now no good could come of it. The truth was that she felt like a liability to her closest friends, that her mere presence in their homes would jeopardize them. So she checked into the Breakers under another name.

Her room cost over three hundred dollars a night and had a Spanish armoire and headboard that dated back to the 1500s. The lock was computerized and she had the only key. She slept better than she had in the month since Jack's murder.

4.

Quin hadn't had a good night's sleep since the beginning of her sixth month and tonight was no exception. She awakened twice with an excruciating pressure on her bladder and couldn't go back to sleep for a long time because she couldn't find a comfortable position. When she finally settled on her side, with a pillow under her stomach, and dozed off, she heard McCleary get up. Merlin immediately jumped onto the bed to claim his spot.

Hepburn, not to be outdone, strolled up Quin's body and settled in the crook of her arm, where she proceeded to preen. Her Persian fur floated through the air like thick motes of dust and made Quin sneeze. "This is real cozy, guys," she said, struggling to a sitting position. "But I'd love to get some sleep." At the sound of her voice, Tracy leaped onto the bed and curled up on her pillow. "Which is clearly impossible." She threw back the covers and got up.

McCleary was in his den, pacing back and forth in front of a large blackboard where they'd been charting everything that had happened in the case. Pinned to the cork strips along the upper edge of it were a copy of the psychological profile Eastman had given him; photographs of both crime scenes; a copy of the photo of Jack and Pearl Hanley that had been on her dresser; and a page from an aviation magazine with a picture of a Citabria on it. Listed on the chalkboard were the numerous facts and variables, including two new sections—CORDOBA/MIGRANT CAMP and ROY FARGO. On the computer screen were the names of the six files they'd been unable to access.

McCleary, paging through Bishop's logbook as he paced, was unaware that she stood in the doorway until she spoke.

"Find anything new?"

He looked up. "Yeah, I think so. Some of the pages have been torn out of here. The more recent entries." He wagged the logbook and grinned. "But other than that, Jack was just being a pilot."

"He was?"

McCleary flipped open the logbook. Every entry listed a flight's point of origin, destination, flight time, and general comments on the trip—weather conditions, flight maneuvers, detours, whatever the pilot deemed pertinent. Since the FAA required certain numbers of hours for various flight ratings, McCleary explained, the logbook was considered a legal document. "I remember how Jack used to talk about how many hours he'd logged and figured that he probably wouldn't cheat himself out of legal hours on these flying parties the caretaker told me about."

He gestured at the chalkboard, under IGLESIA, where he'd jotted three dates. "The caretaker couldn't remember the exact dates when he'd hidden in the barn and watched Jack and his buddies fly off to wherever. These are just approximations. But I think I've found them in the logbook and they weren't torn out because they were last year."

There were six entries: each leg of a round-trip flight was logged. They said RANCH—FLATS or FLATS—RANCH and the flight times varied from ten to twenty minutes, depending on weather and winds aloft.

"But there's nothing out there," Quin said.

"Says Fargo."

"Kate said the same thing."

"I still think we should take a look."

"Right now?"

McCleary laughed and snapped the logbook shut. "First thing tomorrow. And if we're lucky, maybe the lab will have something for us on the contents of the squeeze bottle when we get back."

"Tomorrow. Good. That's a relief. Can we go to bed now?"

He took one last look around the room, reluctant to let it all go. Then he turned off the computer, the lights, and shut the door on their way out, as if he were afraid the information might escape before morning.

20

1.

SHORTLY BEFORE SEVEN Sunday morning, Clicker was parked across the street from St. Mary's Catholic Church, where Frank Abalonee always went to six o'clock mass. Afterward, he would drive over to the Breakers for breakfast.

His ex-wife and daughter often met him there, then the three of them would spend Sunday together. This routine rarely varied. Abalonee was one of those men who thrived on routine, who drew strength and comfort from it. Clicker considered it his greatest weakness.

The church bell tolled at seven on the nose, a plaintive sound that reminded Clicker of the old granddaddy clock that had haunted his childhood. His mother had lived her life by the gongs of that goddamn clock. Up at six, breakfast by seven, everyone out the door by half-past.

The noise of the bell triggered that buzz in his ear again. For an instant, it seemed to become something else, a voice, his mother's voice. He stuck his finger in his ear, moved it fast and hard until the buzzing subsided. He glanced back at the entrance to the church, where people were leaving, and picked up his camera. He rested the lens against the edge of the window and focused on the priest, who was smiling, nodding, shaking hands with his parishioners.

His parents had called themselves Catholics, even though they'd rarely gone to church and had eschewed most of the doctrines. But he had one particularly clear memory of himself and his mother in a church on Saturday evening. She'd made him walk around with her while she did the stations of the cross, bowing her head at each statue, her fingers working the rosary beads, her lips moving in silent prayer while he stood there, his butt stinging from where she'd whipped him before they'd left the house. He could no longer remember why she'd punished him. Most of the time she hadn't seemed to need a reason.

Sometimes small things had set her off. If he came home late from school, if he failed to say *yes, ma'am* and *no, ma'am*, that blackness would descend over her face. She would grab him by the hair and bring out the razor strap and tear down his pants and whip him until he begged her to stop. When he'd reached the point where he endured the whippings without uttering a word, she'd devised new ways to punish him. The locked closet was a favorite. But when she'd realized he didn't mind being in the closet, that he actually enjoyed it because he was alone, away from her, she'd come up with new things. An innovative bitch, his mother.

Abalonee's face appeared in the lens and Clicker focused, snapped the shutter. Spanky Frankie in his expensive threads, his shiny shoes, his designer tie, and those black-frame glasses that were his trademark. Frankie with his big, innocent smile. Hello, Father, your sermon was wonderful.

Clicker wondered if Abalonee had confessed the secret of the flats. *Bless me, Father, for I have sinned.* He could imagine Abalonee getting that far, but Clicker couldn't quite see him divulging the rest. The iniquities he confessed were probably rather ordinary—lustful thoughts, greed, cursing, coveting another man's wife. But he probably tried to atone through his penance—an extra rosary, ten more Our Fathers, perhaps money donated to his favorite charity.

Now Abalonee strolled down the walk, under the trees, hands in his pockets. There was a levity to his stride that was usually absent. Maybe the mass had absolved some of his guilt. Clicker hoped so, for his sake. It would be a shame if Abalonee died with a stained conscience. It was only fair, after all, that he should be allowed to make peace with his God before he died.

The motor drive whirred, catching eight more shots of him before he reached his Mercedes. Clicker set the Nikon aside, waited until Abalonee had driven out of the lot, then followed at a distance. It annoyed him that he was being forced to do this, to clean up another one of Jack's mistakes. Just thinking about it stirred up the anger he'd felt that night at the ranch, when Jack had dismissed his concern with a flick of his hand and a glib, *You want a brew?*

Clicker pressed his foot harder against the accelerator and took a shortcut to the Breakers. He wanted to be there when Abalonee arrived and get a few pictures of him handing his keys to the valet for parking. It was one of those Palm Beach affectations that turned Clicker's stomach.

He parked in the visitors' area, loaded high-speed Tri-X film into the camera, and locked the spent roll in the glove compartment. He sat back to wait for Abalonee. His hand moved absently to his shirt pocket, feeling for the squeeze bottle. One small squirt. For luck. For whatever.

His nostrils tickled in anticipation as he raised the nozzle to his nose. The fingers of his left hand clenched and unclenched against his thigh. Such a dark, sweet thrill, this Bishop magic.

The liquid burned a white-hot path to his brain. He glanced toward the hotel entrance. Colors oozed together like wax, trees blurred, the world tilted to the right, the pavement turned liquid and melted into the grass. The buzzing started as a low whine deep inside his ear and became Pearl whispering: *You did too much, honey, take it from me.*

He wrenched his eyes to the right, to the passenger seat. Pearl was sitting there in the buff, her legs crossed at the knees, her right ankle moving in wide slow circles. Her hair was an electric nimbus around her head. Then she looked at him and he saw her ruined face. Broken teeth, skin hanging in loose flaps, a nostril gone, part of her lip chewed away, an eyeball quivering on her cheek like an uncooked egg. She was dead, but this was real.

He blinked, he squeezed his eyes shut, but when he opened them again, she was still there, shaking a finger at him. "You shouldn't have done it, Click, hon, really. I wasn't going to tell anyone anything."

"You're dead," he hissed.

"And you oughta be," she snapped.

"Don't be nasty, Pearl," admonished a voice from the backseat.

Clicker scrambled around and there was Jack in his blood-stained shirt, Jack smiling, leaning forward. "She's pissed, man, you shouldn't have done her."

He grabbed for the handle, threw open the door, leaped out, stumbled, and ended up on his knees on the warm asphalt. The impact jolted him; he looked around, understood where he was and what would happen if someone saw him. He jumped up, spun, his heart hammering against his ribs, and started to laugh. His car was empty. Of course it was. Empty empty empty, the ghosts were in his head, he had done too much of the drug.

Into the car, he thought. Quick. Get out of here. Go home. Safe at home. Drive slow, real slow. Yes, that's right. Into first. Nice and easy. Now second. Third. Fine, you're doing fine. No cops. Too early for cops.

Two blocks from his house, Jack's face appeared in the rear-view mirror, grinning. "You're going to get caught, ole buddy. You fucked up at Pearl's and left that empty condom pack behind and you shouldn't have taken your beer bottle and you sure as hell shouldn't have gone back there once she was dead, chasing Kate through the house like a maniac, nearly . . ."

Not real not real he's not real none of it is real none . . .

He screeched into his garage, hit the button for the garage door, and was inside the house before it had closed. He ran into the bedroom, shucking his clothes as he went, and leaped into the shower. Cold water. Stinging. Jesus. The floor shifted like sand under his feet. His hands sank into the walls and disappeared to the wrists. "Not real not real," he whispered.

Knuckles rapped at the shower door. His mother. He knew why she was here. He'd broken the rules. The rule of excess, the rule of completing what you start. He would have to be punished. His mother's shadow filled the beveled glass. She demanded that he come out. He told her to go away. She rapped again, harder this time. He started to weep, but he obeyed. He turned off the water. Slid open the door. Wrapped a towel at his waist.

She stood in the doorway, a pack of cigarettes in one hand, the strap in the other.

"Excess, son," she said, and raised the strap.

His mind snapped and he floated away.

When he came to later, he was on the rug at the foot of his bed. In the nearby ashtray were two cigarettes burned to the filter. His skin smarted in a dozen places, spots that wouldn't show when he was dressed.

He had vague memories of his mother's hand pressing the lit cigarettes to his skin, of her voice cutting through him like glass, saying she was sorry she had to hurt him like this, but he needed to learn the rules. Every man needed rules to live by. Did he understand that? Did he? Ask for forgiveness, Clicker, she demanded, tell God you're sorry, go on, say it.

And when he refused, she pressed the cigarette harder against his skin, blowing on the end of it so it glowed.

His eyes swept through the space under the bed, looking for her feet. But he already knew the bitch was gone.

2.

Although the Death Flats weren't on the county map that McCleary kept in his car, the fire tower and the old airstrip were. They lay about twenty-five miles southwest of the Bishop ranch. But he and Quin couldn't locate a road on the map that led to it. The two-lane highway to the migrant camp and the ranch appeared to dead-end ten or twelve miles west of the Bishop property and after that there were only mangroves.

"We're probably going to wish we had a Jeep," Quin remarked as they started out.

"Or a plane."

"Let's rent one at Belle Glade."

"I'd rather not. I have a feeling that word gets around pretty fast out there. The less Fargo knows about what we're doing, the better."

They stopped at a restaurant in the town of Belle Glade so Quin could use the restroom. It appeared to be the local hotspot for Sunday breakfast, eggs and grits and catfish for $1.99. The air stank of hot grease and the coffee smelled burned, but McCleary ordered a cup to go. As he waited for the cashier to ring it up, he saw Roy Fargo and David Bishop getting out of a van in the parking lot. They were yukking it up and looked mighty chummy for a couple of guys who, according to Fargo, knew each other hardly at all. McCleary picked up his coffee, slapped two bucks on the counter, and headed for the side door.

It was in a hallway just off the restrooms, hidden from view by a wall of plants. He stood to one side, watching Fargo and Bishop as they entered the restaurant. The hostess greeted them both by name and said their usual spot was taken today, how about a booth out back? "Sure, whatever, as long as the catfish is good," Bishop replied in Fargo's voice.

The hostess laughed. "Always throws me when you do that, Mr. Bishop."

Yeah, McCleary thought. Like a voice speaking from a burning bush. Maybe God was a ventriloquist.

He ambushed Quin as she hurried from the restroom and they slipped out the side door. "Maybe we should wait around and follow them," she said once they were outside.

"Let's head out to the flats first and we'll swing by the airport on the way back. That's probably where they'll end up."

Fortunately, he'd parked the Miata away from the other cars, where it wouldn't get scratched, and it wasn't in view of the picture windows. As they drove off, Quin said she would never make another snide remark about his fussiness with the car. He could park wherever he wanted, wax the car every day, change the oil every week, he wouldn't hear another peep out of her.

Once they were out of Belle Glade and the trees dropped away behind them, the wind started up. It buffeted the Miata, but the car hugged the road like a spider and on the long stretches of asphalt McCleary opened her up all the way. She shot through the heat, her speedometer climbing.

The scabrous landscape blurred past in shades of deepening brown, the sun poured down, the road stretched to the horizon. Quin, determined to make good on her promise, gripped the seat, her eyes fixed on the road, not uttering a word until the needle brushed one-ten. "I don't think driving was included in my promise, Mac. Could you slow down a little?"

He laughed and kept the speed at seventy until they approached the Bishop ranch. Then he slowed to a crawl and they both glanced at the house, slumbering in the shade of its dying trees. He turned directly south at the ranch and kept an eye on the compass mounted on the dashboard. The road was paved for eight miles, then the pavement didn't so much end as give out, as if from fatigue or indifference.

The ground was packed hard and scarred with dirt-bike tracks. But it was also pitted with potholes and littered with stones and fallen branches from the thin, pathetic clusters of pines that appeared suddenly, growing in no particular pattern.

McCleary angled steadily to the southwest and fifteen miles inland the land dipped suddenly into a steep gully. They got out to see if the Miata could make it across without damaging the undercarriage. A thin stream of water flowed through the gully, vestige of the recent rains. It wouldn't present any problem, but the steep slope on the other side probably would. McCleary decided to follow the gully to the west for a few miles to look for a better place to cross.

Eight miles later the water in the gully turned to mud and they crossed to the other side. Here, the desolation was broken up by mangroves on their right, a wall of green they followed as they backtracked to the southwest again. Not long afterward McCleary spotted the airfield and the fire tower, rising seventy or more feet into the air.

From a distance there was a certain majesty about this man-made structure at the end of a crumbling airfield in the middle of nowhere. But when he pulled alongside it and stopped the car, he could see how the elements had battered it. The wood was rotting, some of the beams had already snapped, and the ladder that shot to the top of it didn't look sturdy enough to support a child.

Beyond it to the south was a clearing, then the mangroves swung inward again, enclosing them and blocking his view. Three hundred yards directly across from the tower, on the other side of the airstrip, were six Quonset huts, crumbling reminders that the army had once used this area for maneuvers. Some of the doors swung open and shut in the wind, their hinges squeaking like mice.

They checked out the huts, refuse piles of empty beer cans,

cellophane wrappers, cigarette butts. High school kids from Belle Glade probably partied out here on weekends, McCleary thought.

"Sorry," Quin said. "But I just can't picture Jack flying out here to suck down beers in a Quonset hut. There's got to be something else."

McCleary agreed. "You bring any other shoes with you?" He pointed to her sandals.

"My running shoes. In the car."

"Why don't you change into them and let's take a look in the mangroves."

She glanced toward the mangroves and made a face, undoubtedly remembering their trip to the Everglades last May. "I'd rather have boots."

"Then you stay here. I'll go take a quick look."

"I've got news for you, Mac. Your looks are never quick. I'll come with you."

McCleary eyed the tower. "I've got a better idea."

She followed his gaze. "Forget it. If you fall, I don't know CPR and we're miles from a hospital."

"Pessimist. It won't take long."

The first half of the climb was easy. The rungs of the ladder hadn't taken the beating the rest of the tower had and didn't so much as creak under his weight. But he made the mistake of looking down at Quin, standing at the foot of the tower, no larger than a doll, and had an attack of vertigo. His vision blurred, his heart pounded, sweat sprang in a wall across his back, nausea churned through him. He clung to the ladder, forcing himself to take deep breaths, his forehead pressed against one of the rungs.

The vertigo passed, but he didn't look down again.

At the top was a square room with walls of pine and glass. The door hung by a single hinge and shards of glass from several broken panes blanketed the floor. McCleary stepped inside, his shoes crunching over glass and dirt and leaves, and gazed south over the Death Flats.

He felt as though he were peering down at a two-dimensional world. Most of the land was paper-flat and utterly devoid of green. The wind had left a million ripples in its wake and had blown the sand into dozens of small, wrinkled dunes. The sun melted over it like butter and heat quivered above it all, tricking the eye, creating the illusion of movement where he was sure nothing had moved in years. It was as if he were seeing the Earth as it might look a millennia from now.

The only relief in the blighted terrain was the mangrove swamp that bordered the flats. It began suddenly to the north of here, an oasis of green that leaped up from all the brown, curved in toward the tower, then angled gradually outward again and south for God knew how many miles and as far west as he could see. If there was a road out there that led through the groves or around it, it wasn't visible from here.

He moved closer to the western window. The wind skipped over and through the thick canopy of branches directly below him, rustling leaves, permitting him an occasional glimpse of water. But as he started to turn away, a glimmer caught his eyes. It was sharper and brighter than sunlight on water, he thought. More like sunlight glinting off metal.

He worked loose a jagged piece of glass in the wood, then stuck his head through the opening to see better. There. The same glint. He moved to the other side of the room, spotted the car, then estimated the distance through the trees. A mile tops.

Even Quin could stand a mile.

3.

She didn't mind insects. She didn't mind sighting an occasional snake as long as it was headed away from her. She didn't even mind sloshing through mud. But she wasn't crazy about doing any of it when she was hungry, and right now she was ravenous.

The mile McCleary had estimated seemed much longer, but probably because they didn't move in a straight line. They twisted and backtracked, following a spit of dry land that wouldn't exist at all if the rains really began. When the mangroves began to thin, dry spots pushed up from the muck like the humps of turtles' backs. Then the mangroves gave way to scraggly pines, palms, ficus, and, finally, dry land.

They came out into a small clearing with a low roof of

braided ficus branches that hid the area from above. The ground was dotted with the stumps of trees that had been chopped down and hauled off. To the south was a tunnel of green that looked as though it had been hollowed out by the wind or machetes or both. She guessed it led to a road over which the trailers had traveled.

A pair of trailers, backed up to the wall of trees at the east. They were old and rusted, one about eighteen feet long, the other no more than twelve. Their doors were padlocked, their windows covered in dust. But there was no question that they were used. Attached to each were a gas tank, probably for a stove, and a forty-gallon water tank. The padlock on the longest trailer didn't stand a chance against a shot from McCleary's Magnum. The explosion echoed, startling a pair of snowy egrets from the trees.

It was hot inside the trailer and the air smelled of mildew. The kitchen table and booths were coated in a layer of dust and an army of ants crawled around the sink. But the empty milk carton in the garbage dated November 8 said the place had been used in the last few months. What it had been used for was anybody's guess.

While McCleary looked through the back of the trailer, Quin checked the pint-sized fridge, which was clean as a whistle. In the cabinets she found a package of paper plates and another of paper cups and a receipt from a Publix supermarket for $82.05, mostly for canned goods and nonconsumable items like matches and candles.

"Hey, Quin, c'mere for a second."

She walked down the short hallway, past a bathroom no larger than a closet, to the small room where McCleary was. The air back here was stifling; very little light penetrated the dust on the window. All kinds of things were piled on top of the cot against the wall—sheets and blankets, pots and pans, boots, old shoes, men's jeans. McCleary was at the head of the cot, holding up a black robe.

"Look at this."

"Yeah, so?"

He slipped it over his head. A hooded cloak, with slits for the eyes, nose, and mouth. "Weird, huh."

200

"Halloween," she said.

"Darth Vader." He pulled the robe off and tossed it back on the cot. "High school kids playing *Star Wars* out here. That's all this place is."

And the army had probably left the trailers when they departed. Of course. Reasonable explanations. But she knew he didn't believe it any more than she did.

21

CLICKER'S CAR ROLLED up and down the deserted streets, the warm night air washing through the open windows. The air smelled good, clean, of beginnings and endings.

It was three hours before sunrise, the best time, the darkest time. The night eased his insomnia and the sting of the wounds his mother had inflicted. Darkness would heal him, protect him; it always had. It also spoke to him of the small, urgent pressures building just beneath the surface of his life. Because he'd followed Jack's rules.

But tonight he would follow his own rules again.

The expensive neighborhood he turned into was like so many in Palm Beach. Clipped lawns the drought had barely touched, sprawling homes, tall hedges bursting with color. This wasn't oceanside living. But it was close enough. That meant patroling cops, no vehicles parked at curbs overnight, no empty lots where he could ditch his car. It made things more challenging.

He turned down a side street and nosed into an alley that ran behind a block of homes. He doused his headlights. The glow of the moon was sufficiently bright to see the thick, billowing shoots of bougainvillea vines that spilled over backyard fences and walls. Trees rose against the sky, tall and graceful sentries of another race. Their arms reached down into the alley as if to touch him.

Before he reached the end, Clicker steered his car close to the fence on his right and stopped in the depression formed where it curved inward. Perfect. The car would be seen only if someone drove through the alley.

From the glove compartment, he removed a pair of latex

gloves, a Walther with a silencer for backup, and a slingshot with a sling that was longer than the one he normally used. He picked up a palm-sized rock on the floor and slipped it inside his windbreaker pocket with the silencer and put the gun in another pocket. He checked the pouch attached to his belt to make sure he had the proper tools, then kicked off his loafers and put on his black canvas shoes.

His killing shoes.

From the backseat, he retrieved his Nikon, hooked the strap over his neck, and started down the alley to Abalonee's home on the next block. In its way a camera was as powerful as a gun. Christopher Wilder had known that; he'd called himself a fashion photographer and had used his camera to lure young women whom he later tortured and killed. Clicker had followed Wilder's cross-country spree with great interest, but in the end Wilder had disappointed him. He'd lost control and had been shot down like some two-bit criminal in a gas-station parking lot in New Hampshire. Clicker did not intend to make the same mistake. His earlier lapse in the Breakers parking lot had frightened him deeply. It would not happen again. Control was everything.

And tonight he would use his camera in a way he never had before.

But as he walked, the squeeze bottle in his tool pouch whispered to him, called to him. Alice's mushroom. The drug had been Jack's camouflage, his lure. His true legacies were the darker, uglier thrills on the flats that had created a camaraderie of corruption among the people who had participated, a corruption of the spirit, a bond of malignant silence. And he'd gone too far. A secret wasn't a secret when more than two people knew about it.

He didn't reach into his pouch. The drug stopped calling to him.

He reached the stucco wall that surrounded Abalonee's place, scaled it easily, dropped soundlessly into the yard. His pores breathed with a sudden freedom, as though he were on the flats again. The trees spoke to him. The grass welcomed him. He sniffed at the air like an animal, alert for menace, surprise, the unexpected—a ferocious dog, a nosy neighbor, a cop car nearby. He sensed nothing and knew he was blessed.

Clicker passed the swimming pool. It caught the reflection of the moon, a gold pendant ringed by clouds, and held his own dark shadow. He snapped on the gloves, flexed his fingers, smiled when the AC unit outside clicked on. It masked the sound of his screwdriver jimmying the lock on the sliding glass door.

He knew the layout of the house; he'd been here a few times with Jack lifetimes ago. His killing shoes crept soundlessly across the living-room floor. The den was off to his right, the half-bath to the left. Yes, it was coming back to him now.

Outside the bedroom door, he paused, brought out the gun, screwed on the silencer. Abalonee wouldn't argue with a gun. His killing shoes sank into the thick carpeting in the bedroom. He felt a brief stab of regret for old Frankie. His only sin was a single night on the flats, which had made him privy to things he had no business knowing.

He thought suddenly of Abalonee's daughter and was sorry she would grow up without a father. Fathers were essential; mothers could be replaced. But he would make amends for that. His son and Kate's would have a father. He would be a model father.

He stepped through the doorway. Neared the bed. Excitement spurted through him. Thanks to the night light in the bathroom—a night light, for Christ's sakes, like a kid—he could see the shape under the sheets. Abalonee's glasses were on the nightstand next to a glass of water and a paperback book. He was on his side, knees drawn up, mouth silently open. Quite a sleeper.

Clicker turned on the lamp, then grabbed Abalonee's hair and jerked his head to the side hard enough so that his body had to follow. Abalonee stuttered, blinked, struggled until Clicker jammed the gun to his throat, then tears swam in his eyes. The sight of them disgusted Clicker. Nothing worse than a grown man who cried when he knew he was going to die, and Abalonee knew, all right, Clicker could smell it on him.

He let go of Abalonee's hair, unsnapped the cover from the camera, focused for the close-up. He snapped photographs without peering through the lens, the gun still up against Aba-lonee's throat.

"Smile, Frankie. For posterity."

"Pl-please," he whispered.

"It's not your turn to talk yet. You'll get your turn. I promise. I'm going to be fair about this. I believe in fairness, really I do. I need to ask you a couple of questions first, though, Frankie. And I know you'll answer them truthfully, because if you don't, your larynx is going to be on this pillow. We understand each other, Frankie?"

"Y-yes."

"What'd you tell the McCleary woman at the brunch?"

"Nothing. I . . . I swear."

"Then what were you talking about for so long?"

"About Jack. How . . . how we went to school together."

"Put your arms at your sides, palms up, Frankie."

"W-why?"

"Do it!"

His arms flopped against the bed like dead fish, palms turned up. Clicker was pleased he'd followed instructions. He kept the gun against his throat as he straddled Abalonee, a knee pressed to either palm. Abalonee grimaced and Clicker took a picture of him in pain. Without the use of his other hand, though, he couldn't frame these photos or experiment with light and shadow. What you saw was what you got. He was sure Kate wouldn't mind.

"Pl-please. I never said anything t-to anyone."

"And I bet it's been a real tough secret to keep, hasn't it, Frankie. I bet you haven't even told it in confession, have you."

"N-no."

"You're lying. I can see it in your face. I don't like liars, Frankie. Jack was a liar and I didn't like him, either. I think you've probably told someone about the flats because you had to. Maybe to that pretty ex-wife of yours?"

"N-no."

"How about to Quin McCleary?"

"No."

"Kate. I bet you told Kate."

"N-no, I swear." Sniffling. Tears coursing down his cheeks.

"Stop your blubbering, asshole." With his free hand, he pulled the rock from his windbreaker pocket. "Say, ah, Frankie."

"W-what?"

"Open your goddamn mouth."

He did. Clicker fit the rock into his mouth and told him to bite down, but not too hard. "Like you're at the dentist, Frankie, and he's taking an impression of your teeth. Very good." His lips closed around the circumference of the rock. "Nice fit. Perfect fit. That rock was made for you, Frankie." He snapped three more photos. "Now I'm going to ask you a couple more questions and all you have to do is blink. Once if the answer is yes, two if it's no. Got it?"

Blink. His eyes bulged in his cheeks, he was breathing noisily through his nostrils and trying to suck air in around the rock.

"Did Jack tell you anything or entrust you with anything before he was killed?"

Blink, blink. Fast, too fast. "Frankie, Frankie. I'm real disappointed in you." He pulled out his slingshot and snapped the sling close to Abalonee's nose. "But because I'm such a nice guy and because I care about being fair, I'm going to give you another chance." Clicker leaned close to him, so close he felt Abalonee's terror leaping from the pores of his skin. "One more time, buddy. Did Jack give you something before he died?"

Blink.

"Are you saying yes just because you're scared shitless?"

Blink. Blink.

"It's the truth?"

Blink.

Clicker eased the rock from Abalonee's mouth. He gasped, sobbed, whimpered, "D-don't k-kill me. I didn't say anything t-to anyone about anything. Ever. I . . . I wouldn't. You know that. I wouldn't . . ."

Clicker popped the sling at his nose again, silencing him. "What'd Jack give you?"

"Key. T-to a locker. Amtrak station. I . . . Please, don't d-do this."

"What's in the locker?"

"Dunno." He sniffed again.

"What'd he say to you when he gave you the key?"

"He . . . he asked me to h-hold on to it for a while. He said he knew I . . . I wouldn't try to double-cross him. That I wouldn't look in the locker. That i-if something happened to him, I . . . I should g-give the key to Kate. Please d-don't hu-hurt me . . ."

"Where's the key? Did you give it to Kate?"

"I lost it."

Clicker smelled the lie on him. "Wrong answer, Frankie. It's a sin to lie, you know. You've got five seconds."

"I . . . I was too ashamed to give it to Kate, so I g-gave it to Quin McCleary."

Clicker's rage was abrupt, fierce, a rush of blood in his head, and he suddenly wasn't holding the gun anymore. He was slamming the rock against Abalonee's mouth, into his mouth, and then he was stretching the rubber on the sling as far as it would go and tightening it at Abalonee's throat, his knees still impaling Abalonee's hands, his body still straddling Abalonee's body, holding him against the mattress as he struggled. Blood poured from his ruined mouth, around the sides of the rock. He bucked and shrieked and twisted, trying to throw Clicker off. He got one of his hands loose and clawed at Clicker's hands and arms and shirt, anything he could grab.

Clicker hardly noticed. He was eaten up by his fury, by this singular mission to fix Jack's mistakes, so many goddamn mistakes, one after another, Pearl and Kate and Abalonee and the flats, year after year he would uncover more mistakes, maybe for the rest of his life he would be cleaning up for Jack the bastard who wouldn't listen to him or anyone.

His vision shrank until only the throat and the length of rubber existed. Rubber slicing through skin, blood bubbling up, red and frothy. It became Jack's throat. Abalonee became Jack dying over and over for using him, for actualizing his darkest fantasies, for bringing in the others, for leaving him no choice but to fix all these mistakes. It wasn't fair. He hadn't asked for this role, hadn't wanted it, but Jack had thrust it on him.

The reek of blood nauseated him and Clicker let go of the sling. He rocked back onto his heels, shocked that he was crying, that his shoulders shook with deep, silent sobs. He slid his hands under Jack's head, cradling it, rocking him, whispering to him, apologizing, trying to explain, listen, please, Jack, just listen.

But Jack gazed up with his dead, dead eyes, his mouth curled around the rock. Clicker's stomach heaved and he barely made it to the toilet before he puked. Scenes from the flats raced across the insides of his eyes, bright and terrible and thrilling. He pushed to his feet, fumbled for the light, stared at himself in the mirror. He was splattered with blood. Jack's blood. Abalonee's blood. Pearl's blood. He tore off his clothes, kicked off his killing shoes, stumbled into the shower.

Hot needles stung his skin. The buzzing whined through his head, he heard his mother laughing at him, but he didn't look around for her. He kept his eyes pinned on the floor of the shower, where blood swirled pink down the drain. He stood there until the water turned cool, then cold, until his mind was clear.

He washed the rubber gloves. Snapped them on again. Scrubbed the shower with Comet. He wiped down the door handles, the light switch, the walls. He stuffed his clothes, the towel, and the bathmat into the wastebasket, then removed the white trash bag, tied it shut, carried it into the bedroom with him.

Something to wear.

He flung open the closet door. Jerked a shirt from a hanger, then a windbreaker, jeans. Nothing fit right. The shirt was too short in the sleeves, the jeans too tight in the crotch, the windbreaker puckered at the shoulders. But he would make do. He had always made do.

His gun and camera were still on the bed, the sling was around Abalonee's throat. Quick. Get them off. Get out of here. He heard his mother's voice warning him about what would happen if he didn't clean up after himself, if he didn't finish the job right. The Rule of Completion. Yes yes yes, he knew all about it.

He shoved the gun into the white trash bag. Unwrapped the sling from Abalonee's throat, wiped the blood on the sheet, stuck it in his pocket. He grabbed the camera, held it up for one last shot, snapped it. Then he shut Abalonee's eyes.

Home again.

Clicker dug a hole next to a tree in the backyard. He took his clothes from the trash bag, cut them into tiny pieces, buried them under a layer of black earth, then dropped in the gun and the silencer. But not the slingshot. It still had work to do.

He filled the hole. Raked leaves and twigs over the surface. It was nearly dawn. Not much time. He went directly to his darkroom, developed his film, printed up the best photographs of Abalonee. He selected two of these and one from the batch he'd taken outside the church yesterday morning. He put them in a large envelope like before.

"You call that fair?" his mother asked. "He's already dead."

His head snapped up. She was leaning against the far wall, a leather strap doubled in her hand. "Go away."

"*Fair* is sending the pictures before he's dead. Clicker. Anyone knows that."

His eyes were on the strap. "That would warn him. And them."

She grinned. Dirt was stuck between her teeth. "If you're worried about warning them, then you're admitting they're smarter than you. Better than you. That they'll figure things out before you get to them. That's where Jack had it all over you. Clicker. He took risks. Big risks. He played the game the way it's supposed to be played. You're just playing a poor imitation."

"But I sent the pictures of the McClearys."

"That's true. You did." She moved toward him, tapping the strap against her open palm. "But they're still alive, Clicker. They've been warned, but they're still alive. So what good is that? You're just a coward. You always were."

The strap lashed out at him, but he was ready for it. He

leaped to the side. It whistled past his ear and his mother laughed and laughed, clumps of dirt falling from her hair. "Coward," she whispered. "Coward. You thought the flats would make you a man, but they didn't, did they, Clicker. And having Jack's wife won't make you a man, either."

He grabbed a tray of developer and hurled it at her. She dissolved. The tray struck the door, developer splashed against the walls, splattering his pictures of Kate, of Pearl, of Jack. His wonderful pictures, ruined ruined ruined. His mother's laughter rose and fell in the cool air, then the room was silent and he was alone again.

He dropped to his knees, slid open the door, removed the panel at the back. He reached into the hole, withdrew a box, dumped out the photographs. *His* legacy. The flats, all of it, right here. And photos of Pearl and Kate and the Mc-Clearys.

Clicker rubbed his thumb over Quin's tummy. Such a pretty tummy. He would love to see it bare. And such pendulous breasts, outlined against the thin filament of the blouse she was wearing. He thought of holding those breasts, touching them, sucking on them, thought of climbing inside her where the baby was, where the baby swam in that sweet, amniotic world.

At one time, he'd had an ordinary life with ordinary pursuits, a life inhabited by friends and goals and dreams. But Jack had changed all that. Now his life was divided. He lived one way in daylight, another way in the dark. Part of him was scattered across the flats, where he was a participant, a collaborator, a conspirator. The rest of his life was here, surrounded by the evidence of what he'd become.

Observer.

Historian.

Blackmailer.

Madman.

22

1.

ON THE MORNING of December 17, Kate checked out of the Breakers, where she'd spent Sunday night, feeling more rested and positive about things than she had in days. It was nice to stop at her own mailbox, pull out the bundle of mail, and better yet to swing into her own driveway.

The house still looked as though it had been designed by an architect with dyslexia, but she didn't care. She no longer thought of it as the home she and Jack had shared; it was *her* home, with her things in it, her memories. When she left, it would be her choice to do so and not because Jack's killer had frightened her into leaving.

Some of her buoyancy left her when she saw Eastman's Caddy parked off to the side, in the Cherokee's space, and there he was, sitting on the front porch. He'd known she'd been staying at the Breakers, she'd told him, and he hadn't called, hadn't bothered her. But now it was ten o'clock Monday morning and her reprieve had ended. It was time to get on with business. Murder and mayhem. The old dread crept through her.

"You look good," he said, tipping his sunglasses back onto the top of his head as she approached.

"I should. All I did was eat and sleep and bake in the sun. How about some coffee?"

"Love some."

As she turned her key in the new lock, she could almost hear the hum of the computerized security system. Inside, the air was cool and still and undisturbed. Kate tapped a couple of buttons on the security panel, disengaging the system. She noticed Eastman's quizzical expression. "You think I'm being paranoid, Fitz?"

"Not at all. I was just wondering why you stayed at the Breakers with this place sealed up like it is."

"I would've felt like a prisoner here."

"Damned if you do, damned if you don't."

"Something like that." She tossed the mail on the kitchen table and put on a pot of coffee. Eastman didn't chatter about the weather or the smell of the coffee or about how he'd spent his weekend. He simply sat at the table waiting for her. When she joined him with the mugs of coffee, his question surprised her. "Did Jack do drugs?"

"He smoked an occasional joint. Why?"

"Late yesterday afternoon I got the analysis from the lab on the contents of that squeeze bottle Quin found in the train-station locker Saturday. One of the primary ingredients was an androgen, specifically a sex hormone, which matched what was in Jack's bloodstream and in Pearl's."

Jack and Pearl: how melodic their names sounded when uttered in the same breath, she thought, as if they were a show business couple. George Burns and Gracie Allen. Liz and Richard. Lucy and Desi. "What were the other ingredients?"

"Cocaine, LSD, Spanish fly. There were traces of a fifth element identical to a drug the state lab in Tallahassee has been puzzling over for months. Homemade stuff that was seized at a drug bust where Garrison was present. It's the link we needed. It doesn't prove that he's guilty, but it's enough to suspend him pending an investigation. His boss will be notified later today by someone in Internal Affairs."

"Does it clear me?"

"No. But it casts enough doubt on the charge against you to force the D.A.'s office to open an investigation on a case they thought was tied up. It's a step in the right direction, Kate."

"My gun still killed him, Fitz."

He nodded, sipped from his mug. "And it's up to us to find enough additional evidence against Garrison to make that fact almost immaterial."

Almost. As in *almost* certain, *almost* dead. It was one of those qualifying words she detested.

"Mike is supposed to meet with the girlfriend of one of the missing migrants today. I'm hoping that will lead us to some additional ammunition against Garrison."

"Suppose it doesn't?"

"Then you just go about your normal routine. If you hear from Garrison, let me know. Otherwise stay out of his way. I'd feel a lot better if you weren't staying in this house by yourself."

She started to protest, but he held up a hand. "Hey, I know how you feel, okay? But I can't predict how Garrison is going to react to this. We removed surveillance yesterday after we got the lab report and initiated the paperwork on the suspension. But until we're over this hump, I wish you'd stay with the McClearys."

"I'm not going to jeopardize them, Fitz."

"Fine. Then you and Quin stay at the Breakers for a couple nights."

"You don't know Quin. Besides, Garrison's not going to do anything to me now. Or to Quin or to McCleary or anyone. He wouldn't dare."

Eastman sighed. It was obvious he'd heard this same line or one like it a number of times over the years. "Do yourself a favor, Kate. Don't underestimate Garrison."

She thought of the silhouette with the valentine-shaped heart in the shooting gallery, of the bullets she'd gone through. "And don't underestimate me, Fitz."

He smiled. "I never underestimate women. All I'm asking is that you think about it, Kate." The beeper attached to his belt interrupted him. "Mind if I use your phone?"

"No, go ahead."

She refilled their mugs as he called his office, then looked through the mail. Most of it was for Jack, naturally. His magazines and newsletters, his brochures and catalogs. Sooner or later, she was going to have to attend to the functional details of death—cancel subscriptions, notify social security, clean his clothes from the closet. But not today.

Kate opened a large envelope and shook the contents onto

the table. Three photos slid out. She stared at them, but her brain refused to process what she was looking at, so she kept staring, waiting for the details to click into place, willing it to happen, and it did. Click, click, click, it happened just that fast. A mouth. A mouth with a rock in it. A throat squeezed bloody. Abalonee.

A noise started deep in her throat, a noise that wasn't quite human, and she pushed away from the table so fast, her chair toppled. It crashed to the floor, startling Eastman, who spun around as she backed away from the table, her hands curled up under her chin. She knew she was still making that horrid noise. She knew it was bursting from her mouth despite her best effort to stop it, swallow it, kill it, shove it back down into the private place where it belonged. It fluttered through the room's silence, not a scream or a shout, but a soft, pathetic wail.

She backed into the edge of the counter, turned, and vomited into the sink. Eastman came up behind her, ran water, wet a towel, and pressed it to her neck. She stood there, leaning over the sink, hands holding up her head, eyes squeezed shut, her tongue thick and sour. Then she straightened up, put her own hand to the towel, and slid it around to her throat, her cheeks, her eyes.

"They've already found him, haven't they? That's what the call was," she said.

"Yes." That was all, just a straight, simple yes.

"Where?"

"At home."

Naturally. Like Jack and Pearl. Killed at home, at night. "Would you stay here for five minutes while I get some clean clothes? Then I'm going over to Quin's."

"You bet."

She took the stairs two at a time, heard him on the phone again, speaking with McCleary. In the bedroom she jerked shirts and skirts and jeans off hangers, shoved them in a shopping bag, tossed it on the bed. She yanked open drawers, pulled out underwear, bras, slips, scooped up shoes from the closet floor. Everything went into the bag. Between these things and what was already in her suitcase, she had enough clothes to outlast this bastard. And what she didn't have, she would buy.

On her way past the bureau, she slapped the framed picture of Jack facedown. When the glass broke, she picked it up, tore out the photo. She ripped it in half, ripped again and again and again. The pieces rained down around her, a corner of his mouth, the tip of his nose, an eye gazing up at her as she fled.

2.

The housekeeper who'd found Abalonee's body was a hefty Jamaican woman who looked as though she didn't spook easily, McCleary thought. But she was clearly upset about this, dabbing at her eyes, shifting her mammoth buttocks around on the kitchen chair, trying to answer Eastman's questions.

". . . he was supposed to be in Europe, was supposed to leave early this morning, uh-huh, he was, I know it was today he was going to leave. Got it posted right up there on the refrigerator so I wouldn't forget. Easy to forget these things, Mr. Abalonee traveling as much as he does. Three months in Europe on business. Last two weeks he's been in New York, came back for a funeral, then he was leaving again. I know I've got that right."

"I'm sure you do," Eastman assured her. "Did he seem worried about anything to you, ma'am?"

She blew her nose noisily into a red kerchief. "Mr. Abalonee was always worried about one thing or another. That's how he was, fretting all the time about his business. Don't know why, you can see he did real well." She opened her flabby arms, the gesture encompassing the entire house filled with antiques. "But Mr. Bishop's killing got him real depressed." Her head bobbed; it made her double chin quiver.

"Did he ever talk about Mr. Bishop with you?" McCleary asked, stepping forward.

"Yes, sir. Sometimes. Sure. Said he was in deep trouble that maybe even the Lord couldn't forgive him for. But the times I seen Mr. Bishop, he didn't look like no man in deep trouble. Real nice, real friendly, hi Mattie, how's it going, how're the kids, like that. Tell the truth, I think Mr. Abalonee was afraid of Mr. Bishop. Uh-huh, that's what I think, all right. He was a funny man, shore enough, afraid of all sorts of things. Here he was, a pilot, but he was afraid of flying on the big jets even though he did it all the time."

"Did Mr. Abalonee own a small plane?" Eastman asked.

"He sold it. Said he didn't have no time for it. But, oh my, what a nice plane it was. Took me for a ride once, he did, and that plane she just lifted right up off the water, a big black bird—"

"He flew a black seaplane?" McCleary interrupted.

"Yes, sir."

"Did it have a design on the side of it?"

The folds in her face creased deeply as she frowned, thinking. "It did, that's right. It was a funny ole thing, a creature that was half bird, half lion."

"You have any idea who he sold it to?" McCleary asked, excited now.

"No, sir."

The FAA, McCleary thought, would have a record of the sale, but without a call number, it would be impossible to trace. "Do you know where Mr. Abalonee kept his logbook?"

"Sir?"

"You know, the book he wrote in whenever he flew."

"Oh. That. Sure. He burned it."

"Burned it? Why?"

"Said he was finished with flying. Don't know why. He did strange things sometimes."

While Eastman finished questioning her, McCleary walked to the back of the house. Forensics was already busy in the bedroom and adjoining bath and no one had moved Abalonee yet. He was lying in a pool of sunlight and dried blood on the king-size bed where he'd died. His mouth was closed around a rock. His throat and neck were crusted with so much blood, it was impossible to tell what had killed him—the rock, a knife, or something else.

His eyes were closed. Like Jack's, like Pearl's. Such brutality, he thought, but the killer had stuck around to shut Abalonee's eyes. Why? Because he couldn't stand the vacant stare of death? Because it was the right thing to do? Because he felt sorry for him? Because his religion said a dead man's eyes should be closed?

It was the kind of gesture rooted in the unconscious, McCleary thought, and the reasons were as singular and distinct as the perpetrators. But he sensed he was missing something obvious that connected with information he had read or heard. The answer pressed up against the edge of his thoughts, teasing him, but when he reached for it, it skipped away from him, as elusive as the killer.

He stepped into the bathroom, watching a woman on the forensics team who was on her hands and knees on the floor, picking up hairs with a tool similar to a pair of tweezers. "Have you been able to lift any prints?" he asked.

"Sure." She didn't look up. "There're always prints. But whether any of them are what we're looking for is something else again, isn't it." She dropped another hair into a plastic bag, sealed it, rocked back onto her heels, and looked at him. "I'll tell you one thing, though. I think he did something different this time. He took a shower after he killed him, then scrubbed down everything he touched with Comet." She gestured toward the container of Comet on the edge of the sink. "The shower was gritty with the stuff."

"Maybe Abalonee cleaned the shower himself."

She shook her head. "Housekeeper says he never lifted a finger to clean. According to her, the container of Comet stays under the sink unless she's here, and when she's finished, she always puts it back. I also got some tissue from under the victim's nails. Maybe we'll get a blood type this time. I'd say things are looking better." Then she smiled and got up and walked into the other room.

As far as McCleary was concerned, things would look better only when they had a name.

When he returned to the kitchen, the Jamaican woman was sitting alone at the table. She lifted one of her immense arms and pointed to the sliding glass door. Eastman and Garrison stood near the swimming pool, looking as though they were about to come to blows. Garrison was hoisting his slacks with one hand and waving the other toward the house. His mouth was moving, but McCleary couldn't hear what he was saying.

Garrison shut up as soon as McCleary stepped outside, looked at him, then at Eastman. "He's got no business being here." As though McCleary weren't present.

"And like I just finished saying, Lou, neither do you." Eastman's voice strained with patience. "Now why don't you just march your ass on over to the station and talk to the captain about things."

Garrison's cheeks turned tomato-red. "Homicide is my department and IAD is yours." He rocked forward, stabbing at Eastman's chest with his index finger. "You got that, nigger boy?"

Eastman knocked Garrison's hand away from his chest. "I've got news for you, pal. You've been suspended. You just don't know it yet." He started to walk away, but Garrison, itching for a fight, grabbed his arm and took a swing at him. Eastman was quicker. His arm flew up, blocking the punch, then he decked Garrison. The lieutenant stumbled, lost his footing at the edge of the pool, and fell back, arms flailing, face seized up with surprise.

He struck the water hard, sank, came up sputtering and shouting obscenities. Eastman stood there until he finished, then pointed at the side gate. "Leave that way, Lou. Can't have you tracking up the floor, huh?" Then he and McCleary went back inside, Eastman grinning and murmuring, "Goddamn, but that felt good."

3.

"This is the last thing I feel like doing," Kate said, referring to the seminar on death and dying.

Quin turned into the visitors' lot at West Palm General Hospital. "It'll keep you occupied for three hours. It's better than moping around the house."

"Yeah, I suppose." She sounded anything but convinced.

They got out and started toward the entrance. Quin looked over at her. Petite Kate in her round sunglasses, her flowered skirt and pale pink blouse, Kate with her shiny black curls, her quick gait, her salubrious good looks. Quin had always felt enormous beside her, the friendly giant. But now it was worse. Now she was the fat lady who waddled, who puffed to keep pace.

"Did I mope with Jack?" Kate asked. "Or nag him? Was I a bitch?"

Quin sighed. "No, Katie. You didn't mope or nag and you weren't a bitch. Jack was the one with the problems, not you."

"But I married him."

"Which means he had some redeeming qualities."

"But why'd he marry me? He couldn't have been in love with me, Quin. He didn't need me."

"That's bullshit." Quin stopped. Kate stopped. "He needed you worse than you ever needed him, you just don't know it yet. You anchored him, Katie. You provided the reality to balance whatever weirdness he was involved in. That's why he was so careful about you never finding out about Pearl. Think about it. Did he ever get hang-up calls at the house? Did he ever reject you sexually? Did you ever smell perfume in his car? Did he ever come home late at night and not tell you where he'd been?"

Kate kept shaking her head, and in a way, Quin envied the ignorance she'd lived with until Jack's death. She'd known about Sylvia Callahan almost from the beginning because McCleary's guilt had eaten him alive. But Bishop hadn't felt remorse or guilt over any of it. His life had been neatly compartmentalized and he'd made sure none of the niches had overlapped. He'd like things tidy. He'd liked having Kate in this peg, Pearl in that one, his professional life here, his ranch parties there, and his flying activities elsewhere. His life, like the mystery of his death, was as sectioned as an orange. Once they found all the pieces and put them together, they would have the truth—and his killer.

Since they were early for the seminar and this was the hospital where Quin would be having the baby, she suggested they go upstairs to the maternity ward. Unlike the rest of the hospital, Maternity was bright and cheerful and everyone smiled. Several women in hospital gowns moved slowly along the hall, obviously in some pain from episiotomy stitches or C-sections. Quin was encouraged that none of them looked fat.

Maybe Sammy Dayton was right about losing fifteen pounds as soon as you gave birth.

A few parents and grandparents stood in front of the nursery window, tapping on the glass, oohing and aahing and whispering. The babies occupied blue and pink bassinets lined up in rows, and all of them looked vaguely Oriental, their tiny features swollen and pink and perfect. Most were sleeping on their stomachs or on their sides, up against rolled blankets. A few were crying, their little fists beating at the air until one of the nurses picked them up.

"Look at her fingers," Kate whispered, pointing at the girl in the bassinet closest to them.

Her shell-pink hands were open against the sheet, the diminutive nails so white they were nearly transparent. "Born with a perfect manicure," Quin whispered back, and they laughed.

But for the rest of the day, the image of those Lilliputian hands and fingers and nails stayed with her, as bright as the future.

Quin stood at the back of the auditorium waiting for Kate, who was still down in front with Sammy Dayton, talking to a group of nurses. She was digging in her purse for stray Cheerios, a stick of gum, a mint, anything to stave off starvation. The seminar had lasted four hours instead of three and all the talk of death and dying had left her famished, as though hunger were her body's way of affirming life.

Someone touched her shoulder, startling her, and she spun, almost expecting to see the man who had sent the photographs. But it was only Wolfe, looking guilty for having startled her.

"Sorry. I didn't mean to creep up on you like that, Quin."

"I'm just jumpy these days." A cloud of after-shave floated around him. "What is that stuff you're wearing, anyway? I should get Mac some."

His gray eyes brightened. "Yeah? You like it? Kate bought me a bottle years ago. She thought it was erotic, so I just kept on wearing it. It's called Night Musk." In the same breath he asked what she'd thought of the seminar.

"I decided that when I go, it's got to be fast and painless, Ray. A heart attack while I'm sleeping. A plane crash."

"I'm with you." He glanced down toward the front of the auditorium, fingers combing nervously at his mustache, and stole a furtive glance at his pocket watch, the white rabbit fretting about time. Quin had the distinct impression he was killing time with her until Kate finished, so it wouldn't look as if he were waiting for her. "But forget the plane crash part," he went on as though there had been no break in the conversation. "I hate to fly. And I bet those final eight or ten seconds as the plane's screeching down are a bitch. Listen, Quin, I was wondering, has Kate mentioned me to you since the three of us were out Friday?"

"She mentions you all the time."

"Really?" The hope in his voice was unmistakable. "In what context?"

Not in the context he would like. "Give her time, Ray."

He shoved his hands in his pockets, his grin sheepish. "I guess I'm always trying to rush things." He started to say something else, but Kate and Dayton joined them. "What was that all about?" Wolfe asked Dayton, nodding toward the dispersing group of nurses they'd been talking to.

"ICU nurses," Dayton replied. "One of them had an older male patient who reported a negative NDE and she wanted to know why there wasn't more written on that aspect of the experience."

"Because it just doesn't happen that often," Wolfe replied.

"Or if it does," Dayton said, "we don't hear about it because the person's so glad to be alive, he doesn't want to talk about it."

Like Pearl Hanley, Quin thought.

"Excuse me," Kate said, and walked out.

Quin and Wolfe stared after her. "What's eating her?" Wolfe asked.

Dayton kneaded a muscle at the back of his neck and didn't look at either of them as he spoke. "Over the weekend, the trustees voted to suspend her."

23

1.

IT DIDN'T MATTER that McCleary had driven this same road during the day. At night, it was another country.

A full moon floated in the windshield like a luminous plate, lighting a landscape surreal in its barrenness. Few trees, no bushes over a foot tall, just the unrelieved flatness of high grass rustling in the wind. This was the kind of place where anything seemed possible—an alien craft landing soundlessly in the middle of the dusty road, a bush bursting into flame, a headless horseman galloping past them in the opposite direction.

The Miata's tires churned up dust that settled on the windshield, the hood, and drifted through the vents. The inside of the car was gritty with it. They were so far from anywhere, the radio emitted nothing but static.

"How much farther?" Quin asked.

McCleary glanced at the odometer. "Another five miles to the turnoff. It's just past the migrant camp."

"And then?"

"Two miles to the house."

She squirmed like a kid on a cross-country trip, dug out her bag of Cheerios, nibbled on some, offered him the bag. He sampled some and made a face. "God, how can you eat those things?"

"They're not that bad, Mac."

"Not bad, boring."

She sniffed. "My unsophisticated palate, I guess. Besides, the fat content's negligible. I'm already eight pounds over my limit."

"What limit?"

"The thirty-pound limit for the pregnancy." She said it as

though it should've been perfectly obvious what she was talking about. She leaned forward and tilted her head, looking up at him.

"What?" He laughed.

"When's our anniversary?"

"July fourteenth."

"Sixteenth."

"Oh, right. Sixteenth."

"What color are my eyes, Mac?"

"Blue."

"When's the baby due?"

"February seventeenth."

She sat back. "You pass."

"Pass what?"

"The reality check."

He frowned. "You think I'm losing touch with reality?"

"I think you drift in and out."

"Thanks."

She munched noisily on another handful of Cheerios.

"You trying to tell me something, Quin?"

"Sometimes I think it'd be nice to have another kind of life, that's all." She shrugged and turned her head toward the window. "A life minus murder."

"We can go back to insurance cases. Those pay well."

"We'd die of boredom. How about something in between?"

"Like what?"

"I don't know. Missing persons, home invasions, surveillance . . ." She shifted in her seat, turning toward him. "Between us, there aren't too many things we haven't investigated. I think we should work on developing an expertise in a couple of areas and then expand to other parts of the country."

"That takes money, Quin."

"Money to advertise, that's all. We choose a couple of cities we'd like to see, make sure our licenses have reciprocity in those places, then advertise in the major newspapers."

"What kind of expertise?"

"I don't know. I guess that's the first thing we need to figure out."

223

"I thought you enjoyed homicide investigations."

"If there wasn't any risk involved, they'd be fine."

"If you don't want risk, go back to teaching."

Her voice assumed a familiar testiness. "Look, the point of this whole thing is that it isn't just going to be the two of us anymore, all right? And it'd be nice if our daughter had two parents."

"She'll have two parents."

"Oh, stop twisting what I say. You know what I'm talking about."

Yes, he knew. The unmentionable.

Neither of them spoke after that. They passed the migrant camp, glowing against the landscape like a giant Japanese lantern. A mile later, he turned off onto a narrow dirt road that led to a hovel of shacks, a makeshift village, a third-world nightmare. Lanterns flickered in windows without glass. Old cars missing parts slumbered in the pale light like ailing pets. Several small children played tag in the dust.

The pungent odor of urine and smoke curled through the air as they got out of the car. The children ran over, then hung back, giggling and shy, their huge liquid eyes nearly hidden beneath locks of thick, dark hair. *"María Milagro está en casa?"* McCleary asked.

"Por allá." The little girl pointed to a dirty concrete bungalow that was a step above the others. A very pregnant young woman of not more than twenty stood in the doorway, watching them warily. *"Señor* McCleary?" she asked.

"Sí. Y mi esposa, Quin."

"Quién?" she asked. *Who?*

"No, Quin."

"Ah. Kwin." She nodded and smiled, her nose wrinkling at the unfamiliarity of the name, then asked Quin when her baby was due. Even though Quin's Spanish was as halting as the young woman's English, they exchanged stories as if they were the only women in the world who'd ever been pregnant. But this immediate camaraderie, he knew, would make things considerably easier.

Inside the house, the lambent light of a half-dozen lanterns washed across an old wooden table where two men were finishing bowls of black bean soup. María introduced her brothers, Juan and Pedro, then turned to the older woman at the rusted gas stove, her aunt Ramona. None of them spoke. The tension in the room was like an invisible wall.

McCleary and Quin sat down at the table while María hustled over to the stove and brought back a chipped plate piled high with cornbread. "Please, eat," said María. "*Tía* Ramona she makes the better cornbread you should ever taste."

"The best," corrected Juan.

María flicked her hand. "Who cares. It is good." She pulled over a stool and straddled it. "The *señora* her baby comes soon, but not so soon as mine," she said, addressing her family, touching her hands to her stomach.

"And yours will have no father," snapped Juan.

Tía Ramona whipped around. *"Cállate, imbécil!"*

"No importa, Tía," María said quietly.

Pedro, the larger and older of the two, stood slowly, then grabbed his brother by the collar, jerked him to his feet, and sent him packing. "Forgive us," he said when he returned to the table. "We have many disputes in this family. My brother believes Diego did not want a baby and that is why he did not come back. I myself believe there is more than that. So when Eduardo Iglesia asked if María would talk to you, we decided it is the best thing to do."

"Diego worked at the camp?" McCleary asked.

"Sí, señor. We all work there. Ramona she cooks, I myself clean in the offices, and now that María cannot pick in the fields, she is watching children for the women." He sat down.

"How long ago did Diego leave?"

"Eight months," María replied. "And I know he would not just leave me. He very much wanted a son. I know this in my heart. *Jefe* Cordoba he tells Diego there is a special job for much money in Orlando. For a few weeks, he says. So Diego he goes. I hear nothing. Then one month after he is gone, a *gringo* comes to the offices one day when the *jefe* is on vacation, no? He asks Pedro about Diego."

"I tell him Diego goes for a better job in Orlando." Pedro said, picking up the story. The *gringo* asks if Diego has family. A girlfriend, I tell him. She is pregnant. He asks if he can talk

225

to the girlfriend, so I bring him here. He gives María three thousand pesos. American pesos. Cash money. For the baby. I hear that the sister of another worker who has gone to Miami was also visited by a *gringo*. I talk to the sister. I know from what she says about this man that he is the same one who gave María money. I find out that the man's name is Frank Abalonee."

One Sunday a few weeks later they were all having lunch when Mr. Abalonee showed up here at the house, Pedro went on. He and Abalonee went outside to talk and Abalonee told him to spread the word to the other workers not to take any of the special-project jobs that Cordoba offered. "But that is difficult, *señor*. Cordoba tells the men that these jobs they pay much more than the fields, the men they need money, they go. *Señor* Abalonee he does not tell me why the workers should not take the jobs, but I know it is because they do not come back."

"Maybe they just don't want to come back," Quin suggested.

"Then Diego he would send for me," María said. "I know."

Pedro nodded, agreeing. "But there is more. One day I ask the *jefe* about these special projects. He tells me they are not my business; my business is to clean the offices, and if I cannot do that, he will find someone who can. I not ask questions again. But I listen. I hear things about other workers who have left for special projects many months past and have not come back."

"How many men?" McCleary asked.

"I myself know of six."

"I, too, hear things," Ramona said in Spanish. She shuffled over to the table with a pot of coffee and mugs. "In the kitchen one hears many things. And when these things are about Cordoba, I believe them. He is a *cabrón*," she spat. "An evil, greedy man. And there are records. Tell him, Pedro, tell him about the records."

"In his office there are records."

"Records on what?"

"The truth."

As though the truth were indisputable, cast in stone, McCleary thought. Perhaps in this case it was.

"How do you know about the records?"

"Because of what happened with *Señor* Bishop," Ramona replied. "Tell him, Pedro."

"You knew Jack Bishop?" Quin asked.

"Ah, *señora*," Ramona clucked. "Everyone knew *Señor* Bishop. He was like a king, no?"

About a week before Bishop was killed, Pedro said, he had worked late to finish waxing the lobby floor. It was about six, everyone had gone home, he thought he was alone in the office. Then he heard voices coming from the back of the building and realized Cordoba and someone else had come in the rear door.

The two men were arguing and sounded as though they were about to fight. Alarmed, Cordoba went back to see what was going on. The door to Cordoba's office was open a crack, and inside Pedro saw Bishop leaning over the *jefe*'s desk, clutching the front of his shirt, shouting in his face.

"Shouting what?"

"It is not right to repeat what he said in front of the ladies, *señor*."

Ramona sighed. "We have heard worse, *mi amor*."

Pedro thought about it and stared at the table, as though the words were inscribed there. "*Señor* Bishop was saying, 'I'm not paying you more than five grand, you stupid fuck, and if you don't take that, I'll go somewhere else.' Then Cordoba he jumps up and threatens the *señor*."

"Physically?"

"No, through the mail."

"Blackmail, you mean."

"Yes, blackmail. With evidence. *Señor* Bishop he laughs and says he has his own evidence and that the *jefe* has one week, that is all. I hurry back to the front, and minutes later, I hear *Señor* Bishop's car drive away."

"So you think these records are what Cordoba was going to blackmail Bishop with?"

"*Sí*. There is a safe somewhere in Cordoba's office. It is always locked. The payroll is in there. But his secretary she is

227

good friends with my wife and she says the combination it is a birthdate for someone in his family."

"What makes her think that?"

Pedro shrugged. "Perhaps because she has worked for Cordoba many years, perhaps because she knows but is afraid to speak up, I cannot say for sure." He slipped a key from his shirt pocket. "This is for the back door of the offices." His fingers dug into the pocket again and brought out a scrap of paper on which five birthdates were scrawled. "I hope you can help us as we have helped you."

McCleary picked up the key, folded the scrap of paper. "Count on it."

2.

It was still early, just eight o'clock, and Kate sat on the McClearys' back porch watching a couple of neighborhood kids fishing in the lake. They had a large hurricane flashlight between them in the grass, sitting on end so its beam shot up toward the black sky. Its dispersed light spilled thinly across the surface of the water, allowing them to see the fish nibbling at their bait.

Beyond them, in the distance, lightning flashed erratically against the dark, illuminating thunderheads that climbed to thirty thousand feet or more. These giants were indigenous to South Florida. You just didn't see them in the northern part of the state where she'd grown up. Or the kind of lightning that accompanied them, long jagged bolts that leaped from sky to ground in the space of a single breath and struck more than fifty people a year.

It was the kind of statistic Jack had always had at the tip of his fingers. He'd seemed to believe that knowing such things had enhanced his credibility. She had a quick lucid image of him falling back on the bed one night and saying:

Ask me anything, Katie.

What's the sound of one hand clapping?

No fair, that's a koan.

Give me an answer.

Okay. Death. Death is the sound of one hand clapping.

Death. It all came back to death. Jack's death, Pearl's death,

Abalonee's death, near-death studies. She got up, locked the sliding glass doors behind her, went into McCleary's den. She stood in front of the blackboard, studying everything that was laid out. Facts, theories, suspicions, the profile on the killer. Then she sat down at his computer, booted up, accessed the file he'd named *Jack*.

MOLE	CLICKER
ACE	GRIFFIN
NOVEMBER	NABISCO

Somewhere in these six words was the answer. But to understand what these terms had meant to Jack, she would have to think like Jack. And she was no longer sure how Jack had thought about anything.

Compartmentalized, Quin had said. All right, then. Each word was a separate compartment. A symbol for something else. Her eyes skipped down the list to GRIFFIN. Next to it she typed BEAST.

ACCESS DENIED.

MYTHOLOGICAL BEAST.

ACCESS DENIED.

PLANE.

ACCESS DENIED.

CITABRIA.

The screen scrolled. She held her breath.

ENGINE RUN, 1800 RPM WITH CONTROL COLUMN HELD BACK TO PREVENT SPRAY DAMAGE. 80/87 FUEL, MAX GROSS WEIGHT 1650 POUNDS. WHEN CONVERTING FROM LANDPLANE TO SEAPLANE WITH EDO 2000S, GROSS WEIGHT INCREASES FROM STANDARD 1650 POUNDS TO 1800. WHEELED TAKE-OFF REQUIRES 231 FEET TAKE-OFF DISTANCE AND 457 FEET TO CLEAR A 50-FOOT OBSTACLE AT SEA LEVEL. NO PUBLISHED CHARTS FOR TAKE-OFF DISTANCES FOR SEAPLANE. BUT AFTER EXPERIMENTING, I FOUND THAT AT SLIGHTLY OVER 50 MPH, THE PLANE LIFTED FROM LAKE OKEECHOBEE IN ELEVEN SECONDS. WITH BACK SEATS AND FRONT PASSENGER SEAT REMOVED,

WITH FUEL TANKS HALF FILLED, FIVE MEN FIT COMFORT-
ABLY AND WEIGHT LIMITATIONS WERE OVERCOME. WITH
SIX MEN, PERFORMANCE WASN'T AS GOOD, RUDDERS WERE
SLUGGISH BUT OKAY FOR WATER LANDINGS.*

That was it. But she was suddenly sure there was more, there
had to be. Jack wouldn't hide a goddamn disk in a plant if there
wasn't. Since Abalonee had owned the plane, she typed in his name.
ACCESS TO LEVEL 2 DENIED.

ABALONEE BALONEY, she typed. Jack's high school nickname for the man.

The screen blanked, then: LEVEL 2. ABALONEE SAYS THE
PLANE'S FOR SALE, AM I INTERESTED IN BUYING? NOPE, BUT I
KNOW WHO MIGHT BE.*

DEATH FLATS, she typed.
ACCESS TO LEVEL 3 DENIED.
SCHRÖDINGER'S CAT.
ACCESS TO LEVEL 3 DENIED.

She tried a dozen words after that, anything that came to
mind. The names of famous pilots, terms in near-death studies, Pearl, herself, Jack's name, and none of them worked.
Desperate, she typed, ROY FARGO.

LEVEL 3. FOR ALL HIS BRAVADO AND RATINGS, FARGO
ISN'T MUCH OF A PILOT. HE GETS INTO A TIGHT SPOT,
PANICS, ACTS STUPIDLY. DOESN'T KNOW HOW TO IMPRO-
VISE. IN CONTRAST, ABALONEE IS TOO CONTROLLED, TOO
PRECISE, TOO MUCH BY THE BOOK. YET HE'S WILLING TO
TAKE A RISK NOW AND THEN. FARGO, ON THE OTHER
HAND, IS MARRIED WITH KIDS. MAYBE THAT MAKES HIM
LESS OF A RISK TAKER.*

Did that mean Fargo had bought the plane from Abalonee?
She kept reading the last three sentences, certain that Jack
was alluding to something other than flying. She tried more
names, everyone she could think of. David, Stephanie, Wayne
Shepard, Wolfe, Sammy Dayton, the McClearys, herself, Jack,
his parents, but she couldn't get beyond level three. Perhaps
there wasn't a level beyond that. Maybe none of it meant a

damn thing, it was just Jack playing mind fuck games with himself on the computer.

The phone rang and she picked up the receiver, her eyes still on the screen. "Hello?"

Silence.

Her head began to pound, her fingers tightened over the receiver. She thought: *Hang up, it's him, just hang up*. But her hand was frozen. She listened to that terrible hollowness, that silence, waiting for him to speak, wanting him to speak. Then: "Kate?"

It was David. "You just scared the hell out of me," she said.

"My phone's been screwing up all day. I never heard it ring. I've been calling your house since this afternoon, kiddo. I was beginning to get worried."

"I'm going to be staying here for a while."

"Good, that's good. I think you should. That old house is too big for one person. Can you get away from the center sometime in the next few days for lunch?"

"Sure, I've got plenty of time. I've been suspended." Her voice surprised her; it held no rancor.

David said all the right things, that he was sorry, that it wasn't fair, but she had the impression that he already knew about her suspension. Wolfe or Sammy might have told him, but she doubted it. They would both leave it up to her to inform other people.

They set a time and a place for lunch, the day after tomorrow. Then she hung up and sat there, disturbed by the call, by the way her friendship with Jack's brother had unraveled in the weeks since his murder, wondering how many other relationships in her life would become suspect before this ended.

If it ended.

She turned off the computer and walked out of the den, the rumble of thunder and the promise of rain moving closer.

24

1.

CLICKER WOKE THAT morning to the sound of thunder and rain. A torrent of rain. It beat against the roof and windows, swept in gusts through the street, rushed through the gutters at the sides of his house, and poured into his yard. The storm possessed power, like the night, like a camera, a slingshot, a gun.

The storm was a sign that the floodgates had opened, the drought had ended. It was time to act.

He showered, dressed, ate breakfast. Then he returned to the bedroom and opened the drawer of his nightstand. Where the squeeze bottle was. Two generous spurts, one in either nostril. He stood at the window, waiting for the drug to overtake him. Already he felt it pumping through him like some ancient magic. He pressed his hands to the windows, fingers splayed. His skin was transparent. He saw blood rushing through the veins and capillaries, heard his bones breathing, smelled the firing of synapses as his nerves crackled and popped, seeking new connections.

The surface of his brain began to ripple, change, transform. His body was purging itself, molting its ordinary skin, becoming that pure, simple vessel through which all life flowed. His soul was now a conduit between heaven and hell, between life here and life *there*, where Jack and Pearl were.

Hello, Jackie boy.

Hello, Pearl.

Then his mother spoiled it. She crept up behind him in that silent way she had, her body not even disturbing the air through which she moved. It was as if she'd been born to some other element, to water perhaps. She pointed a long, bony finger at the tree in the middle of the yard. The tree under which he'd buried the evidence of Abalonee's murder.

"It's all going to wash up, Clicker."

"Go away."

"I'm just telling you the truth. Abalonee's blood is going to wash across that bed of fallen leaves, into the hedges, and splash into your neighbor's yard and then you're going to be in deep shit, Clicker honey."

He rubbed his palm in wide circles against the glass, clearing away the condensation. Rain streamed through the branches of the tree, the wind whipped leaves and twigs out from under it, the ground there had turned to mud. She was right. He hated to admit it, but even he could see what was going to happen if the rain kept up. If the wind kept howling. If the ground got any wetter.

The garage. He jerked his slicker from the hook on the door, grabbed the shovel, tossed it in the wheelbarrow. He shrugged on his slicker, pushed the wheelbarrow out into the milky morning light. Into the rain. Toward the trees where his sins were buried.

His mother's laughter fluttered after him, high and shrill, the sound of a hyena. He hated her for being right, for intruding, for being here. His hatred consumed him as he slammed the end of the shovel into the ground where the hibiscus hedge grew. He heaved a pile of dirt into the wheelbarrow, sank it into the dirt again, heaved again. Dig and heave, dig and heave until the wheelbarrow was half full. He tossed the shovel on top of the dirt, pushed the wheelbarrow across the yard.

Rain struck his face. It streamed down inside his slicker, wetting his clothes. His shoes sloshed with mud. Again and again he crossed the yard, loading and unloading dirt, digging, heaving, raking the dirt over his sins and Jack's mistake.

After a while, he could no longer tell the difference between his sweat and the rain and tore off his slicker, his clothes, his shoes and socks. Liberated, his body sang and the drug flowed through him and he became the dirt that he dug and dumped and raked. He saw what it saw: his own face leaning over it, rain running into his eyes, wet leaves trembling above him. He felt his own fingers burrowing, assaulting, violating, and

233

tasted the salt of his own sweat as it mixed with rain and seeped into the ground, the soil. He became the roots that twisted through the dirt, the worms and bugs that hid just beneath the surface, the dead leaves that rotted into mulch. And in the end he became the mound that his fingers and hands had sculpted, a thing of complex beauty, a sentient being, and he laid down against it and wept.

House again. Shower. Clean clothes. Dry, Jesus, he was dry, and the phone was ringing. These two things—his dryness and the phone—were not connected, he knew they weren't, but it seemed as if they were. The sound was loud, abrasive, and bounced back and forth inside his skull like a Ping-Pong ball. It made his ears ring.

He stopped midway across the room, shaking his finger inside one ear to make the horrible ringing stop, then he couldn't remember what he was about to do. The phone reminded him. He snatched up the receiver. Listened. As the voice spoke, he turned toward the window and stared at his mound, his lovely, huge, marvelous mound where all his secrets were buried.

"You hear what I said?" the voice asked.

"Sure."

"And?"

"Sounds good."

"You can do it?"

"Yes."

"You're sure?"

As though the idea were new. An original. He almost laughed. "Yes, I'm sure," he said, and hung up.

He glanced at the clock. Kate would be up by now. He punched out the McClearys' number and cleared his throat. He reached the goddamn machine and slammed the receiver down. No one home. Or maybe Kate was there and not answering the phone. Or maybe they'd all slept in because of the rain. He called the McClearys' office and was shocked when Kate said, "St. James and McCleary, can I help you?"

Like a secretary. His finger touched the button, quickly dis-

234

connecting. Improvise. Take a risk. His mother's taunt. Fine. He would show her.

Clicker turned slowly in place, his smile growing as he turned, his thoughts zipping along, a train gathering speed. He looked at the room through eyes that were changed, in a body that had been transmuted, and knew he wouldn't be sorry to leave here. It was time.

He spent most of the day making preparations, thinking of the risk he would take, turning it over in his mind, scrutinizing it for flaws, weaknesses, surprises.

He saw none.

2.

McCleary spent the morning in front of the computer at the office, trying to access the *Jack* files. He tried every combination of every person in Kate's life with the list of six words and came up with zero. He went back to the *Griffin* file she'd broken into last night, read through it.

The type of plane—Citabria—had gotten her into the first level of the file. A nickname—Abalonee Baloney—had cracked the second level, and another name—Roy Fargo—had accessed the third level. It was possible Bishop had used the same pattern in the other files. But before tackling one of them, he tried his list of names to see if any of them would admit him to the fourth level.

None did.

He exited the file and sat for a few minutes studying the six words. Mole, Ace, November, Clicker, Griffin, Nabisco. He picked up the phone and buzzed the front desk, where Kate was filling in.

"Got something, Mike?"

"Not yet. What month was Jack born in?"

"August. And I was born in February. I already thought of that."

"What about his parents? His brother and sister? When were they born?"

"None of them was born in November."

"Okay, thanks."

He hung up, walked over to the blackboard he'd brought

from home. His eyes skipped across the prodigious accumulation of facts, pausing here, there, looking for something. He hoped for the slow burn of a hunch and felt it finally, right between his eyes, the skin there tightening as if from a sunburn. His gaze stopped on the photograph of Bishop's Bonanza that Fargo had given him, with Fargo, Shepard, and Bishop standing there laughing, arms around each other, good ole boys. Across the side of the plane were the call letters, N-929.

NOVEMBER NINER-TWO-NINER. That was how Bishop had announced himself the few times McCleary had been in the plane with him. November. Goddamn.

He sat in front of the computer again. Next to NOVEMBER he typed BONANZA and level one of the file opened up. It was a description of the aircraft similar in content to what Kate had found under CITABRIA. At the end of the entry, following the previous pattern, McCleary typed Bishop's name.

ACCESS TO LEVEL 2 DENIED.

A nickname, he needed a nickname. He buzzed Kate again, asked her if she'd had a nickname for Bishop. "Something like Abalonee Baloney," he said.

"He was always just Jack to me."

"Did anyone else have a nickname for him?"

"Maybe I'd better come back there."

She and Quin hurried in a few moments later. "Type, nickname, name," he explained. "That appears to be the pattern for the first three levels of the file."

"Try Jackie. That's what the family use to call him."

JACKIE.

LEVEL 2, AUGUST 8, 1983. CLICKER AND I HAULED IN THE TRAILERS TODAY. I BOUGHT THEM USED IN JACKSONVILLE FROM AN OLD FARMER WHO TOOK CASH FOR THEM. I THINK THEY'LL DO JUST FINE. WE EQUIPPED THEM WITH GAS TANKS FOR THE STOVES AND 40-GALLON WATER TANKS, ENOUGH FOR BASIC NEEDS.

WE HAVEN'T TALKED ABOUT THE SPECIFICS YET, ABOUT HOW WE'RE GOING TO DO THIS. IN FACT, WE HAVEN'T TALKED MUCH AT ALL ABOUT THE DETAILS. EVERY TIME

WE START TO, A SENSE OF THE FORBIDDEN PREVENTS US
FROM FINISHING THE CONVERSATION. BUT I HAVE NEVER
FELT A DEEPER SENSE OF CAMARADERIE WITH ANOTHER
HUMAN BEING.*

McCleary typed: JACK BISHOP.

ACCESS TO LEVEL 3 DENIED.

"Any suggestions?" He glanced at Kate. Her face was so
white, her features seemed in danger of vanishing.

"No." She rubbed her hands over her arms.

Quin spoke up. "Jack's full name is Jackson, isn't it?"

"Only on his birth certificate."

JACKSON.

LEVEL 3. FEBRUARY 2, 1985. WE ARE NOW FOUR. CLICKER
THINKS IT'S A BIG MISTAKE TO BRING IN OTHERS. HIS
FAVORITE LINE IS THAT A SECRET ISN'T A SECRET ONCE
IT'S SHARED BY MORE THAN TWO. MY ARGUMENT IS THAT
A SECRET BINDS THOSE WHO KNOW IT. AND HE CAN'T
DISPUTE THE FACT THAT THE FOUR OF US ARE UNIFIED
ON THE FLATS. WE ACT AS ONE BODY, ONE MIND. IT
WORKS.

SOMETIMES, WHEN IT IS JUST CLICKER AND ME, PEARL
JOINS US. THE THREE OF US SLEEP TOGETHER IN THE
LARGER TRAILER THEN, AN ARRANGEMENT THAT WAS
PEARL'S IDEA AND THAT I DON'T MUCH CARE FOR. BUT
IT KEEPS HER HAPPY. SEX DOES FOR HER WHAT THE FLATS
DO FOR ME.

UNFORTUNATELY, SHE CREATES BARRIERS BETWEEN
CLICKER AND ME. IT'S THAT AGE-OLD COMPETITIVE
THING, I GUESS, TWO MEN, ONE WOMAN, THE ETERNAL
TRIANGLE. NOT THE SAME BALLGAME AS THE RANCH PAR-
TIES, NOT AT ALL. THOSE ARE MEANT TO BE EXPERIMEN-
TAL AND PRIMARILY EXPERIMENTAL IN TERMS OF HOW
THE GROUP INTERACTS. THIS IS DIFFERENT.

AT TIMES, SHE DELIBERATELY USES HIM TO TAUNT ME,
PROPPED BACK ON HER ELBOWS ON THE QUILTS AND
BLANKETS, HER LONG BARE LEGS BENT SLIGHTLY AT THE
KNEES, HER HAIR BLACK AGAINST THOSE PALE SHOUL-

DERS, CLICKER'S HANDS AT HER BREASTS, THE LENS OF
HIS GODDAMN CAMERA AIMED AT THEM FROM THE TRI-
POD, RIGGED TO A DELAY BUTTON THAT HE CAN REACH.
MORE THAN ONCE, I'VE JUST LEFT THE TRAILER AND
WALKED FOR HOURS ACROSS THE FLATS. I NEED SOME-
THING TO BALANCE THIS. NEED IT DESPERATELY.*

No one spoke. The sounds in the room seemed abnormally loud: the hum of the computer, the tick of the clock on the wall, Kate's breathing. And beyond the room the drumming of the rain. McCleary finally broke the silence. "Any idea how to crack the fourth level?"

"Yes." Kate's voice was calm, controlled. "I was the balance. Put in my name."

KATE BISHOP.

ACCESS TO LEVER FOUR DENIED.

"Not Bishop," Quin said. "Her maiden name. Wells."

KATE WELLS.

LEVEL 4. APRIL 9, 1986. I MET HER TWO MONTHS AGO, IN
THE PARKING LOT AT THE NDE CENTER. HER NAME IS KATE
WELLS. ONE WAY OR ANOTHER, I'M GOING TO MARRY HER.
PEARL KNOWS ABOUT HER. SHE'S INCENSED.**

"I think the two stars mean there aren't any more levels in this file," McCleary said.

"Then where are all the missing years?" Quin asked.

"I think they're scattered throughout the other files," Kate said. "But we're not going to find names there. Just the nick-names." She leaned over McCleary, exited the November file, brought the cursor even with CLICKER. "I think this is the guy who killed Jack." Next to it, she typed CAMERA.

NIKON F4. A detailed description of the camera and its ca-pabilities was given. At the end of the entry, they tried dozens of nicknames to gain access to the second level, but none of them worked.

"Do you know anyone with a Nikon F4?" McCleary asked.

She laughed bitterly. "Mike, I wouldn't know a Nikon F4 from a Kodak. At those weekend parties at the house, every-

238

one had cameras. It could be anyone and God knows what kind of nickname would get us into the file. We can't do anything else with this until we know more.''

''Hey, anyone here working today?'' Eastman called out from the front.

''Back here, Fitz.''

Kate exited the file and turned off the computer. ''It's embarrassing enough to have you two reading this stuff. Fitz doesn't have to see it. I think I'll go get some lunch. You hungry, Quin?'' Quin laughed; it brought a momentary smile to Kate's face. ''Yeah, I guess that's a stupid question, huh.''

''Give me two minutes to get my things,'' Quin said. ''Meet you outside.'' She lingered in the doorway when Kate had left and her ghost blue eyes had that *I-need-to-know-something* look in them. He expected a question about Sylvia Callahan and wished she wouldn't always relate cases to their personal lives.

''What is it?'' he asked.

''You going to leave for the migrant camp from here?''

''We'll probably get a bite to eat first and then head out before dark.''

''Call me on Fitz's car phone when you're finished at the camp, okay? Kate and I will be at the house.''

''Sure.''

She came over and put her arms around him and said she loved him, that was all. No questions, no interrogation about Callahan, just three simple words. Then she left and he felt as though he were about to board a plane that was doomed to crash, a crash Quin had dreamed about and dismissed.

Ridiculous, he thought, and went out to greet Eastman.

3.

Clicker drove by the McClearys' development twice. The road turned sharply north just beyond it, veering away from the lake, which curved gently to the south. Beyond the lake lay nothing but mango trees. Eventually, if the pattern of development in South Florida held true, the trees would be razed, the road would be extended through it, and some new housing development would spring up overnight. But for now the grove of mango trees was the ideal place to stash his car. He would return later to pick up his suitcase and money.

He checked to make sure he had everything—tools, slingshot, gun—then shrugged on his navy-blue slicker and got out of the car. His weapon this time was a Smith & Wesson .38, easy to carry, easy to conceal.

There were two ways he could approach the house, each with advantages and disadvantages. He could cut in behind the development and traipse through a couple of backyards to reach the rear of the McClearys' place. It was the most direct route, but if any of the neighbors were home, he'd be inviting trouble.

The other option was to just walk up to the front door, then head to the back when he was positive no one was around. This seemed the least risky of the two.

He moved briskly along the sidewalk that paralleled the road, rain washing over the hood of his slicker and sliding into his face. He didn't mind. This was a perfect South Florida rain, warm and friendly. Now and then, thunder rattled the air and lightning cracked through the leaden sky, but he welcomed it. The storm fit his mood.

As he neared the house, he was certain he'd made the right decision. The property was deeper than it was wide, so the front door of the house was actually to the side. The garage was closed. No car parked outside. Not a car in sight anywhere.

He flicked up the latch on the gate and strolled along the walk, admiring the plants that grew at the side of house. Hibiscuses, crotons, thick clumps of grasses, philodendrons. He liked the lushness. He would have to settle someplace lush, the Caribbean, maybe, or even the West Coast around Seattle. If Kate was nice to him, he would take her with him. But he didn't want to think about any of that now. When it came time to make those decisions, he would know what to do.

Clicker rang the bell. Waited. If Kate or Quin answered the door, he would smile, he would say he just wanted to check on them, make sure they were okay, and they would ask him in for a drink or dinner. One or both of them would comment on his cologne, his clothes, and he would tell Kate how sorry he was that she'd been suspended. She would tell him it didn't matter and he would see the lie in her eyes. He would find out when McCleary was expected. He would improvise. It would be okay.

But no one came to the door.

He walked to the porch at the back of the house. The McClearys hadn't screened it yet, but there was patio furniture out here and a gas grill. In Miami, if these thing were outside at all, they were usually bolted to the concrete.

Clicker turned, gazed out at the lake, the trees, the road, troubled by how visible he was. He peered through the glass, hands cupped at the sides of his face, and spotted a safer place to get in.

An atrium on the other side of the house with a wooden gate.

Jesus, a simple wooden gate.

Maybe in his new life he would teach seminars to home-owners on simple security measures to diminish the odds of robbery. It was particularly bad in Florida, where the lifestyle lent itself to patios and atriums and, yes, multiple sliding-glass doors. Clicker himself had been robbed only last year and the bastard had gotten in through the sliding glass door; he'd just lifted the sucker right off the track.

Like he was going to do.

Inside the atrium now. Two sliding doors, the one he'd seen from the back and another that opened into the nursery. The first had a plank of wood in the track that fitted between the edge of the door and the jamb, which would make it more difficult to lift the door from the track. But the nursery door didn't. He checked for metal pins or bolts at the top and bottom. Just one, at the top. It wasn't insurmountable, but it would take longer.

First, with the smooth edge of a screwdriver, he popped the lock. A cheapo brand, he thought, one of the ways developers cut costs. He leaned into the glass, shoved hard to the left. The door cracked just enough for him to wedge his fingers in. He gripped the other side, then shook the door until he knocked the pin loose—not out, but loose. Another shake and the pin fell out, dangling on its short metal chain like a fish on a hook.

He shrugged off his slicker and removed his wet shoes and

socks. Then he rolled them up in his raincoat, slid the door left, stepped inside. A black cat sat in the middle of the room, gazing up at him. "Scat," he shouted, and it scrambled through the slats of the Levolors and out into the atrium. The last thing he needed was a goddamn cat sniffing around wherever he hid.

But as he walked out of the nursery, he saw two more cats. The fluffy one with the squashed face took off. But the calico's back arched; it hissed and stood its ground. Cats were like squirrels. They had fleas. They carried diseases, maybe even rabies. They served no purpose.

He set his bunched raincoat down, slipped the slingshot from his pocket, fitted a rock into it.

He pulled back. Aimed.

And the fucking cat sprang at him, its claws bared, its shriek from the depths of hell.

Claws sank into his cheeks, his hands, his arms, and his throat before he jerked the thing away from him and hurled it twenty feet across the room. It landed on all fours and raced away, still shrieking, and slammed into the screen of an open window in the bedroom. For a beat or two, it hung there, legs splayed against the screen, a flying squirrel. Then the screen tumbled out and the cat fell with it.

Clicker ran into the bedroom, stuck his head out the window. The animal was gone, the screen was on the ground, rain was blowing into the room. The windowsill and the rug under it were already wet because the window had been open all this time. Good. Get the screen back in, he thought, and no one would be the wiser.

The screen didn't fit right, but as long as no one leaned on it, he thought it would stay put. He returned to the nursery doorway and picked up his raincoat and shoes. He cleaned up the water that had puddled on the floor from his raincoat, then went in search of a hiding place.

25

1.

THEY TOOK EASTMAN'S '53 Caddy. What the car lacked in grace and beauty was compensated for by its solidness, the way it claimed the road like a tank. Inside, though, it was strictly contemporary—cellular phone, quadraphonic sound, seats comfortable enough to sleep in.

McCleary didn't fully appreciate the car until they were on their way to the migrant camp. The wind tore across the miserable two-lane highway sounding like a 747 on its way to hell and the old Caddy withstood the assault without so much as a shudder. "I think I love this car," McCleary said.

Eastman laughed. "She gets twenty-five miles to the gallon because she was built before high-compression, gas-guzzling engines came into vogue. She's been refurbished a couple of times, but I figure she'll outlast me." He switched on the defroster; the window cleared in seconds. "Still can't see a rat's ass. This rain's going to make things messy. You bring extra clothes?"

"In the pack." McCleary reached back and pulled the knapsack into the front seat. It was new, a replacement for the pack he'd lost on the nightmare trip to the Everglades this past spring. The canvas was still stiff and smelled like the sporting-goods shop where he'd bought it. From one of the side pockets he pulled out two pieces of an apparatus that had been given to him by a hit woman the summer he'd lost his memory.

Custom-made in Zurich, it was powered by a battery that was charged by plugging it into an outlet, like a laptop computer, but for twice the length of time. It emitted a thin, high-powered laser similar to what was being used experimentally on heart patients with clogged arteries. In the medical proce-

243

dure, lasers were shot through a catheter fed into the heart and burned out the fatty deposits in the arteries. Adapted, this cut through virtually anything except lead and did it in about fifteen seconds. As McCleary snapped the two pieces together, Eastman glanced over.

"Looks wicked. What is it?"

McCleary told him. Eastman let out a soft, appreciative whistle. "And it works?"

"I haven't found anything yet it can't open."

Eastman adjusted the rearview mirror. "You see anything back there?"

McCleary turned. "Nope. You paranoid, Fitz?"

"I thought I saw headlights behind us a while ago. They must've turned off."

"Nobody but crazies are out in this."

"Yeah." Eastman laughed. "That's what worries me."

As they rounded a curve, McCleary expected to see the huge pumpkin glow of the migrant camp. Instead, the wet darkness was broken up by the flicker of candles and lanterns. "Power's out at the camp. Better slow down so we don't miss the turnoff. The road's just past the main gate."

Eastman doused the headlights, turned on the dims, hung a left onto the road that paralleled the administration building. It was a river of mud, but the Caddy splashed through it without missing a beat. Eastman turned right into the pines and killed the engine.

McCleary pulled on his poncho, slipped the laser into a side pocket, slung the pack over his shoulder. He snapped a clip into Quin's Browning, glad they'd exchanged weapons. It was lighter than his Magnum. He tucked it in a pocket close to his hip, zipped it shut. "Ready?"

"Let's do it."

Within two minutes, they were at the southwest corner of the fence, knees sinking into mud blacker than coal. There was nothing to stop the wind. It whipped out of the south, flinging rain against them, whining in their ears. McCleary was afraid the water might short-circuit something in the laser, so he used the wire cutters on the fence while Eastman held the flashlight steady. He cut away a section at the bottom, then

244

bent the wire back and held it up while Eastman shimmied under. McCleary passed him the pack and followed.

The key Pedro Milagro had given him unlocked the rear door of the building and they stepped into a vestibule. But no one had mentioned the second door or the dead bolt that held it in place. "That gadget of yours work on dead bolts?" Eastman asked.

"It's simpler to take out a chunk of wood around it."

"Which is going to show."

"Sure as hell, Fitz."

"Christ. It's one thing to get in and out and no one knowing about it, Mike."

"You want Garrison or not?"

"Turn it on, white boy."

Ten seconds to burn out a square of wood, and they were in. They hurried down the hall to Cordoba's office, and while Eastman stood watch outside, McCleary unlocked the office door. The smell of cigar smoke lingered in the air. The beam of his flashlight touched the painting on black velvet and dropped to the desk, where Cordoba and his family gazed out from the photograph in the cheap ceramic frame. A safe, he thought, and his eyes fell to the kneehole under the desk, where the rug hid scuffed vinyl.

2.

She and Quin ate at a Mexican restaurant in West Palm and, over dinner, talked about old times. They avoided any mention of the present, as if by mutual consent, and for a while Kate almost forgot that she'd been married to a man she'd never really known.

But afterward, as the Cherokee splashed through the nearly flooded streets toward Quin's, the marriage was all she could think of. The marriage and the things she had chosen not to see, not to question. Like a near-death experience, it possessed imponderable riddles with many possible answers but no absolutes.

She made it to the house before Quin, who had turned off at the market to pick up a few groceries. Since she didn't have a garage-door opener, Kate pulled to the far left of the driveway, leaving Quin enough space to get by, then darted through the rain to the side of the house.

The flower beds had flooded and rainwater rushed over the sidewalks, carrying wood chips and buds and dead insects. The gate swung open in the wind, its song as mournful as the whistle of a train in the dead of night, and clattered behind her as she ran through.

Merlin was huddled in a corner of the porch, his fur so wet he looked to be nothing but skin and bones and amber eyes. "Hey, boy, what happened to you? How'd you get out, anyway?"

He meowed when she picked him up and nipped at the back of her hand as if reprimanding her for not getting home sooner. "I bet one of you guys knocked out that screen in the bedroom, right?"

Kate unlocked the door and Merlin suddenly leaped from her arms and shot across the yard, a black bullet bound for the lake. She started to go after him but thought better of it. He'd be home when he got hungry.

Inside, she turned the dead bolt and headed straight for the shower, stripping off her wet clothes as she went. Oddly, the air smelled faintly of Wolfe's after-shave; Quin must have finally bought McCleary a bottle of the stuff. But it reminded her that she should call Wolfe later.

Since that night in the center's parking lot, she'd avoided thinking too much about him, about what had happened, about a future with him. Or any kind of future, for that matter. It seemed that she existed only in the present tense, in a kind of tight, indeterminate now that had been shaped by an immediate past that Jack had orchestrated.

She started the shower, then stripped off her wet underwear and stepped under the hot spray. A burst of rain exploded against the bathroom window, startling her, smearing the glass like spit. She jerked the Levolors shut. Jumpy, she thought. Then she heard the door squeak and a flutter of cool air stirred the curtains and kissed the back of her neck. Her head snapped around. She backed up to the wall clutching a bar of soap as though it were a weapon. "Quin?"

Hepburn peeked around the edge of the curtain and Kate

laughed. "You just took five years off my life, cutie. What's eating your pal Merlin, anyway? And where's Tracy? He hasn't put in an appearance yet."

The cat meowed and clawed at the curtain, trying to shove it aside. When she didn't succeed, she gave up and jumped onto the toilet seat, where she preened and purred. Her dark shape against the curtain, the loud noise of her purr, were vaguely comforting.

Kate shampooed and rinsed her hair, and when she looked for Hepburn's shadow again, it was gone. First Merlin, now Hepburn, the two of them as spooked as she was. Kate turned off the shower, pushed the curtain aside, and there he was, standing in the bathroom door. Her towel was hooked over his arm and he whipped it off and held it up. "Looking for this, Kate?"

3.

The safe was there, all right, solid steel and set in stone, impervious to probably everything except nuclear attack. But none of the five birthdates was the combination. "It's the handwriting," Eastman opined. He was crouched on the other side of the safe, the scrap of paper in his hand. "The ones could be sevens, the sevens could be ones."

"No, Latins make horizontal crosses on their sevens. I think it's the fives and the eights. Hard to tell which is which."

"Then let's substitute the eights for fives and go through them again."

On the third date, McCleary heard the telling click of the combination. He pulled open the lid and Eastman held his flashlight above the safe. On top were several dozen photos of a woman in a string bikini. On the back of one was a message scrawled in Spanish that roughly translated as: *To Arturo, my cocksman. I will never forget Acapulco. Love, Conchita.*

"Arturo Cordoba, family man," Eastman muttered, and set the photos aside.

Under Conchita were hundred-dollar bills, neatly bundled, like hay. McCleary picked up one of the piles. "I say there's about five grand to a stack, Fitz. What do you say?"

"Makes sense to me. That's what Bishop was paying him for his special projects. There should be six stacks."

McCleary counted. "Ten." Fifty grand wasn't a bad start on retirement.

Beneath the money were ten files. They removed them one by one, checking the names against the list of six names Pedro Milagro had given them. They were all there, but even Milagro hadn't known about the other four men.

McCleary paged through the file on Diego Hernandez. In his photo he looked like a young adult version of the countless street urchins that were fixtures on the streets of South American cities. But in the eyes that had once been predatory, McCleary recognized uncertainty, submissiveness, a spirit that had been nearly broken by the fields, by the promise of the American dream that hadn't been fulfilled.

His bio said he was twenty-three years old, single, a native of a Mexican town McCleary had never heard of. He'd arrived at the camp sixteen months ago, a transfer from another camp in Miami. Last spring, he was sent on a "special project" to Orlando. Stamped across the sheet in black letters was TRANS-FERENCIA. But stapled to the bio was a red flag with SCHRÖ-DINGER'S CAT printed neatly across it.

"So we have a name for the project. So what," Eastman said. "We still don't know what the hell it entails."

"There's got to be something more. Cordoba threatened to blackmail Bishop, and there's not enough here to do anything but incriminate himself."

While Eastman went through the loose papers at the bottom of the safe, McCleary sat at Cordoba's desk and searched the drawers. They yielded nothing. He stared at the photograph of Cordoba with his family and watched the *jefe*'s smile tilt to the left and the right as he turned the cheap ceramic frame around in his fingers. Empty threats. That was the only thing Cordoba had.

"Anything in those papers?"

"Blank forms," Eastman replied.

McCleary set the frame back on the desk and noticed that the picture had slipped out the side. As he worked it back into the frame, he realized there was something behind it and pulled it out.

A second photograph.

It was extremely grainy. indicating that it had been blown up considerably, and had been taken at night, probably with infrared film. It showed a figure kneeling on the ground, illuminated by headlights or the beams of powerful flashlights, he couldn't tell which. The person's head was covered with a hood and Jack Bishop held a gun to his temple.

McCleary got up and knelt beside the safe. "Take a look at this, Fitz."

"Jesus, Cordoba wasn't bluffing."

This was Cordoba's insurance policy, all right. He was "selling" migrant workers to Bishop for five grand apiece for some good-ole-boy fun on the Death Flats and he'd documented it.

Remembering how eloquently Bishop had once spoken about hunting with his father as a boy, he guessed that the workers who survived Russian roulette were then hunted down by Bishop and his boys. He knew it had to be tied in with Bishop's near-death research, but he didn't understand how. Obsessions, though, were rarely comprehensible even to the people who had them. The real tragedy was that Bishop, a man who'd had everything, had become so fixated on the riddle of death, his obsession had killed ten innocent people and damaged other lives in the process.

"I'm taking this with us," Eastman said, and stuck the picture in his wallet. "Everything else stays. I'll get a search warrant first thing in the morning. In fact, maybe I can catch the judge at home and get things rolling. Meet you out by the car."

"Right."

Eastman left and McCleary returned everything to the safe. As he locked up the office and started down the darkened hall, he heard the wind banging the rear door. Eastman hadn't shut it tightly when he'd left.

Then he heard footsteps. Eastman, back already. But he stopped, switched off his flashlight, backed up to the wall.

"Fitz?"

Softly: "Yeah, man."

Something was wrong with his voice. It sounded as though rubber bands were wrapped around his vocal cords. "What happened?"

"Nothing."

The whole thing felt wrong to him—the voice, the air, the door banging in the wind. Eastman wouldn't be careless enough to leave the door open. A likelier scenario was that someone had been waiting outside and that person now had a gun at Eastman's head.

Desk to the right, he thought, and moved toward it. He dropped to a crouch behind it. Papers rustled in the draft from the open door. He exchanged the flashlight for the Browning. Safety off.

"You got the judge?" He kept his voice soft to make it more difficult to pinpoint in the dark, transferred the gun to his left hand, and pulled out the laser with his right. "On the phone?"

"Right, McCleary. C'mon, let's split."

Fitz never called me McCleary.

He raised the laser, hoping he was aiming at the stack of loose papers in the wire basket, which the wind was stirring, and prayed Eastman would be quick enough to seize the advantage. Heart hammering, he pressed his thumb against the button on the laser, pushed it up as far as it would go. A beam shot out and ignited the papers almost instantly. Then he was up and racing back through the hall toward the front door.

A shot nicked wood from the jamb inches above his head. *Silencer.* He stumbled, caught himself, skidded around a corner, and fired a volley of shots before he reached the lobby. He could smell smoke now and knew the wind whistling through the open rear door was fanning the flames. There were at least two men behind him and maybe a third, but none of them shouted. Neither did Eastman, and that worried him.

He crashed through a row of metal chairs in the lobby, threw the dead bolt on the door, charged out into the rain. McCleary already knew that a padlocked gate stood between him and the administration building parking lot. He also knew he didn't have time to use the laser on it. He slipped it between his teeth, slammed into the fence, and scrambled up the wire mesh.

Rain struck him in the face, the wind fought him, the blackness was a cloak that blinded him. Just as he neared the top, his hand exploded with pain. He dropped the Browning and knew he'd been hit. He crabbed to the right, struggling to stay on the fence, his hand shrieking. His fingers wouldn't work, he couldn't grab the mesh. He reached with his left hand, gripped the top of the fence, pushed with his feet, and hoisted himself over.

For an instant, he straddled the top of the fence, dizzy with pain, fear, and saw the men behind him. Two men. He couldn't tell who they were. It didn't matter. He threw his leg over and dropped. He struck the ground on both feet, jarring his body to the bone, fell onto a knee, leaped up, and ran toward the pines. Where the Caddy was.

But before he'd made it through the river of mud the road had become, headlights impaled him and the Caddy roared out of the dark, a hungry beast. He kept running, his arms pumping at his sides, but the Caddy reared up over the shoulder, blocking him. A big man with an Uzi leaped out of the driver's door and Garrison flew from the passenger side, a sawed-off shotgun leveled at McCleary's chest. "Don't be an asshole," he shouted.

Running up behind him, raincoats flapping wetly, were two men, and one of them was David Bishop. He grinned and, in a perfect replica of Eastman's voice, said, "Hello, McCleary."

"The name's Mike."

"So that's where I fucked up." He motioned toward the car with his automatic. "Get in."

McCleary, cradling his injured hand, moved toward the car, and Bishop shoved him into the backseat, where Eastman was crumpled against the side window. The doors slammed. Bishop and the other man hopped onto the trunk and rode a hundred feet to the end of the road, where a Firebird waited.

Then the Caddy swung into a turn and raced for the highway.

"Figured it out yet, detective?" Garrison asked from the

front seat, his shotgun aimed at McCleary's chest. In the back-wash of the headlights, McCleary could see only his grin, a half-moon painted on his deeply lined face.

"Mole, Ace, November, Clicker, Griffin, and Nabisco."

The half-moon shrank to nothingness. The shotgun was suddenly up against his throat, pressing against his Adam's apple, eating up his air. "Where'd you get those names?"

The pressure eased a little. McCleary coughed and rubbed his throat. "Jack's computer. There's a copy of the disk with IAD."

"Bullshit." The shotgun withdrew a foot and the Caddy swerved out onto the highway, rear end fishtailing, then leaped forward into the dark.

Garrison's smile didn't appear again.

4.

He had taken her into the guest room. Now she was huddled at the edge of the bed, clutching the towel against her, as he gripped a handful of hair and held her head back so hard, the muscles in her neck ached. The gun was a light pressure at her throat.

"Where's Quin, Kate?" He rocked toward her, breathing hard, his eyes flickering from her face to the swell of her breasts, which the towel covered, to the part of her legs where the towel didn't reach. She realized that the sight of her like this, nearly naked, helpless, excited him. "C'mon, where?"

"At the office. She's still at the office. Working late."

"Uh-huh." A slow smile grew across his face and cut it in half. He let go of her hair and touched the barrel of the gun to her thigh, easing the towel up. "For how long?"

"I . . . I don't know."

Now he stroked her thigh with the back of his other hand, his free hand. "So pretty. My pretty Kate. Jack loved your body better than Pearl's. He told me that. He told me a lot of things. Private things."

She pulled her leg away from him. Pulled, not jerked. She was terrified of startling him. But he leaned closer to her, forcing her back into the quilt, pressing the gun up against the side of her neck, gripping her chin. His thumb slipped over

252

her cheek. "I can make you come like Jack never could, Katie. And we won't even need scarves."

He laughed and slipped his fingers inside the towel, easing it down over her breasts. Her head was sinking into the quilt and she stared at the ceiling, focusing on it. She forced her awareness to the back of her mind, compressed it into a tiny square, like a handkerchief. But it wasn't enough. Her skin still crawled when he covered a breast with his hand, when his fingers pinched at her nipple, when his hand moved down to her thigh and up under the towel.

"I can play with you if I want to, Katie. Like a cat."

She didn't say anything. He told her to place her arms at her sides. She did. Then he straddled her, trapping her arms under his legs, and set the gun aside. He brought out a squeeze bottle, uncapped it. "You're going to come where I am, Katie." She didn't struggle, didn't speak. He gripped her chin, slipped the nozzle into her nostril, squeezed.

She sneezed; some of the liquid flew out in a fine spray. "You still got enough. You'll see." He got off her, covered her with the towel, leveled the gun at her again, waited.

Lights exploded insider her eyes, the ceiling melted, colors oozed down the walls like wax. When she looked at him, his features shifted and quivered, his smile slid into a corner of his mouth, the pores of his skin opened like craters. *Hallucinations. It's the drug. Take it easy. Ride it out.*

"How's your head, Katie?" His words sounded slurred and slow, like a 45 played on 33 speed. "Feeling good, Kate? Hmm? Feeling warm and thick inside? The drug was Jack's idea. At first, it was androgens mixed with prescription stuff. The androgens hit you in the libido and give you that vital aggressive edge. The ranch parties were a good outlet in that respect. Then when Garrison joined us, we experimented, a little of this, a little of that, and presto! We suddenly had magic.

"The drug connects us, Katie. I can feel what you feel. It's especially true on the flats. When a person's terrified. When he knows he's going to die. Then there's the empty click of the gun and that rush of euphoria when he realizes he survived, then his extreme fear when the hunt begins and all those instincts rearing up, pushing him harder and faster . . . That's the beauty of it, see, all that elation and terror and awe the person's feeling pours into you and suddenly you're experiencing that quantum consciousness without having to die to do it. You understand, Katie? It's important for you to understand. I want you to understand. You will understand." He backed across the room to her closet. "We're going on a little trip." He yanked clothes off the hangers, threw them at her. "Get dressed."

Her body felt rubbery as she sat up. She kept blinking to clear her vision, but it didn't help. The room was breathing now, the walls pulsing like the walls of her heart. In rhythm with her heart. The room *was* her heart.

"I said, *get dressed*." He whipped the towel away from her, rocked toward her again. "Can't dress yourself? Is that it? Am I going to have to help you, Katie? Hmm? You want me to help you?" He gripped her by the shoulders, shaking her, his voice rising and falling inside her: *Do you? Do you?*

She forgot about who he was, about what he had done to Jack, Pearl, Abalonee, and suddenly her legs jacked up and she kicked and her heels slammed into his stomach, knocking him back. She scrambled up, clothes fluttering to the floor like tremendous autumn leaves, but it was already too late. He was faster. He caught her around the legs and she went down. He held on, flipped her over, and squeezed at her throat, squeezed hard and long as he hissed things at her, things she couldn't hear because her brain was screaming for air. But she could see. She could see the way rage had changed his face, seized it, claimed it, and knew she was going to die here, now, on the floor of Quin's guest room.

Then his hands flew away from her throat as though someone had grabbed them. She gasped for air, gulped at it, sucked at it, coughing and rubbing her throat. "Can't. The rules. The goddamn rules. Get up real slow, Katie. You're going to get dressed. We're leaving."

The gun was pointed at her. His eyes were feverish. She pushed up slowly on her hands, rubbed at her throat, and knuckled her eyes, trying to clear the cobwebs, the visions.

He shoved the clothes at her, then stepped back, watching her dress.

"It started a long time before Jack even knew you, Katie." His voice echoed in her head. "I'm going to tell you the story in the car. You deserve to know the full story. That's only fair. And I really am a very fair man."

She didn't dare look away from the gun. If she kept watching it, she would see the bullet coming, she thought.

"Where?" she whispered, covering herself with her arms.

"The flats," he said. "We have an appointment. And I'm always on time. C'mon, up, up, fast."

Jeans. A shirt. No bra, no panties, no socks for the sneakers. But she was still alive.

For now. For this moment. This split second. And that was all that mattered.

26

1.

AS QUIN TURNED into her development, she was thinking about the bags of food in the backseat and the $85.27 she'd blown on it. No meats, no milk, no eggs, no bread, no staples at all. This was strictly fun food, junk food, cookies, foods she'd denied herself since she'd discovered she was pregnant.

She didn't know what had come over her in the store. She'd intended to pick up a jar of popcorn, cheese, juice, something for breakfast, that was all. But suddenly she was wheeling the cart up and down aisles, remembering the sweet marvel of chocolate chip cookies, of how good a square of cheese tasted on a Dorito, of how peanut butter went well with thin slices of banana, of the thick, creamy chill of chocolate ice cream. Kate had never shared her passion for munchies, but she would pick at whatever was in front of her. So tonight would be like those years they roomed together. Snacks, old horror movies, talk until dawn. Or at least until McCleary called or got home.

She passed beyond the island of trees that separated the entrance from the exit and saw the house, seventh in on the right. Kate's Jeep was backing out of the driveway, bright lights screaming.

"What the hell," Quin muttered, watching in the rearview mirror as the Jeep swerved left out of the development and tore down the road, a bat out of hell. A call, she thought. She'd gotten a call and it had spooked her. In that case, she'd be back when she was sure Quin had gotten home.

Quin pulled into her driveway, pressed the remote button for the garage door. As it trundled up, Merlin and Tracy leaped from the flower beds and raced into the garage. Tracy huddled in a corner, wincing against the glare of the headlights, and

Merlin clawed at the utility-room door. Quin parked next to the Miata, squirmed out from behind the wheel, and waddled over to Merlin. "You're a mess, big guy. Did you get out when Kate opened the door?" Tracy trotted over, rubbing against her legs, begging to be picked up. "God, all this affection."

She unlocked the door and the cats ran into the house. They'd gotten trapped outside in storms before and they'd never been this freaked, she thought, and followed them inside, momentarily forgetting the groceries. She stood for a moment in the kitchen, listening to the house. Its air and sounds were still new to her, but even so, she sensed the wrongness here. Then she looked up and saw the note tacked to the fridge.

Sorry we missed you. Love, Clicker.

Quin shouted for Kate; the house tossed her voice back to her. She hurried to the glass doors that opened onto the lake and shoved the slats of the Levolors aside, hoping to glimpse the Cherokee barreling down the road. Nothing. Not a headlight in sight. Then, on the other side of the lake, in the mango groves, light flickered, went out, flickered again. She grabbed the remote phone off the counter, punched out Eastman's number, went back to the blinds, watching. The phone on the other end rang and rang.

"C'mon, c'mon, someone answer. Please."

"Detective Eastman's office. This is Sergeant Rawlings."

"Sergeant, my name's Quin St. James, and my husband has been working with Detective Eastman on the Jack Bishop case and I need help. The—"

"On what case, ma'am?"

"Bishop," she snapped, eyes fixed on the grove. "And he's been investigating Lieutenant Garrison, who just got suspended. You with me now, Sergeant?"

The phone beeped, indicating the conversation was being recorded.

"Uh, yes, ma'am." She couldn't tell whether the caution that had crept into his voice was due to discretion or because he thought he had a nut on the line. "What seems to be the problem?"

The problem. Give this turkey the problem in ten words or

less. "The man who killed Bishop just abducted his widow and—"

"Excuse me, ma'am, what was your name again?"

The lights were headed out of the grove again. "St. James, and . . ." She knew. She knew where they were headed. "The Death Flats, the old fire tower, you know where I mean, Sergeant? About twenty miles southwest of the Bishop ranch, out near Lake Okeechobee. You got that?"

"Ma'am, if you could hold on a minute while I get someone else on the—"

She turned off the phone and dropped it on the kitchen counter as she dashed for the door. The Miata. She would take the Miata. It was faster. More dependable. She grabbed her purse from the Toyota's front seat, jerked the keys from the ignition, hurried around the front of her car to McCleary's.

The tires shrieked against the wet pavement as she peeled out of the garage and into the rain.

2.

McCleary knew their destination.

He'd known the moment the Caddy headed west toward the Bishop ranch. Now the ranch was coming up on the right, a ghostly blur in the wash of headlights, and the Caddy turned left, the Firebird hugging its tail. He was going to find out the secret of the flats, all right, but not in quite the way he'd imagined.

Eastman moaned and lifted his head from the window and Garrison's sawed-off shotgun slid through the warm, damp air and found Eastman's nose. It pressed up against it, forcing Eastman's head back. "Now you listen real good, nigger boy. I'd just as soon spill your brains right here, but that wouldn't be sporting, now would it. So you're going to sit real still like your buddy McCleary and you're going to do exactly what I tell you. Got it?"

"Yes." His voice was clear, but very, very soft.

"Give me those cuffs, Jeff." He snapped his fingers at the driver without taking his eyes off Eastman or McCleary. A set of handcuffs appeared. Garrison thrust them at Eastman. "Put them on McCleary. And you, squash those wrists together.

258

You know the routine, being ex-Homicide and all." He laughed.

McCleary pressed his wrists together, grimacing at the flash of pain through his hand. It had stopped bleeding, but it was beginning to swell. Eastman snapped the handcuffs on him, his eyes telegraphing an apology.

"Give me the other pair, Jeff. And McCleary here is going to put them on his nigger buddy."

Talk to him, McCleary thought. Keep his finger away from that trigger. "You're Mole."

"You got that right, smart boy. Maybe you're even as smart as Jack, huh. One thing's for sure, you're gonna be as dead as Jack, isn't he, Jeff."

The thug at the wheel just laughed.

"Jack was November," McCleary went on.

"*Very* good, smart boy. I'm impressed." Garrison's head seemed large and round in the dim light and it bobbed up and down like a ball. "What else you figured out?"

"Griffin. That was Abalonee."

"Wrong, you got it wrong."

"Gong, gong, he's got it wrong," the thug sang.

"Abalonee was a chicken shit," Garrison said. "Guy who killed him did everybody a favor."

"Yeah? And who would that be, Lou?" said Eastman. "You?"

"Hell, not me, man."

"And I don't suppose you killed Pearl, either."

"Nope."

"Ace. The high card," McCleary said. "That'd be David Bishop. Ace musician, ace ventriloquist."

The half-moon grin claimed the lower part of his face. "Hey, you are *very* good, smart boy. Ain't he good, Jeff?"

"Gold star for the smart boy," Jeff said, and laughed and drove on through the night, toward the Death Flats.

3.

He spoke to her as he drove, his voice drifting through her like water that congealed to glass the moment it was inside her. With every bump in the road, the glass cut more deeply,

259

the ropes at her wrists and ankles pulled tighter, and her hallucinations worsened, as though the constant jarring was knocking them loose from someplace inside her she hadn't known existed.

She was on the floor in the back of the Cherokee, and her head kept banging up against the window. Every time she breathed, she inhaled bits of lint and dust from the floor. But she forced herself to listen, to understand. Her only weapon now was information and how she could use it against him when she had the chance.

". . . it was never meant to go so far, Katie. That was Jack's fault. In the beginning, when it was just the two of us, it was like a game, you know? Well, not exactly a game, really, I guess you couldn't ever call it a game. It was more of an experiment."

He paused. She knew he was jamming the nozzle of the squeeze bottle into his nose again. She moved her wrists, trying to loosen the ropes, but they were behind her and her right arm was nearly numb from lying on it and the ropes were too tight. She kept her eyes on the tire iron under the passenger seat; the drug made it quiver and breathe and dance. She rested a moment, then moved her wrists some more.

". . . we found it out there on the flats, Katie. The quantum state of NDEs. We *found* it. You have any idea what that means? Katie? Are you listening?"

"Yes." She squeezed her eyes shut and began moving her ankles, up and down, up and down. *C'mon, ropes, loosen, please.*

"Ask me anything you want to know. Anything. And I'll tell you the truth, Katie. I swear."

"Why'd you kill Jack?"

"Because of you. Because he was eaten up with the flats. When it was just him and me, there was a bum now and then, a vagrant, no one who'd be missed. They taught us things. And it didn't happen that often. Three, four times a year. But then we bought those trailers and not long after that he brought Pearl into it, and she, Jesus, she used to pit us against each other. You women are good at that, Katie. I think it's genetic, the thing women do to men. You even did it to Jack and me for a while, but you didn't realize it. With you it wasn't conscious. But Pearl knew what she was doing, she always knew . . ."

Kate pressed back as far as she could, her eyes seeking the windows, lights, trying to get some idea of where they were, how close to the flats they were. But she could only crane her neck so far before the pressure on her hands became too great.

"Then not long after Pearl, he brought Cordoba and Garrison in. That was his biggest mistake. Cordoba's nothing but a greedy sleaze. He didn't even appreciate what we were doing on the flats. Jack just paid him and Cordoba stood there grinning and counting his money saying, '*Sí, señor*, I take care of everything. Not to worry.' And Garrison, my God, he was even worse. You should've seen him out there on the flats, Katie, sweating and breathing hard, getting all worked up. He was like some lowlife prison guard who enjoys kicking ass. Can you understand what I'm saying, Katie? When it was just the two of us, we were perfecting and polishing an art, we were working toward an understanding of what life and death are. You know, Katie?"

You know, you know: The words rang in her head as the ropes at her wrists seemed to loosen a little. Her heart soared. She moved them harder, faster, faster.

"Listen, I didn't want to have to bring you out here to see this, I really didn't want to, but if I hadn't said yes, I'd become the next Abalonee. They'd hunt me. They would. They're good at it. They know how to hunt. But one on one I'm better. I've always been better. So if you're nice to me, Katie, no one will hurt you out there. I won't let them. I have a plan. I know what I'm doing. I have money. Plenty of money. I've saved. We'll go to the Caribbean. I know people who can forge documents, get new identities, the works. Don't worry about a thing. Really."

Another pause. More of the drug. Driving faster now. Hitting potholes. No lights.

She moved her wrists faster. *Faster.*

4.

Quin didn't dare stop. She felt that as long as she kept the Cherokee in sight, nothing would happen to Kate. It was one of those childhood truths: If you could see that the space under your bed was empty, then the bogeyman couldn't be there. Like that.

But as the lights of Belle Glade fell away behind her, as the rain began to slacken and the wind started up, her courage started to slip. She was a pregnant woman with a gun, that was all. No match for the man in the Jeep unless she had an edge of some kind. Especially if he was headed for the flats, through the muck and the mangroves where those trailers were.

But the bottom line was that the Miata's gas tank was scraping empty. She would never make it as far as the flats.

Quin swung around in the middle of the road and drove back to the airport. The car sputtered seconds after she pulled into the lot and died before she'd nosed it into a space. She left it where it was and hurried across the lot toward the terminal building.

Thanks to the front that had passed through, the temperature was fifteen or twenty degrees cooler and for the first time in months she felt comfortable outside. Her body breathed. Moving was no longer an effort.

The terminal building was unlocked, but there were only a few people inside. The hands of the big clock on the wall stood at 8:30. She passed a phone and briefly considered calling the Belle Glade police. But she would have to explain everything from the beginning and that would take time, too much time. Worse than with Sgt. Rawlings.

Down the hall. Past flight service. Out the double doors to Fargo Flights. Lights burned in the windows. Quin hesitated, hand sliding into her purse, fingers touching McCleary's Magnum.

Madness, whispered the voice of reason. Yes, probably. But Fargo would know exactly where to go. She flicked off the safety, kept her hand against the gun as she went inside.

No one was behind the desk. She slammed the heel of her hand against the bell on the counter. "Anyone here? Hello?"

Roy Fargo poked his head out of the back room. Fargo with

262

his sunburned hick face, his tire of fat at the waist, Fargo dressed in boots and army fatigues. "Well, well." He grinned and sauntered out, a raincoat slung over his shoulder, a set of keys in one hand, a vanilla wafer in the other. A *Nabisco* vanilla wafer.

"If it isn't the detective. I was just on my way out."

"Dressed like that, I'd say you're headed for the flats, Mr. Fargo. Big rendezvous out there tonight or something?"

His smile thinned. He blinked fast. "I'm about to lock up."

"And you're going to take me with you, Nabisco," she said, and pulled out the Magnum. His astonishment would have been comical under other conditions. But her heart was thudding against her ribs, her mouth had flashed dry, her palms were damp. "Out from behind the desk, Mr. Fargo."

"Just take it easy, Mrs. McCleary." Plump hands patting the air. Big grin. A mouth filled with teeth like yellowed piano keys. "You don't want to go swinging that thing around."

Granted, she didn't cut an imposing figure with the gun. But nothing pissed her off worse than someone who didn't take her seriously. "That's right, I don't. So why don't you just come on out here, Mr. Fargo. We're going flying."

Blinking again, as though he couldn't quite believe he was being held hostage by a pregnant woman. "We are?"

"That's right, Mr. Fargo. And if you try anything funny while we're in the air . . . Well, I'm sure you know what kind of damage a Magnum does at point-blank range."

"Whatever you say, Mrs. McCleary."

5.

McCleary knew the Caddy wasn't following the same route to the flats that he and Quin had; it had turned too often. But he couldn't see anything except the light fog that swirled like smoke across the ground.

Now the car turned again and the dark shapes of the mangroves appeared on McCleary's left. Another turn and the headlights bore down on the trees, then the Caddy bounced into them. Low branches clawed the roof, the windows. McCleary realized they were inside a wet, green tunnel of leaves that led to the clearing where the trailers were. But where the tunnel was in relation to the airstrip was anyone's guess.

"How about this tunnel, isn't it something?" Garrison asked. "Can't see it unless you know it's here. And there's another to the south that leads to the flats."

"Impressive," Eastman murmured.

Garrison sank the end of the shotgun against Eastman's neck. "Keep your mouth shut, nigger boy. No one gave you permission to speak."

The thug who was driving said, "Take it easy, man. You don't want to mess him up before we get there."

"Good point, Jeff." The shotgun retreated a foot. "But who the hell asked you?"

The Caddy began to slow, the branches thinned, the road emptied into the clearing. The fog was much denser here, curling around the trunks of the trees, snaking across the ground in thick braids. The Caddy swung around, headlights washing across the trailers and a solitary car parked at an angle, nose facing in, away from the trees. Lantern light flickered in the windows of the larger trailer.

As they pulled alongside the car, the door of the big trailer swung open and a tall figure in a flight suit with a hood strode toward them, arms waving.

"Hit the lights," Garrison barked, and he and the driver got out and stood by the open doors.

"How bad's the hand?" Eastman whispered.

"Useless. Got any ideas?"

"Take one of them down when we get the chance, hit the car if possible. There's a car key in my pocket and one taped to the inside of the visor."

"If we can't make the car, we head for the fire tower. It's through those groves behind the trailers."

The tall figure stooped down and looked into the car. "Welcome to the flats, boys." It was Stephanie Bishop, and she was gripping a thirty-ought-six as though she'd been born with one in her hand. "Now just get out of there nice and slow-like, hmm? And don't do anything heroic, please. We got lots of trigger-happy fingers around here."

264

"Smart boy thinks he's figured it all out, Steph," said Garrison.

"Yeah? So who am I, detective?"

He took a stab. "Griffin." And when she was Griffin, she dressed like a man.

"Goddamn, detective, you *are* good. Now if you can follow directions half as well, you might live another hour. Get out."

The pain in his hand woke up and flashed, screaming, through his arm, then settled into a hot, agonizing throb. The fog swirled past his ankles, thick as clam chowder now. Garrison asked Stephanie where the others were. She said she didn't know and jammed the shotgun into the small of McCleary's back, urging him toward the large trailer. Garrison was right behind Eastman.

"Bet you didn't know my sister-in-law and your wife are joining us, did you, detective," said Stephanie. "We're going to have quite a little party."

Her laughter fluttered up toward the dripping ceiling of leaves and branches, chilling him.

27

1.

SHAPES LOOMED IN the fog and they were all huge and menacing, demons with claws that lunged for the Cherokee, demons who wore Jack's face and Pearl's and Abalonee's and even a demon who looked like his mother. Not real, Clicker told himself, the drug was doing this, he'd done too much of it, gotten carried away.

But it wasn't much farther now. He could smell his own excitement, the anticipation, the promise of the flats. The dark thrill awaited him like a lover, around this turn, that curve, through this sweet, dark tunnel of green. "Kate? Kate? It isn't much farther. Are you okay? Can you hear me?"

He worried when she didn't say anything and turned around, peering down at her. He couldn't see her face, but he knew she was breathing; the drug permitted him to hear her soft, even breaths. The movement of the Jeep had lulled her to sleep. A good sign. He didn't want to hurt her. He would if he had to, if she made him, but it would pain him deeply to do such a thing. They had come so far, he and his pretty Kate. He had claimed her, she was his, he loved her, they would save each other, have a life together.

The tunnel ended and he saw the trailers, the cars, dark shapes in the fog. He stopped next to the Firebird, climbed down, opened the back door. "Kate?" She didn't move, her eyes were closed, the lower part of her body was still covered by the sheet he'd thrown over her earlier. He wasn't sure now that she was breathing. Panic squeezed at his throat. He leaned closer to touch her and realized something was wrong with the way she was laying. But his thoughts were slow and sluggish, and by the time he remembered that he'd tied her hands behind her, not in front of her, it was too late, she'd bolted forward, her hands loose, free, and swinging a tire iron.

The blow struck him on the shoulder, blood rushed through the backs of his eyes, and he lunged for the tire iron, grabbed it, jerked it from her hands. She rolled back and kicked at him. Her shoes slammed into his chin and he stumbled back, blood filling his mouth, and hit the ground.

Fog swirled to his elbows, around his neck, curled insidiously into his nostrils. He heard his mother cackling. He leaped up and charged around to the other side of the Cherokee. She was already tearing for the closest trees.

There was enough illumination from the headlights for him to see as he raced after her, rage fueling him. Seconds before she reached the trees, he found one final burst of speed, his feet literally left the ground, and he tackled her. They went down. Rolled. She kicked, screamed, but he straddled her, trapped her arms, and looked down at her. Her hair was wild, her chest heaved for air. He saw hatred in her eyes. Hatred for him.

"You shouldn't have done that, you should've been nice to me, we could've had a good life, Katie, a real good life, that was stupid, it—"

She spat at him. Saliva oozed down his cheek. He slapped her and she cried out and he liked the way it sounded and slapped her again. Then he jerked her to her feet, twisted her arm behind her, and pushed her toward the trailer.

2.

McCleary couldn't have been more shocked if Santa Claus had walked in the door. Sammy Dayton looked like a madman: eyes glazed, hair drenched, dark pockets in his face where the lantern light didn't reach. He shoved Kate into the booth at the dirty table, then sank into a nearby chair.

Stephanie Bishop strolled over to him, hands on her skinny hips. "That was quite a little show, Sammy, you and Kate fighting like that. David wanted to go out and give you a hand, but we thought it'd be a good idea if you dealt with it yourself. Manhood and all that." She laughed and Dayton's homicidal eyes snapped toward her.

"Shut up," he hissed.

"Oh, fuck off." She looked at Garrison. "I told you he'd screw up and wouldn't be able to get both of them."

"What happened to Quin?" Garrison asked.

"She wasn't home." His words were slurred.

"Not *home*?" Garrison leaned into his face. "What do you mean she wasn't *home*, Sammy? You were supposed to get both of them."

Dayton shoved Garrison away from him and stood. "Your breath stinks, Lou. Where's Roy?"

"Not here yet," Bishop replied. "I say we start without him."

"The sooner the better," Stephanie agreed, and pulled a plastic bottle from her jumpsuit pocket, twisted the cap, stuck the end in one nostril, then the other, then passed it to her brother. "And I say we start with the pretty little Kate. Unless Sammy's got any objections, of course." Her smile was quick, furtive.

"No objections. But I do her." He brought out a .38, spun the chamber, and ejected all but one bullet. Then he snapped it shut, spun it again, and grinned. "Got the picture yet, Mike?"

He thought of the photograph of the hooded figure, gun at his temple. Yes, he had the picture.

"David and I will take Mike," said Stephanie. "What about it, bro?"

Bishop nodded.

"And Lou, honey, you get your black boy. I say we take off their cuffs now; they aren't going anywhere with us here, and once we're on the flats, it'll give them a fair chance."

"Fuck fair," snapped Garrison.

"No, she's right," Dayton said.

Overruled, Garrison just shrugged and jerked a thumb toward one of the thugs from the Firebird. "Get it." Then he tossed Stephanie the keys to the handcuffs and she freed McCleary and Eastman as the thug lumbered to the back of the trailer and returned with the black cloak he and Quin had found. He unsnapped the hood and tossed it to Garrison. Not Darth Vader at all, McCleary thought dimly.

Garrison tossed it to Dayton, who told Kate to stand up. He handcuffed her, then fitted the hood over her head. Her eyes peeped through the slits, wide and terrified, and yet, in the very center, McCleary saw something else. The flame of fury. Good, he thought. Stay angry, Kate. It'll keep you alive.

Dayton touched the back of Kate's head. Softly, he said: "If the bullet doesn't get you, Kate, you'll have a five-minute lead. That's the rule of the hunt. Then it's just you and me on the flats. Jack was good out there. But I'm better."

"You won't get away with it," Eastman said, speaking to all of them, but his eyes were on Garrison. "IAD knows too much."

"IAD doesn't know shit," Garrison barked, his eyes glazed and feverish from the drug. "Come on, Sammy. Let's get the show on the road."

Dayton's fingers closed over the back of Kate's neck and he pushed her roughly toward the door, the others bringing up the rear, with just one of the thugs left behind.

Eastman caught McCleary's eye. *We can take this mother,* he mouthed.

Maybe, McCleary thought, eyeing his useless hand.

3.

Fargo wasn't very bright. He should never have told her about Eastman and McCleary. But once he had, he was bright enough to know that she was serious about the Magnum and that she would kill him if she had to.

Fortunately, he thought she knew how to fly, so he didn't try any scare tactics in the air. If he had, Quin was sure her heart would have given out from fright. Since the others were expecting him, he set the plane down just outside the clearing, on the crumbling airfield near the firetower. His landing was awful; the fog was so thick he couldn't see the ground and they bounced, lifted, bounced hard, and he cut the power. "Keep your hands on the wheel where I can see them, Mr. Fargo."

He did.

"What's the easiest way in there?"

He told her.

"How far it is?"

"Quarter mile, maybe less."

"Lean forward."

He leaned. She winced, then slammed the butt of the gun over his head. He slumped against the wheel. She found a flashlight and a length of rope in the baggage compartment. She tied his hands to the wheel, gagged him with a handkerchief, then returned to the baggage compartment and rummaged through the box of odds and ends for things she might use.

Weird things were in this box. Firecrackers, for instance. Freeze-dried food. Flares. Clothes. Boots. And at the bottom an automatic pistol and four clips with ten shots apiece in them. She took the firecrackers, the flares, the gun and clips.

Not much of an edge, but it was the best she could do.

Then she lit out for the clearing, talking silently to the baby as she moved, promising her that it would never come down to this again.

4.

"Wait for Roy," David said. "That was his plane."

"Fuck Roy," Dayton snapped. "Let's get on with it."

He could already smell Kate's fear, that faint strange stink that seeped out with her sweat, the same odor they all had. He pushed her to her knees, loving the feel of her shoulder against his hand and the way she trembled, the power he possessed. Her terror flowed through his pores, up into his nostrils, his mouth, filling him.

He pressed the barrel of the gun to her temple and a part of him flew back eighteen years to the moment of his own death in that scuba-diving mishap. He felt himself sucking on that empty tank of oxygen, the weights on his belt dragging him under, his lungs screaming for air. A special kind of terror, extreme, intense—and liberating. In all the years since, it seemed his entire life had been geared to understand those few moments and to re-create the rush of horror and exaltation. That was Jack's gift to him.

As his finger squeezed back slowly on the trigger, the song of life rushed through Kate, he felt it, and then it leaped into him, clean and fresh and powerful. He was suddenly at the border of life and death with her, hovering there, suspended between breaths, between moments.

Let it come.

5.

The thug sat with his metal chair tipped back against the wall, watching them. His hand was on his weapon, the silencer protruding from the end of it like a pig's snout and resting against his thigh. A rather easy posture, McCleary thought. He obviously didn't think either of them would be stupid enough to make a move.

Eastman nodded at McCleary, who set his dead hand on the surface of the table. It looked like a slab of raw meat. "Hey, could I have one of those dish towels to wrap around my hand? It's starting to bleed again."

"So suck on it."

"Christ," Eastman said. "You can't be that lazy. I'll get it if you don't want to move." He started to stand and the thug's gun popped up and his chair came away from the wall.

"Stay put, nigger. I'll get him the goddamn towel." He stood, sidled back toward the sink, his eyes on them every second. Then, for just a fraction of an instant, he looked away to reach for the towel and Eastman and McCleary sprang at him.

Eastman slammed into him from the side and they toppled into the gas stove and kept on falling. McCleary kicked for his gun, missed when the two men struck the floor, lunged again, and the gun went off, as soundless as a falling star. The slug ripped through his right side at almost point-blank range and burned a path through him, nicking his liver and crashing through the fourth rib on his left side before it exited. The pain seared through him, driving him to his knees, and as he was falling, he thought of Quin saying *I love you* and of how he had thought of a doomed plane and knew for sure now that he was on it.

But then Eastman was jerking him to his feet, dragging him to the back of the trailer, saying, "C'mon, Mike, c'mon, we're going to get out of this."

271

He held him up with one hand as he knocked out the broken glass in the window with the other. Fresh air rushed over him, dizzying him, and he knew he was falling again, into the scent of water, earth, but it didn't hurt when he landed. Fog closed around him, a white fist, a white box, and now Eastman was pulling him through the leaves, moving him under the trailer, whispering, "Hold on, Mike, hold on."

Then Eastman was gone and he was folded into the white, neat as a letter in an envelope, and he closed his eyes and drifted into it, into all that white, wondering why he didn't hurt anymore.

6.

When he jerked back on the trigger, Kate felt a surge of euphoria unlike anything she'd ever known. It was as if her body had suddenly been filled with helium and she was being lifted by a strong wind.

The hood was whipped from her head. She blinked hard and fast, the faces around her blurred, the night air licked at her cheeks. Sammy grabbed her roughly by the arm, yanked her to her feet, backed away from her. "Five minutes." His voice was steel. "That's all. *Move.*"

Her eyes snapped to each face in the circle, to hands holding guns aimed toward the ground. She took a step back, certain Sammy or one of them would aim and fire. *"Get going, bitch!"* hissed Stephanie, and moved toward her, waving her arms. *"Scat!"*

She spun and ran, ran for the trees. She crashed into them, tripped, and sprawled in the leaves, momentarily unable to rise. *Alive I'm alive oh God get up fast fast . . .*

"Four and a half minutes, Mrs. Bishop!" Garrison shouted, and she stumbled to her feet and ran on.

Behind her, she heard the Cherokee cranking up and was suddenly certain that Sammy had never intended to shoot her, that he knew exactly where the single bullet was in the chamber. Of course. He wanted to hunt her down on the flats, just the two of them, alone.

7.

Quin heard Garrison shouting, saw the Cherokee swinging around, headlights washing through the clearing. She couldn't go after it, but she could slow the bastard down. She struggled to her feet, lit a string of firecrackers, and hurled them away from her.

The explosions threw the people in the clearing into a panic. They scattered like bugs, hurling themselves to the ground, scampering toward their cars for protection. She got off two shots at the Jeep before someone fired in her general direction. She dropped to the ground and scuttled forward. She heard more shots coming from somewhere near the trailer. McCleary, she thought. McCleary and Eastman had gotten out. They were free. Her heart soared and she crept on, branches snagging her clothes, wet leaves sucking at her shoes, shouts rising from the clearing.

8.

McCleary had never been so cold. He couldn't feel his legs, couldn't flex his fingers, couldn't lift his head. He thought he heard shots, but they seemed more like a memory of sound. He opened his eyes and Quin was leaning over him, raising his head, saying something to him, but he couldn't hear her. He didn't understand how she had gotten under the trailer with him. It hurt to think about it and he closed his eyes and floated away again.

9.

One of the shots had hit the Cherokee's windshield dead center, shattering it. Slivers of glass were embedded in Dayton's thighs, he felt them, hundreds of sharp little daggers drawing blood. But he knew how to vanquish pain. His mother had taught him well. He simply turned it off in his head and sped on through the tunnel of leaves.

Only one of the headlights was functional and it stripped the blackness from the trees on his left and impaled her. His pretty Kate, racing against time, racing for her life, just like all the others. The hunt. Her life for his.

"You can do it, Click," said Jack, perched at the edge of

the passenger seat, his head poking through the jagged peaks of glass, his finger stabbing. "There, she's over there. Swerve left, Clicker, fast, to the left."

Dayton swerved, a tree rose up in front of him, he swerved again, and lost sight of her. *"Faster!"* Jack shouted. "There, see her there?"

Yes. Yes, he saw her, all right. Saw her shooting from the trees, headed for the flats. Dayton laughed. Jack laughed. They looked at each other, Jack in his bloodied shirt, Jack with the wind whipping through his hair, Jack, like the old days when it was just the two of them.

The Cherokee flew free of the trees, as swift as a cold, smooth stone hurling from his slingshot. The single headlight struck Fargo's plane, abandoned near the end of the airfield, and he slammed on the brakes. The engine died with a shudder. Dayton stared at the plane, his head throbbing. He thought of Kate and Wolfe, of how she had chosen Wolfe over him. Jack over him.

"She's hiding in the plane," Jack whispered. "The bitch is hiding in the plane. I'm right behind you, buddy."

He killed the headlight. Slipped the slingshot from his pocket. Opened the glove compartment and brought out one of his stones. Steady now. The joy of the flats flooded through him. He felt Jack at his side, covering him.

"Watch your step," Jack whispered.

"Go easy," said Pearl, coming up on his left.

He approached the plane at a crouch, head-on. His night vision was perfect. The wind blew dirt across the cauling, the windshield, and he could see a shape inside. Kate. Waiting for him, just as he had known she would wait. Kate, thinking she would outsmart him.

Kate, Jack's Kate.

"Go under the plane," Jack whispered.

"She won't be expecting it," said Pearl.

He touched the propeller, loving the cool, hard reality of the blade; the taste of triumph filled him. Not much farther. He would fuck her before he killed her, and he would make her beg for her life.

He pulled his head down to duck under the propeller and

he heard a high, almost shrill whine. He knew what it was, he knew what had happened, but before he could leap out of the way, the propeller began to move. Then turn. Then spin.

The blunt edge of the first blade slammed into his upper back. The second blade severed his hand at the wrist. The third blade struck just above his collar, and nearly decapitated him.

He was dead before he hit the ground.

10.

Blood.

That was all Kate saw. Blood spraying the plane's windshield, blood flying away from the propeller, blood everywhere. She jerked the throttle back, robbing the engine of gas, and it stopped. There was just the wind, whistling through cracks and vents, and the staccato wheeze of her own breath.

Then, distantly, she heard the chatter of a helicopter.

11.

McCleary was rising, lifting up, up out of the fog and into the dark with the ease of a bird. He was flying, racing toward the moon. He'd never seen a moon as large as this, as bright, as luminous. Its light was everywhere, bleeding across the sky, eating up the darkness, moving into him, through him: he *was* the light, weightless, boneless, racing at an impossible speed. The light spit him out into a clear blue sky and he tumbled like a leaf to the crest of a green, green hill.

Sylvia Callahan was sitting there, nibbling at a blade of grass, legs drawn up under her flowered skirt. Her hair was longer than he remembered, pulled away from her face, setting off the fine, delicate bones.

"Callahan."

"Sylvia, as Quin would say." She laughed. "How are you, Mac? It's been a while." She stood and hugged him hard. Her skin was fragrant with the scent of lilacs or pears, which mixed with the sweet fragrance of the grass when they sank to the ground.

He couldn't stop looking at her. She was lovelier than his memories, softer, and yet changed, changed in a way he

275

couldn't define. He started to ask what she was doing here but heard a steady *beep beep beep* in his head and a voice saying, *Pulse forty-one and dropping, BP sixty over thirty.* It had nothing to do with him, with her.

"I don't understand," he said.

"Sure you do, Mike. You just don't want to deal with it."

She talked slowly, patiently, as if he were a boy of ten and she were his older, wiser sister. Her voice was music. It moved through him like light. But behind her voice was the other voice, louder now, irritating, harder to ignore. *Pulse twenty-two. BP fifty-three over twenty-four. We're losing him.*

Callahan held her fist up to the light, against the blue, and opened her hand. A small beautiful bird fluttered out singing a melody so lovely, it nearly broke his heart. It swooped low over their heads dropping things from its beak. The objects struck the grass, took root, grew.

They were photographs.

When he looked at them closely, he saw himself, scenes from his life that he recognized, other scenes that he knew hadn't yet happened. The figures in the pictures moved and talked. They expanded until they seemed to stretch across the curve of sky, a living panorama.

He saw his unborn daughter as an infant, a toddler, a young girl. She was moving toward him, laughing, arms outstretched, her face a perfect amalgam of his and Quin's. He heard Quin whispering his name, weeping, then she was in one of the living photographs, against a wall, a hand at her mouth. She was watching people doing something to a man on a bed. He understood that the man was himself and that he was dying.

"Make your choice, Mike," said Callahan.

He didn't want to die.

He wanted his life, such as it was, he wanted Quin, he wanted to know his daughter. He wanted these things with a fierceness he hadn't thought possible. He jumped up and tore away from Callahan, down the hill, down toward the violet horizon. The soft, tall grass rustled with his movements. He stumbled, felt himself falling, tumbling past the blue and the green into a vast darkness. Agony seized him. Bolts of lightning swept through his chest. His body convulsed.

We've got a pulse.

Then a tide of pain washed over him and he went away again.

12.

"May I see him now?" Quin asked the nurse.

"Just for a few minutes."

It was fifty-two hours later. She knew. She had counted. She had watched the hands of the clock in the waiting room crawl from hour to hour, through dark and light and dark and light, over and over.

She'd dozed for a while in the waiting room and came to when one of the nurses had led her into the room the residents used for catnaps. She'd slept deeply for ten hours and awakened suddenly to find Kate and Wolfe in the room.

No change in Mac, Kate had said, and handed her clean clothes. Wolfe set a tray of food in front of her. She polished off everything on the plate, showered, talked briefly to Eastman when he arrived. Garrison and his two thugs had been picked up, and the judge had set the bail on the Bishops and Roy Fargo at one million apiece. Quin thanked him for telling her. But at the moment she didn't give a rat's shit in hell what happened to any of them.

She stepped into room seven in the intensive care unit. Her throat closed up. McCleary was as still as a corpse on the bed. He was on oxygen, connected to a million tubes and catheters. Machines monitored his vital signs and spit out streams of paper with his brain waves scribbled across them like inscriptions in an alien language. He hadn't regained consciousness and no one could guarantee that he would.

Quin pulled over a chair and sat beside the bed, looking at him, that was all, just looking as though the force of her will alone could make his eyes open. She touched his hand, held it. It was cool and limp in her own. She believed he could hear her, so she talked to him, recounting things they'd shared. Did he like the name Michelle for the baby? She said she thought it was a good, solid name. Since they didn't know any Michelles, they wouldn't have any preconceived notions about what sort of person a Michelle would be and that was important, wasn't it?

His fingers twitched against her hand, one of those involuntary muscles spasms the doctor had already told her about. But she stared at his fingers nonetheless, and when they twitched again, she leaned close to him and whispered, "Mac, can you hear me?"

The machine beeped and hummed and purred.

"Mac?"

His fingers moved—not a twitch, but an actual sliding against her palm. Then they tightened around her hand and held on fast and hard, a ship that had moored at last.

Epilogue

Announcement

Born: Michelle Maia McCleary
Where: West Palm Beach, Florida
When: February 17, 1991
Time: 8:10 p.m.
Weight: six lbs., six ounces
To: Quin St. James McCleary &
           Michael McCleary

About the Author

T.J. MacGregor lives in South Florida with her husband, novelist Rob MacGregor, and their daughter. She is the author of five other books in the Quin St. James/Mike McCleary mystery series: *Dark Fields*, *Kill Flash*, *Death Sweet*, *On Ice*, and *Kin Dread*.